The History of Methodism within the Bounds of the Erie Annual Conference of the Methodist Episcopal Church

Volume 1

SALZWASSER
VERLAG

Samuel Gregg

The History of Methodism within the Bounds of the Erie Annual Conference of the Methodist Episcopal Church

Volume 1

Reprint of the original, first published in 1865.

1st Edition 2022 | ISBN: 978-3-75259-018-0

Verlag (Publisher): Salzwasser Verlag GmbH, Zeilweg 44, 60439 Frankfurt, Deutschland
Vertretungsberechtigt (Authorized to represent): E. Roepke, Zeilweg 44, 60439 Frankfurt, Deutschland
Druck (Print): Books on Demand GmbH, In de Tarpen 42, 22848 Norderstedt, Deutschland

THE

HISTORY OF METHODISM

WITHIN THE BOUNDS OF THE

ERIE ANNUAL CONFERENCE

OF THE

METHODIST EPISCOPAL CHURCH.

BY REV SAMUEL GREGG,

AUTHOR OF "INFANT CHURCH MEMBERSHIP," AND "EARLY RIPE FRUIT."

"Bright visions of the golden past
Fly back on wings of love to me."

VOLUME I.

New York

1865.

Engraved by L. Mackenzie from an original painting

REV. ROBERT RICHFORD ROBERTS.

PREFACE.

THE history of Methodism, when completed, will form one of the brightest pages of ecclesiastical history our redeemed world has produced. To accomplish this as it should be, each section of the work should gather up its own materials and preserve them until our *great general historian* gets ready to compile the whole into one extended chain of connected facts, which his pen will beautify, until like a glittering rainbow it will span the moral heavens, and give promise of the future immortality of its happy subjects. In sending forth this volume from the press, we desire to say to the reader that we have long felt the importance of rescuing from a threatened oblivion an account of the great work of God along the south shore of Lake Erie, in which so many good men have spent their lives in toil and sacrifice for the great Redeemer, but delayed the undertaking, hoping that some person, with more leisure at command and higher qualifications for the work would devote himself to the task. But no indications of that kind appearing, and fearing that a longer delay would render it impossible to obtain the facts from living witnesses of the scenes to be narrated, we were induced some six years since to commence quietly collecting the materials for the present volume. We were also inclined to this work because Providence had placed us in circumstances through our whole natural life peculiarly favorable for obtaining the necessary information. Our parents and grandparents moved into the very center of the Erie Conference about the time when the first societies were being formed, and became identified with them, and in their humble log-cabin furnished a welcome home to the devoted itinerants of that day.

As far back as memory runs we were accustomed to sit by the knee of our venerable paternal grandmother, who was converted in Ireland under the preaching of the Rev. John Wesley, and of hearing her describe the different preachers she had heard both in Ireland and in America, and especially since she came to the West. And our excellent mother, who united with the Church in the wilderness in her sixteenth year, used often to relate to us the scenes she had witnessed, and describe the ministers she had heard, and the revivals of religion she had known. And then our father obtained license to preach when we were quite young, and traveled and preached extensively as a local preacher, and assisted in revivals and in forming classes, and from him we obtained much valuable information. And it was our good fortune to embrace religion and to unite with the Methodist Episcopal Church when but sixteen years old, and become a close, constant, and greatly interested observer of all that was transpiring in the Church of our choice, and an almost enthusiastic admirer of the ministers we were accustomed to hear preach. We have now spent thirty-three years in the work of the itinerant Methodist ministry without losing a single month by sickness or any other circumstance, occupying fields of labor in every part of our territory, sometimes on its bleak mountains and along its flowing rivers, and at others in its beautiful villages and flourishing cities. We have never in that time missed the session of a single conference, and have uniformly been in our seat and attentive to the business being transacted. We have also been a constant reader of those Church periodicals in which accounts of the progress of the work have been published, and have gleaned from them all we could get. We are also under many and great obligations to some of our ministerial brethren who have greatly assisted us in procuring the materials used in this work. We have carefully consulted such autobiographies and historical works as could give us any available information. We only regret that we could devote so small a portion of our time exclusively to this history. We have been compelled to accomplish it all in connection with the labor of a heavy pastoral charge, doing most of our writing at night while others were enjoying "sweet repose." We regret also that we have not been able to give a more perfect account of our work; many of the societies are not so much as named. But we have obtained all the information we could get from all sources within our reach, and have used all we could obtain.

But we are over the most difficult part of our work. It will be much easier to get information hereafter from living witnesses of facts and scenes to be used in our next volume; so that, if Providence shall spare our life, we hope in due time to present the reader with another and better volume than this. Till then may blessings without number fall like showers upon those that favor us with a perusal of these pages.

CONTENTS.

SECTION V.

FROM 1810 TO 1812.

SECTION VI.

FROM 1812 TO 1815.

SECTION VII.

FROM 1815 TO 1817.

SECTION VIII.

1817 AND 1818.

SECTION IX.

FROM 1819 TO 1822.

SECTION X.

FROM 1822 TO 1825.

THE

HISTORY OF METHODISM

WITHIN THE

BOUNDS OF THE ERIE ANNUAL CONFERENCE.

SECTION I.

THE TERRITORY OCCUPIED BY THE CONFERENCE, AND ITS FIRST SETTLEMENTS.

"O 'tis a noble heritage, this goodly land of ours;
It boasts indeed no gothic fane, nor 'ivy-mantled towers;'
But far into the closing clouds its purple mountains climb,
The sculptures of Omnipotence, the twins of time.
And then its intertwining lakes, its forests wild and wide,
And streams, the sinews of its strength, that feed it as they glide;
Its rich primeval pasture grounds fenced by the stooping sky,
And mines of treasure, yet undelved, that 'neath its surface lie."

THE Erie Annual Conference of the Methodist Episcopal Church was formed by the General Conference which met in Cincinnati, Ohio, May, 1836; but its history extends back beyond that period nearly forty years, and it is through this incipient state of its existence, while undergoing the process of formation, that the reader will be conducted in the present volume.

We commence by giving a description of the country and its first settlements, to show how the *Methodist ministry*, traveling and local, followed up the tide of emigration, carrying the Gospel of peace to the destitute pioneer settlements, enduring with the people, for the Master's sake, the hardships and sacrifices incident to such a state of the country.

The conference is "bounded on the north by Lake Erie, on the east by a line commencing at the mouth of the Cattaraugus Creek; thence up said creek to the village of Gowanda, leaving said village in the Genesee Conference; thence to the Alleghany River at the mouth of the Tunungwant Creek; thence up said creek southward to the ridge dividing between the waters of the Clarion and Sinnemahoning Creeks; thence southward to the head of Mahoning Creek; thence down said creek, exclusive of Milton Society, and including Putneyville in Bethlehem Circuit, to the Alleghany River; thence across said river in a north-westerly direction to the Western Reserve Line, including the north part of Butler and New Castle Circuits, and also including Petersburgh; thence west to the Ohio Canal; thence along said canal to Lake Erie, including Akron and all of Cleveland lying east of the Cuyahoga River."*

This territory includes corners of three states: New York, Pennsylvania, and Ohio. The eastern portion, lying in New York and Pennsylvania, except the lake shore region, is quite rough and mountainous, producing large quantities of lumber, coal, and iron ore, and is well watered by the Alleghany, Clarion, and Mahoning Rivers and their tributaries; the western part is comparatively level, furnishing excellent grazing lands, and producing large quantities of butter and cheese, and is also well watered

* See Discipline, p. 161.

by the Cuyahoga, Chagrin, Mahoning, and Grand Rivers.

As early as the year 1750 the French had taken possession of this territory as a part of the great valley of the "Mississipi," which they claimed in connection with the "colonies in Canida," and had erected three fortresses, and garrisoned them with soldiers for its protection.* One of these forts was called "Presque Isle," after an island of that name near the south shore of Lake Erie, forming the beautiful bay at Erie, Pa. The fort stood on the bank of the lake, about one mile below the city of Erie. Another of these forts stood near the village of Waterford, Erie County, Pa., about twelve miles south of Erie, and was called "Fort La Bœuf," perhaps after some French officer of that name. The third fort stood near the mouth of French Creek, just below the village of Franklin, Pa., and was called "Fort Venango." The soldiers garrisoned in these forts were the first white men in this part of the country.

The first native white man that penetrated this western wilderness was Mr. GEORGE WASHINGTON, who in the year 1754 was sent by Governor Dinwiddie of Virginia to see the officer in command of the "French forces" at "Fort La Bœuf," to induce him, if possible, to leave the country peaceably, it being claimed by the Commonwealth of Virginia. But not succeeding in his peaceful negotiations with the French commander, Mr. Washington returned by passing down French Creek, and then down

* Willard's History of the United States, p. 123.

the Alleghany River to "Fort Du Quesne," where Pittsburgh now stands, and thence across the mountains to his home in Williamsburgh, Va., having been providentially preserved, while all the rest of the company that started with him lost their lives by sundry accidents which befell them by the way. May our land, thus honored, long cherish the name, imitate the example, and disseminate the principles of the great and good *General George Washington!*

Mr. James Smith, a citizen of Bedford, Pa., who was captured by the Indians just before Braddock's defeat, spent the winter of 1755–6 at "the Cuyahoga,"* not far from where the city of Cleveland now stands. His savage captors had a cabin near here large enough to accommodate thirteen squaws and eight hunters.

The earliest expedition of English troops through this country occurred soon after the fall of Canada into the hands of the English. During the war a regiment of rangers had been raised in New Hampshire. A detachment of this regiment was sent west to take possession of Detroit under the command of Major Robert Rodgers. The detachment reached "Presque Isle" (now Erie) in the month of October, 1760. It took up its march for Detroit on November 4, the troops proceeding along the south shore of Lake Erie in open boats. At the same time Captain Brewer started along the lake shore with forty head of beef cattle, procured in Pennsylvania for the use of the troops. At the mouth of the Grand River Major Rodgers landed his troops, and was soon after met by the

* Lecture by Hon. E. Whittlesey.

celebrated Indian chieftain Pontiac, who stood in the path, backed by his warriors. Pontiac immediately demanded of Major Rodgers the reason why he presented himself here with an armed force? The major replied that the great king of Great Britain had overthrown their French father, the grand Onnontio, and had taken possession of his dominions in Canada. Pontiac replied that the French did not own this country on this side of the lake, as he had never granted it to them. Upon being informed that he did not intend to disturb the country, but only to pass through it on his way to Detroit, Major Rodgers, with his command, was permitted to pass, and the Indians accompanied them through to Detroit, and rendered important assistance in driving the cattle.*

After the conquest of the French possessions in North America by Great Britain,† this tract of country was ceded by the French to Great Britain by the treaty of Paris in 1763, and the claim of the English monarch ‡ to the "north-western territory" was ceded to the "United States" by the treaty of Paris, September 3, 1783.

After the boundaries of the States of Pennsylvania and New York were fixed along their western line, the State of Connecticut continued to claim as a part of her chartered dominion a vast body of land lying west of these states; but following the magnanimous example of Virginia — who, in 1784, ceded to the general government all lands claimed by her west of

* See Hon. E. Whittlesey's Lecture.

† See History of Ohio, p. 6.

‡ Ibid., p. 9.

the Ohio River, also in 1786 ceded her claim of soil and jurisdiction to all lands lying west of the western line of Pennsylvania, except "one hundred and twenty miles directly west of Pennsylvania, on the south shore of Lake Erie,"* (this fine territory she reserved in her possession until the year 1801, when Ohio was made one of the states of the Union,)—Connecticut ceded her claim to Ohio; and this circumstance gave it the name by which it is distinguished from other portions of the State of Ohio, "THE CONNECTICUT WESTERN RESERVE," a large portion of which lies within the bounds of the Erie Conference. During the Revolutionary war this territory, lying back far in the Western Wilderness, as it then was called, was not disturbed by the British foe, or the action of contending armies. Various Indian tribes held it in undisturbed control.

The year 1795 was remarkable for two events which occurred of great importance to this territory. The first was the action of the Legislature of the State of Pennsylvania, granting four hundred acres of land to any person who would make an actual settlement for five years, clear and fit for cultivation twenty-five acres, build a small house, and pay at a specified time twenty dollars to the state for each hundred acres. This act caused an immediate emigration to commence from the east to the west side of the Alleghany Mountains. A land-office was established at "Presque Isle Fort," thenceforth called *Erie*, after the lake of that name, on whose southern shore it was situated. Captain John Kelso

* History of Ohio, p. 9.

and Mr. Rufus S. Reed were among the first enterprising and substantial settlers of the place.

The second event referred to was the treaty formed with the Indians by General Anthony Wayne, after defeating them in several hard-fought battles in the northwestern part of the State of Ohio. This caused the Indians, to a great extent, to cease their depredations upon the white settlements, and soon emigrants from the east began to seek homes along the southern shore of Lake Erie in Ohio, making their way in many instances over the rough threatening waves of Erie in small and fragile crafts of different kinds.

The French forts referred to were now converted into trading posts, and became radiating points from which the white settlements were gradually extended in all directions into the surrounding country, the traders rendering valuable assistance by furnishing the inhabitants with provisions and implements of husbandry in exchange for furs, skins, and wild meat. We must now introduce to the reader a man who was not only a pioneer in the settlement of the country, but who stands more intimately connected with the early history of Methodism within the bounds of the Erie Conference than perhaps any other person, and who subsequently arose to a very high position in the Methodism of the United States of America, and will be known and loved while the Methodist Episcopal Church continues her glorious existence upon this continent.

Robert Richford Roberts was born in Frederick County, Md., August 2, 1778. His father removed his family into the State of Pennsylvania, and settled them on a farm in Ligonier, Westmoreland County, in 1785. Owing to the newness of the country, the scarcity of schools, and the moderate circumstances of the father, the early literary advantages of young Roberts were quite limited; but by the diligent exertions of his excellent mother, his education was kept constantly advancing. In the year 1788, when young Roberts was about ten years of age, the Methodist ministers began to preach in Ligonier, and notwithstanding the violent prejudices of the father, he ventured out to hear them preach, and soon became much interested in their preaching. It was not long before three of his sisters experienced religion and united with the Methodist society in that place, and through their earnest entreaties both the father and mother were induced to attend the Methodist preaching, which soon resulted in their conversion to God, when they also united with the Methodist society, and took the preachers, meeting and all, to their house. Young Roberts now enjoyed the society and religious instruction of these faithful men of God exceedingly, and notwithstanding his constant employment as a laborer on his father's farm, so applied himself to reading such books as they furnished him as to accumulate a very valuable amount of intelligence. He was converted to God in the fourteenth year of his age, in the spring of 1792. He says: "One day about sunrise in the month of May I was in the corner of the fence praying, when I humbly trust my sins were forgiven, and God for Christ's sake accepted me. Before that time I have frequently had sweet intimations of the goodness of God. My heart was tender, and I felt as if I could love God and his people. But yet until that morning my mind was not at rest. Then everything seemed changed. Nature wore a new aspect as I arose and went to my work with cheerfulness, though I own I did not then know whether I had received all that I should look for in conversion. I never had such alarming views of my condition as some have experienced. My mind was greatly opened, and although I had always led a moral life, I firmly now thought that my heart must be changed. Owing to my youth I cannot now remember the precise day of my conversion, though the scene as it occurred that morning has ever been deeply printed on my memory." * But so diffident was this promising young man, that, much as he loved the Church, and highly as he valued the means of grace, he did not offer himself for membership in the Church for more than a year after his conversion. It then happened strangely. Rev. Mr. Bell, preacher in charge of the circuit, one day at the close of class-meeting inquired of the leader if there was any objection to the reception of Brother Roberts on probation, and being answered that there was none, proceeded to place his name on the class-book, an act for which Mr. Roberts afterward said he never was sorry. † Mr. Roberts now sought instruction from every source within his reach, and attended the best schools in the country, so far as he could be spared from the labors of the farm. In the spring of 1796, when Mr. Roberts was about eighteen years of age, he started out in company with his brother, Thomas

* Elliott's Life of Roberts, p. 25. † Ibid., p. 27.

Roberts, and three other young men of his neighborhood, on an exploration tour into the western part of the State of Pennsylvania, where land was abundant and cheap, with the intention of securing each a tract of new land if the country suited them. They traveled on foot, and carried their provisions in knapsacks on their backs, with guns on their shoulders for the purpose of securing wild meat by the way as they might need it. They crossed the Alleghany River near where Freeport now stands, and passed up Buffalo Creek. Two of their company soon became discouraged and returned home; but the other three, with young R. R. Roberts for their leader, renewed the search, and on the third day came upon the old Venango road, leading from Pittsburgh to "Fort Venango," and continued to pursue it until they arrived at the fort. Here the company remained over the Sabbath; not, however, enjoying the rich and delightful means of grace now to be enjoyed by the weary traveler who chances to spend a Sabbath in the cozy little village of Franklin, nestling among the high hills which surround it, close by where the old fort used to stand, but the day was spent in witnessing a scene of drunkenness among the Indians, who had collected about the fort to sell their skins and furs to the traders for whisky. From the garrison they proceeded up French Creek to the mouth of Cassawago Creek, when they bore off to the left, and after traveling some time in a southern direction, crossing several streams, they came at length upon the head waters of the Little Shenango, where they found a large body of land which pleased them well, and where they soon determined to commence a settlement. They accordingly proceeded to erect a cabin near the bank of the Shenango, about three quarters of a mile north of the residence afterward occupied by Mr. John Leach, Sen. During this long and adventurous journey our youthful pioneers were several times lost in the wilderness, without compass or anything else to assist them in determining their latitude and longitude; often encountering furious wild beasts, with but little knowledge of their character, or experience or skill in hunting them. The lands along French Creek were mostly taken up, and settlements at several places had been commenced. Soon after Mr. Roberts and his associates pitched their tent on the bank of the Shenango they passed over on to the waters of Cassawago Creek, and followed it down to its junction with French Creek, where Meadville now stands. A settlement had already been commenced at this place by two brothers from New Jersey by the name of Mead, from whom the place was afterward named. During the summer of 1796 Mr. Amos Judson and Mr. William Miles settled in the vicinity of Fort La Bœuf, where Waterford now stands, and Mr. James Pollock settled four miles below on the bank of French Creek, and Mr. Martin Strong settled about the same time four miles north-west of Waterford, on the road to Erie; thus opening a continuous line of settlements from the Alleghany River to Lake Erie. Also a settlement was commenced this season at the mouth of Walnut Creek, a few miles above Erie, on the Lake shore; but who the persons were that formed it we have not been able to ascertain. In the spring of 1793 Colonel James Hillman, residing in Pittsburgh, Pa., and who had for years past been carrying on a successful trade with the Indians of the Western Reserve, bringing his goods and liquors up the Mahoning River in canoes, and returning in the same way ladened with skins and furs in exchange, was one day descending the river alone, and as he came near where Youngstown now stands was surprised to see a smoke arising from the shore, and on landing he found Mr. Young, proprietor of the township, in company with Mr. Wolcott, who had just arrived. Mr. Hillman soon after returned and erected a dwelling-house and removed his family to Youngstown, then the only family residing between the Alleghany and the Lake shore, at the mouth of the Cuyahoga River.

Early in the summer of 1796 a company of surveyors were sent out from the State of Connecticut, which landed first at the mouth of Conneaut Creek, on the fourth day of July, and the following September proceeded up the lake to the mouth of the Cuyahoga River, and surveyed and laid out the city of Cleveland, naming it after General Moses Cleveland, the general agent of the land company. By the 18th of October the party had completed their survey and returned home, leaving Mr. Job V Stiles and family, and Mr. Edward Paine, who were the only white inhabitants in the place during the following winter. Their nearest neighbors were two families at the mouth of Conneaut Creek, a distance of seventy miles. Both settlements suffered severely for the want of food.

The year 1797 witnessed many valuable improvements in the settlements previously commenced, as well as the formation of several new ones. It was also a year of almost incredible sufferings to the people thus scattered through a vast wilderness country, with no adequate supply of provisions within their reach, and exposed alike to the relentless cruelties of their savage neighbors, the fury of wild beasts, and the enmity of venomous serpents. An experienced "backwoodsman" has truly said: "The first settlers could not have sustained themselves had it not been for the wild game in the country. This was their principal subsistence, and this they took at the peril of their lives, and often some of them came near starving to death. Wild meat without bread or salt was often their only food for weeks together. If they obtained bread, the meal was pounded in a mortar or ground in a handmill. Hominy was a good substitute for bread, or parched corn pounded or sifted, then mixed with a little sugar and eaten dry. On this coarse fare the people were remarkably healthy and cheerful. Almost every man and boy were hunters, and some of the women of those times were expert in the chase."* Early in the spring of 1797 Messrs. Thomas and Lewis Roberts, in company with Rev. Jacob Gurwell, a local preacher in the Methodist Episcopal Church, and several other persons, arrived in the little settlement commenced the previous year on the Shenango by Mr. R. R. Roberts and his two comrades. But finding the country almost wholly destitute of provisions, Mr. Thomas

* See Life of Rev. J. B. Finley.

Roberts, with one or two others, soon returned to Ligonier for a new supply, and being detained much longer than was expected, their provisions in the settlement became entirely exhausted, and all except Mr. R. R. Roberts left the settlement, and he remained there three weeks living on squirrels' meat and salt, until he became so emaciated that he could endure it no longer, and started on foot for French Creek. But when about five miles from his cabin he unexpectedly met his brother, Thomas Roberts, accompanied by his sister, Elizabeth Roberts, returning well supplied with provisions. The meeting, as the reader can easily imagine, was a truly joyful one, causing them all, and especially the kind-hearted Elizabeth, to weep freely. And when Miss Elizabeth Roberts became the mistress of the log-cabin at Shenango, there was not another female residing within twenty miles of the place. But her industrious habits, generous disposition, and dignified Christian deportment soon secured to her the confidence and esteem of all who knew her, and gave her an influence for good long and widely felt in the Shenango settlement. When any were afflicted or in want Elizabeth Roberts had a heart that could sympathize and a hand ready to furnish relief to the extent of her ability. "She openeth her mouth with wisdom, and in her tongue is the law of kindness." Prov. xxxi, 26.

SECTION II.

THE CONTINUED IMPROVEMENT OF THE COUNTRY, AND THE INTRODUCTION OF METHODISM FROM 1798 TO 1802.

"I venerate the man whose heart is warm,
Whose hands are pure, whose doctrine and whose life,
Coincident, exhibit lucid proof
That he is honest in the sacred cause.
To such I render more than mere respect,
Whose actions say that they respect themselves."

1798.

THE year 1798 witnessed a degree of healthful improvement in the settlement of the country very encouraging to those persons who had evinced the fortitude to make permanent investments in the soil, and to risk their lives in the wilderness. Settle ments were commenced this year in Newburgh, Euclid, Burton, Vernon, and in a few other towns in Ohio. The hardships endured by the people in some of these new settlements were terrible, and have imposed on us a debt of gratitude of incalculable dimensions, who are now living in the midst of luxuries upon the very soil they rendered rich and beautiful by their sacrifices and toil. Up to this time most of the provisions used in the Shenango settlement had to be brought from Meadville, Pa., in packs carried by the men on their backs, a distance of more than twenty miles, and paying at the rate of two dollars a bushel for corn, and other things in proportion. But during the fall of this year a blind path was opened from Pittsburgh through Butler and Mercer Counties to Meadville, making it much easier to get supplies from Pittsburgh on pack-horses than to bring it, as they had previously done in canoes, up the Alleghany river and French Creek to Meadville, and then the remainder of the way on their backs. Mr. R. S. Reed, of Erie, Pa., commenced his fortune by transporting provisions on pack-horses from Buffalo, N. Y., to Erie, Pa., a distance of more than a hundred miles, along a rough path upon the lake shore.

During the summer and fall of this year every person in Cleveland, Ohio, was sick, either with fever and ague or bilious fever, diseases with which this section was troubled for several years, but which have gradually disappeared as the country has become improved.

In the spring of this year the parents of Mr. R. R. Roberts moved from their old homestead in Ligonier, Westmoreland County, Pa., to Shenango, Pa., where all their children were now living. They were also soon followed by several of their neighbors, among them were the Stevensons, Walkers, M'Lanes, Dumars, who were regular members of the Methodist Episcopal Church. About the same time Rev. JACOB GURWELL, a native of Ireland, and a local preacher in the Methodist Episcopal Church, of moderâte talents, but an excellent Christian man, together with Rev. THOMAS M'CLELLAND, also an Irishman, and a local preacher of very respectable preaching talents, settled in the same neighborhood.

These two local preachers commenced preaching the Gospel in rude log-cabins and in groves, and wherever a little group could be convened, and some time in the summer of 1798 they formed a class consisting of such persons as had brought letters of membership with them, appointing Robert R. Roberts leader; this being the first class, and he the first leader, within the present bounds of the Erie Annual Conference of the Methodist Episcopal Church. It is said that Mr. Roberts was so extremely timid that he could not be prevailed upon to speak to the class in the ordinary way for several months after his appointment; but eventually he overcame this embarrassment so far as to become a very acceptable class-leader. We are here furnished with another instance of the great value of that class of men holding the relation of local preachers to the Methodist Episcopal Church. Relying upon no particular charge for their support, but laboring with their hands for the maintenance of their families, their love to the Master, and the desire to do good, leads them out frequently into new and destitute settlements, where they can break the bread of life to the destitute. It was in this way Methodism was first planted upon this continent by Philip Embury and Robert Strawbridge, both local preachers from Ireland. We shall have occasion frequently to refer to this class of pioneer laborers in breaking up the ground in advance of our regular itinerant ministry. True, after the country becomes densely populated, and the work well supplied with the regular ministry, the services of the local ministry is not in as great demand as formerly; yet these results are to some extent unavoidable, and should never be allowed to engender strife among brethren.

The reader will doubtless be pleased to see in this place a list of the names of the persons who composed this nucleus of Methodism in the Erie Conference. They were Robert R. Roberts, leader; Rev. Thomas M'Clelland and wife, James Stevenson and wife, William Sindsig and wife, Lewis Roberts and wife, John Honnel and wife, John M'Granehan and wife, William M'Granehan and wife, John Caughey and wife, John Rogers and wife, William M'Lean and wife, William Steward, and Nancy Wilson, twenty-four in all. Emigration continued to flow in, and especially members of the Methodist Episcopal Church, and the settlement extended to the south, so that another class was soon formed, which was called the "south class," composed of the following members: George M'Fetridge and wife, Thomas Dumars and wife, James Dumars and wife, John Waters and wife, Rev. Jacob Gurwell and wife, Probson Gibbins and wife, Thomas Jolly and wife, James Walker and wife, Morris Dunlavy and wife, William Gurwell and wife, to which was added in 1802 John Leech and wife, twenty-two in all. The local preachers above referred to took the entire watchcare of these classes, supplying them regularly with preaching for several years before the regular itinerant ministry reached them. They also found their way occasionally into new settlements, and carried the bread of life to hundreds that must have perished without it before other ministers could reach them. Thus was the "wilderness and the solitary place made glad by them, and the desert did rejoice and blossom as the rose."

1799.

The year 1799 furnishes a few interesting facts connected with the natural and religious improvement of the country. This year a company formed in Connecticut came on under the supervision of Mr. Nathaniel Church, and surveyed the ground where Canfield, the seat of Mahoning County, now stands; and Mr. Judson Canfield, from whom the place was named, in company with Mr. Elijah Wadsworth, moved their families from the East, and commenced the settlement of the place. Also in the spring of this year Mr. Lewis Day and son, and Mr. Lewis Ely and family, moved from the State of Connecticut, where both Mr. Day and Mr. Ely had belonged to the Methodist Episcopal Church, and settled in the town of Deerfield, Portage County, Ohio, being the first emigrants that ever came to the Western Reserve in a wagon.

Settlements were commenced this year in Warren, seat of Trumbull County, and in Ravenna, seat of Portage County, Ohio; also in the towns of Hudson, Mentor, Mantua, Chester, Willoughby, Windsor, Austinburg, and Harpersfield, in Ohio, and one on Elk Creek, and another in Springfield, called Lexington, Erie County, Pennsylvania. The Western Reserve was now pretty well dotted over with new settlements, but there were but a few families in a place, and a long distance apart, without roads between them; each exposed to Indian depredations and the intrusions of wild beasts, and no provisions in the country or means of getting them, so that it was a year of great suffering.

In the month of January, 1799, Mr. R. R. Roberts, in company with his brother, Lewis Roberts, returned to Ligonier, Westmoreland County, Pennsylvania, on a trading expedition, and in February following was married to Miss Elizabeth Oldham, of York County, Pennsylvania, who returned with him to Shenango, and became henceforth the noble and cheerful partner of his privations and toils to the end of life. It may be of use to some youthful bride of the present day, in planning her first bridal tour, to consult the experience of Mrs. Roberts, who, about two weeks after her marriage, mounted a good horse, with a few bed-clothes and cooking utensils lashed on around her saddle, and set off with the two brothers, who were similarly mounted, for Shenango. "Toward evening one day, as they were on their way, Mr. Lewis Roberts with his pack-horses proceeded somewhat in advance of his brother and his wife. Night came on, and the path was so obscure that Robert and his wife were compelled to stop and remain in the woods until morning. To Mr. Roberts this was no difficult matter; to his bride the event was only new, as she was made of as good materials as he for enduring hardships of this character. No person of her sex was ever better prepared to take a first lesson in such an adventure. Lewis had all the provisions on his extra horse, and of course they must pass the night supperless, though they had eaten nothing since breakfast, which was taken early in the morning. They encamped in the open air, and in the rigor of winter. When they were about to fall asleep, wrapped in their blankets and overcoats, the wolves began to howl around them most lustily, and so near them that they were afraid to go to sleep lest their noisy neighbors would favor them with a more intimate visit.

The night, of course, was spent sleeplessly, and not without some fearful apprehensions that the wolves might devour them. "Robert," said she, "they will certainly eat us before morning." "No, Betsy," was the reply, "they will be afraid to approach us, and if they do, this half-burned stick with its red blaze will terrify them, so that they will never face it to assault us." As soon as it was day the packs were placed on the horses, Mrs. Roberts mounted, and Mr. Roberts hunted the way, leading his horse until they recovered the path, and soon arrived at the hut where Lewis had spent the night, which, upon seeing, proved to be so very filthy that they congratulated themselves that their resting-place, after all, was the more desirable of the two. The family had been favored with a recently killed bear, and all things around had the impress of the greasy dainties. After riding a short distance further they stopped in the woods, sat down in the snow, and ate their cold breakfast, thanking a kind Providence that it was no worse with them."* After arriving at Shenango, Mr. Roberts, though very reluctant, was prevailed upon to resume the office and duties of class-leader, and in

* Elliott's Life of Bishop Roberts, pp. 75. 76.

his religious exercises evinced so much talent and pious zeal that many of the members of his class became convinced that "a dispensation of the Gospel" was divinely committed unto him, a fact with which his own mind had been deeply impressed for several years, but a consciousness of his want of the necessary qualifications for the work of the ministry had kept him back from any public effort of that kind. The society in Shenango continued to prosper under the efficient labors of the two local preachers who had formed it and had labored together harmoniously for its welfare.

During the summer of 1799 the author's grandfather, Samuel Gregg, who had several years before emigrated from Ireland, and settled his family in Center County, Pennsylvania, removed them across the mountains and through the wilderness, along a blind path, to Oil Creek, and purchased a farm on the banks of that stream, a few miles below Titusville, in Venango County, Pennsylvania. In crossing the Clarion River his oldest son, David Gregg, was drowned. The entire family, with all their effects, were brought on pack-horses. Mr. Gregg was not a member of any Church, but his wife, our paternal grandmother, was converted under the preaching of Mr. John Wesley and united with the Methodists in Ireland, and had united with them again in America; and on arriving at her new home on Oil Creek embraced the earliest opportunity to invite the Methodist ministers to her humble log-cabin in the wilderness, which for several years was both their lodging place and sanctuary.

1800.

The year 1800 greatly increased the number of inhabitants in this new territory notwithstanding all the hardships and sufferings they had to endure. Painesville, Lake County, Ohio, was made the nucleus of a flourishing settlement this year.

Mr. Roberts continued to be exercised more and more in his mind on the subject of preaching the Gospel. Perhaps the destitute condition of the extensive new country around him, now so rapidly filling up with inhabitants, had a great tendency to call his attention in that direction. Frequently after digging up a few grubs, or cutting down a few trees, he would sit down and give up his mind to solemn reflection the remainder of the day. At other times, while his horses were left standing for a long time in the plow, he would be seated on the beam, "musing on ministerial duties and other sacred subjects, or would be standing in an attitude for public speaking, as if addressing a congregation, or perhaps kneeling in the corner of the fence pleading with God in secret prayer for divine guidance." *

In the minutes of the conferences for this year Rev. P. B. DAVIS, of the Baltimore Conference, was appointed to the Shenango Circuit, but for some reason he did not embrace the classes in the Roberts neighborhood in his circuit. Perhaps he had as many appointments as one man could fill without them, and consequently left them still under the care of the two local preachers residing in the place, who

* Elliott's Life of Bishop Roberts, p. 89.

also established an appointment and formed a class on French Creek, a few miles below Meadville, Pennsylvania, at a place called Mumford's Settlement. The names we have not been able to procure; it did not continue many years.

Rev. OBED CROSBY, a local preacher in the Methodist Episcopal Church in the State of Connecticut, visited the town of Vernon, Trumbull County, Ohio, and spent a few weeks making preparations for the settlement of his family in that town, which was accomplished the next year. He undoubtedly preached a few times during his stay.

Rev. JOSEPH BADGER, a very devoted and laborious Presbyterian missionary, commenced preaching this year in the town of Vernon, and continued for several years to labor with good success in different parts of the Western Reserve.

We have now arrived at the period of time when the itinerant Methodist ministry was first introduced into this country, forming an important point in its religious history, and furnishing some of the sublimest specimens of Christian heroism. How very appropriate in their case was the language of the poet:

> "Though in a bare and rugged way,
> Through devious, lonely wilds I stray,
> Thy bounty shall my pains beguile,
> The barren wilderness shall smile."

Although there were eight annual conferences held in 1800, there were no fixed boundary lines between them; the preachers were at liberty to attend whichever conference was nearest or most convenient to their work. The Baltimore Conference was the first to occupy this territory, because the first members of the Methodist Episcopal Church who came here were from that part of Pennsylvania which received its ministers from Baltimore.

1801.

The Baltimore Conference sat in Frederick County, Maryland, at a place called Pipe Creek, commencing the 1st of May, 1801, at which the following appointments were made.

Pittsburgh District, Thornton Fleming, Presiding Elder.

Erie Circuit, James Quinn.

Shenango, Joseph Shane.

The Pittsburgh District embraced the settled territory now covered by the Western Virginia, Pittsburgh, and Erie Conferences, but we give here the names of but two of the eight circuits it contained, because these only were within the present bounds of the Erie Conference. The Erie Circuit, on which Mr. Quinn was appointed, was not yet formed, nor was there a class formed within the territory it was designed to embrace, or anywhere along the southern shore of Lake Erie. The two circuits when formed embraced all the country west of the Alleghany River from the Ohio to Lake Erie.

The Rev. THORNTON FLEMING, Presiding Elder on the Pittsburgh District, was the first man that ever labored in that capacity in this territory. He was born in Williamsburgh, Va., October 12, 1764, embraced religion and united with the Methodist Episcopal Church in 1784, and was received on trial in the Baltimore Conference, which sat in Baltimore Sept. 10, 1788, and into full connection and ordained a deacon in 1790, and an elder in 1792, and after traveling and preaching extensively on large circuits, he was in 1801 appointed presiding elder on the Pittsburgh District. We very much regret that he has not furnished the Church a more ample account of his labors, privations, hardships, sufferings, and success on the district he so ably served; but like the pioneers in Methodism generally, he found but little time to write. The only quarterly meeting held by Mr. Fleming this year within our bounds, of which we have any knowledge, was at the Mumford settlement on French Creek, and on the Shenango Circuit, in the early part of the year, at which Mr. R. R. Roberts received a license to exhort; but notwithstanding the deep feeling he had possessed for some years on that subject, he could not be prevailed upon to exercise his gifts in that way, being naturally very timid.

Rev. JAMES QUINN, appointed to the Erie Circuit this year, was born in Washington County, Pa., April 1, 1775, was converted to God and united with the Methodist Episcopal Church when about seventeen years of age. He was admitted on trial in the Baltimore Conference in 1799, received into full connection and ordained a deacon in 1801 by Bishop Asbury, and sent by him to form the Erie Circuit. After his appointment was announced, "Bishop Asbury called young Quinn to him, clasped him in his arms and pressed him to his bosom, gave him a Discipline, and said, 'Go, my son, and make full proof of thy ministry.'" * With this solemn charge pressing upon his heart our young itinerant started immediately for the field of labor assigned him. He was accompanied in his tedious journey as far as Pittsburgh by Rev. Joseph Shane, appointed to the Shenango Circuit. The whole journey was performed on horseback, along steep and rugged mountain paths. From Pittsburgh Mr. Quinn directed his course alone to Meadville as direct as possible, intending to make that place the center of his circuit. After a careful reconnoissance of his field of labor Mr. Quinn says, "The Presbyterian Synod of Pennsylvania had sent out ministers who had laid out all or most of all the settlements into congregational districts; and wherever they could gather a sufficient number of members, organized Churches and ordained elders, so that they seemed to have taken possession of the entire country."† This fact is introduced here not to the discredit of our Presbyterian brethren, but in commendation of their Christian zeal and enterprise in Western Pennsylvania. But it was unfortunate both for them and us that we entered upon this work too much in the spirit of religious rivalry, instead of looking upon and treating each other as fellow-laborers in the Master's vineyard. Mr. Quinn entered upon his work with true apostolic zeal, and soon was enabled to see "streams breaking forth in the wilderness." His circuit, when formed, contained twenty appointments, requiring him to travel four hundred miles every four weeks. The first class he formed was

* See Quinn's life, p. 57. † Ibid., p. 59.

near a place called Lexington, in Springfield township, Erie County, Pa. It was formed at the house of Mr. John Mershon, and its members were John Mershon and wife, Andrew Stull, Daniel Monroe, and Elizabeth Monroe, brother and sister of Rev. Joshua Monroe of the Pittsburgh Conference. Not one of these persons now remains on earth. Father Mershon, the leader, after serving God and his Church for more than fifty years died in peace, and went to unite in heaven with that "company which no man can number." A person not then a member says, "I heard Rev. J. Quinn preach at the house of Stephen Maxfield, a cabin twelve by seventeen feet, no floor in it, a black ash bark roof, the room overhung with pumpkins prepared to dry." Such were many of his preaching places.

Mr. Quinn says, "I suffered a little in the flesh this year. Breadstuff was very scarce, and what flesh we ate was chiefly taken from the woods with the rifle; but about midsummer we got plenty of potatoes. Once, however, having been several days without bread or meat, I indulged, when very hungry, in eating too freely of half-ripe blackberries, which caused an attack of bilious colic, that held me two days; but on the third day an old lady cured me by giving me weak ley made of hickory ashes. Upon the whole, I look back with as much pleasure upon the labors and sufferings of that year as any of the many years I have been employed in the vineyard of the Lord."*

Mr. Quinn in a letter says, "In the course of the

* Quinn's Life, p. 59.

year I spent a week with Brother Shane on his circuit for the purpose of administering baptism, as I was a deacon, and he only a probationer, and unordained. Here I became acquainted with Robert R. Roberts, of whom I had heard so many good things in Ligonier. He took me to his house or cabin, and opened his mind to me freely on the subject of his call to the ministry. But he had great misgivings, and felt deeply sensible of the awful responsibility of the office, and of his own inadequacy to fill it. I told him I believed that God had called him to the work, and that he would probably never be satisfied in his own mind until he had made a trial; and, moreover, that the Church could have no action in his case until she had evidence of his gifts for edification. A few nights after this we held a watchnight, to which he came on foot, the distance being from his house six or seven miles. Here we prevailed on him to give an exhortation, which was about the first. He delivered it in the costume of a backwoodsman, but it was worthy of gray hairs and broadcloth. All present were perfectly amazed, and Brother M'Clelland, who had been a traveling preacher in Ireland, said to me, 'That is the man. He ought to be in the work. He understands the doctrines of the Gospel well, and is a natural logician.'"

For some reason unknown to us the presiding elder removed Mr. Quinn to the Pittsburgh Circuit about Christmas, and employed in his place Rev. JOSEPH A. SHACKELFORD the balance of the conference year. During the following winter a revival of religion took place in the township of Washington, Erie

County, Pa., and a class was formed near the Conneaut Lake by Mr. Shackelford. Rev. Russel Stancliff and wife were among the first members, both of whom have long and well sustained the interests of the Methodist Episcopal Church.

Mr. Stancliff was licensed to preach in 1806, was ordained a deacon by Bishop George in 1819, and an elder by Bishop Roberts in 1828. As a local preacher he had but few equals in his day. Noble and dignified in appearance, with talents as a speaker of the first order, he was listened to with pleasure and profit by thousands now with him on the other side of the flood. After serving the Church for more than fifty years, he died in peace in 1856.

Mr. Shackelford formed another class the same winter about seven miles south of Mr. Mershon's; the leader's name was Blackmar. The names of the members not known. They were rather transient, and the class became reduced, until 1806, when the Randalls and Keeps, with other substantial persons, became connected with it, since which time its history has been glorious, until it received a crushing blow from Wesleyanism about 1843. Another class was formed about the same time thirteen miles further up the Conneaut Valley at M'Dowell's, but the names of the members are not known. There were four other classes formed on the Erie Circuit this year by Messrs. Quinn and Shackelford, but where they were located, or who were members of any of them, we cannot tell. They returned to conference at the close of the year sixty-five members.

Rev. Joseph Shane, appointed to the Shenango

Circuit this year, was admitted on trial in the Baltimore Conference in 1800, and was received into full connection and ordained a deacon in 1802; but for some reason he located in 1804. According to the best calculation we can make there must have been at the close of this year on the Shenango Circuit a membership of sixty within the bounds of the Erie Conference.

Rev. OBED CROSBY, who had the preceding year visited the town of Vernon, Trumbull County, Ohio, removed his family to that town during the summer of 1801. He came from the State of Connecticut by the way of Pittsburgh, Pa., in an open wagon drawn by an ox team, and soon after leaving Pittsburgh one of his oxen died, and he was compelled to yoke up a cow the remainder of the journey. On arriving at Vernon he found one Methodist family there, and immediately formed a class, consisting of Obed Crosby and wife, Ewing Wright and wife, and a Miss Bushnell, five in all. This was the first Methodist society on the "Western Reserve." The place of meeting was near the line of Vernon and Hartford, and the members increasing in Hartford more rapidly than in Vernon, it was finally removed into Hartford, and bore its name. Mr. Crosby, after laboring hard to establish the Church of his choice in the country around him, finally died in peace in 1814. The entire membership within the boundaries of our conference at the close of this year was one hundred and thirty. Mr. Quinn, who was now on the Pittsburgh Circuit, says that "some time in March, 1802, Brother Roberts came to one of my appointments, informing me that he had had no rest in his mind since we parted, and that he had determined to leave all, and that he was now on his way with his wife to offer himself to the Baltimore Conference. This startled me a little, for he had never been licensed either to exhort or preach,* neither had he a recommendation from the society or any quarterly conference. I paused a while. He observed the expression of hesitancy in me, and I also an affecting embarrassment in him, which I endeavored to remove by observing that as Shenango was missionary ground, and the circuit had not been fully organized, I thought we could get his case brought before the Quarterly Conference of one of the old circuits, and as Brother Fleming, the presiding elder, would hold a quarterly meeting at Doddridge's Meeting-house, on Ohio Circuit,† the following Saturday, I would write to him and the Quarterly Conference, and I doubted not they would take action in his case. He spent the night in restless tossings to and fro, and in the morning concluded he had better return home. At length he reluctantly took the letter and went to the quarterly meeting. Brother Shane providentially was present on the occasion, upon whose recommendation, along with my own, the conference licensed him to preach, and recommended him to the Baltimore Conference, at which he was admitted on trial." The conference met in Baltimore, April 1, 1802.

* Mr. Quinn was evidently not aware that Mr. Roberts had received license to exhort from Mr. Fleming. See Elliott's Life of Bishop Roberts, p. 90.

† Dr. Elliott, p. 97, says it was at "Holms's Meeting-house on Short Creek."

Rev. JAMES QUINN continued to labor in the Baltimore Conference until 1804, when he was transferred to the Western Conference, and in 1812, when the Ohio Conference was formed, he became a member of that body, of which, except two years in which he was located, he continued an active, useful, and influential member until his death, which occurred December 1, 1847.

Mr. Quinn, it is said, was "more than usually comely," in height "about five feet ten inches," and otherwise "well proportioned." At the commencement of his sermon he was "cool" and deliberate, but as he advanced he became animated, and his "countenance kindled into light, and at times it would become lighted up to almost a glare." His voice was melodious, "his style chaste," his sermons usually "doctrinal." He filled many prominent appointments in his conference, was for many years a presiding elder, and was chosen to represent his conference in the General Conference seven times.

The reader will be anxious to know how our preachers were supported on these large laborious circuits. From 1800 to 1816 their allowance was as follows:

"1. The annual salary of the traveling preachers shall be eighty dollars and their traveling expenses.

"2. The annual allowance of the wives of the traveling preachers shall be eighty dollars.

"3. Each child of a traveling preacher shall be allowed sixteen dollars annually to the age of seven years, and twenty-four dollars annually from the age of seven to fourteen years; *nevertheless*, this rule shall not apply to the children of preachers whose families are provided for by other means in their circuits respectively." *

To what extent the above amount was paid we cannot now tell, as no report is given in the General Minutes at this early day of the amount received; but judging from the number and circumstances of our members, and from the deficiencies of later periods in our history, the preachers could not have received more than two thirds of the amount allowed them. How they lived and supported their families is hard now to conjecture.

* Emory's History of Discipline, p. 238.

SECTION III.

FROM 1802 TO 1806.

"It looked but like a human hand;
Few welcomed it, none feared;
Yet as it opened o'er the land
The hand of God appeared."

1802.

THE Baltimore Conference, which sat in Baltimore April 1, 1802, made the following appointments:

Pittsburgh District, Thornton Fleming, Presiding Elder.

Erie, John Cullison.

Shenango, Asa Shinn.

It has been truly said that "When God plants the Christian faith in a new country, he employs for that work a ministry which follows up the pioneer hunter, the adventurer, and the emigrant. Along the western frontier in early times hastened the herald of the Cross, with Bible, hymn book, and saddle-bags, to occupy the ground in advance, and to point the rude children of the wilderness to the momentous concerns of the world to come. Men were needed then who could excel the old trapper in shooting at a mark, and yet lead the rude hunter to the feet of Jesus." Fleming, Gruber, Finley, and Cartwright were men of that stamp, well calculated to lead the host of young men, thrust out by the good providence of God, into this great western wilderness to cultivate it for God.

Mr. Fleming visited each circuit in his district once a quarter, holding a quarterly meeting in each, accomplishing his journeys on horseback, along rugged mountain paths, fording bridgeless streams, lodging at times in the woods, suffering immensely from cold and hunger. But the history of these sufferings and toils he had not time to write. On he sped from place to place, leaving it for the recording angel to make the record, and the Judge Eternal to read it in the great day of final reckoning, when he will say, "Well done, good and faithful servant."

Rev. JOHN CULLISON, appointed to the Erie Circuit this year, was admitted on trial in the Baltimore Conference in 1797, and received into full connection and ordained a deacon in 1799, and an elder in 1801, and continued faithfully to labor in the itinerant field until 1804, when for some reason unknown to us he located.

Rev. ASA SHINN, appointed to the Shenango Circuit this year, was admitted on trial in the Baltimore Conference in 1801. Shenango was, therefore, his second appointment. He was received into full connection and ordained a deacon in 1803, and an elder in 1805. Mr. Shinn was born and raised among the mountains of Virginia, and consequently enjoyed but few literary advantages; was quite awkward in his appearance, but possessed a mind of uncommon strength and brilliancy, which he cultivated with commendable diligence, which soon brought him into public notice and favor, and placed him among the first ministers of the famed Baltimore Conference. Indeed he possessed reasoning powers seldom surpassed.

The writer has now in his possession two valuable books written and published by him, which indicate a talent for logical discussion of a very high order. One is entitled "The Plan of Salvation," and the other "The Supreme Being."

Mr. Shinn became warmly interested in the great "Radical" movement which resulted in a large secession from the Methodist Episcopal Church in 1828, and the formation of the "Protestant Methodist Church," in whose communion he continued until death. His labors, however, were greatly interrupted by mental aberration, with which he was afflicted several years before he died.

Rev. HENRY SHEWEL, a local preacher, a native of New Jersey, but for a time residing in Redstone, Pa., removed in the spring of 1802 to Ohio, and settled in Deerfield, Portage County. The last forty miles was through an unbroken wilderness without a single inhabitant. He found a few Methodist families in that town who gladly received him as their spiritual guide. Mr. Shewel was one of the very best specimens of old-fashioned local preachers. His education was quite limited, and his language very imperfect. But his strong memory was well stored with a knowledge of the Holy Scriptures, which enabled him to bring out of "the treasury things new and old." His great theme was Christian experience. Enjoying a deep and rich experience himself, and possessing an ardent temperament, with almost unbounded zeal, attended with much of the divine unction, enabled him when dwelling upon this subject especially to produce a most thrilling effect upon his congregations;

and for many years he served as a pioneer in carrying the Gospel into the new settlements as they were being formed. Some time during the summer of 1802,* Mr. Shewel collected together the few members of the Methodist Episcopal Church in Deerfield, and formed them into a class. They were Henry Shewel and wife, Lewis Ely and wife, Ephraim Hubbard and wife, Simeon Card and wife, Lewis Day, and Daniel Diver and wife. This little heroic band, after witnessing the rise and spread of the work of God which they assisted in starting on the Western Reserve, have one by one passed away from earth, and again united in purer social and Christian fellowship in that world of heavenly bliss, where

> "Perfect love and friendship reign
> To all eternity."

In the fall of 1802 Mr. James M'Mahan, from Huntingdon, Pa., settled his family one mile and a half west of Westfield, Chautauqua County, N. Y., which was the first white settlement in that county. The following spring Mr. John M'Mahan and Mr. Edward M'Henry were added to the settlement.

Hon. JOHN LEECH came to reside in the Shenango settlement in May, 1802, reared a log-cabin, and entered it with his family. Before he could get it chinked, or bedsteads set up, Bishop Whatcoat came to the settlement, preached in his cabin, and remained all night. A pole thrust between two logs the length of the bed from the end of the cabin,

* In Bangs's History of Methodism the date of this society is fixed at 1801. But our information is derived from persons who were in circumstances to know the time.

winding the bed-eord round the pole and the log horizontal to it, and plaeing the bedding on this rude structure. furnished the pioneer bishop with a lodging-place in the wilderness, around which angels kept watch.

The membership on the Erie Circuit this year amounted to..	109
Shenango..........................	65
In all	174
Last year..........	130
Increase..	44

1803.

The Baltimore Conference sat in Baltimore April 1, 1803, at whieh the following appointments were made:

Pittsburgh District, Thornton Fleming, Presiding Elder.

Erie, Noah Fidler.

Shenango, George Askin.

Deerfield, Shadraeh Bostwiek.

Some time the following summer Mr. Fleming held a quarterly meeting on French Creek at Mumford's, then eonneeted with the Erie Cireuit, which was attended by a large eoneourse of people, eoming, some of them, a distance of fifty miles or more. The author's father, then a young man, attended that meeting, walking on foot from his home on Oil Creek, over thirty miles, and never regretted it to the end of his life, for at that meeting he was powerfully and happily eonverted to God. A large number of persons attended the meeting from Oil Creek and along the Alleghany River, and several from a settlement lying partly between those streams called "Pit-hole," and among them a lady by the name of Kinnear, who during the meeting became convicted of sin but could obtain no relief. On the Monday following, as the whole company were pursuing their journey homeward, along a blind path, some on foot and others on horseback, as they reached the top of a high hill light suddenly broke into the soul of the penitent lady, and the blessing came so sudden and powerful that she instantly began to clap her hands and to shout "Glory, glory to God!" when the whole company became so filled with joy as to join in the shout, and there in the wilderness was the command of the prophet in Israel fulfilled when he said, "Let the inhabitants of the rock sing, let them shout from the tops of the mountains." A class was formed this year by Mr. Fidler at Mr. Henry Kinnear's, near where the Titusville and Meadville road crosses Sugar Creek, in Crawford County, Pennsylvania. This class was finally removed to the house of Jonathan Benn, who became a useful local preacher, and lived and died much beloved on account of his excellent Christian character. Another class was formed about twelve miles north-east of Meadville, in the Daniels neighborhood. Abram Daniels, who became a traveling minister, was one of its first members. Mr. Fidler also crossed the Pennsylvania line into Ohio, and established an appointment, and formed a class in the town of Hubbard, composed of Rev. AMOS SMITH, a very useful local preacher recently from the East, and wife, and Rev. WM. VEACH, also a local preacher of excellent reputation, and wife, Mr. Parish and wife, Mr. Frazee and wife, Amos Snyder, Thomas Snyder, Joshua Snyder, Wm. Burnet, and Enos Burnet, and a few others. This class met for a number of years about one mile and a half west of the center of the town, and subsequently another class was formed about the same distance east of the center, but both have several years since been united at the center of the town.

Rev. NOAH FIDLER, appointed to the Erie Circuit this year, was received on trial in the Baltimore Conference in 1801, and into full connection and ordained a deacon in 1803, and an elder in 1805. Mr. Fidler was an excellent man and a very useful preacher, but for some reason unknown to us he located in 1807. A short but brilliant career.

Rev. GEORGE ASKINS, appointed to the Shenango Circuit this year, was admitted on trial in the Baltimore Conference in 1801, and into full connection and ordained a deacon in 1803, and an elder in 1805. Mr. Askins continued a faithful laborer in the Lord's vineyard, traveling and preaching on new and large circuits, enduring privations and hardships to us almost incredible, until February 28, 1816, when he passed from earth to heaven in a most triumphant manner, exclaiming, "Glory, honor, praise, and power be to God forever!" We have no account to give of his labors this year, except that about one hundred members were added to the Church on his circuit.

Rev. SHADRACH BOSTWICK, appointed to Deerfield this year, was born in Kent county, Maryland, March 30, 1769. We have no information relative to his conversion and call to the ministry. He was admitted on trial in the Baltimore Conference in 1791, and into full connection and ordained a deacon in 1793, and an elder in 1795. Mr. Bostwick was removed gradually to the north-east from year to year until, in 1796, when the New England Conference was formed, he fell into that conference, where in 1798 he was appointed presiding elder, but as the custom then was no name was given to the district. In 1801 he was appointed to the "Pittsfield District," this being the year when the districts were first regularly named, and was reappointed to that district again in 1802. Mr. Bostwick had married a daughter of Mr. Daniel Diver, who had emigrated to Ohio and settled in Deerfield, and was a member of the class formed in that town in 1802, by Father Shewel. Mr. Diver proposed to Dr. Bostwick also to come to Ohio and assist in introducing Methodism into the new country, and offered to give him a piece of land on which to locate his family. Mr. Bostwick had obtained a good knowledge of medicine, and would also be of great advantage to the new settlement in that respect. Accordingly in 1803 Dr. Bostwick was at his own request transferred to the Baltimore Conference, and appointed a missionary to Deerfield. The society at Deerfield experienced a gradual growth through his efficient services. And notwithstanding the time he must necessarily give to the erection of a house, clearing and cultivating land, together with the practice of medicine, upon which he immediately entered, he found time to penetrate the forests into other towns, where he established appointments, organized societies, and accomplished much good among the people. He was induced to visit Youngstown, Mahoning County, Ohio, where he found a small log-house built by the citizens, and occupied by the Presbyterians for a church, in which he asked permission to preach but was promptly and positively refused. Judge Rayen, a prominent citizen of the place, though not a professor of religion, invited the doctor to preach in his barn, which he consented to do until a better place was provided. Soon after Dr. Bostwick commenced preaching in Youngstown he formed a class consisting of Moses Crawford and wife, John Hogue and wife, Isaac Powers, a Mr. Braden, and others. These persons have all gone to join the doctor in heaven. Judge Rayen never became a member of the Church, but continued to be its friend and supporter; and in his death, which occurred in 1857, gave evidence of feeling the need of a Saviour by the earnest manner in which he besought his mercy. His excellent wife, however, soon became a member of the class, and lived and died a faithful Christian, and many years since entered into that rest that remaineth to the people of the Lord.

Mr. Isaac Powers, one of the members of this class, and extensively and favorably known by the preachers in the Erie Conference, has favored us with the following interesting account of his conversion. He says, "I joined this class, not because I had religion or considered myself a fit subject for membership in the Church, but as a means of obtaining salvation. This step was taken deliberately. The purpose was then formed to be a Christian. The family altar was then erected, and my house became a house of prayer, and a house for the weary itinerant. Pursuing this course, a measure of peace was sometimes felt, but it was a momentary gleam. The burden still pressed my heart. Charles Wesley expresses my feelings when he says:

'O that my load of sin were gone!
O that I could at last submit,
At Jesus' feet to lay me down,
To lay my soul at Jesus' feet.'

"While thus struggling under the weight of condemnation, a vision of the night impressed upon my mind the true mode of deliverance. I found myself walking out upon a horizontal beam, which projected over a most dark and fearful precipice. A glance around and downward revealed to me a position of most awful peril. To turn around was impossible because of the narrowness of the beam; to advance was equally impossible, for it extended to no safe footing, but terminated abruptly right over the yawning abyss. Despair was about taking place when something said, 'Trust in God and he will save you.' I awoke with this impression on my mind, that an implicit trust in the Redeemer was the way for a sinner to be saved. This act I was enabled a few days after to perform, and sudden as the lightning's gleam my darkuess vanished, and light filled my soul. The entire face of nature was changed. Everything was praising God, and in the simplicity of my soul I thought everybody would soon embrace the Saviour."

The class in Youngstown met for a time in the house of Mr. Crawford, who was the leader, then for a time at the house of Mr. Hague, at the head of Front-street.

The membership on Erie Circuit this year was........	168
Shenango..	236
Deerfield	16
Total	520
Last year	239
Increase..................................	281

1804.

The Baltimore Conference sat in Alexandria, April 24, 1804, at which the following appointments were made :

Monongahela District, Thornton Fleming, Presiding Elder.

Erie, Andrew Hemphill.

Shenango, Joseph Hall.

Deerfield, Shradrach Bostwick.

Our fathers were so strangely inclined to name both circuits and districts after some river, mountain, or creek, that the name of Pittsburgh District must this year be changed to Monongahela District, after a river that unites with the Alleghany at Pittsburgh. The district, however, embraced the same territory that it did before, and enjoyed the continued services of the same presiding elder.

Rev. ANDREW HEMPHILL, appointed to the Erie Circuit this year, was admitted on trial in the Baltimore Conference in 1803, and received into full connection and ordained a deacon in 1805, and an elder in 1807. He continued in the regular work until the Master called him home to heaven, which occurred August 27, 1837. The last three years of his ministry were spent on the Carlisle District. He was in the best sense of the word a revival preacher; affectionate in his address, simple in his manners, original in thought, pure in heart; his only aim seemed to be to see how many souls he could bring to Christ. His last dying words were, "Happy, happy." Mr. Hemphill was a member of the General Conference in 1824, 1828, and 1832. It was some time in the fall of this year that the author's mother, then Miss Sally Stevenson, a young lady of sixteen, was happily converted to God in a prayer-meeting held at our grandfather Gregg's on Oil Creek; and soon after this occurred Mr. Hemphill organized a class in the same house, but we are able to give but three of the members: John Gregg, Hannah Gregg, and Sally Stevenson. Mr. Hemphill also formed a class a few miles from Oil Creek, in a place called Pit-hole, composed of the Dawsons, Sigginses, Hendersons, Kinnears, and Alcorns, nearly all of whom have gone to their rest in heaven. Some time in the fall of this year Mr. Hemphill, in company with Mr. William Conley, who served as a guide, traveled from where Titusville on Oil Creek now stands to Franklin, Venango County, Pa., along a blind path. On arriving at Franklin, where he had an appointment to preach, he was refused the privilege of occupying the school-house, and consequently took his stand under a tree on the common, where he sang, prayed, and then preached to a small congregation, some sitting, and others standing on the green grass. This is supposed to be the first Methodist sermon ever preached in that village, since so famed for Methodism.

Rev. JOSEPH HALL, on the Shenango Circuit, was admitted on trial in the Baltimore Conference in 1801, and into full connection, and ordained a deacon in 1803, and located at the end of this year, most likely for the want of sufficient health to endure the hardships of the itinerancy in so new and rough a country.

Mr. WILLIAM RICHARD, a member of the Methodist Episcopal Church, and a licensed exhorter, moved his family this year from Center County, Pa., and settled them in Lawrence County, Pa., about four miles north of Newcastle, and one mile east of Shenango Creek, and commenced holding meetings in his own house, and the Lord greatly blessed his labors. The circuit preacher was invited, and preaching established, and soon a class was formed consisting of William Richard and wife, Robert Simonton and wife, Arthur Chineworth and wife, Mary Ray, Rachel Fisher, John Bibben and wife, Michael Carman and wife, William Underwood and wife, Robert Wallace and wife, Philip Painter and wife, and Rebecca Farber. The class increased rapidly.

Mr. Marinus King and family, all Methodists, moved into the neighborhood, and united with the class soon after it was formed, and in 1830 gave the Church an acre of land for Church purposes, on which a small log school-house was standing, which was fitted up and occupied as a place of worship, which gave it the name of "King's Chapel." The class soon increased to seventy members.

Dr. Bostwick continued his valuable services upon the Deerfield Circuit, extending his appointments as far west as Hudson, Summit County, Ohio, where he preached in the house of Capt. Gaylord. One day a gentleman by the name of Thompson happening to call at Mr. Gaylord's, and finding Dr. Bostwick there, commenced a terrible tirade upon Methodist ministers, because they did not receive uniformly a college education. The doctor heard him a few minutes, and then told him that he "had been through college." Mr. Thompson seemed much pleased that he had found one educated Methodist minister; and after congratulating the doctor upon his good fortune in being so far in advance of his brethren, he was about leaving, when the doctor took him by the hand, and said that the way he had "went through college" was a very short way, for he went in on one side of the building and went out at the other."

Dr. Bostwick had become deservedly popular as a physician, with a constantly increasing practice in medicine, which he could not consistently leave, and our rules not permitting him longer to remain on the Deerfield Circuit, he concluded, at the close of this year, to locate and serve the Church in a local capacity, relying upon his profession for his support. In his local capacity he continued to travel and preach extensively, and with great acceptability and usefulness. Thousands of persons on the Western Reserve who enjoyed his services esteemed him as an excellent Christian man, and a zealous and devoted minister of Jesus Christ. In 1807 he removed his family to Canfield, Mahoning County, Ohio, where he continued to serve the Church as a minister, and the community as a physician, until September 10, 1837, when he "ceased at once to work and live."

The membership on the Erie Circuit was this year.	349
Deerfield	30
Shenango	206
Total	585
Last year	520
Increase	65

1805.

The Baltimore Conference sat in Winchester, Va., April 1, 1805, at which the following appointments were made:

Monongahela District, James Hunter, Presiding Elder.

Shenango, Robert R. Roberts.

Erie and *Deerfield*, David Best, J. A. Shackelford.

We now must take our leave for a short interval of Mr. Fleming, who was stationed this year at Annapolis, and introduce to the reader Rev. JAMES HUNTER, who was admitted on trial in the Baltimore Conference in 1796, and into full connection and ordained a deacon in 1798, and an elder in 1800. He remained upon this district but one year, and then for some reason unknown to us was returned to a circuit. In 1808 he was appointed to the Carlisle District, on which he labored four years, and again returned to the regular work until 1815, when he located. We can give no account of his death.

Rev. DAVID BEST, in charge of the Erie Circuit, was soon after conference removed to the Shenango Circuit. He was admitted on trial in the Baltimore Conference in 1801, and into full connection and ordained a deacon in 1803, and an elder in 1805, and transferred to the Philadelphia Conference in 1808.

Rev. ROBERT R. ROBERTS, whose early history has already been recorded, was admitted on trial in the Baltimore Conference in 1802, and appointed junior preacher on the Carlisle Circuit, with James Smith for his colleague. In 1803 he was on the Monongahela Circuit, with P B. Davis. In 1804 he was received into full connection, ordained a deacon, and appointed in charge of Frederick Circuit in Maryland. It was not customary in those days to receive men with families into the conference, or to allow young men to marry until they had traveled four years. This was in consequence of the great difficulty of procuring a comfortable support for two married men on a new circuit. But Mr. Roberts had no family except a wife, who had been accustomed to close economy and great hardships; he was therefore received. But his support was so meager that he determined to take his wife back to her home in Shenango, and make the best provision he could for her support. Accordingly, in the fall of 1804, Mr. Roberts returned with his wife and household goods to the old log-cabin, where he made arrangements for the erection of a grist mill the following season, and it was on this account that he was this year appointed to the Shenango Circuit. But finding the appointments immediately around his own house connected with the Erie Circuit, he applied to the presiding elder, and obtained a change with Mr. Best, placing the latter on the Shenango Circuit, and Mr. Roberts in charge of the Erie Circuit, in company with Mr. Shackelford. Mr. Roberts was now once more quietly ensconced in his own rustic log farm-house, which, though humble in its dimensions and general appearance, yet having toiled hard to procure it, there was a charm in it to his heart which led him to feel that

"The old farm-house, where roof of faded red
Is seen beneath the snow-white cherry-trees
That fringe it round, and slowly, sweetly shed
Their floating blossoms on the whispering breeze,
Is more enticing in its calm retreat
Than stately mansions in the crowded street."

But he returned to his wilderness home not as the rustic backwoodsman or the timid class-leader he was when he left it. The three years he had spent in the ministry, in close application to study, and constant practice in preaching, had made him an able and eloquent expounder of the "truth as it is in Jesus," to whom his old neighbors and classmates listened with wonder and delight. The Erie and Deerfield Circuit at this time was more than four hundred miles in circumference. And this journey, to be accomplished every four weeks, was along blind paths found by marked trees, across swollen unbridged streams, over rugged precipices and high hills, now winding around steep, rocky mountain sides, and then plunging through deep miry morasses, sometimes camping in the woods all night, wearied and hungry, resting his head upon the root of some forest tree, while his faithful horse stood tied up without a mouthful to eat, and not unfrequently encountering wild beasts, rude savage men, and venomous serpents. One evening, in company with his wife, he put up at a "waste cabin," and spent the night without food, and only a little hay for their horses. Another night they spent in a most miserable cabin, cooking their own victuals, and making their bed for the night on a heap of unwinnowed flax-seed, covering themselves with their own overgarments. But Mr. Roberts was the man for such hardships and herculean labors. With a very large well-built physical frame, and great muscular strength, together with undaunted courage, accustomed from a child to great hardships, and thoroughly versed in the peculiarities of pioneer life, he appeared to be a well prepared and divinely chosen instrument for the peculiar work assigned him. Although engaged a portion of his time in the erection of his mill and the cultivation of his farm, on which he relied principally for the support of his family, the amount of valuable service performed upon his circuit this year was incalculable.

For some reason unknown to us, the presiding elder did not come to the last quarterly meeting, which was held in Shenango, and resulted in a glorious revival of religion, during which about thirty souls were added to the Church, and among them a member of the Presbyterian Church, who not long previously had driven his daughter from his home for attending a Methodist meeting; but now both father and daughter gave themselves for life to the Methodist Episcopal Church.

Rev. Joseph A. Shackelford, Jr., preacher on the Erie Circuit, was admitted on trial in the Baltimore Conference in 1804, and into full connection and ordained a deacon in 1806, and located in 1808. He was an excellent preacher, and greatly beloved by the people on the Erie Circuit, where he was instrumental in the conversion to God of a large number of souls. Why his itinerant career was so short we cannot tell at this distance of time.

Mantua, Portage County, Ohio, received the Gospel first from the lips of Mr. Bostwick in 1803, after which it was made an appointment for preaching. Mr. Roberts and Mr. Shackelford were instrumental in forming a class in this town in 1806, consisting of Basel Winsor, Joshua Mills, Paschal P M'Intosh and wife, Rufus Edwards, Silas Pinney and wife, which still continues to flourish.

The number of members this year on the Erie Circuit were.	555
Shenango.	277
Total.	832
Last year.	585
Increase.	247

SECTION IV

FROM 1806 TO 1810.

Is it not yet a very little while and Lebanon shall be turned into a fruitful field?—ISAIAH xxix, 17.

THE Western Reserve, with its New England inhabitants and peculiarities, seemed to be illy adapted to a rapid spread of the doctrines and usages of the Methodist Episcopal Church. And the same remark is true in a limited sense of Western Pennsylvania. The early settlers were puritanical in their descent, with strong predilections for the old and well-established system of partial salvation, the general features of which the old Puritan divines had dyed, as it were, into their very souls. Methodism was more elastic and latitudinarian in its nature and tendencies, and hence it was looked upon as an antagonistic agent bordering on heresy which ought to be sternly resisted. Acting in accordance with these views, the most violent attacks were made upon our doctrines and usages by the clergymen of the country, which rendered it necessary for our ministers in those days to study closely the writings of Mr. Fletcher, and discuss over again those very doctrines of his day, and faithfully was the work accomplished.

1806.

The Baltimore Conference sat in Baltimore, March 14, 1806, at which the following appointments were made:

Monongahela District, Thornton Fleming, Presiding Elder.

Erie, Robert R. Roberts, James Watts.

Shenango, James Reed.

The rule in our Discipline which prohibits the return of a presiding elder to a district he has traveled "four years," until he has been absent "six," is of modern date, and did not apply in Mr. Fleming's day; hence after an absence of one year he is now back again, to the great joy of preachers and people all over the district.

Rev. JAMES WATTS, junior preacher on the Erie Circuit with Mr. Roberts, was admitted on trial in the Baltimore Conference in 1804, and into full connection and ordained a deacon in 1806. Very little information can now be obtained respecting the labor performed by Mr. Watts this year, except that it was of the severest character. The Erie Circuit was this year so enlarged as to require six weeks to go around it, preaching generally once each day and twice on the Sabbath. And yet these two faithful pioneer ministers were frequently engaged in penetrating still further into the wilderness to find new settlements that they might furnish them with the bread of life. Meadville, Pa., had increased to be a flourishing village. The Presbyterians had become strong and numerous, but the Methodists, as their usual custom then was, had neglected the village, giving all their time and attention to the country. Mr. Roberts tried to gain a foothold there. The only place he could procure to preach in was a tavern, where he occasionally held forth on a week evening. One evening, as he was preaching to a small congregation against the prevailing desire for unrighteous gain, he said that "if he wanted riches he would not go to hell for them, for if they were to sweep hell over they could not find a sixpence." A shrewd little man sitting in one corner, with a squeaking voice, cried out, "Then, sir, money is about as scarce there as here." A smile ran through the congregation, but the gravity of the speaker was undisturbed. What a change has since taken place in Meadville!

Mr. Roberts started off on a tour of exploration up the Alleghany River as far as Warren, Pa., where a settlement had been made the year previous by Mr. Gillman, who for many years made the Methodist ministers welcome to his house, as some of his descendants do to the present time. From Warren he proceeded up the Conewango Creek to a settlement then known as the "Beech Flats," near the Pennsylvania state line, where he preached at the house of Mr. Isaiah Jones, and as he returned preached in several new settlements, and was undoubtedly the first Methodist minister that preached the Gospel in Warren County, Pa. The class formed at Conneaut, in Erie County, Pa., had increased rapidly, so that there was now a large congregation in that place. One cold, wintry day, with deep snow, Mr. Roberts was late in getting to his appointment, and found the congregation waiting, and proceeded at once to preach and then to meet class without any refreshment. He was then prevailed upon to stay and preach in the evening. Seeing no preparation for supper, and "having eaten nothing since morning," he felt keenly the cravings of hunger, and quietly slipped "into the kitchen," and supplied his wants with such things as he could find; and it was a fortunate move for him, for the meeting was so "interesting" that it lasted to a late hour.

The next day, as Mr. Roberts "was starting for Lexington," now known better as West Springfield, Pa., where he had an appointment to preach the day following, which was the Sabbath, "the lady at whose house he had been stopping proposed accompanying him a few miles on horseback to visit some friends." As "the snow had fallen" to a considerable depth the road was scarcely discernible, and in "passing through a beech woods" the "lady's horse" stepped on some roots, with which his foot became fastened, so that he could not extract it. Mr. Roberts, however, "went to the nearest house and borrowed an ax, and by applying it to the roots soon extricated the animal." But this circumstance "detained him" so long that "night came on when about eight or ten miles from his appointment. There was no path or track," or anything to indicate his course save "marks made on the trees." While hunting his way along in the dark he came to "a small cabin and found only some children in it, the parents being from home. He asked if he could stay all night, and was informed that he could." He hesitated some; "the appearance of things in and around the cabin" was by no means inviting, and yet to proceed was impossible, as he could not see the marks on the trees. To advance he might be compelled to lie in the woods; to stay was but little better. The children were "very dirty, being covered with bear's grease," having partaken freely of the meat and fat of a good-sized bruin during the day, distributing the greasy substance profusely upon the scattered, broken pieces of furniture. He finally determined to stay. Soon after the mother came, and her appearance was but little better. She also gave him permission to stay, but "informed him that they had no bread in the house, nor anything to make it of." It was not long "until the father came home from hunting," and was glad to see the stranger, and treated him with marked kindness. "He had no grain for the horse," but gave him some hay. "For supper the woman put a plentiful supply of the bear's meat into a large kettle over a blazing fire, filling it up with potatoes. When this mixture was well boiled, a quantity was put into dishes, and set on a table made of a slab. They sat down to this repast; but such was its uninviting appearance that though suffering with hunger, Mr. Roberts could eat but little. They had no bed for their reverend guest to sleep in, and as a substitute, they took a moderate supply of straw and spread it on the floor before the fire, his saddle-bags serving as a pillow, and his great coat for a covering." He spent the night as comfortably as he could. "Next morning the same dish was prepared for breakfast, but in rather better order, which rendered it more palatable, and an increase of hunger had sharpened the appetite of the preacher, so as to overcome his fastidiousness. During his stay" Mr. Roberts conversed freely with "the father of this family" on the subject of religion, who seemed to be greatly interested in what he said. The man had enjoyed religion in other days, but "in his secluded" condition he had enjoyed but few religious privileges, and had consequently grown careless. But this visit of a man of God aroused him again to duty, and was no doubt the means of his salvation. "At his request Mr. Roberts baptized several of his children."* Early on Sabbath morning Mr. Roberts set out for Lexington, arriving just in time for service. "Three persons in this place who had experienced religion some time previously" desired to be baptized by immersion. Mr. Roberts had never witnessed the administration of baptism in this way, and was at some loss to know how to proceed appropriately. "The weather was exceedingly cold." But "after preaching they went to Conneaut Creek, where he immersed them." He then had to walk about a mile to his lodging-place, and by the time he arrived his clothes were frozen stiff, but he suffered no perceptible injury.† Mr. John Randall, who became a very valuable member, was one of the persons baptized. This reference to baptism by immersion reminds us of an occurrence we heard of some thirty years since in the very place where it is said to have occurred. About twelve miles north of Meadville, Pa., in the town of Randolph, was a Baptist Church of some strength, and also a growing Methodist society under the pastoral care of Mr. Roberts and his colleague. A great amount of controversy was kept up between the two congregations on the subject of

* See Elliott's Life of Bishop Roberts, pp. 138, 139.

† Ibid., pp. 139, 140.

"immersion being the only mode of Christian baptism," and on "the final perseverance of the saints." Mr. Roberts became completely disgusted with the way in which those who advocated these doctrines constantly obtruded them upon the attention of the public, and as far as possible avoided them. This course, however, did not suit the impetuous friends of controversy, and Mr. Roberts was urged to preach his sentiments touching these points. He finally promised that he would tell what he thought about them at his next appointment in that place. The notice was published, and a large congregation assembled to hear him. Mr. Roberts took his text and proceeded with his discourse as usual, saying nothing upon the topics in dispute, until his congregation began to show signs of disappointment. He finally paused in his discourse and said, "You are expecting me to give you my opinion to-day on two doctrinal points, on which some of you place a great deal more stress than their importance demands. I will give you my opinion of those doctrines by relating a little circumstance which occurred the other day. As I was riding through a piece of woods in the dusk of evening I came to a pond of water on one side of the road, and just in the edge of that pond stood a noted advocate of those two doctrines. As I approached he was crying out 'Rep-ro-ba-tion, rep-ro-ba-tion,' and suddenly he plunged into the water, and after immersing himself in it he came up crying 'Fin-ished sal-va-tion, fin-ished sal-va-tion.' And I thought that if any one else had a mind to listen to such nonsense, or to waste time in replying to it, that I would not, and so rode on and left him, perhaps thinking that he had beaten me in the argument." And so left the subject.

Not far from the Shenango settlement lived a Rev. Mr. M'Lean, a Seceder minister and a thorough-going Calvinist. In a conversation with Mr. John Leach he said "the Methodists are an ignorant people, and greatly deluded; and I could convince them of their error in one sermon if I had an opportunity." Mr. Leach promised that he should have the opportunity desired. Accordingly an appointment was published at the house of Mr. Walker, and the Methodists generally attended. Mr. Roberts also was present. Mr. M'Lean took for his text, "Contend earnestly for the faith once delivered to the saints." He undertook to discuss this subject by inquiring, "I. Whether Christ died for all the sins of all men." He maintained that he did not; for if he did then all would be saved, which he showed was not true. "II. Or whether he died for some of the sins of all men." If this was true, then he argued none could be saved. "III. Or for all the sins of some men." This he affirmed; by which he showed some only would be saved. When the sermon was concluded, Mr. Roberts arose and requested the privilege of replying to it, promising not to occupy more than half an hour. Mr. M'Lean gave consent, and Mr. Roberts gave out, and the Methodists present sang with spirit, that excellent hymn,

"Blow ye the trumpet, blow,
The gladly solemn sound."

Mr. Roberts was well read in the old Calvinistic controversy as waged by Rev. John Fletcher in his "Checks to Antinomianism," and proceeded to deal out blows that soon made his reverend opponent feel very uneasy, and in about fifteen or twenty minutes he arose and said that it was contrary to the rules of his Church to hear a Methodist preach, and requested his people to leave immediately with him; and so away they went, producing all the noise and confusion they could. Mr. Roberts soon closed, carrying the public sympathy generally with him.*

The conference year was closed up pleasantly, and Mr. Roberts became satisfied that the cultivation of his farm, building a grist-mill, and traveling a circuit from four to five hundred miles in circumference, was more than any man could accomplish and do it well, and so resolved to leave his home again and devote himself entirely to the work of the ministry, which he did from this time forward with wonderful success. His progress from this time was remarkably rapid. In 1807 he was appointed to the Pittsburgh Circuit, where he labored one year with great success. In 1808 he was appointed on the West Wheeling Circuit, enjoying another year of good success. This year, in company with Rev. T. Fleming, he represented this part of the work in the General Conference which sat in Baltimore May 1, 1808, and was the last General Conference where all the elders met, and when a delegated General Conference was permanently established to meet once in four years. In

* Elliott's Life of Bishop Roberts, pp. 141, 142.

1809 he was stationed in Baltimore; in 1810 at Fell's Point; 1811 at Alexandria; 1812 at Georgetown. He was also elected by the Baltimore Conference a delegate to the General Conference which sat in New York, May 1, 1812. In 1813 he was transferred to the Philadelphia Conference and stationed in Philadelphia, where he was reappointed in 1814. In 1815 he was appointed presiding elder on the Philadelphia District, to which he was reappointed in 1816. He was also elected by the Philadelphia Conference a delegate to the General Conference which met in Baltimore May 1, 1816, where he was elected to the office of a bishop in the Methodist Episcopal Church, to which he was consecrated May 17, 1816.

I will here say without fear of contradiction from any source, or of giving offense to any one, that in the whole eventful history of Methodism in Europe and America, where so many brilliant Gospel luminaries have been raised up, that no man ever rose from such obscurity, amid so many embarrassing circumstances, in so short a time, to such an eminent position, and maintained it to the end of life with so much credit to himself and usefulness to the Church. Among the many things for which the writer of these pages will forever be thankful to a kind Providence, will be the privilege of enjoying the acquaintance of this great and good man. We have sat in three annual conferences where he presided, and have heard the Gospel several times from his eloquent lips. Among all the men we ever saw his gigantic frame was the most ancient in appearance and dignified in looks and movements, and yet he was as simple as a child.

> "Among the faithless, faithful only he;
> Among innumerable false, unmovod,
> Unshaken, unseduced, unterrified.
> His loyalty he kept, his love, his zeal."

Rev. JAMES REID, in charge of the Shenango Circuit, was admitted on trial in the Baltimore Conference in 1804, and into full connection and ordained a deacon in 1806, and an elder in 1808. He continued in the regular work, except a few years in which he was in a supernumerary or superannuated relation on account of poor health, until he died.

The Erie Circuit returned a membership this year of....	647
Shenango	309
Total	956
Last year	832
Increase	124

1807

The Baltimore Conference, which sat in Baltimore March 2, 1807, made the following appointments:

Monongahela District, Thornton Fleming, Presiding Elder.

Erie, C. Reynolds, A. Daniels, and T. Divers.

Shenango, James Watts, Thomas Church.

The Erie Circuit this year was a six weeks' circuit, with three preachers.

Rev. CALEB REYNOLDS, in charge of the Erie Circuit this year, was born in the State of Maryland in 1785, and through the preaching of the Methodist ministry was converted to God in 1802. He was received on trial in the Baltimore Conference in 1805, and into full connection and ordained a deacon in 1807, and an elder in 1809. Mr. Reynolds was a laborious Christian minister, and many souls were brought to God under his faithful ministry. He continued in the regular work, except two years in which he was in a supernumerary, and two years in a superannuated relation on account of ill health, until 1827, when he departed this life in holy triumph.

Rev. ABRAHAM DANIELS was licensed to preach and recommended to the Baltimore Conference by the quarterly conference of the Erie Circuit, and was the second man sent out from this territory into the itinerant ministry. He was received on trial in the Baltimore Conference March 14, 1806, and appointed junior preacher on the West Wheeling Circuit, and now in 1807 second preacher on the Erie Circuit. At the end of this year he was received into full connection and ordained a deacon, and in 1810 an elder.

Mr. Daniels was large in stature, robust in health, possessed a clear, strong mind, and was a stern defender of Methodist doctrine and discipline, and might have become one of our first and best men. But becoming discouraged with the hardships and sacrifices of the itinerant work, he located in 1813, and returned to his former home in Randolph, Crawford Co., Pa., where he finally died, we trust, in the Lord.

Rev. TIMOTHY DIVERS, third preacher on the Erie Circuit, was received on trial in the Baltimore Conference in March, 1806, but was discontinued at the end of the year.

Rev. THOMAS CHURCH, second preacher on the Shenango Circuit, was received on trial in the Baltimore Conference in 1802, and into full connection and ordained a deacon in 1804, and an elder in 1806, and was transferred to the Western Conference in 1809, and located in 1810.

The number of members on the Erie Circuit this year is..	665
Shenango	275
Total	940
Last year	956
Decrease	16

1808.

The Baltimore Conference sat in Georgetown, D. C., March 2, 1808, where the following appointments were made:

Monongahela District, Thornton Fleming, Presiding Elder.

Erie, Job Guest and William Butler.

Shenango, James Charles.

The Erie Circuit is again compressed into a four weeks' circuit, with two preachers, perhaps by transferring some of its appointments to some other circuit, a fact also indicated by the decrease of members at the close of the year, compared with last year.

Rev. JOB GUEST, in charge of the Erie Circuit, was admitted on trial in the Baltimore Conference in Baltimore at its session in March 14, 1806, and into full connection, and ordained a deacon in 1808, and an elder by Bishop M'Kendree in 1810. Of his labors on the Erie Circuit we have been able to obtain but little information, but of his character and success generally as a Gospel minister there is evidence in abundance to show that he possessed more than ordinary talents and piety, and that large success generally accompanied his labors. For more than fifty years he continued to travel and preach, extending his labors from the shore of Lake Erie on the north to the Chesapeake on the south and east, much of the country at the time a dreary wilderness, and from which many thousands will rise up in the great day of the Lord and call him "blessed." His biographer truly says that "he was rich in all the virtues that adorn ministerial character." He died in peace December 15, 1857.

Rev. WILLIAM BUTLER was admitted on trial in the Baltimore Conference at Baltimore March 2, 1807, the Erie Circuit being his second appointment. At the end of this year, in March, 1809, he was ordained a deacon, and received into full connection, and ordained an elder in 1811. Relative to his labor on the Erie Circuit we have been able to gather no information of importance. He continued faithfully to travel and preach until 1843, when he received a superannuated relation, which he continued to sustain until January 11, 1852, when he closed his useful life in a very triumphant death at Carlisle, Pa., where he first united with the Methodist Episcopal Church more than fifty years previously. From a diary which he kept it appears that nearly four thousand persons had been added to the Church on the different fields where he had labored. "They that turn many to righteousness shall shine as the stars forever."

From 1796 up to 1812 Western New York was nominally within the bounds of the Philadelphia Conference, though most of the time entirely unoccupied. In 1808 a circuit was formed by that conference called the "Holland Purchase," which embraced all of the State of New York west of the Genesee River, to which the Rev. GEORGE LANE was appointed. Some time in the winter of 1808–9, learning that a few members of the Methodist Episcopal Church had settled a short distance east of the present village of Fredonia, in the west part of Sheridan, in Chautauqua County, Mr. Lane started up from Buffalo in a one-horse sleigh to visit and preach to them. On his way up he overtook Mr. Gould and wife in a two-horse sleigh, who were members of the Methodist Episcopal Church, and resided in the place just mentioned, and who had been east on a visit, and were returning home. The snow was deep, and, as is usually the case in that region, badly drifted. Night came on them while in the woods some distance below the Cattaraugus Creek, and they became so buried in the snow that they could get their sleighs no further. After disengaging their horses from the sleighs, each person mounted a horse, and rode on the bare back to Mack's Tavern, where they spent the remainder of the night. Next morning they succeeded in getting their sleighs, and before night reached Mr. Gould's house, where Mr. Lane spent a few days and preached several times, and during his stay in the place formed a class consisting of Stephen Bush, Daniel Gould and wife, and Elijah Risley. This was undoubtedly the first Methodist preaching and the first class formed in Chautauqua County, State of New York, which has since that time been a very fruitful field for Methodism, and very productive of *Methodist ministers.**

The number in society on the Erie Circuit this year was ..	646
Shenango	282
Total	928
Last year	940
Decrease	12

1809.

The Baltimore Conference met in Harrisonburgh, Va., March 2, 1809, at which the following appointments were made:

Monongahela District, Thornton Fleming, Presiding Elder.

Erie, J. Charles, J. M. Hanson, J. Decellum.

Chenango, Jacob Dowell, Eli Towne.

The Erie Circuit is again a six weeks' charge, with three preachers.

Rev. THORNTON FLEMING this year closed his labors on the Monongahela District, which he had now served two terms of four years each, one year intervening. He continued a faithful laborer within the bounds of the Baltimore Conference until the Pittsburgh Conference was formed in 1825, in which he continued to labor until 1834, when, on account

* For these facts I am indebted to the Hon. E. T. Foot, formerly of Jamestown, New York, but now of New Haven, Conn., who received them from Mr. Lane.

of declining health, he was placed in a superannuated relation. He spent fifty-eight years in the ministry, fifteen of which he was presiding elder. If his slumbering ashes could speak from the grave, or his happy spirit from heaven, he could describe to us many scenes of toil, sufferings, sacrifices, hard-fought battles, and animating victories in the cause of Christ which occurred on the very soil we as a conference now occupy, of thrilling interest; but unfortunately he has left no record of them on earth; we must, therefore, wait until we receive them from his lips in the world of light to which his happy spirit fled in holy triumph November 26, 1846. Mr. Fleming was a member of the General Conference in 1828.

Rev. JAMES CHARLES, in charge of the Erie Circuit, was admitted on trial in the Baltimore Conference March 2, 1806, and was received into full connection and ordained a deacon in 1808, and an elder in 1810. This was a very prosperous year on the Erie Circuit.

Rev. J. M. HANSON was admitted on trial in the Baltimore Conference March 2, 1809, and appointed second preacher on the Erie Circuit, where he labored with great acceptability. He was received into full connection and ordained a deacon in 1811, and an elder in 1813. Mr. Hanson became an eminent and useful minister, filling the most important stations and districts in the Baltimore Conference.

Rev. JOHN DECELLUM was this year admitted on trial in the Baltimore Conference, and appointed third preacher on the Erie Circuit, and at the close of the year was discontinued.

On the Western Reserve our progress was slow, its "New England inhabitants were slow to yield their Calvinistic prejudices in favor of a system of religious faith which recognized no divine favoritism among men, making all alike sinful, and giving all an equal chance for heaven." England needed such religious champions as the Wesleys, Coke, Nelson, Maxwell, and Bramwell to arouse a formal Church, and such giant controversialists as Fletcher, Clarke, and Watson to inaugurate anew the pure apostolic system of faith which for centuries had been buried beneath the rubbish of the "dark ages." So New England must needs have a Lee, a Broadhead, a Pickering, and a Fisk to meet the "hordes of ecclesiastical Samsons, whose mighty sway, at the introduction of Methodism into the new world, gave its friends reason to fear that a plant of such unnatural and rapid growth would scarcely survive their scathing criticisms for a single year;" but the "sect everywhere spoken against" not only held its own, but made steady progress in Puritan soil, and in its aggressive achievements soon found its way over the Alleghany Mountains, and with the march of ceaseless immigration made for itself a home in the great lake region of the north-west. But wherever our cause spread there was a polemic warfare waged, which would have been most disastrous to the Church in the wilderness but for the host of mighty men Providence raised up upon the ground for her defense. Without institutions of learning, or the means of creating them, in which to prepare instruments for the work, God raised up men of giant intellects, whose knowledge of the holy Scriptures and of the plan of salvation therein taught made them mighty in defense of the truth. Quinn, Bostwick, Fleming, Roberts, and Hemphill, with scores of others who succeeded them in this work, have accomplished for Methodism in the West what Lee and his compeers had done in the East. The settled peace we now enjoy is to a large extent the result of the hard-fought battles of those trying times; and instead of condemning their controversies, we should thank God that this work was accomplished before we came upon the stage, and by men so much better fitted, both by nature and by grace, for that kind of work.

Rev. JACOB DOWELL, in charge of the Shenango Circuit, was received on trial in the Baltimore Conference in 1807, and into full connection and ordained a deacon in 1809, and an elder in 1811.

Rev. ELI TOWNE, second preacher on the Shenango Circuit, was received on trial in the Baltimore Conference in 1804, and into full connection and ordained a deacon in 1806, and an elder in 1808. His labors in this work ended this year.

The number of members reported this year was.......	989
Last year..	928
Increase....	61

SECTION V.

FROM 1810 TO 1812.

"Would I describe a preacher, such as Paul,
Were he on earth, would hear, approve, and own,
Paul should himself direct me; I would trace
His master strokes, and draw from his design.
I would express him simple, grave, sincere;
In doctrine uncorrupt; in language, plain."

1810.

THE Baltimore Conference met in Baltimore March 9, 1810, at which the work in this region was arranged as follows:

Monongahela District, Jacob Gruber, Presiding Elder.

Erie, Joshua Monroe.

Hartford, James Charles, James Ewen.

Shenango, James Watts.

The Monongahela District was bounded on the east by the Alleghany Mountains, south by the Greenbrier Mountains, west by the limits of the white settlements in Ohio, and north by Lake Erie. It contained ten circuits, two of which, with part of a third, lay within the bounds of Erie Conference, each of which had to be visited once in three months by the presiding elder on horseback. Erie Circuit is divided. The western part, lying chiefly in Ohio, is called "Hartford."

Rev. JACOB GRUBER, the new presiding elder, appointed to the Monongahela District, was born

February 3, 1778. His parents were of German descent and dialect. In learning to speak both languages his English became quite broken, which, together with some constitutional eccentricities, rendered him at times quite musical, though connected as it was with so much practical good sense as to render him always interesting and instructing. He was convicted and converted to God when about fifteen years old, through the labors of the Methodist ministry, and was compelled literally to forsake father and mother, home and friends, in becoming a member of the Methodist Episcopal Church. He was admitted into the Baltimore Conference on trial in the spring of 1800, and into full connection and ordained a deacon in 1802, and an elder in 1804, and appointed presiding elder on the Greenbrier District in 1807, and now, 1810, transferred to the Monongahela District. He was a man of untiring energy and industry. "His principles were moulded and his habits formed in the school of early Methodism, and after the model of some of the most efficient Methodist ministers. And although generally harsh and often severe, perhaps to excess, yet he was always sincere and honest. Of him it may in truth be said, he was 'in labors more abundant.' Thoroughly read in the writings of Wesley, Fletcher, and Clarke, and catching the living inspiration from the lips of Asbury, Whatcoat, and M'Kendree, he was always ready to defend the doctrines and institutions of Methodism with a degree of strength that made our enemies dread him wherever he went. In exposing false doctrines, and unmasking false religion, though rather caustic for the public ear, he was usually extremely successful." *

Rev. George Brown, editor of the "Methodist Protestant," says, "Jacob Gruber was a man of great physical, mental, and moral energy. We never knew a more laborious Christian minister, or one of more practical ready wit. He met all occurrences as they arose before him with as much readiness as if a month had been allowed him for preparation. His sermons were always fresh beef in the market. Old truths seemed new when cast in his original mould. His congregations never slept under his preaching, for he was both an interesting and profitable expounder of the living oracles. Revivals followed his course, for all his efforts were directed to the great work of saving souls. Young preachers under his care, by precept and example, were taught to be working men. A lazy preacher was to him an abomination. At his camp-meetings, his rule was never to allow a gun to be fired from the stand that would not go off in the altar among the mourners. Like a general at the head of his army have we often seen him at the head of his camp-meeting forces, in the altar all night long, singing, praying, and shouting on to victory. And yet Jacob Gruber was a perfect original in his eccentricities. He often did things that no one else could do." The following incident will illustrate that last assertion. It was received from a reliable person who was present and heard it. On coming to one of his circuits to quarterly meeting on his first round after conference, he heard repeated

* See Conference Minutes, vol. iv, p. 556.

complaints from the people on account of the length of the sermons preached by their young minister. Mr. Gruber concluded to say nothing to him until he had a chance to hear for himself, and accordingly put him up to preach on Saturday evening in a barn where the meeting was being held, and taking his seat with him in the rough stand, listened to him more than an hour on the first head of his discourse. As he branched off on to the second head he remarked that, "here a vast field opens to my view." Just then Gruber lifted his hand and said, "Coot Got, put up dem pars and don't let him into dat pig field or we'll not get him out to-night." The sermon was stopped short without exploring the "vast field," much to the gratification of the congregation.

Erie Circuit, which, after conference, was made a four weeks' circuit by the appointment of Rev. J. Dowell by the elder to travel with Mr. Monroe, embraced Erie, Crawford, Venango, and Mercer Counties in Pennsylvania.

Rev. JOSHUA MONROE, in charge of the Erie Circuit, was admitted on trial in the Baltimore Conference in Georgetown, District of Columbia, in March, 1808, and into full connection and ordained a deacon in 1810, and an elder in 1812. When the Pittsburgh Conference was formed in 1825, Mr. Monroe became a member of that body, to which he now belongs. After spending fifty-six years in the ministry, he now sustains (1864) a superannuated relation, loved and respected by all who know him. Mr. Monroe has been elected by his conference to represent them in the General Conference three times. Mr. Monroe says that "Erie was now a four weeks' circuit, of about two hundred miles, with twenty-three appointments. The most prominent of these were, Brush's meeting-house, in West Springfield, Erie County; Leech's, on Little Shenango; Mumford's, near Meadville; Pit-hole; Mrs. Mitchell's, in Venango; and Ford's, on French Creek Flats, in Erie County. Our appointments were all in private houses, except Mercer, where we used the school-house, and Brush's meeting-house. This was built of round logs and covered with clap-boards." This church, located in the neighborhood of Mr. John Mershon, in West Springfield, Erie County, Pa., was undoubtedly the first Methodist meeting-house within the bounds of our conference. We cannot now tell when it was built, but some time previous to 1810.

Rev. James Ewing, second preacher on the Hartford Circuit, was admitted on trial in the Baltimore Conference in March, 1809, and into full connection and ordained a deacon in 1811, and an elder in 1813, and located in 1814.

Rev. Jacob Dowell was sent in 1810 to form a new circuit, called "Indiana," but not succeeding, was sent by the elder to the Erie Circuit in company with Mr. Monroe. He continued to travel and labor until 1816, when he located.

Rev. George Stuntz, of Springfield, Erie County, Pennsylvania, was powerfully awakened by a sermon preached by Rev. Jacob Gruber, Presiding Elder, at a quarterly meeting held in the Brush meeting-house in the month of July, 1810, from the text, "Be not deceived, God is not mocked," etc., and immediately joined the class on probation and commenced praying in his family, but obtained no peace of mind until the following September, at a camp-meeting held by Mr. Gruber on the banks of French Creek, below Meadville, Pennsylvania, where many souls were converted. He went to the altar repeatedly, but still found no relief; partook of the sacrament, but instead of finding in it a blessing as he expected, was tempted to believe that he had eaten the body of the Lord "unworthily," and exclaimed in the bitterness of his anguish, "Is mercy clean gone? Will he be favorable no more?" In this state of despair he went outside of the encampment and prostrated himself under an oak tree to "bewail his sad fate." While there he says, "I ventured my all on Jesus, by faith saw the Saviour, was relieved of my burden, light and joy inexpressible filled my soul, and all things appeared new to me." He was licensed to exhort in April, 1814, and to preach in Salem meeting-house July 22, 1815; was ordained a deacon by Bishop George September 18, 1820, and an elder by Bishop Soule in 1836. Father Stuntz has been a most efficient and acceptable local preacher for fifty years. His sun must soon set, we hope in a clear sky.

Rev. James Watts, after leaving the Erie Circuit, which he traveled in company with Mr. Roberts in 1806, was two years on the Shenango Circuit, and was then transferred to the Western Conference, where he labored two years on the Will's Creek Circuit, and was then transferred back to the Baltimore Conference, and again appointed to the Shenango Circuit, as we now find him.

Mr. Gruber held a camp-meeting during this year in the eastern part of the town of Hubbard, near what has since been known as the Veach meeting-house, Trumbull County, Ohio. Mr. Isaac Powers, belonging to the Methodist society in Youngstown, Ohio, was present, and says: "The meeting was a powerful one. One night there was an extraordinary display of divine power. My wife came to me, and taking me by the hand requested me to go forward with her to the altar and ask Rev. Mr. —— to pray for her. I was astonished, knowing her uniform opposition to such things. I, however, readily complied. The minister directed her to kneel, which we all did. He prayed earnestly in her behalf. In the midst of the prayer she sprang to her feet and shouted aloud the high praises of God. I took her by the hand and was conducting her back to the tent when something suddenly impressed me that I had no religion. I became most miserable. The noise around became exceedingly offensive, and I resolved at once to go out of its hearing; started, but the further I went the more plainly it was heard; so it seemed at least. My misery was doubly intensified. The very 'pains of hell gat hold of me.' Not only my mind but my body was sorely oppressed. Every joint in my body seemed wrenched from its socket. I found it impossible to run away from my wretchedness, and turned back to the camp, entered the tent where they were engaged in singing and shouting, and in rather an angry mood said to them, 'You are serving the devil in good earnest.' The ill-natured remark somewhat dampened the ardor of their spirits. In a short time

I asked my wife to take a walk with me. She arose to go, at the same time taking James Bradford, her brother-in-law, by the arm, and inviting him to accompany us, which he did. She told me afterward that she was afraid of me, such was the vindictiveness of my looks. At the solemn hour of midnight we started off from the encampment. We had not proceeded far before my feelings strangely relaxed, and in a few minutes I was entirely relieved of the terrible burden which seemed to be crushing me to the earth. My mind now being relieved from my own misery, I discovered that my friend, Mr. Bradford, was groaning under a terrible burden of agony. At length he exclaimed, 'O, if I do not get religion to-night I shall be in hell before morning!' We halted, and he requested us to pray for him. He fell flat upon his face and groaned and cried for mercy. My wife led in prayer in his behalf, and I followed her. Before the second prayer was concluded Mr. Bradford bounded, I feel confident in saying, ten feet from the place where he lay. He did not get up first upon his feet and then make the leap, but it was rather a bound from a prostrate to a standing attitude, as if thrown by some strong invisible hand, which he always afterward declared was the fact, at the same time he roared with a stentorian voice, 'Glory to God!' He at once started off for the camp-ground, not walking, but 'leaping and praising God.' His conversion was a marked one. He obtained the pearl of great price, and I am quite confident he never lost it. He has gone to his rest."

The result of this camp-meeting was an addition

of fifty persons to the Church. This was a year of great success generally; there were revivals on each of the circuits, and new classes formed, and congregations raised up. During the summer of 1810 Mr. Tillinghast Mowry moved from Connecticut and settled in the town of Milton, Portage County, Ohio, one mile west of the Center, where his house became a welcome home for the Methodist preachers who were sent to labor on the Hartford Circuit, and was for many years a preaching place. Father Shewel, still residing in Deerfield, Ohio, after toiling daily through the week with his hands for the support of his family, would on Sunday morning find his way through the woods on foot to the new neighboring settlements to break to the hungry souls in the wilderness the bread of life. He established a preaching appointment at Mr. Mowry's, and several persons were soon converted, and a class was formed consisting of T. Mowry, leader, and his wife, Jacob Allen and wife, Joseph Depue, Margaret Hudson, and a Mr. Cole and wife, with perhaps a few others. This appointment was soon added to the Hartford Circuit, and supplied with circuit preaching.

Mr. Monroe on the Erie Circuit succeeded in forming a class this year in Gravel Run, now called Rockville, Crawford County, Pa., but we have not succeeded in getting the names of the first members. Their meeting place for a long time was at the house of Mr. John Shearer.

Mr. Monroe also succeeded in forming a class, and in permanently establishing Methodism in Franklin, Venango County, Pa. The class consisted of William

Conley, wife, and daughter, John Looper and wife and William M'Lehany and wife. Mr. Conley was leader, and was soon after licensed to preach, and for several years was a useful local preacher.

Mr. Watts on the Shenango Circuit formed a class this year in Newcastle, Pa., and established a preaching appointment in that place. The class consisted of John Beven and wife, Michael Carman and wife, James Squire and wife, and Nancy Wallin. This class has had a glorious history up to the present time.

We have before mentioned the fact that Rev. G. Lane, of the Philadelphia Conference, formed a class in Sheridan, Chautauqua County, New York. But this class remained without regular preaching until the present year; and in the mean time Mr. Justin Hinman, a very pious and intelligent man, had settled in the village of Fredonia, and had united with this class.

Early in the spring of 1810 an entire class of ten members removed from the East and settled in the town of Villanovia, Chautauqua County, New York. This class consisted of John Arnold, leader, and his wife, Father Kent and wife, Daniel Whipple and wife, Roderick Wells, John P Kent, James Kent, and Ann Kent.

Mr. John P Kent, of the Villanovia class, in company with Mr. Justin Hinman, of the Sheridan class, attended the sitting of the Genesee Conference, which met for the first time this summer in the village of Lyons, New York, and held its session in Father Dorsey's corn barn, to secure if possible a preacher to labor in Chautauqua County, New York. The application made personally to the bishop was successful. Three preachers were appointed to the "Holland Purchase," embracing all of the State of New York west of the Genesee River, one of whom, familiarly called BILLY BROWN, was to labor in Chautauqua, and soon afterward entered upon his work with zeal. Mr. Brown was admitted on trial in the Philadelphia Conference in 1809, and being within the bounds of the Genesee Conference when it was organized, was by it received into full connection and ordained a deacon in 1811, and an elder in 1814, located in 1817, and in 1823 removed to Ohio, where he labored extensively for many years as a local preacher. Mr. Brown possessed a great knowledge of the Holy Scriptures, and loved to search and expound difficult and obscure passages that other people would pass over with indifference. He was also remarkable for his faith in prayer; was very odd in his actions and gestures, eccentric in his ideas and illustrations, was much sought after by some, and greatly disliked by others. He died suddenly in 1850. As Chautauqua was connected with other work, and their members reported together, we have no means of knowing how many members there were in Chautauqua this year.

On the Erie Circuit there were reported a membership of..	501
Hartford	334
Shenango	306
Total	1,141
Last year	989
Increase	152

1811.

The Baltimore Conference held its session in Baltimore March 20, 1811, at which the work for this region was arranged as follows:

Monongahela District, Jacob Gruber, Presiding Elder.

Erie, James Watts, James Ewing.

Shenango, Abel Robinson.

Mr. Gruber continued to prosecute his labors on the district with untiring diligence and remarkable success. Many were the seals of his ministry this year.

Several camp-meetings were held on the district which were seasons of great good; one, in the vicinity of Franklin, Pa., is spoken of as a meeting of much interest; and at the close of the year a great lamentation was made in consequence of his removal from the district. Mr. Gruber spent thirty-two years of his ministerial life on circuits, seven years on stations, and eleven on districts; making fifty years spent in active, earnest toil in the Master's vineyard. Mr. Gruber was a member of the General Conference in 1812 and 1816. Unable to attend the Baltimore Conference in 1850, he sent a request that, "after fifty years of hard work, he might enjoy a jubilee." He was accordingly superannuated, and gradually sank away by disease until his once robust constitution became reduced to a helpless condition. He was graciously sustained throughout his extreme sufferings, and often rejoiced amid paroxysms of great agony. The hour of his departure came and found him ready to meet its claims. A few hours before he died he inquired of a preacher present whether he thought it possible for him to survive through the night, and was answered in the negative; whereupon he exclaimed, "Then to-morrow I shall spend my first Sabbath in the Church above;" and with great emotion continued,

> "Where congregations ne'er break up,
> And Sabbaths never end."

He had once before expressed to some of his friends a wish that when he was about to depart, if it could be ascertained, a few brethren and sisters should be present and "see him off," and all join in singing,

> "On Jordan's stormy banks I stand,
> And cast a wishful eye," etc.

He was asked if he felt that he was on the banks of Jordan? He replied, "I feel that I am." The hymn was sung by all present; but before it closed his spirit had peacefully left the house of clay. He died May 25, 1850.*

Rev. WILLIAM KNOX, in charge of the Hartford Circuit, was born in Ireland June 8, 1767, was converted and united with the Methodists in 1784, was licensed to preach in 1787, came to this country in 1800, was received on trial in the Baltimore Conference the same year, and into full connection and ordained a deacon in 1802, and an elder in 1804. He remained on the Erie Circuit but one year, when by a division of the work he fell into the Ohio Conference, within whose bounds he continued to labor until the formation of the Pittsburgh Conference in

* See Life of Gruber, p. 376

1825, when he became a member of that body. Here he labored until 1845, when on account of failing health he was superannuated. After serving the Church with great fidelity and usefulness for fifty years, during which time it is said he seldom disappointed a congregation for any circumstance, he died in peace and joyful hope October 6, 1850. "Servant of God, well done."

Rev. ABEL ROBINSON was admitted on trial in the Baltimore Conference March 20, 1811, and appointed to the Shenango Circuit; was received into full connection and ordained a deacon in 1813, and an elder in 1815. We shall have occasion to refer to him again.

Rev. ELIJAH METCALF, one of the preachers appointed to the Holland Purchase by the Genesee Conference, labored this year in Chautauqua County, N. Y., occasionally extending his labors down into Warren County, Pa., preaching in a new settlement on the Conewango, and at Mother Reece's on the Alleghany River, one or two miles below Warren, and also on the Brokenstraw Creek, where the parents of the author then resided, having moved from Oil Creek to the Brokenstraw in 1808. The Hartford Circuit in Ohio, under the labors of Messrs. Knox and Monroe, was extended some distance west, and a class was formed in the town of Northampton, Summit County, consisting of Abraham Vanhining (leader) and wife, William Prier, Elizabeth Perkins, John Cockran, and Catharine Prier. Soon after this class was formed another class was organized in the town of Stow, to which Mr. Vanhining was transferred and appointed leader, leaving Mrs. Vanhining in charge of the class in Northampton, a position for which she was well qualified. The class in Stow finally established its preaching place on Darrow-street, in the town of Hudson, where it flourished several years. During the year a class was formed also in Fredonia, Chautauqua County, N. Y., consisting of Justin Hinman and wife, Daniel Gould and wife, William Ensign and wife, Jeremiah Baldwin and wife, and a few others.

Erie Circuit returned this year	585
Hartford	444
Shenango	436
Chautauqua	30
Total	1,495
Last year	1,141
Increase	354

1812.

The Baltimore Conference sat in Leesburgh, Va., March 20, 1812, at which the following arrangement of the work was made:

Ohio District, Jacob Young, Presiding Elder.
Erie, James Watts, Jacob Gorwell.
Shenango, William Knox.
Trumbull, Thomas J. Crockwell, J. Somerville.
Grand River, Abraham Daniels.

The district is now called "Ohio," after the Ohio River, along whose waters it extended for a long distance below Pittsburgh. It contained four circuits now in the bounds of the Pittsburgh and West Virginia Conferences, and four in the Erie Conference, making eight in all.

The Hartford Circuit was divided, making two circuits in Ohio: Grand River, extending along the lake shore from the eastern line of Ohio to the mouth of a river by that name; and the Trumbull Circuit, embracing the south part of the old Hartford Circuit, lying mostly along the waters of the Mahoning River.

Rev. JACOB YOUNG, the presiding elder on the Ohio District, was born in Alleghany County, Pa., March 19, 1776. "When about ten years of age," he says, "I became greatly alarmed; I arose one night from my bed and sat some time by the fire, in distress of mind almost beyond endurance. But suddenly a change took place, and my burden appeared to fall off; something whispered in my ear, 'be of good comfort, your sins are forgiven.' I then went to bed with great comfort, and for a number of months was a very happy boy." When about fifteen years of age, Mr. Young's parents moved into Henry County, Ky., where, having lost his religious enjoyment, our young friend became very fond of dancing, gambling, and other kindred vices. But, fortunately, the Methodist preachers began soon to visit that place, and he, with many others, was induced to go and hear them. A powerful revival of religion commenced, and Mr. Young became powerfully awakened; and while at a neighboring house one evening an appropriate hymn was sung for his especial benefit; and while they sang the first verse, he says, "My physical power gave way. I fell upon the floor, and there I lay several hours, having no recollection of anything that passed, only that my mind was dark and my soul greatly distressed. Toward midnight the light appeared to shine from the south part of heaven, and God in mercy lifted up the light of his countenance upon me, and I was translated from the power of darkness into the kingdom of God's dear son, and rejoiced with joy unspeakable and full of glory. I arose from the floor praising God with a loud voice."* After passing through a variety of mental conflicts on the subject of preaching the Gospel, he was induced to enter upon the pursuit of useful knowledge by attending the best school within his reach, and by reading such books, in connection with the Bible, as would best prepare him to be useful and happy. He says: "I was licensed to preach in September, 1801. The day I was licensed was a precious day to my soul."† The presiding elder that licensed him was Rev. William M'Kendree, afterward Bishop M'Kendree. During the summer of 1802 he was employed by the presiding elder to labor on a circuit in Kentucky, where he was duly recommended to the traveling connection, and was admitted on trial in the "Western Conference," which sat at Cumberland, Tenn., October 2, 1802, and into full connection and ordained a deacon in 1804, and an elder in 1806. He continued to labor with increasing ability and usefulness in the Western Conference until the spring of 1810, when he was transferred to the Baltimore Conference, where, after two years' acquaintance, he was appointed presiding elder on the Ohio District. Mr. Young says the "Baltimore Conference this year held its

* Young's Autobiography, p. 42. † Ibid., p. 60.

session in Leesburgh, Va.; and while we were sitting in conference, Congress was sitting in Washington agitating the war question. About the time we left Leesburgh they declared war with Great Britain. Part of my field of labor lay near the seat of war."* About the first of May Mr. Young started from his home in the State of Virginia for his district. He passed through New Lisbon, Canfield, Youngstown, and Hubbard, in the State of Ohio; thence across the Pennsylvania line to Salem, formerly called Shenango; thence up into the region of Oil Creek, where he held his first quarterly meeting in a barn, a crowd of people being present—Rev. James Watts, preacher in charge, and Rev. W Connelly, a local preacher from Franklin, Pa., assisting. Mr. Young says: "I found the neighborhood under revival influence, and had a comfortable quarterly meeting. Next week I returned to the Western Reserve, and held a quarterly meeting in the town of Hartford. Thomas Crockwell and John Summerville were the preachers; the prospect looked rather discouraging." The week following he says: "I made my way through mud and water to the town of Burton, and held a quarterly meeting in Seth Hays's barn. Here I found a very large congregation, considering the newness of the country. This was a profitable meeting. Abraham Daniels was the preacher." During this round he says, "I did not receive twenty dollars." A very small sum to support a family upon three months.

* Young's Autobiography, p. 276.

After spending a few days at home he says: "I procured another horse, and set out on my second round of quarterly meetings, pursuing nearly the same route, holding quarterly meetings every week, often preaching at night, and frequently our meetings would continue till after midnight. Revivals became common throughout the whole district, especially on Shenango Circuit, under the labors of the pious Abel Robinson. The work also prospered well on the Erie Circuit. I had not proceeded far on this round when I heard the cry of distress from many families. Breadstuff had become very scarce, and sold at very high prices; flour in some places was sixteen dollars per barrel, and meat was about as scarce and high as bread. Along the lake shore the alarm of war spread terror among the inhabitants. I went next to the mouth of French Creek on the Alleghany River." This was at Franklin, Pa. "Here," he says, "Rev. William Connelly undertook a mission to Brokenstraw and the mouth of the Conewango, where the people were expecting a quarterly meeting, though there were no preachers in that part of the country. The Genesee preachers had left them out, and they were like sheep without a shepherd." These streams enter the Alleghany River in Warren County, Pa., and the quarterly meeting, I have ascertained, was held on the banks of the Alleghany River, a short distance below the village of Warren. The author's father, at this time residing on Brokenstraw Creek, attended this quarterly meeting, and informed Mr. Young that an awakening had taken place in his neighborhood, which led Mr. Young to visit that place at the close of the meeting. Mr. Young says: "When I arrived on the ground I found a stand erected near the bank of the river, very convenient seats, and a kind of a large tent into which we could retire. About ten o'clock the people began to gather in great numbers, some on horseback and some on foot, and a goodly number came down the Alleghany in canoes. Here, for the first time, I met with the Rev. John P Kent, who was then a smooth-faced boy, and I suppose about as polite as any young French gentleman in Paris, and as kind and accommodating. He had a large company with him, of which he appeared to be chief man. One of his company was a local preacher by the name of Arnold. Just as I was about to commence divine service up rode Bishop M'Kendree as large as life, filled with health and animation. He had two preachers with him, George Harmon and Brother Metcalf. He just took time to shake hands and ask me how I was, then mounted the stand and preached one of his flaming and awakening sermons. Harmon exhorted, and we had a prayer-meeting. Many tears were shed, and a good deal of shouting was heard. M'Kendree and all the preachers but myself rode off to Warren to procure refreshments. There were two places called public houses there, but I called them low grog-shops. The bishop rode up to one, and they played the fiddle at him. He went to the next, where he made out to stay all night. I preached in the evening, and held a prayer-meeting, and the congregation dispersed, leaving me a little like my divine Master, for I had not where to lay my head. No one asked me to go with him. After wandering about a while I found an old log barn with some half-rotten hay in it. There I laid me down and slept till daylight. Before sunrise I was invited to take breakfast on the bank of the Alleghany River, where a number of people had encamped. They had neither tables nor chairs, but they spread their cloths on the ground. We worshiped God together, took a hearty breakfast, and conversed freely on our prospects of getting to another world. The congregation gathered early, and the preachers with them, and we had an excellent love-feast. That morning I gave out preaching for eleven o'clock, and while the congregation was collecting and becoming seated, M'Kendree stood up, with his back against a tree, and preached us a sermon about fifteen minutes long. The people gazed upon him as though he had been some heavenly visitor. He then took the stand, and after singing and prayer, he held forth to great advantage for upward of an hour. His text was, 'I call heaven and earth to record this day against you, that I have set before you life and death, blessing and cursing: therefore choose life that both thou and thy seed may live.' After a short intermission Brother Harmon preached. I then opened the door and took a number into the Church. Having dismissed the congregation, we mounted our horses and rode away to Brokenstraw and stayed that night with Squire Mead." This was one mile and a half west from Youngville, Warren County, Pa. "The bishop preached again a good little sermon, and we all retired to rest."* While here Mr. Young formed a class consisting of John Gregg and wife, Jacob Goodwin and wife, William Arthur and wife, Anna Mead and her son Philip Mead, Betsey Ford, Polly Arthur, and Polly Campbell, eleven in all. Mr. Young traveled with the bishop to Franklin, Pa., thence to Salem, Pa., then crossed the state line into Ohio, and went to Youngstown, where they parted. Mr. Young went to Ashtabula, Ohio, and attempted to hold a quarterly meeting, during which the news came of Hull's surrender of Detroit, and the people were so alarmed that the meeting was broken up, and a camp-meeting, previously appointed, was abandoned, and but little more was accomplished on the district until the session of the Ohio Conference.

Mr. Young says: "When I was placed on the Ohio District in March it belonged to the Baltimore Conference. But the General Conference, which met in May following, transferred the district, with the incumbent, to the Ohio Conference." He had accomplished two rounds only on the district when the Ohio Conference met in Chillicothe, October 2, 1812. The above fact will show the reader why our territory and work stands connected with the Ohio Conference hereafter, and also why the preachers are changed in the fall instead of spring.

Rev. JACOB GORWELL was admitted on trial in the Baltimore Conference in 1811, and in 1812 appointed junior preacher on the Erie Circuit with James Watts, and in 1813 admitted to full connection and ordained a

* Young's Autobiography, p. 284.

deacon, and was appointed to the Shenango Circuit, where he labored one year, and located March, 1815.

Rev. THOMAS J. CROCKWELL, in charge of the Trumbull Circuit, was received on trial in the Virginia Conference in 1807, and into full connection and ordained a deacon in 1809, and an elder in 1811, and then located one year. In 1812 he was readmitted into the Baltimore Conference and appointed to the Trumbull Circuit, where he labored but one year. He located again in 1814.

Rev. JOHN SUMMERVILLE, junior preacher on the Trumbull Circuit, was an Irishman, was converted to God in Chambersburgh, Pa., was licensed to preach by Rev. Jacob Gruber in 1811, and admitted on trial in the Baltimore Conference in March, 1812, and appointed to the Trumbull Circuit. We shall have occasion to speak of him again.

Rev. ABRAHAM DANIELS, on the Grand River Circuit, closed up his itinerant labors this year by receiving a location at the ensuing conference.

Rev. BENJAMIN G. PADDOCK was appointed to the Chautauque Circuit by the Genesee Conference, which sat at Niagara, July 23, 1812. He was a man of superior talents, piety, and usefulness. He formed a class in the town of Hanover, Chautauqua County, N. Y., in what is known as the Angel Settlement, (James Jewet was leader,) and another in Omer, town of Villanovia, same county. For some reason the Genesee Conference ceased to send preachers into Chautauqua at the close of this year, and it was henceforth supplied with preachers from the Ohio Conference.

The following narrative will show what Methodist ministers had to suffer in planting the Church of our choice in this region in an early day.

Rev. THOMAS BRANCH, born in Preston, Connecticut, commenced preaching in the winter of 1800, and was admitted on trial in the New York Conference in June, 1801, in company with Martin Ruter and Elijah Hedding. So rapid was his progress, and eminent his talents, and great his usefulness, that in 1806 he was appointed presiding elder on the New London District, outstripping both of his illustrious compeers. In 1807 he was transferred to the Vermont District, where he continued to labor with great success for four years. His zeal was too great for his strength, and toward the close of his term on this district his excessive labor brought on pulmonary consumption. Hoping to improve his fast declining health by a change of climate, he obtained a transfer to the "Western Conference," and was stationed in Marietta, Ohio. In the spring of 1812 he started on horseback for his new distant field of labor. On arriving at North East, Erie County, Pennsylvania, he found himself so far reduced in strength that he could proceed no further. There were no Methodists in this town at this time, or within twenty miles of it, with whom he could stop, or of whom receive kind attention.

A Presbyterian Church had been organized, and were occupying a small log house as a place of worship but a short distance from where their present more sightly edifice now stands. As soon as Mr. Branch's condition became known, some of the citizens visited his sick room. It was his constant practice to converse on the subject of religion, and pray with all who called; and when several persons would happen in together he would preach to them, sometimes sitting in his chair, and at other times lying upon his bed. In this way an extensive religious awakening was produced in the settlement, which called forth the most determined opposition, especially from the Presbyterians. But this precious man of God soon died, and, like Lazarus, was "carried by angels to Abraham's bosom." The day of his burial found a few of his friends present who had been blessed through his instrumentality, and who desired in turn to give him a respectable Christian funeral and burial. But the little log church could not be procured for that purpose, nor were they permitted to inter his body in the newly inclosed cemetery, nor could they procure a respectable team or carriage with which to carry the corpse to the grave. At the hour appointed a prayer was offered, and the coffin placed on a wood-sled and drawn by a yoke of oxen about one mile and a quarter west from the present village of North East, and on the north side of the Erie and Buffalo road this sainted man was buried in a beautiful grove. To the honor of the people of that town be it said, they have long since so enlarged the cemetery as to bring within its inclosure the grave of the lamented Branch. The writer was permitted several years since to visit the place, and shed a few tears over the turf that covers his sacred dust.

> "Rest here, blessed saint, till from his throne
> The morning break, and pierce the shade."

Soon after the death of Mr. Branch the preachers on the Erie Circuit established an appointment for preaching in North East, and formed a class consisting of Perrin Ross (leader) and wife, Mr. Russell and wife, Mrs. Brown, and a few others, to which, in a short time, the Tuttles, Nashes, and Sillimans were added, and Rev. Enoch Burdick, a local preacher from Canada, settled there, a small brick church was erected, and the Church has maintained a prosperous existence there ever since, and many happy spirits have gone up from that town to join the triumphant host in heaven.

We must close this section in the middle of the year so as to have the next section commence with the first session of the Ohio Conference, which was formed by the General Conference in May, 1812, and to which this work was attached for thirteen years.

SECTION VI.

FROM 1812 TO 1815.

"Soon and forever the work shall be done,
The warfare accomplished, the victory won!
Soon and forever the soldier lays down
The sword for the harp, the cross for the crown."

1812—Continued.

THE Ohio Conference held its first session in Chillicothe in October, 1812. The appointments were as follows:

Ohio District, Jacob Young, Presiding Elder.
Erie, John Graham.
Shenango, James Watts.
Trumbull, James M'Mahan.
Grand River, John M'Mahan, Robert C. Hatton.

After making a short visit with his family, Mr. Young says: "I then commenced my first regular round. But nothing very worthy of remark took place during this entire round, only the Lord was with us in nearly all our public and private exercises. This was a year of great peace and prosperity, but our success was not quite equal to last year. On my second round I found all the preachers at their work faithfully, blessed with fine health, and the Lord was with them in the power of the Holy Spirit. On some of the circuits revivals were very extensive, and many were converted. As far as temporalities were concerned, we began to feel the effects of hard times.

War between the United States and Great Britain was progressing. Provisions of all kinds were very high. At times we felt discouraged, and some thought of retiring from the work; but their courage revived, their wives were zealous for the cause, and exhorted their husbands to weather the storm. Winter months came on, snow fell deep, weather extremely cold; sometimes we had not much to eat, and suffered greatly at night for clothes. I was much puzzled to find my way from one settlement to another. Sometimes I was in danger of being lost, and of lying out all night, but by the good providence of God I always found a shelter. Spring opened about the time I commenced my third round. The snow and ice melted, and streams of water ran down. The weather was clear and delightful. As well as I can recollect we had no special revivals on this round, but the churches were edified and built up in their most holy faith. One spirit seemed to actuate the whole ministry, and frequently when I would leave one circuit the preacher would go with me to the next quarterly meeting, and sometimes lay members would pilot me through the unsettled parts of the country. I never shall forget the acts of Christian friendship shown to me by preachers and people on that district. I closed my third round much to my satisfaction. The last quarter of the year was made up mostly of camp-meetings, which were attended with great displays of divine power. Time would fail to give a minute account of all the camp-meetings during this round. I will therefore confine myself particularly to one held on French

Creek, near Meadville. The people in that country appeared to be hungry for a camp-meeting. They selected a beautiful spot of ground, and built a great many very comfortable tents. The congregation was very large on the first day. Many ministers were present. Bishop M'Kendree was with us and preached every day, and took a lively interest in the night meetings. The literati of Meadville were nearly all in attendance. General Mead was one of our company. They were delighted above measure with the bishop's preaching. The rowdies began to trouble us on Saturday afternoon. As I went around to keep order, two gentlemen from Meadville requested me to give myself no trouble about keeping order, but to carry on the religious exercises as we had been doing, and they would keep order throughout the congregation. General Mead went on the stand and requested the people to be orderly, showing them the consequence if they did not comply with our rules. We had no more trouble during the meeting. The good work of the Lord went on with very little intermission day and night. Many professed to be converted. Sabbath was a great day. The bishop gave us the Lord's supper. The Lord honored his table by pouring his Spirit on the congregation. We continued the meeting until Tuesday morning; then the bishop gave us his valedictory. We closed the meeting under pleasing circumstances, took our departure, rode to John Leach's, where the bishop preached to a small congregation on Wednesday."*

* Young's Autobiography, pp. 298–301.

Rev. JAMES WATTS closed up his valuable labors in this region the present year, but continued to preach within the bounds of the Ohio Conference until 1816, when he was transferred to the Baltimore Conference, where he continued in the regular work until 1827, when he was appointed presiding elder on the Rockingham District, where he remained four years. He then returned to the regular pastoral work until 1852, when on account of declining health he was superannuated. After spending fifty-three years in the ministry, forty-eight of which were in active service, he died in great peace and full assurance of faith and hope in 1857. He labored between four and five years within the bounds of this conference.

Rev. JOHN GRAHAM, in charge of the Erie Circuit, was received on trial in the Ohio Conference at its session in October, 1812, and appointed to the above charge. We shall have occasion to speak of him again.

Rev. JAMES M'MAHAN, in charge of the Trumbull Circuit, was received on trial in the Western Conference in 1810, and into full connection in the Ohio Conference and ordained a deacon in 1812, and an elder in 1814.

Rev. JOHN M'MAHAN, in charge of the Grand River Circuit, was brother to James M'Mahan, and both of Irish origin. John was received on trial in the Ohio Conference in 1812, and into full connection and ordained a deacon in 1814, and an elder in 1816. He continued to labor in other parts of the Ohio Conference until 1828, when he was expelled from the connection. Soon after the session of conference, for reasons now unknown, the Trumbull and Grand River Circuits were connected, and the two M'Mahans labored together, James being in charge of the whole work. The name given to the circuit was New Connecticut.

Rev. Robert C. Hatton was received on trial in the Ohio Conference in 1812, and appointed second preacher on the Grand River Circuit, but was soon after transferred by the presiding elder to the Erie Circuit. He was received into full connection and ordained a deacon in 1814, and an elder in 1816.

Rev. John Norris, a local deacon in the Methodist Episcopal Church from the State of Connecticut, settled in the town of Windsor, Ashtabula County, Ohio, in the month of June, 1812, and immediately commenced preaching in that town and in Mesopotamia. In the fall of that year a class was formed in Windsor, consisting of John Norris, wife, and two daughters, A. Crandell and wife, Seth Young, Cornelius Norris and wife. Soon after this a class was formed in Mesopotamia, Ohio. Mrs. Sarah Sanderson is the only member whose name we can now give.

Rev. Lemuel Lane, a local preacher from the Western Reserve, was employed by the presiding elder this year to labor on the Chautauqua Circuit, embracing a few appointments in Warren County, Pa. He formed a class at Silver Creek, Chautauqua County, N. Y., consisting of A. Clothur and wife, S. Spink and wife, and a few others.

A class was formed in Ashtabula, Ohio, consisting

of Thomas Benham and wife, Samuel Benham and wife, Adna Benham and wife.

Another class was formed this year about six or seven miles north of Meadville, Pa., in what has long been known as Father Brown's neighborhood, consisting of Simeon Brown and wife, Oleon Chase and wife, E. Douglass and wife, John Grimes and wife, William Smith, and Anna Glenn.

A small class was formed in Boardman, Ohio, by one of the M'Mahans. Oswell Dutchen was one of the members.

The membership at the close of this year was.......	1,498
Last year..	1,495
Increase....................................	3

1813.

The Ohio Conference met in Steubenville, Ohio, September 11, 1813, Bishop M'Kendree presiding. The work was arranged, and the appointments made as follows:

Ohio District, Jacob Young, Presiding Elder.

Erie, Abel Robinson.

Shenango, Jacob Gorwell.

New Connecticut, John Solomon, Oliver Carver.

Chautauqua, John M'Mahan.

After conference adjourned Mr. Young spent a short time with his family, residing at this time about fifteen miles south of Steubenville, and then commenced his first round on his district. He says: "By the time I came to Erie, on the Lake, the weather had become intensely cold, and the war was still going on between England and the United

States. The people were yet very uneasy along the Lake shore, more than half way down to Pittsburgh. They had not recovered from the panic of last year, occasioned by Hull's surrender of Detroit. And to heighten our trouble through the country, the fever had broken out in the camp at Black Rock, run up the lake, and spread out through the country. They called it the cold plague. It was far worse than either the British or the Indians. There was no guarding against it. It was almost as bad as the cholera in later days. It made its appearance in Hartford, Trumbull County, Ohio. The first that fell a victim to it in that place was an eminent minister by the name of Crosby." Rev. Obadiah Crosby was the first Methodist minister that found his way to the Western Reserve, and formed the first class west of the Pennsylvania state line, in 1801, near the line of Vernon and Hartford townships, Trumbull County, Ohio. Mr. Young says: "I preached his funeral sermon and buried him. I went on to Burton, returned next week to Hartford, and found another of the old citizens lying a corpse. I preached his funeral sermon and buried him. Went on to Youngstown and held my quarterly meeting, and then returned to Steubenville; found the cold plague spreading in every direction; it was nearly as bad in Wheeling as in Meadville. It spread throughout the great valley of the West, and carried thousands to their graves. I suffered much more with cold this winter than ever before. Sometimes I would have to give fifty cents for a peck of oats for my weary horse; and I have paid as high as four dollars for shoeing my horse. I was often entirely out of money, but some one always took compassion on me and supplied my wants. I commenced my third round under more favorable circumstances, but we had but little revival the whole year. I commenced my fourth round early in the summer. During this round we held many camp-meetings; one on that favorite spot on French Creek, near Meadville, where I had had a glorious camp-meeting the year before. The Lord was pleased to give us another good meeting, but not quite equal to the one the year before." *

Rev. JOHN SOLOMON, in charge of New Connecticut Circuit, was received on trial in the Ohio Conference, at Steubenville, September 1, 1813, and appointed to the above circuit, and in 1815 he was received into full connection and ordained a deacon; and an elder in 1817, and located in 1821.

Rev. OLIVER CARVER, second preacher on the New Connecticut Circuit, was also received on trial in the Ohio Conference in September, 1813, and into full connection and ordained a deacon in 1815, and located in 1816.

In the spring of 1814 Father Shewel removed his family from Deerfield and settled in Rootstown, Portage County, Ohio, near the eastern line of the town, and commenced preaching in several places in the vicinity. At a place called Bacon Hill, in the south part of Randolph, he formed a class consisting of John Tickner, leader, and his wife and father, Cozans Bacon, Sally Bacon, Ebenezer Cutler and wife, Ezekiel Tupper and wife. Mr. Shewel also established an

* Young's Autobiography, pp. 308–311.

appointment in his own log-cabin, where a class was soon formed, consisting of Henry Shewel and wife, Nathan Sears and wife, Stephen Coulton and wife, Samuel Redfield and wife, Margaret Shewel, Salina Shewel, and Nancy Coe. Mr. Shewel also preached for a time in an old log school-house in Rootstown, near the Cleveland and Pittsburgh Railroad depot. In this neighborhood he found an old lady, by the name of M'Knight, who was converted to God under the preaching of Mr. John Wesley in one of his visits to Ireland. She died in great peace in 1819, being more than a hundred years old. During the summer of 1814 Mr. Shewel established an appointment for preaching in the western part of the town of Ravenna, Portage County, Ohio, about one mile from the present village, where he formed a class consisting of Mr. Abel and wife, and his son and wife, Mr. Granger and wife, and Mr. Grear. Thus did this faithful old pioneer find his way into the new settlements, breaking up new ground, and after raising up societies he would hand them over to the preachers on the circuit, and then seek out new places of labor. Father Shewel was a source of terror to the wicked, and often incurred their displeasure by his severity. He was also accustomed to deal heavy blows at Calvinism. One good Presbyterian lady was so exasperated at the severity of his remarks one day that she said, "Father Shewel was no more fit to preach the Gospel than a chestnut-burr was fit to be an eye-ball;" but soon afterward hearing a man who had been very wicked date his conversion to Father Shewel's preaching, recalled the uncharitable expression, and became a great admirer of the man. In the spring of 1814 Mr. Harvey Stow, of Braceville, Trumbull County, Ohio, while working in his sugar camp, became powerfully awakened, and in the midst of great distress of mind sought the Lord earnestly in prayer, but found no relief; but one day, while carrying a sap-trough on his shoulder, he suddenly commenced singing, and when he came to these lines,

> "Jesus all the day long
> Was my joy and my song,"

his soul found instant relief, and he became so exceedingly happy that his sap-trough came tumbling down, and he shouted and praised the Lord until he made the woods ring and the hills echo. Thus the leaven continued to spread.

"Chautauqua" Circuit received its name from a beautiful lake of that name in the extreme western corner of the State of New York. The county in which it is located also bears its name. It is about sixteen miles in length and from one to four miles wide, and is about thirteen hundred and five feet above the ocean, with Mayville, the county-seat, at its head, and Jamestown, a thrifty manufacturing village, at its foot, where a branch of the Conewango Creek is formed, furnishing an immense water-power for machinery. The name Chautauqua is of Indian origin.

> An Indian maid in early days, 'tis said,
> Torn from her tribe, some stranger home to fill,
> From her rude captor's stern embrace she fled;
> Her fleet foot bore her o'er a rugged hill

Which overlooked thy banks, and swiftly sped,
  Pursuers after; peerless stood she there;
Defied her foes; then plunged; her bridal bed
  She sought within these crystal depths so fair;
  Her name Chautauqua still do thy sweet waters bear.

O. M. Kellogg, M. D.

The Chautauqua Circuit at this time embraced most of the territory now covered by the Jamestown and Fredonia Districts. Over this vast territory did the preachers on the old Chautauqua Circuit use to travel on horseback, through drifted snow and piercing blasts in winter, and in mud and mire in the fall and spring, enduring an amount of suffering, and requiring an amount of heroism little thought of by the preachers who now pass over the same ground in their easy carriages.

The close of this year showed a handsome increase in members.

Erie Circuit returned	596
New Connecticut	600
Shenango	344
Chautauqua	150
Total	1,690
Last year	1,498
Increase	192

1814.

The Ohio Conference met in Cincinnati, September 8, 1814; Bishop Asbury presiding, in very feeble health. The appointments were as follows:

Ohio District, Jacob Young, Presiding Elder.
Erie, John Solomon, John Graham.
Shenango, John Elliott.

New Connecticut, James M'Mahan, Lemuel Lane.
Chautauqua, Burrows Westlake.

Mr. Young gives no account of his labors on this part of the Ohio District during the first and second rounds, but says, "I began my third round of quarterly meetings in fine health and good spirits, till I came to the Mahoning River; here I was attacked with fever and ague. I traveled on, grappled with the disease, and preached almost every day until I reached Warren, Trumbull County, Ohio, and there I had to halt and send for the doctor. My next quarterly meeting was in the town of Burton, and as my labors had always been wonderfully blessed in that place, I could not think of missing the meeting. I told the doctor I wanted him to break the fever as soon as he could. On Thursday evening I took a large dose of calomel, followed by a large portion of jalap. On Friday morning I obtained a quart of port wine, four ounces of genuine Peruvian bark, mounted my horse very early in the morning, took a large portion of wine and bark every two hours, rode thirty-two miles, preached at night, went through the labors of the quarterly meeting with comfort; and the best of all God was with us. Nothing remarkable took place during the round.

"I commenced my fourth round under more auspicious circumstances. Our quarterly meetings were attended with great displays of the goodness and mercy of God. I look back with great satisfaction on the three years and six months I spent on this rough but delightful field of labor." *

* Young's Autobiography, pp. 315, 316.

Rev. JOHN ELLIOTT, in charge of the Shenango Circuit, was admitted on trial in the Ohio Conference in Cincinnati September 8, 1814, and appointed to the above circuit, and at the end of the year was discontinued.

Rev. JOHN GRAHAM, second preacher on the Erie Circuit, was admitted into full connection and ordained a deacon in 1814, and an elder in 1816. He continued to labor within the bounds of the Ohio Conference until 1825. When the Pittsburgh Conference was formed he became a member of that conference, where he labored until 1833, when he located.

Rev. BURROWS WESTLAKE, in charge of the Chautauqua Circuit, was received on trial in the Ohio Conference in September 1814, and into full connection and ordained a deacon in 1817, and an elder in 1819. He continued to labor in the Ohio Conference until 1836, when he was transferred to the Indiana Conference, and died in 1845.

Rev. LEMUEL LANE, second preacher on the New Connecticut Circuit, was admitted on trial in the Ohio Conference September 1814, and appointed to the above circuit, where he labored with great acceptability.

During the year Mr. Lane formed a class in the town of Nelson, Ohio, composed mostly of persons who had belonged to the Methodist Episcopal Church in the East, who had settled in that town. They were Rev. Asahel Mills, a local preacher, Isaac Mills and wife, Sylvanus Hulet and wife, Benjamin Prichard, Elisha Taylor and wife, Prudence Taylor, Oliver Mills, Anna Mills, Orilla Kennedy, Catherine Trusdale, and Betsey Bates. The class was soon considerably increased. Mr. Lane's text on the occasion was, "Fear not, little flock, for it is your Father's good pleasure to give you the kingdom." Miss Bates was soon afterward united in marriage with Mr. Lane.

Another class was formed this year in the town of Wethersfield, Ohio, where the village of Nilestown now stands. Mr. Ebenezer Roller, residing in that place, attended a camp-meeting near Zanesville, Ohio, where he experienced religion, and then invited the preachers on the New Connecticut Circuit to preach in his house, which they continued to do until the class was formed.

In July, 1815, Rev. James M'Mahan preached the first Methodist sermon in Braceville, Ohio, in the bar-room of Mr. John Croy's tavern, the house now (1862) occupied as a parsonage. Soon after this a two-days' meeting was held in the woods near Mr. Edward Oviat's, at the close of which a class was formed consisting of Harvey Stow and wife, Samuel Oviat, Sarah Oviat, William Johnston, and William Cole. For many years Mr. Harvey Stow's house was the place of preaching, and Mr. Stow has filled the office of steward for near fifty years without intermission.

Mr. Graham formed a class this year near Springfield Corners, in Erie County, Pa., consisting of Philip Bristol, leader, and wife, Alexander Davis and wife, Samuel Davis and wife, Samuel Ball and wife, and Benjamin Sandy and wife.

This year was made memorable to the people generally on account of the close of the war, and the return of peace with Great Britain. The treaty of peace was concluded December, 1814, although it was not known in this country nor did hostilities cease until the decisive battle at New Orleans under Gen. Andrew Jackson, January 8, 1815.

Members reported this year were, Shenango...	367
Erie	588
Trumbull and Grand River	1,110
Chautauqua	157
Total	2,222
Last year	1,690
Increase	532

1815.

The Ohio Conference met in Lebanon, Ohio, September 14, 1815, Bishops Asbury and M'Kendree presiding. The appointments were as follows:

Ohio District, David Young, Presiding Elder.

Shenango, John Summerville.

Erie, R. C. Hatton.

Grand River, Samuel Brown.

Mahoning, John Waterman, Shadrach Ruark.

Chautauqua, Lemuel Lane.

The district contained nine circuits in all; five of them only lay within the bounds of the Erie Conference. The Grand River and the Mahoning are again separated, having been greatly enlarged the previous year.

Rev. David Young, appointed to the Ohio District this year, could not enter immediately upon his work on account of some private business requiring his attention within the bounds of the Muskingum

District, which he had previously traveled. Rev. Jacob Young, who this year was appointed to the Muskingum District, says: "As we both had to go to the General Conference in the spring, and as my four years on the Ohio District would not expire until spring, the bishop told us we need not change districts until we returned from the General Conference. So I went back with great delight to my old district. I passed the autumn and winter on the Ohio District, to the mutual satisfaction of myself and the Lord's people."

At the close of the General Conference which sat in Baltimore May, 1816, Rev. JACOB YOUNG entered upon his work on the Muskingum District, thus closing forever his very useful labors on the Ohio District. Mr. Young spent fifty-four years of his life in the work of the ministry, and much of the time he was upon large districts. He possessed a vigorous mind, with a robust constitution, and a noble, generous heart. He loved the Church and her ministry only less than he did the Master. He was nine times sent as a delegate to the General Conference of the Methodist Episcopal Church. He died in great peace in the month of September, 1859.

"Grant us, Lord, his life to live,
That we like him may die."

Rev. SAMUEL BROWN, appointed to the Grand River Circuit, was received on trial in the Ohio Conference in 1812, and into full connection and ordained a deacon in 1814, and an elder in 1816. He continued a faithful laborer until 1820.

Rev. JOHN WATERMAN, in charge of the Mahoning Circuit, was born in New Hampshire June 29, 1790, embraced religion in his eighteenth year, was licensed to preach at Athens, Ohio, in 1814, and was received on trial in the Ohio Conference September 8, 1814, and appointed to the Cincinnati and Miami Circuit, and in 1815 to the above circuit. He labored but one year in this territory, but it was a year of great success. He was received into full connection and ordained a deacon in September, 1816, and an elder in 1818. When the Pittsburgh Conference was formed in 1825 he became a member of that body, ranking among its most talented members, but was transferred back to the Ohio Conference, where he closed his useful life and labors on August 6, 1837.

Rev. SHADRACH RUARK, second preacher on the Mahoning Circuit, was received into the Ohio Conference September, 1813, and into full connection and ordained a deacon in 1815, and an elder in 1817. He spent but one year in this part of the work, but it was a year remembered by many souls as the time of their conversion to God. He continued a faithful laborer in the vineyard until 1830, when he located.

Rev. R. C. HATTON, in charge of the Erie Circuit, resided at the little village of North East, Pa., where he is still remembered by many of the inhabitants. He was subject at times to a singular depression of spirits, when he would imagine very queer things, which made him appear strange, and caused the people to talk much; but when free from this embarrassment he was a remarkable preacher. Not handsome, but dignified and noble in his appearance, with a fine address, a stentorian voice, and a vivid imagination, he could describe the day of judgment, the sufferings of the lost, the joy of the saints, in language that would thrill an audience.

Rev. WILLIAM YOUNG, a local preacher from Ireland, settled his family this year in "King's Chapel" neighborhood, in Lawrence County, Pa., where he lived and labored until September 14, 1829. He died in great peace of mind and full assurance of faith.

The whole number of members this year was ..	2,104
Last year..................................	2,222
Decrease	118

The General Conference in 1816 increased the allowance of all the preachers and their wives to one hundred dollars each, leaving the amount to their children as before.

SECTION VII.

FROM 1815 TO 1817.

"But, pilgrim, be sorrowful no more;
A little while, then we shall soar
Like white-winged sea-birds in the infinite deep:
Till then the Father will our spirits keep."

1815—Continued.

AT the close of the General Conference, in the spring of 1816, Rev. DAVID YOUNG was not able yet to go to the Ohio District, and consequently a new man was sent to perform the fourth round on the District, whose name and early history we now have the pleasure of introducing to the reader.

Rev. JAMES B. FINLEY was born in the State of North Carolina July 1 1781. When quite young his father, who was a Presbyterian minister, moved his family into the State of Kentucky, and settled in a place called Cane Ridge. But when approaching manhood James B. Finley, followed by the whole Finley family, moved into the North-western Territory, then an almost unbroken wilderness, now the flourishing State of Ohio. He married in 1801, and settled in Highland County, Ohio. According to his own account, Mr. Finley's habits of life were extremely rough and irreligious; associating much with Indians and rough backwoodsmen in hunting, fishing, and sporting in various ways. He became fond of the most daring adventures with savage men and wild beasts. Possessing a large, well-built physical frame, with extraordinary muscular strength and activity, he became renowned as a hero in single combat. About the close of the last century a great revival of religion extended throughout the southern and western states, and especially in Kentucky. It commenced among the Presbyterians, but soon the Methodists and other denominations became deeply interested in it. Such vast crowds of people were accustomed to assemble for worship that no church in the country could contain them; consequently places were prepared in the woods, and the people would often become so deeply interested as to remain together several days in succession, under the most intense excitement. It was these meetings that gave rise to camp-meetings among the Methodists, which have accomplished so much good in all parts of our country.

In the month of August, 1801, Mr. Finley set out, in company with some of his associates, to attend a camp-meeting at Cane Ridge, his former home in Kentucky. On arriving on the ground he says: "A scene presented itself to my mind not only novel and unaccountable, but awful beyond description. A vast crowd, supposed by some to have amounted to twenty-five thousand, was collected together. The noise was like the roar of Niagara. The vast sea of human beings seemed to be agitated as if by storm. I counted seven ministers all preaching at the same time; some on stumps, others on wagons, and one, the Rev. William Burke, now of Cincinnati, was standing on a tree which had, in falling, lodged against another. Some of the people were singing, others praying, some crying for mercy in the most piteous accents, while others were shouting most vociferously. While witnessing these scenes a peculiarly strange sensation, such as I had never felt before, came over me. My heart beat tremendously, my knees trembled, my lip quivered, and I felt as though I must fall to the ground. A strange supernatural power seemed to pervade the mass of mind that was there collected. I became so weak and powerless that I found it necessary to sit down. Soon after I left and went down to the woods, and there strove to rally and man up my courage. After some time I returned to the scene of excitement, the waves of which, if possible, had risen still higher. The same awfulness of feeling came over me. I stepped up on a log, where I could have a better view of the surging sea of humanity. The scene that then presented itself to my eye was indescribable. At one time I saw at least five hundred swept down in a moment, as if a battery of a thousand guns had been opened upon them, and then immediately shrieks and shouts that rent the very heavens. My hair rose up on my head, my whole frame trembled, the blood ran cold in my veins, and I fled to the woods a second time, and wished that I had stayed at home." For the purpose of quieting his feelings, Mr. Finley hurried away to a tavern in the vicinity, where a company of desperate men were engaged in drinking, gambling, and fighting. After some time had elapsed he says: "I got to the bar and took a dram and left, feeling that I was as near hell as I wished to be, either in this or the world to come. The brandy had no effect in allaying my feelings, but if anything made them worse." Returning to the ground, his feelings became still more intense as he wandered around gazing upon the exciting scene before him. He spent the following night in a barn near by in a most wretched state of mind, and in the morning, finding one of his companions, he said to him, "Captain, let us be off; I will stay no longer;" and immediately they started for home. As they journeyed along both were too much occupied with their own reflections upon the wonderful scenes they had so recently witnessed to be inclined to converse about them. Mr. Finley says that "when we arrived at the Blue Lick Knobs, I broke the silence which reigned mutually between us." He said: "Captain, if you and I don't stop our wickedness the devil will get us both." At this remark tears gushed freely from both their eyes. The following night was spent without either rest or slumber at a place called May's Lick. Mr. Finley says: "As soon as day broke I went to the woods to pray; and no sooner had my knees touched the ground than I cried aloud for mercy and salvation, and fell prostrate. My cries were so loud that they attracted the attention of the neighbors, many of whom gathered around me. Among the number was a German from Switzerland who had experienced religion. He, understanding fully my condition, had me carried to his house and laid on a bed. The old Dutch saint directed me to look right away to the Saviour. He then kneeled by my bedside and prayed for my salvation most fervently in Dutch and broken English. He then rose and sang in the same manner, and continued singing and praying alternately till nine o'clock, when suddenly my load was gone, my guilt removed, and presently the direct witness from heaven shone fully upon my soul. Then there flowed such copious streams of love into the hitherto waste and desolate places of my soul, that I thought I should die with excess of joy. I cried, I laughed, I shouted; and so strangely did I appear to all but the Dutch brother that they thought me deranged. After a time I returned to my companions, and we started on our journey. O what a day it was to my soul! Then did I realize the truth of that hymn I have so frequently sung:

"'I feel that heaven is now begun;
It issues from the sparkling throne—
From Jesus' throne on high:
It comes in floods I can't contain;
I drink, and drink, and drink again,
And yet am ever dry.'"

Upon returning home Mr. Finley could find no Church to whose doctrines he could subscribe, they being mostly Calvinistic. The Methodists had not established themselves in his neighborhood as yet. He was at times strongly impressed that it was his duty to preach the Gospel; but belonging to no Church, and not possessing the necessary qualifications, he finally determined to abandon entirely all thought of preaching, which was soon followed by the loss of all his religious enjoyments, the abandonment of all religious duties, and a return to his former wicked habits. Seven years were spent in a backslidden and desperately wicked state. In the month of December, 1808, at the urgent solicitation of his wife, he went with her several miles to a Methodist prayer and class meeting. The earnest zeal and kind Christian sympathy manifested by the good people at this meeting removed his former prejudices toward the Methodists, and thoroughly awakened him to a sense of his wretched condition; and when he returned home he commenced reading the Bible, fasting, and praying. On the following Thursday night, about midnight, in the woods, where he had been a long while engaged in prayer, he once more obtained peace and comfort to his soul, and returning home, slept quietly the remainder of the night. He says: "Just at day-break I awoke, and I never shall be able to tell the gratitude I felt to God that I was permitted to awake out of hell. I thought I would express my feelings to my wife; when, to my astonishment, I found her convulsed with sorrow, and bathed in tears. I immediately arose for the purpose of going to my barn to pray. Just as I passed the corner of the house on my way, suddenly God poured upon me the Holy Spirit in such a manner, and in such a measure, that I fell my whole length in the snow, and shouted and praised God so loud that I was heard over the neighborhood. As soon as I was able to arise I returned to the house, and my wife having risen, I caught her in my arms and ran round the house shouting, 'Salvation! Salvation! God has again blessed me with his pardoning love.' For an hour I could do nothing but praise the Lord. While thus exercised I felt as though some one had spoken to me, 'Go preach my Gospel.' I instantly replied, 'Yes, Lord, if thou wilt go with me.'" Soon after this Mr. Finley went to hear a Methodist minister preach, and an opportunity being given to unite with the Church, he gladly embraced it, and thus identified himself, with all his interest in time and eternity, with the Methodist Episcopal Church. He entered at once upon the performance of his Christian duties with such evidences of extraordinary talents, and such a promise of future usefulness, that he was soon properly recommended and duly licensed to preach, and on the first day of May, 1809, by the request of Rev. John Sale, presiding elder of the district, left his home for the Scioto Circuit, which he traveled up to the session of the Western Conference, which sat in Cincinnati, Ohio, September 30, 1809, when he was received on trial and appointed to the Wells Creek Circuit, and in 1810 to Knox Circuit. In 1811 he was received into full connection and ordained a deacon, and in 1813 an elder. He was in charge of the Cross Creek Circuit, when in the summer of 1816 he was sent to accomplish the service of the presiding elder on the Ohio District, the fourth and last round for the conference year.

His first quarterly meeting was on the Mahoning Circuit, but at what place we are not informed. He says that "during the communion the Spirit was poured out in rich effusion. Here I met with Brothers Waterman and Ruark, and on Monday, 13th, rode with the former to Hubbard, and stopped at Brother

Parish's, where I spent the evening in reading and prayer.

"*Tuesday*, 14th.—I rode through Hartford to Brother J. Leach's on the Shenango. This was a lonesome road, and I was much tempted and tried in mind. I prayed all the day to be delivered, and did find some relief.

"*Wednesday*, 15th.—I rode through Meadville, on French Creek, to Gravel Run. Here I put up at Brother Ford's. Living in this country is very hard, there being but little for man or beast. This day I am not so tempted. I slept well, and rose early to offer myself to God without reserve.

"*Thursday*, 16th.—I rode to Brother King's, on the flats of French Creek, three miles from Waterford. Here I was comforted, and felt a blessed hope of heaven.

"*Friday*, 17th.—I rode through Waterford to R. K.'s; himself and wife were formerly Methodists. I exhorted them to seek the Lord, and set out again to run the race set before them. I prayed with them, and went on to Erie. This town occupies a handsome site, and has a good harbor for vessels. Here I met L. Lane, and tried to preach at night to a number of hardened sinners.

"*Saturday*, 18th.—Set forward for North East, and stopped at Brother Russel's. This family loved the Lord." North East was the place for the quarterly meeting for the Erie Circuit, which commenced on this day.

"*Sunday*, 19th.—I tried to preach to a large congregation from Acts iii, 19. The Lord helped me, and we had a gracious season. I trust the fruits of this meeting will be seen in the gates of heaven, when all time is ended.

"*Monday*, 20th.—Rode through Canadeway, now Fredonia, to Brother Baldwin's. In family prayer the Lord visited us in mercy, and our prospects of a better world were greatly increased.

"*Friday*, 21st.—Rode sixteen miles further down the lake to Brother Webb's. This is a new country, everything scarce and dear, and hardly to be had at all. Corn two dollars per bushel, wheat three dollars per bushel, and pickled pork twenty-five cents per pound. These new settlers must learn to live by faith, and many of them have, and are a people zealous of good works. Here, according to the best calculation, I am about two hundred and fifty miles from home, and yet here is the same throne of grace, the same Saviour, and Christians of the same spirit and heavenly temper and calling.

"*Wednesday*, 22d.—This day I preached to an attentive, weeping congregation; after which I baptized six by immersion, and it was a solemn time, and afterward visited a sick brother. He was happy in God his Saviour, and was resigned to his will, waiting to depart and be with Christ, which is far better. This evening rode five miles to a neighborhood on Silver Creek, where the Lord is reviving his work, and many of these new settlers have been converted to God. It has been the observation of my life that new settlements are the most favorable to revivals of religion.

"*Thursday*, 23d.—This morning I felt much revived and encouraged. My communion with God was sweet, yes, sweeter than honey or the honey-comb. I spent part of the forenoon in visiting the young converts, and in praying with them. At twelve o'clock I tried to preach to a large, attentive, and weeping congregation, and I trust not in vain, and baptized six by immersion, and several joined the Church. In the afternoon I rode twelve miles to Brother Baldwin's, and had a good night's rest.

"*Friday*, 24th.—Started for Chautauqua Lake in company with Brother Lane, and after traveling several miles through a swampy country, we arrived at a Brother Southard's, where quarterly meeting is to commence to-morrow." This was upon the north-east side of the lake.

"*Saturday*, 25th.—This day it began to rain, and looked as though a storm was on hand. I sought before the mercy-seat for a suitable preparation of heart for the duties which lay before me, and I felt the Lord precious to my soul. At twelve o'clock I tried to preach from Matt. viii, 11, 12, and it was a very open time with me; the Lord helped me. There was a great move in the congregation. Saints rejoiced, and sinners cried aloud for mercy. After preaching we held our quarterly meeting conference. At five Brother Smith preached, and I exhorted after him, and then we held a prayer-meeting, and the shouts of new-born souls were heard before we closed." The "Brother Smith" referred to was an excellent local preacher, who lived near the head of Chautauqua Lake. He was lame. The writer re-members having seen and heard him preach some years after this. Once at a quarterly meeting he undertook to preach from Rev. xii, 1: "And there appeared a great wonder in heaven; a woman clothed with the sun," etc. He had not proceeded far when he became badly "brushed," as preachers say sometimes when they cannot proceed to their liking. He closed his sermon by saying, "The bee is capable of teaching us many important lessons, and I think I have learned one from them to-day. You will scarcely ever find a bee trying to extract honey from the red clover, and yet it is certain that the red clover blossom contains more honey than the white. The reason of this is, the bee knows that his bill is too short to reach the honey in the red clover, and therefore wisely contents himself with getting what he can from the white. My text to-day is like the red clover blossom, full of honey, but my bill is so short that I cannot reach it, and I will hereafter try to confine myself to texts that my bill can penetrate, so as to reach the honey." Let me commend this remark to young ministers troubled with short bills.

"*Sunday*, 26th," Mr. Finley continues, "at nine o'clock our sacrament commenced, and we had a good time; but Satan was engaged at our love-feast. One of the old man's sons, who was kept out, became enraged, and tried to break open the door, and then went to the window and broke it, and hurt an old man much. . Notwithstanding this interruption, the meeting was one of interest and power. At twelve o'clock I commenced preaching from the first psalm and the first three verses. During the time of my preaching, in which I laid it down as heavy as I could on the sinner, some one called me a liar. Satan was enraged to the very highest pitch, his kingdom was shaking, and I felt that God and heaven and angels were with us, and on our side, and the devil's kingdom trembled. Such was the constancy of the rain that few could leave, and we had a house full. All night was spent in exhortation, singing, and prayer. It was a night never to he forgotten.

" *Tuesday*, 28th.—Rode to Brother Stone's," (about four miles south from Wesleyville, Erie County, Pa., on a ridge called " Gospel Hill,") " and put up to rest till to-morrow. Sister Stone is an old lady, and a well-tried Christian. She embraced religion in early life, and became a member of the Methodist Episcopal Church when it was a reproach and by-word, but she knew in whom she believed, and walked with God in newness of life. She is now a mother in Israel, and we Methodist preachers find in her a mother, and in her house a welcome home. For years after this I made her house my home when I could reach it. She sent for Squire Reese and his wife to spend the afternoon with us, and we had a comfortable time."

During the year 1834 we enjoyed frequently the hospitality and congenial Christian society both of Mrs. Stone, and of Mr. Reese and wife. All of them, however, have some years since passed over the flood, and are now with Finley in heaven.

" *Wednesday*, *29th.*—This day I feel at peace with God and all men. At two o'clock I tried to preach to the people from Hebrews ii, 3, and some were awakened to see their condition and to pray.

"*Thursday*, 30*th*.—This morning my soul is stayed on God. I rode to Erie, where I saw the vessels which Commodore Perry took from the British navy on Lake Erie. They were literally torn to pieces. The Niagara is the largest, and seems to have received the hottest fire. They all lay out in the basin, sunk, a mile from town. From Erie I rode to Brother Randall's, on Conneaut, where our next quarterly meeting is to be held, thirty-two miles up the lake.

"*Friday*, 31*st*.—At twelve o'clock our meeting commenced. I tried to expound John xii, 21, 22. Brother Ira Eddy exhorted. In the evening Brother Stancliff preached, and Brother Westlake exhorted. This was a time of great power. On the Sabbath I tried to hold forth from John vi, 50. At the close some fell, others shouted, and some were in a rage. At night the Lord's people were filled with his heavenly presence in an astonishing manner, and while some were shouting and praising God in the house, others were in the yard giving glory to God in the highest."

Thus in a little more than three weeks Mr. Finley traveled nearly from one end of our conference to the other and back again, holding four quarterly meetings, and traveling and preaching almost every day in each week. He does not give the name of the month in which this labor was performed, but we are inclined to think it was in August, 1816.

The class previously formed at Father Shewel's, in

Rootstown, Ohio, was divided this year. The members residing in the town of Randolph were formed into a class which continued to meet for preaching and class and prayer meetings at the house of Mr. Samuel Redfield, in Randolph, Ohio, for sixteen years, and was then removed to the center of the town, and those members residing in Rootstown were formed into a class at the center of that town, where they worshiped for many years in a school-house. Among the first members of the class at Rootstown were David Collins and wife, Sylvester Jerome and wife, Wilks Paine and wife, and a Mr. Benton. Another class was formed this year in Forrestville, New York, of which Rufus Washburn was leader, and his wife, and William M'Clenathan and wife, were among the first members. The class has had a successful and glorious history up to the present time.

In the spring of 1816 several brothers, who were members of the Methodist Episcopal Church in the State of Connecticut, moved and settled in Chardon, Ohio, where a class was formed the following September, consisting of Zeadock Benton and wife, Ariel Benton and wife, Otis Benton, Gideon Morgan and wife. Preaching was in the court-house until 1835, when a church was built. The society in Newcastle, Pa., succeeded in the erection of a meeting-house this year. It was a plain log structure, which answered a noble purpose in its day, but has been succeeded, first by a frame house, and since by a good brick church. Notwithstanding the good success which had attended the ministrations of the word on the different fields of labor the numbers reported show a large decrease, owing no doubt to the fact that at the last conference new circuits were formed which were composed in part of portions of the Erie, Shenango, Trumbull, and Grand River Circuits lying beyond the bounds of this conference.

The numbers reported this year were, Erie....	664
Chautauqua..	322
Shenango..	337
Trumbull and Grand River.	486
Total.....	1,809
Last year..	2,014
Decrease.	205

1816.

The Ohio Conference commenced its session in Louisville, Ky., September 3d, 1816, when the following appointments were made:

Ohio District, James B. Finley, Presiding Elder.
Shenango, Robert C. Hatton.
Erie, Curtis Goddard, John P Kent.
Grand River and Mahoning, Henry Baker.
Chautauqua, Daniel D. Davidson.

Mr. Finley now being regularly appointed to the Ohio District, becomes permanently connected with our history. As a man, his muscular frame was large and compact, rather tending to corpulency, but not enough so to prevent the most stirring activity. His features were rather coarse, his eye large and full of expression, his hair sandy and standing erect, with a good-sized mouth, and a voice like thunder, and a zeal that never seemed to tire. His mental powers also were strong and clear, his feelings easily aroused, and in preaching his whole being would become engaged, and his impassioned eloquence was at times overwhelming. His appearance and movements were at once calculated to command respect, and even admiration. He could control a set of rowdies at a camp-meeting the best of any man we ever saw attempt it.

His first round of quarterly meetings was as follows: For Grand River and Mahoning Circuit, at Hartford, November 2, 3; for Erie Circuit, at Oil Creek, Venango County, Pa., November 9, 10; for Chautauqua Circuit, at Brokenstraw, Warren County, Pa., November 16, 17. Nothing is said of the quarterly meeting on Shenango Circuit. He says the other meetings "were seasons of great interest, and attended with divine manifestations."

The second round commenced in January, 1817. He says, "I suffered much with cold, which I had contracted by exposure to the chilling blasts of the northern lakes. Our meetings were all attended with the presence and power of God, and the preachers were all in the spirit of revivals. At North East we had a most glorious time both among saints and sinners. The snow was about two feet deep, and continued for a long time, affording great facilities for sleighing, which were improved. Vast numbers came to Church, and many were converted. At this place I visited the grave of the Rev. THOMAS BRANCH. My feelings were of a peculiarly solemn character as I stood by that lone grave of the stranger minister in a strange land. His meek and quiet spirit won for him the friendship of all. Indeed it may be said,

"None knew him but to love him,
None named him but to praise."

Mr. Finley says nothing of the third round. The last round, which occurred during the summer of 1817, was mostly taken up with camp-meetings, some of which were seasons of great interest. One was held in the vicinity of Fredonia, N. Y., commencing July 24, 1817, and lasted four days. Mr. Finley says: "Brothers James M'Mahon and Smith accompanied me to labor in word and doctrine. At this meeting we expected from the wicked much opposition, as they collected together a band the previous year and drove the people away. One of the rules for the government of the meeting was, that at the sound of the trumpet at nine o'clock at night all were to retire to their tents, and those who had no place to lodge were requested to leave the ground. At dark the rabble gathered, and one of their number was designated as their captain by a piece of white paper attached to his hat, and a white club in his hand. The company made but little disturbance until preaching was over. Seeing that there were indications of hostility on their part, I blew the trumpet, and requested all to go to their tents, while those who had none must leave the ground. The captain of this banditti refused to go, and summoned his men to come to his aid. I ordered the constable to take the captain a prisoner, but he swore he would knock down the first man that touched him. He had hardly finished the declaration when I seized him and threw him on the ground, and, disarming him, gave him over to the officer. The company seeing the fate of their captain fled in dismay from the ground. In a conversation with the prisoner I learned what his plans were, and how sadly he was disappointed in not being able to carry them out. He plead so hard for mercy, and promised so faithfully never to engage in such a wicked work again, that I let him go. We kept up the watch all night, fearing they might return, but they did not disturb us. Some were in favor of an attack; but one of the company reported that as I was a Kentuckian, I carried a long dirk in my waistcoat pocket, and that I would as soon stab a man as not. The hour for preaching arrived, and as there were rumors coming in from various quarters that the rowdies were gathering, I preached on the subject of civil and religious liberty. Of course this led me to speak of our pilgrim fathers, and the danger and sufferings endured by them in crossing a watery deep to plant the stand ard of equal rights on this desert soil, and that they might leave unstained what here they found—freedom to worship God—they pledged their lives, their fortunes, and their fame. I remarked if there were any in whom flowed the blood of '76 present to-day who would protect us in the exercise of our religious rights and privileges, to come over on our side and defend us from the rabble. Just at that moment Judge Cushing, who was sitting in the congregation, arose, and addressing the people, said, 'I have fought for this liberty, and I will maintain it with my life; and I give due notice, as a servant of my country, that I will enforce the laws of the State of New York to the utmost against any one who shall disturb this people in their worship.' From this time on the meeting was the most orderly one I had attended. The Sabbath morn broke upon the earth in all its sacred stillness. Brother M'Mahon commenced the morning services, and preached at eight o'clock in demonstration of the spirit and power. I followed at eleven o'clock, and Brother Smith at five. At every coming together of the congregation the work of the Lord progressed with power, and during the night in the tents many were born into the kingdom of God."

The next camp-meeting was near Rockville, Crawford County, Pa. In describing the closing up of this meeting Mr. Finley says: "The great battle was fought on Sabbath night. It was a close and hot engagement, lasting all night. The army of Diabolus was attacked in front, flank, and rear, and literally cut to pieces, so that, in military parlance, there was a total defeat, a perfect rout." At this place our people succeeded this year in the erection of a place of worship. It was a humble-looking log structure, but in it many excellent revivals of religion have occurred, and perhaps the best days Methodism ever saw in that community was in that same log-house.

Rev. R. C. HATTON, in charge of the Shenango Circuit, soon became disaffected toward the Church, and left the circuit.

Rev CURTIS GODDARD, in charge of the Erie Circuit, was received on trial in the Ohio Conference at its session commencing September 8, 1814, and into full connection and ordained a deacon in 1816, and appointed to the Erie Circuit. He was ordained an elder in 1818.

Rev. HENRY BAKER, in charge of the Grand River and Mahoning Circuit, was admitted on trial in the Ohio Conference at its session commencing September 8, 1814, and into full connection and ordained a deacon in 1816, and an elder in 1818, superannuated 1824, and located 1827.

Rev. JOHN P KENT, second preacher on the Erie Circuit, was admitted on trial in the Ohio Conference at its session in Lebanon, Ohio, September 14, 1815, and into full connection and ordained a deacon in 1817, and an elder in 1819. For some cause now unknown Mr. Kent was removed during the year from the Erie to the Grand River Circuit, where he labored in connection with Mr. Baker. While on this circuit Mr. Kent became belated one evening, and was obliged to stay all night in the town of Austinburgh with a Presbyterian deacon. During the evening Mr. Kent inquired of the deacon whether there were any Methodists in that neighborhood. The deacon answered promptly "No," and then said, "I hope there never will be." "Why so?" said Mr. Kent. "Because," said the deacon, "they are such an ignorant, noisy, fanatical set of people I hope we will never be disgraced with them." Mr. Kent was very careful not to make known his Church relations that evening. Next morning, when the time for family worship came, the deacon handed the Bible to Mr. Kent, and requested him to "read and pray." After reading a chapter Mr. Kent sang one of his lively Methodist hymns. His voice was very sweet and melodious, and the hymn was sung in the spirit, filling all that heard it with delight. He then kneeled and prayed most fervently. The whole family were melted to tears, and the inquiry was soon made "if he was not a Methodist preacher?" The answer was prompt, "I am;" when suddenly apologies in rich profusion were made for the deacon's ungenerous remarks about the Methodists, and a very cordial invitation extended by all the family for the young minister to call whenever he could.

Rev. D. D. DAVIDSON, in charge of the Chautauqua Circuit, was received on trial in the Ohio Conference at its session commencing September 3, 1816, and into full connection and ordained a deacon in 1818, and an elder in 1820. Mr. Davidson was a physician before entering the ministry, and hence was usually called Dr. Davidson. The Methodist Episcopal Church had no other doctors at that time, for, as Lorenzo Dow once said, "she did not need them, for her divinity was not sick." Mr. Davidson was tall and slim, with a sharp, shrill voice, which he used freely, and with great effect. He held a two days' meeting in the spring of 1817 in a barn belonging to the widow of Darius Mead, Esq., where Bishop M'Kendree, in company with Rev. Jacob Young in 1812, had the controversy with the Calvinists, and then formed a class one mile and a half west from Youngsville, Warren County, Pa. The meeting was one of great power, and a goodly number were converted, among them a favorite uncle, whose Christian name we bear, but who, many years since, went

"Away from a world of distress,
Away to the mountains above."

Rev. JOHN GREGG, the writer's father, received license to preach in the Methodist Episcopal Church at the last quarterly conference on Chautauqua Circuit this year, signed by James B. Finley. He continued to serve the Church as a local preacher, traveling and preaching extensively through that new and rough country for about thirty years, when he exchanged earth for heaven. In the winter of 1817 a class was formed three miles below Warren, Pa., on the north bank of the Alleghany River on this wise.

Rev. IRA EDDY, then a young man just licensed to preach, was employed by the Presiding Elder to labor on Chautauqua Circuit in connection with Mr. Davidson. Having some relatives residing in the village of Warren, Mr. Eddy was invited to preach there occasionally. On his way up the river from Youngsville he lost a shoe from his horse, and the animal soon became too lame to proceed. About three miles below Warren, right on the bank of the river, stood a blacksmith's shop, the sight of which greatly relieved the feelings of our young itinerant. He halted, and inquired if he could get a shoe set. The blacksmith replied, "Not to-night." Mr. Eddy assured him that he could go no further in that condition. The smith, not in the least suspecting the character of the young man, told him that if he would stay all night he would shoe his horse in the morning. Mr. Eddy gladly accepted the invitation, dismounted, and put up his horse, little thinking what kind of a host he was stopping with. When the blacksmith had finished his day's labor he came into the house, and when about retiring to bed Mr. Eddy respectfully asked the privilege of praying with the family. The rough-looking blacksmith stood for a moment amazed, as if he scarcely knew what reply to make. He then went reluctantly and picked up an old Bible and handed it to Mr. Eddy. While at prayer Mr. Eddy was greatly blessed, and prayed with unusual fervor, and both of the parents became much affected, even to tears. The young minister was then directed to a trundle-bed, where he spent the night as comfortably as possible. In the morning, before the smith went to work, Mr. Eddy again read the Scriptures and prayed with the family, having again great liberty in prayer, while the family, the parents especially, were melted to tears. After prayer the blacksmith took some coals of fire and went to the shop to shoe the horse, according to promise. As the good woman wiped away her tears, she said to Mr. Eddy, "I thank you, stranger, for the prayers you have offered for us, for," said she, "I never before saw my husband weep. He is," said she, "a dreadful opposer of religion, and especially of the Methodists, having been brought up a Calvinist." Mr. Eddy felt certain that the old man's heart had been warmed, and concluded that it was best "to strike while the iron was hot," and accordingly started for the shop. He entered it just as the smith was taking a piece of red hot iron from the fire. As he had it upon the anvil, and was about to strike, his feelings overcame him, and dropping his hammer, the blacksmith said, "Sir,

I would be willing to be chained to this anvil-block and labor all my life as hard as a slave in Algiers if I could but enjoy what you do." This opened the way for our young itinerant, who immediately commenced preaching a full and free salvation to him on the one simple condition of faith in Christ, to which the blacksmith listened with apparent astonishment, until his iron became cool, and he was obliged to heat it again. But while the smith was engaged with his hammer in making the nails and setting the shoe, Mr. Eddy was engaged in applying the hammer of truth to his heart. As the last nails were being driven Mr. Eddy ventured to make known the fact that he was a Methodist preacher. The blacksmith immediately besought him to leave an appointment and come and preach in his house to his neighbors. The appointment was made, and the young preacher hastened away to his appointment in Warren. At the time appointed, as Mr. Eddy came in sight of the blacksmith's shop, he saw both the old man and woman standing on an eminence, eagerly looking for him to come. On riding up to them they both greeted him with tears of joy as well as with open arms, telling him as they grasped his hand how "God had pardoned their sins and changed their hearts." On entering the house Mr. Eddy found it crowded with people anxiously waiting to hear his message of mercy. A revival of religion had already commenced, and this meeting gave it a new impetus, and in a short time a class was formed consisting of Joseph Mead and wife, Mr. Owens and wife, Martin Reece, wife, and mother, Benjamin Mead, and David

Mead. The number was soon increased to twenty-six members.

A class was formed this year by Mr. Baker on the Grand River Circuit, in the town of Southington, Ohio, consisting of Roderick Norton, wife, and others.

Rev. Robert Montgomery, a local preacher in the Methodist Episcopal Church, was instrumental in forming a class in the summer of 1817 in Geneva, Ashtabula County, Ohio, consisting of Thomas Stevens, leader, James Morrison, Jr., and wife, Abisha Laughton, S. Laughton, Phebe Custon, Anna Morrison, and Samuel Quinton.

In the spring of 1817 Mr. B. B. Clarke, a valuable member of the Methodist Episcopal Church in the State of New York, moved his family into Clarion County, Pa., and was the first Methodist in that county. Not long after a few other families connected with the Methodist Episcopal Church settled in different parts of the same county. They soon found each other out, held meetings together, and were formed into a class, which met at the house of Mr. John Lawson, near the mouth of Redbank. It consisted of B. B. Clarke, leader, John Lawson and wife, Mr. Bead and wife. This class was for several years connected with the Mahoning Circuit, Baltimore Conference.

There was a class formed about this time in Springfield, Erie County, Pa., known as the "Randall Class," which was the nucleus of the present Methodist Episcopal Church in Albion, which consisted of John Randall, leader, and wife, Rev. George Stuntz and wife, and some others.

The membership on Erie Circuit this year was	626
Shenango.	316
Grand River and Mahoning	625
Chautauqua	500
Total	2,067
Last year	1,809
Increase	258

SECTION VIII.

1817 AND 1818.

"'Tis thine own work, Almighty God,
And wondrous in our eyes."

1817

THE Ohio Conference met in Zanesville September 3, 1817, at which the work was arranged as follows:

Ohio District, James B. Finley, Presiding Elder.

Erie, John P Kent, Ira Eddy.

Grand River and Mahoning, D. D. Davidson, Ezra Booth.

Chautauqua, Curtis Goddard.

The Shenango Circuit was divided between the Erie and Beaver Circuits, and hence the name appears no more on the minutes of the Conference. Mr. Finley, the presiding elder, says: "In the true spirit of Gospel ministers the brethren went to their respective fields of labor. Great were the toils and hardships they were called to endure. The winter was extremely severe, the cold being almost beyond endurance; yet the Lord crowned the labor and sufferings of his ministers with success. The country was but sparsely settled, the rides were long and roads rough, the fare hard and provisions scarce; but in the midst of all the Lord was with them. To preach once every day and lead class, after having traveled from ten to twenty miles, and two or three times on the Sabbath, leading as many classes, with the privilege of being at home three days out of thirty, would now be regarded as severe work."

A few miles south-west of Akron, Ohio, Mr. Finley says, "On the lands of Dr. Clarke, near the Portage, was held this year the first camp-meeting that was ever known in this part of the country." He says, "M'Mahan, Davidson, Booth, and Brooks were present," and "the word preached was attended with power to the hearts of the people." In the town of Hudson, Ohio, he says, "At a quarterly meeting held in Major Gaylord's barn, a sharp-featured little man came on Saturday and took his seat. I was advised that he was an Orthodox clergyman. I tried to preach a free grace sermon on Revelations xxii, 17. After I had finished the discourse I invited him to come forward and conclude the meeting. Instead of doing so he rose up in his place and said, 'Let us pray.' After congratulating the Lord on his greatness and the power of his righteous decrees, which never could be altered, he began in the plenitude of his benevolence to pray for poor, ignorant, misled people and their instructors, informing the Lord that they were doing more harm than infidelity itself, and hindering the progress of the pure Gospel. When he was done I asked him, in the presence of all the people, who those ignorant, deluded people and their instructors were to whom he alluded in his prayer. 'Did you,' said I, 'mean the Methodists and their teachers?' To all this he answered nothing. 'Then,' said I, 'come out to-morrow, and I will show up the gross and irreconcilable inconsistencies and absurdities of unconditional election and reprobation.' When the time arrived there was a great crowd. I took the Saybrook platform and read the creed, and brought it to the test of the Bible. The whole audience was greatly excited, and when I closed the people gathered in groups and entered into controversy, which continued until the next meeting hour arrived. I then preached the true doctrine, that 'Jesus, by the grace of God, had tasted death for every man,' and that all might be saved. This was the beginning of a glorious revival of religion; seventy-five professed to find peace in believing." Mr. Finley says that "On the 4th of June," 1818, "a camp-meeting commenced at Lexington, on Erie Circuit. All came together in the spirit, and the work commenced at the first meeting. The divine influence kindled and spread in every heart. On Sabbath many were awakened to a sense of their lost condition, and were prompted to cry for mercy. The evening was set apart for a prayer-meeting, and many came forward to the mourners' bench and were converted to God by scores. Among the number was a native of France. This poor old soldier of Napoleon Bonaparte had wandered out into the western wilderness, houseless and homeless, without a knowledge of God. He had stood in the thickest of the battle, breasted the hottest of the fire, and heard the deafening roar of the artillery without trembling; but when he came to hear the thunders of Sinai his lip quivered, his knees trembled, and he fell in the battle of the Lord. After suing for mercy, and crying for quarter all night, it pleased God, at the rising of the sun, to pour upon him pardoning mercy. No sooner had heaven come down into the heart of the old worn and weary veteran than he arose, and his whole face beamed with joy. His shouts of praise ascribing glory to King Jesus were truly remarkable. In broken English he tried to tell the bystanders what God had done for his soul. He told them he had eaten bread in three kingdoms, and that morning he was eating bread in the fourth, even the bread that cometh down from heaven. 'I fight,' said he, 'under de Emperor Napoleon; but now me fight under de Emperor Jesus. Vive le Emperor Jesus!' Great good was accomplished at this meeting." This camp-meeting was on the Grand River Circuit, which now, it seems, extended into Pennsylvania a short distance.

Mr. Finley says, "On the 10th of June our camp-meeting for Erie Circuit commenced fourteen miles below Erie." This must have been at North East, Pa. He says, "A camp-meeting had never been held in these parts before, and many were induced, out of curiosity, to attend the meeting. It commenced under favorable circumstances, and many were awakened and converted. Sabbath, however, was the great day of the feast. When the preacher addressed the vast congregation from Rev. xx, 12, 'And I saw the dead, small and great, stand before God; and the books were opened: and another book was opened, which is the book of life: and the dead were judged out of those things which were written in the books, according to their works,' there was not one inattentive soul on the ground. The whole congregation was melted into tears, and deep groans and cries for mercy were heard bursting forth from hearts convinced of sin and judgment. Occasionally shouts of victory and triumph were heard from the pious, who waited the happy change. The evening was devoted to praying and laboring with mourners. After the ring was formed, and we commenced our address to the throne of grace, the Holy Spirit fell on us, and multitudes within and without the ring fell under the shocks of divine power. Many mariners from Erie were there, and some of them became the subjects of awakening grace. I heard one say to the sheriff, 'Mr. B. is down crying for mercy.' To this he replied, 'If the Methodists can make him a better man it is more than the commonwealth of Pennsylvania can do, for he has been in nearly all the prisons in the state.' This called my attention to Mr. B., whom I found in great distress, earnestly seeking the salvation of his soul. I gave him all the instruction I could, and soon the light of heaven broke on him, and the Sun of righteousness arose with healing in his beams. He was soundly converted to God; he lived and died a good man."

The next camp-meeting Mr. Finley attended was on the Chautauqua Circuit, one mile west from Youngsville, Warren County, Pa., on the land of Mr. William Mead, and a short distance west and north of his house. He says: "At the commencement of this meeting I was much discouraged, but the Lord was greater to me than all my fears, and never did I have a more clear and satisfactory evidence of the fact that man's extremity is God's opportunity. Sabbath morning arrived, and as the sun was gilding the eastern sky, the trumpet called us to the concert of prayer. While we were looking up to heaven for a blessing, God graciously poured out his spirit, and we realized the opening of the gates of life. Preparatory to preaching, I walked out into the wilderness, or rather desert, for the ground was covered with rocks, for the purpose of meditation. While reclining among the rocks and fern, which grew in great abundance, I heard a sound, which to the practiced ear, carries more terror perhaps than any other. It was the rattle of death. The weather being exceedingly warm I had taken off my shoes and stockings, and my feet being somewhat elevated, exposed my legs. Looking in the direction of the alarm I saw the glaring eyes and forked tongue of the *Americana horribilis* within a foot or two of me. It was coiled and ready for a strike. The great Creator has so formed this dreadful creature that it cannot strike without warning, and this doubtless saved my life, as it has the life of thousands. Seeing my danger I instantly sprang, and with one bound was far beyond the reach of its deadly fangs. After dispatching the rattlesnake I returned to the camp, thankful to God for deliverance. During the day the work of the Lord went on with power, and many were saved by the regenerating grace of God. Monday morning we held a solemn communion, and I think it was the most glorious season I ever beheld. The most hardened sinners trembled and wept and looked on, while the followers of Him who, in Gethsemane and on the cross drank the bitter cup, were commemorating his dying love. Two men from different parts of the country, with their companions, came to the meeting with the avowed purpose of disturbing the people of God in their worship. One of these men was from near the mouth of the Chautauqua Lake, and the other from the Alleghany River. The former, Captain W—x, brought with him a supply of whisky. Both of these men came into the congregation and took their seats. While the minister was preaching the Holy Spirit attended the word, and Captain W was smitten, like Elymas the sorcerer, with blindness. An awful feeling came over him as the horror of darkness surrounded him. He felt as if God was about to call him to judgment; and although he had been a Universalist, and had tried to believe and teach others these delusive doctrines, yet he now felt himself hanging over the fearful gulf, and nothing but life's brittle thread kept him from dropping into perdition. He afterward remarked that his feelings were awful beyond description. After some time his sight returned, and he arose and left the congregation. Notwithstanding his conviction, his stubborn heart was unwilling to yield, and obstinately persisting in the rejection of mercy, he resolved to seek oblivion in the cup. But the most potential draughts of the maddening poison could not obliterate the traces of the Spirit's conviction from his heart. Soon with redoubled force the power of God again came down upon his sin-smitten soul. Unable to bear the deep and utter wretchedness which drank up his spirit, he resolved if God did not kill him to return home. While on his way home the constraining spirit of God operated so powerfully that he was forced to cry out in the bitterness of his soul for mercy. He did not reach home until some time in the night, and when he did arrive his family were much alarmed. No sooner did he enter the house than he fell upon his knees and continued his cries for mercy. The alarm was so great that the whole neighborhood was soon collected together. All night that man cried to God, and just as the gray streaks of morning were breaking from the chambers of the east the Lord in mercy spoke peace to his soul. His family and many of the neighbors were converted, and the result was the conversion of thirty in that neighborhood, whom I subsequently organized into a class, and made the captain's house a preaching place." The following list contains the most prominent members of the class referred to by Mr. Finley: Lyman Crane and wife, Henry Crane and wife, John Steward and wife, Michael Frank and wife, Philetus Stevens and wife, Stephen Wilcox and wife, Ephraim Wilcox and wife. One of the men by the name of Wilcox was the person referred to by Mr. Finley. He resided about three miles south-west from Jamestown, New York. Mr. Finley says that "the man from the Alleghany River, W N., was powerfully awakened on Sabbath, and being unable to withstand the powerful influence, he fled for his home. Just before reaching the door of his habitation, he was struck down by the power of God and was carried into the house by some of the family. Soon the alarm spread, the neighbors were collected, and a messenger was dispatched to the camp-ground, a distance of nine miles. Two or three brethren went to the house and found him in a convulsed and speechless state. Soon after their arrival he seemed to awake to consciousness, and exclaimed with a loud voice, 'O hell! hell! hell!' He then fell away into the same unconscious state. His countenance bore all the deep marked traces of despair. The brethren sang and prayed alternately, and those who watched his features could discover the deep emotions of his soul. At times a faint ray of light would kindle on his cheek, but soon it was gone, and like the lightning from a storm-cloud, which shocks the soul and disappears in darkness, it only rendered his features more gloomy. It seemed as if despair would settle down sullenly upon him. After hours of religious exercises, such as singing and prayer, deep, agonizing prayer to God in behalf of the struggling soul, all at once the dark cloud passed away, his countenance was lighted up with an unearthly radiance, and opening his eyes he exclaimed, 'O heaven! heaven! heaven!' Then springing to his feet he shouted, 'Glory! glory! glory!' Many were awakened and converted in this neighborhood. He related the exercises of his mind during his unconscious state afterward. He said his mind was as bright and clear as it ever was; that he distinctly saw hell and its miseries. He felt that he was doomed; but just as hope was leaving him, he saw the Saviour pleading for him. During this plea he said his suspense was awful beyond expression; but when it was ended and mercy obtained, he saw heaven and glory open upon him." The writer was present and remembers this camp-meeting well, although he was a small boy at the time. That sermon on Monday had a very different effect on some other persons present. Mr. Finley dealt some severe blows in his sermon on whisky makers and venders, which gave great offense to some persons engaged in that business, especially a Mr. M. C. D., who ran a distillery a few miles distant. The writer was requested by a young man, whose name was Mr. J. W., to accompany him to the pasture field to look after his horses. We left the ground for that purpose, and had proceeded but a few rods from the inclosure when we came upon a company of men, perhaps six or eight in number, talking very loud, with frequent oaths. We drew up to hear the conversation, and heard Mr. M. C. D. threaten with a terrible oath that if he ever had an opportunity he would "pound that preacher until he would learn to let his business alone." Mr. J. W replied that if they remained there much longer using such language he would bring Mr. Finley there and let them try their courage. They dared him to do it. Mr. J. W started upon the run for the campground. The writer, a good deal scared, but anxious to see the affray, clambered up on to a stump where he would be able to see the combat and be out of danger. Soon we saw Mr. Finley coming up the main aisle as fast as he could walk, with his right hand raised and clenched, and the other swinging by his side. On he came until he reached the crowd, who on account of the shape of the ground did not observe him until he was close up to them. As he sprang in among them with his hand raised in an attitude to strike, he cried out, "Disperse and leave this encampment at once; disperse, I say, every one of you." Instantly the whole gang fled like the herd of swine when the Saviour permitted the devils to enter them, not into the sea, but the adjoining woods. Mr. Finley turned and walked back to the ground, saying, "The wicked flee when no man pursueth."

A lady who was present at a camp-meeting held by Mr. Finley, near Rockville, Pa., says that "while Bishop M'Kendree was preaching, three young men took their seats with their hats on, on the ladies' side of the ground, and commenced talking and laughing. Mr. Finley slipped softly up, until he came suddenly to them, with his hand clenched and drawn, and said, 'Off with them hats, and away from this side of the ground immediately.' The young men seemed to try which should obey first.

A gentleman who was present at a quarterly meeting a few miles south of Franklin, Pa., says that after preaching on Sabbath evening several mourners came forward for prayers; and while preachers and people were engaged in prayer, several young rowdies were disposed to make what disturbance they could. One of them, a stout, fearless-looking young man, got up on a seat in the rear of the praying circle, and stood there smoking a cigar. Mr. Finley, observing him, arose from his knees, and ordered him to "Stop smoking and get down." The young fellow refused to do either. Mr. Finley then sprang over a bench or two and caught him with one hand in his collar and the other on the opposite shoulder, and brought him suddenly from the seat on to the floor, and started with him for the door. The rowdy caught hold of Mr. Finley with both hands and moved along, intending with the aid of his comrades to take the elder out of the house with them and there abuse him. But as they approached the door, Mr. Finley took a sudden turn on his opponent, and at the same time knocked his feet from under him, and sent him head foremost out of the door and down two or three steps on to the frozen ground, and then wheeling round shook his clenched hand at the other rowdies, saying, "There, I could cram a cellar full of such fellows." The young men rushed out of the door, and after helping up their bruised comrade, made their escape.

Rev. SAMUEL R. BROCKUNIER, a large young Dutchman, full of zeal, and of very promising talents, was sent by Elder Finley about midwinter to take the place of Mr. Goddard, whose health had failed, on the Chautauqua Circuit, and Mr. Brockunier remained on the circuit until conference, when he was admitted on trial in the Ohio Conference, and has spent a long and useful career within the bounds of the Pittsburgh Conference.

Rev. IRA EDDY was born in Sherburne, Rutland County, Vt., March 31, 1796, and was converted to God near Mayville, Chautauqua County, N. Y., March 8, 1813, in the nineteenth year of his age. Such was his religious zeal and self-sacrificing spirit that the people of God soon became convinced that "a dispensation of the Gospel was committed unto him." He was licensed to exhort, and immediately entered into the work with all his might. He was employed by Elder Finley during the fall of 1816 and winter and spring of 1817 with Mr. Davidson on the Chautauqua Circuit, but in June was sent to the Shenango Circuit to take the place of Mr. Hatton, where he labored until September, 1817, when he was admitted on trial in the Ohio Conference, and appointed second preacher on the Erie Circuit. He was ordained a deacon and received into full connection in 1819, and made an elder in 1821.

Rev. EZRA BOOTH, second preacher on the Mahoning Circuit, was admitted on trial in the Ohio Conference September, 1817, and into full connection and ordained a deacon in 1819, and an elder in 1821.

Rev. CURTIS GODDARD, on the Chautauqua Circuit, left this part of the work at the close of this year, but continued a member of the Ohio Conference, performing valuable service in different portions of that extensive field until 1834, when for some reason unknown to us he located.

This year there was a great revival on one part of the district. Mr. Finley says that "on the Mahoning Circuit two hundred were added to the Church." The work commenced at a camp-meeting held in Deerfield, July, 1818. During the meeting there were no perceptible evidences of a revival, though all the meeting was solemn, and the word was preached with the demonstration of the Spirit and with power; but shortly after the meeting closed the bread which had been cast upon the waters began to show itself. In the course of three months the society increased from sixteen to upward of one hundred. Among the converts were some of the principal men of the town. The society at Youngsville, Warren County, Pa., commenced the erection of a church this year. It was a small plain frame building, situated on the south side of the main road about half a mile west of the village, sat with its side to the road, and the place of entrance was on the back side of the house. It was so awkwardly arranged that the society never finished it. A log meeting-house was erected this year in the Shenango Settlement, Mercer County, Pa. Another log meeting-house was built about this time in Father Carrol's neighborhood, about ten miles east of Mercer.

The members returned this year were, Erie Circuit.	505
Grand River and Mahoning	678
Chautauqua	532
Total	1,715
Last year	2,067
Decrease	352

1818.

The Ohio Conference commenced its session in Steubenville, Ohio, August 7, 1818. The work was arranged and the preachers appointed as follows:

Ohio District, James B. Finley, Presiding Elder.

Erie, D. D. Davidson, Samuel Adams.

Mahoning, Calvin Ruter, John Stewart.

Chautauqua, John Summerville.

Tuscarawas District, Charles Waddle, Presiding Elder.

Grand River, Ira Eddy.

Cuyahoga, Ezra Booth, Dennis Goddard.

We now have parts of two districts extending over the territory of the present Erie Conference. The number of circuits five instead of three, and the number of preachers ten instead of six. The Grand River and Mahoning Circuit is divided into two, and out of the western part a new circuit was formed, embracing the whole region watered by the Cuyahoga River, whose name it bears. Mr. Finley says he was "astonished to find what God had wrought at Deerfield and the neighboring towns. The work spread like fire in a prairie, and at every meeting victory turned on Israel's side. I held a two-days' meeting in Brother Manary's barn, and the work was powerful and overwhelming. All opposition seemed to have ceased, or was borne down by the tide of religious influence. The following May I attended a quarterly meeting in the same place, and there were at least five hundred persons in the love-feast. In this meeting the saints lifted up their voice in praise to God, and the sighs of penitents, mingled with the songs of joy, were grateful to angelic ears."

Old Dr. Bostwick was present at the meeting, and seemed as Moses on the summit of Pisgah. He saw by faith the land that was afar off, and with shoutings exclaimed, in the language of the poet, "'Tis grace that supports, or glory would crush me." It is supposed that at least fifty souls were happily converted to God during this meeting.

Rev. James B. Finley. As this year closed up the labors of Mr. Finley within the bounds of the Erie Conference, it will be proper here to give the reader a short account of his subsequent useful life. From 1819 to 1823 he was presiding elder on the Lebanon

District, bounded by the Ohio River on the south, and the immense forests of Michigan on the north. From 1823 to 1827 he was missionary among the Wyandot Indians in the north-western part of the State of Ohio, near Sandusky. Here his labor was remarkably successful; hundreds of these Indians were converted through his instrumentality. In 1827 and 1828 he was again on the Lebanon District, still, however, superintending the Indian Mission at Sandusky. In 1829 and 1830 he was stationed in Cincinnati. In 1831 and 1832 he was presiding elder on the Miami District. In 1833 he again labored in Cincinnati. In 1834 and 1835 he was presiding elder on the Chillicothe District. From 1836 to 1838 he was again on the Lebanon District. From 1838 to 1842 he was presiding elder on the Dayton District. From 1843 to 1845 on the Zanesville District. The next three years he was moral instructor in the Ohio Penitentiary. In 1849 he was superannuated, 1850 stationed at Yellow Springs, 1851 again superannuated; 1852 and 1853 stationed at Clinton-street, Cincinnati; 1854 he sustained a supernumerary relation, and in 1855 he superannuated; 1856 he was appointed conference missionary. In May, 1856, he was a member of the General Conference in Indianapolis, Indiana, where the writer was permitted to renew his acquaintance with this venerable man, after which his health continued rapidly to decline, until on the night of September 6 his happy spirit took its flight from earth to heaven. Mr. Finley spent some fifty-seven years in the ministry, and was a member of eleven General Conferences.

"Servant of God, well done!
Thy glorious warfare's past;
The battle's fought, the race is won,
And thou art crowned at last."

Rev. CHARLES WADDLE, Presiding Elder on the Tuscarawas District, was admitted on trial in the Western Conference, which sat in Cincinnati in October, 1811, and into full connection and ordained a deacon by the Ohio Conference in 1814, and an elder in 1816. He was a man of very respectable talents, and a very useful and acceptable minister.

Rev. D. D. DAVIDSON, in charge of the Erie Circuit, finished up his valuable labors within our bounds this year, but continued his itinerant work in the Ohio Conference until the Cincinnati Conference was formed, of which he is now (1864) a superannuated member, residing at Dayton, Ohio, commanding the love and esteem of all that know him. But few men have been permitted to labor as long for Christ or gather as many souls into his kingdom as Mr. Davidson has done.

Rev. SAMUEL ADAMS, second preacher on the Erie Circuit, was admitted on trial in the Ohio Conference at its session in Steubenville, Ohio, August 7, 1818, and into full connection and ordained a deacon in 1820, and an elder in 1822. When the Pittsburgh Conference was formed in 1825 Mr. Adams became a member of that body. We shall have occasion to refer to him again.

Rev. CALVIN RUTER, brother to Dr. Ruter, was admitted on trial in the Ohio Conference at its session in Zanesville, September 3, 1817, and into full connection and ordained a deacon in 1819, was transferred to the Missouri Conference in 1820, ordained an elder in 1821. In 1832, when the Indiana Conference was formed, he became a member of that body, and was its secretary for six years. He was a member of the General Conference at each session from 1832 until 1856. He died suddenly of disease of the heart June 11, 1859, and "ceased at once to work and live."

Rev. JOHN STEWART, second preacher on the Mahoning Circuit, was admitted on trial in the Ohio Conference at its session in Zanesville, Ohio, September 3, 1817, and into full connection and ordained a deacon in 1819, and an elder in 1821, when he was transferred to the Missouri Conference, but was returned to Ohio in 1822, where he continued to itinerate through nearly every part of the state, being presiding elder nine years, and laboring without interruption forty-three years, when he became superannuated.

Rev. JOHN LEWIS, a local preacher of respectable preaching talents, and of great zeal and piety, moved from the east and settled his family in the town of Harmony, Chautauqua County, N. Y., and through his labors, in connection with the Rev. J. Summerville, there was an extensive revival of religion in the town, and a class formed consisting of Rev. John Lewis and wife, Daniel B. Carpenter, Isaac Carpenter and wife, John Pember and wife, Joseph S. Pember, Henry Pember, and Lucinda Terry. Mr. Lewis died February 20, 1864, aged eighty-nine.

Rev. DENNIS GODDARD, brother to Rev. Curtis

Goddard, was admitted on trial in the Ohio Conference at Steubenville, August 7, 1818, and appointed second preacher on the Cuyahoga Circuit, was received into full connection and ordained a deacon in 1820, and an elder in 1822. We shall refer to him again.

In the year 1816 Mr. Hubbard Hulbert, a member of the Methodist Episcopal Church, with his family, settled in the town of Franklin, Portage County, Ohio, and soon after invited Father Shewel to preach in his house, which he continued to do until some of the neighbors became converted; and one or two other Methodist families coming into the place, Messrs. Booth and Goddard were induced to establish an appointment there, and to form a class consisting of Amasa Hamline and wife, Hubbard Hurlbert and wife, David Lilly and wife, and Ephraim Rue and wife.

About this time a class was formed at Springfield Corners, Erie County, Pa., consisting of Walter Darby and wife, Aaron Wills and wife, a Brother Lumpkin, and a few others.

Some time this year Mr. Billings Clark moved from Massachusetts with his family and settled in Concord, Geauga County, Ohio. His wife, Mrs. Caroline Clark, and her sister, Miss Nancy Brigden, were both active members of the Methodist Episcopal Church, and immediately interested themselves in the religious welfare of the neighborhood. A Methodist society had been formed previously, but was broken up by internal dissensions. Rev. Ira Eddy, preacher on the Grand River Circuit, was invited by Mr. Clark to preach in his house, which thenceforward became the home of Methodist preachers, and for several years their preaching place. Soon a revival of religion commenced, which resulted in the formation of a class consisting of Asa Mallory and wife, Lemuel Baldwin, Simeon Winchel, Caroline Clark, and Nancy Brigdon. The last named lady in about one year after this became united in marriage with Mr. Eddy, and has shared with him the hardships and trials of forty years in the itinerant work. The next time Mr. Eddy came round the work had spread, and six more united with the class, and among them was Mr. Billing Clark, who joined only as a seeker, but was soon after happily converted to God. Mr. Clark and wife are still (1864) devoted Christians, residing in the town of Edinburgh, Portage County, Ohio.

Mr. Eddy also formed a class in the town of Mentor, Geauga County, Ohio, consisting of Noah Nowland and wife, Mr. Brass and wife, Mr. Wilson and wife, and Mr. Jewet and wife.

Several families belonging to the Methodist Episcopal Church in the State of New York moved the previous year to Ohio, and settled in Willoughby, and were formed into a class by Mr. Eddy this year. They were Rev. Henry Woolsey and wife, Benjamin Woolsey and wife, Mrs. Richards, and a few others. Mr. Summerville also formed a class in the town of Busti, Chautauqua County, New York, consisting of Palmer Phillips and wife, Joseph Phillips and wife, Asa Smith and wife, with several other persons. The class grew rapidly.

Number of members this year..................	2,576
Last year..................................	1,730
Increase..................................	846

SECTION IX.

FROM 1819 TO 1822.

"More and more it spreads and grows,
Ever mighty to prevail;
Sin's strongholds it now o'erthrows,
Shakes the trembling gates of hell."

1819.

THE Ohio Conference met at Cincinnati, Ohio, August 7, 1819, at which the work was arranged and the appointments were made as follows:

Ohio District, William Swayze, Presiding Elder.

Erie, Philip Green.

Lake, Robert C. Hatton. Benjamin P Hill was a supply by the appointment of the presiding elder.

Chautauqua, John Summerville.

Mahoning, James M'Mahan.

Lancaster District, Charles Waddle, Presiding Elder.

Cuyahoga, Ezra Booth, James Murray.

Grand River, Ira Eddy.

Each of the above districts contained eight circuits; but only two on the Lancaster District extended into this territory, and four on the Ohio District.

Lake Circuit was formed out of portions of the Erie and Chautauqua Circuits, and extended up and down the shore of Lake Erie from North East to Silver Creek.

Rev. WILLIAM SWAYZE, Presiding Elder on the

Ohio District, was born in Sussex County, New Jersey, November 18, 1784, near the village of Asbury, named after the venerable Bishop Asbury. In the seventeenth year of his age he went to reside near the City of Baltimore, where he was induced by a pious colored man to go with him to the Methodist Episcopal Church. The preacher was the Rev. J. Chambers. The sermon interested him greatly, and he became powerfully awakened. After having sought earnestly for some time for salvation, but in vain, as he was standing one day on a scaffold near the top of a building in the City of Baltimore, engaged in painting, he says: "Pressed by this unutterable load, suddenly I felt a touch on my forehead like the blaze of a candle, (but without pain,) which immediately ran through my whole body like an electric shock. My load was gone, and I felt as calm as infant innocence. I looked east, west, north, and south—all appeared glorious—a new city, a new world."* It was immediately impressed upon his mind, as if a voice had uttered it, "Son, thy sins which were many are all forgiven thee." Soon after this he offered himself for membership in the Methodist Episcopal Church at Fell's Point, Md., and was received by Rev. Philip Bruce, the pastor.

He could no longer content himself unless at religious meetings of some kind, taking an active part in them with such zeal and fervor as soon convinced the people that God had a special work for him to perform. He received a license to exhort, and commenced calling sinners to repentance with

* Swayze's Narrative, p. 41.

great earnestness. After much fasting, prayer, and reading the Scriptures, he consented to receive a license to preach, and as fast as the way opened he commenced preaching with an ability that was surprising to the people. After passing through some sore afflictions, malicious persecutions, and providential deliverances, he determined to give himself up entirely to the work of the ministry. Receiving a present of a horse and outfit, he started off on a preaching tour through the States of Delaware, New Jersey, New York, Massachusetts, and Vermont, preaching as he went with great power and wonderful success. In May, 1807, he was admitted on trial in the New York Conference, and appointed, in company with Rev. DANIEL OSTRANDER, to the Dutchess Circuit, embracing parts of three states. It would be very interesting, if our space would permit us, to follow this zealous, talented young minister through the various fields of labor he occupied in the New York Conference, and see with what untiring zeal and remarkable success he labored for the conversion of sinners to God. He became emphatically a "son of thunder," attracting great crowds of people to his ministry, and with a power and pathos but few have ever equaled, moving and exciting them, some to tears, others to cry for mercy, while others would shout for joy. He was received into full connection and ordained a deacon in 1809, and an elder in 1811, and continued to labor in the New York Conference until May, 1815, when he was transferred to the Ohio Conference and appointed to Columbus, Ohio, where he remained two years. In 1817 he was sent to the

Deer Creek Circuit, where he remained until placed upon the Ohio District. Mr. Swayze was a very remarkable man, differing greatly from Finley, Young, and Gruber, but in moving, melting eloquence not inferior to either of them; tall, straight, and slim in person, with great power of endurance. His complexion was dark, black eyes, deeply set, and very expressive. His voice possessed great compass, and was perfectly at his control. At times it would be soft and mellow, musical and pleasing; then it would become like peals of thunder, or the roar of a lion. Himself full of feeling and interest, and possessing a wonderful command of the feelings of others, he would at times sway the multitude of astonished listeners like trees by a hurricane. The first half hour of his sermon was usually dry and dull, then he would begin to warm up, always imparting his warmth to his auditors, then rising rapidly in the sublimity of his theme, impressiveness of his manner, clearness and force of his utterance, carrying his congregation up with him, until they would rise from their seats and rush toward the speaker, some weeping, others shouting, here one pleading for mercy, and there others falling like dead men. But the grandest scene would be at the close of the sermon, when he made his grand rally for mourners to come to the altar for prayer. At camp-meetings we have seen from fifty to one hundred persons gathered around the altar at once. Then what prayer-meetings would follow, with perhaps a hundred penitents pleading for mercy, and two or three hundred Christians pleading with all their might and all at once for them, making the roar of Niagara a tame affair in comparison. Mr. Swayze could never contentedly close a quarterly meeting or a camp-meeting without having a big break in the ranks of the wicked. He was not a close student, nor a brilliant sermonizer, but no man could excel him in getting sinners converted to God. We will venture here the opinion that more souls along the southern shore of Lake Erie have gone up to shine like stars in the heavenly sky through the instrumentality of Rev. William Swayze than any other man dead or living.

Rev. PHILIP GREEN, in charge of the Erie Circuit, was admitted on trial in the Ohio Conference in September, 1817, and into full connection and ordained a deacon in 1819, and an elder in 1821. Mr. Green was a stout-built man, with coarse features, plainly clad, and a stern appearance. He had a sharp, piercing voice, which he used rather too freely. He was a good man and a good preacher. After spending over forty years in the regular work within the bounds of the Erie, Pittsburgh, and West Virginia Conferences, he now (1864) holds a superannuated relation to the last named body. Mr. Green was removed to the Chautauqua Circuit the last half of the year by the presiding elder.

Rev. ROBERT C. HATTON not only became disaffected toward the Church and left Shenango Circuit in 1817, but he also located at the next Ohio Conference, and soon after withdrew from the Church, but soon became convinced of the error of his ways, retraced his steps, and was readmitted into the Ohio Conference in 1819, and appointed to Lake Circuit.

Rev. James Murray, second preacher on the Cuyahoga Circuit, was received on trial in the Ohio Conference in August, 1819, and into full connection and ordained a deacon in 1821, and an elder in 1823, and located in 1825.

Rev. Palmer Phillips, residing in Busti, Chautauqua County, N. Y., was licensed to preach this year, and continued to labor zealously as a local preacher until 1831, but, becoming dissatisfied with the doctrine of the divinity of Christ as held by the Methodist Episcopal Church, withdrew from her communion.

Some time this year a lady belonging to the Methodist Episcopal Church in the State of New York came to reside in Painesville, Ohio, and hearing that there was Methodist preaching in Concord, went up and invited Mr. Eddy to send an appointment to Painesville. Mr. Eddy consented to preach on a week-day evening. When the time arrived several of the Concord members accompanied Mr. Eddy to his appointment. The meeting was in a schoolhouse, which was well filled. Mr. Eddy preached with his usual fervor and zeal, and at the close of the sermon a lady by the name of Bliss spoke with much feeling, and Mrs. Clark closed the meeting with prayer. These exercises greatly surprised the people, having never heard a woman speak or pray in meeting before. This was the commencement of Methodist preaching in Painesville. Mr Eddy formed a class this year in Bloomfield, Ohio, consisting of a Mr. Thayer and sixteen other persons, and another in Bristol, names not remembered, and also one in

Austinburgh. Daniel Dudley, and Mr. Wilton and wife were among the members. He also formed a class in East Farmington, consisting of Joel Hyde and wife, Eli Hyde and wife, Ira Hyde and wife; and still another class was formed this year by Mr. Eddy in Mayfield, Ohio, consisting of Mr. Adam Overrocker, wife, and daughter, Michael Overrocker, Daniel Richardson, wife, and daughter, Henry Francisco and wife, John Richardson and wife.

During the summer of 1819 Mr. John Bridle, a member of the Methodist Episcopal Church, settled with his family in Warren, Trumbull County, Ohio, and being anxious to secure Methodist preaching in that place, went on foot to Youngstown to a quarterly meeting the first week in November, and during the meeting made arrangements with both the elder and the preacher in charge to visit Warren and preach to them. Accordingly, at the time appointed Elder Swayze and Mr. James M'Mahan came to Warren, and on Thursday evening Elder Swayze preached in an old school-house, and the next day Mr. M'Mahan formed a class in the old log jail, consisting of John Bridle, leader, and wife, Sarah Cowen, A. Stewart, R. Rockway, Achsa Knapp, John Barnes and wife. Preaching was established in the court-house on Saturday evening, and the following spring several persons were converted and added to the class: Josiah Soulc, Nancy Harsh, Betsy Hall, Ebenezer Rodgers, and Benjamin Stevens and wife. A small class was formed this year in Clarksville, Mercer County, Pa., consisting of Samuel Clark, leader, wife, son, and daughter, Samuel Clark, jr., and wife, William M'Knight and wife, and widow M'Knight. The General Conference, in May, 1820, changed the boundary line between the Genesee and Ohio Conferences, running it from Erie, Pa., to Waterford, thence down French Creek to the Alleghany River, placing all north of this line in the Genesee Conference. Hence for a time we were fragments of two conferences.

Membership this year	3,144
Last year	2,576
Increase	568

1820.

The Genesee Conference sat in Niagara, Upper Canada, July 20, 1820, at which the following appointments were made:

Genesee District, Gideon Draper, Presiding Elder.

Lake, John Summerville.

Chautauqua, Philetus Parkus.

The Ohio Conference sat in Chillicothe, Ohio, September 8, 1820, at which the following appointments were made for this work:

Ohio District, William Swayze, Presiding Elder.

Erie Circuit, Ira Eddy, Charles Elliott.

Mahoning, James M'Mahan, Ezra Booth.

Grand River, Philip Green.

Cuyahoga, Alfred Brunson.

We now have two conferences, two districts, six circuits, with two presiding elders and nine preachers on this field of labor.

Rev. GIDEON DRAPER, Presiding Elder on the Genesee District, was admitted on trial in the Philadelphia Conference in 1803, and into full connection and ordained a deacon in the Baltimore Conference in 1805, and an elder in 1807. He was appointed presiding elder on the Susquehanna District in 1809, and in connection with this district fell into the Genesee Conference when it was formed in 1810, and continued on this district until 1812, when he was appointed presiding elder on the Genesee District, where he remained until 1816, when he returned to the regular work, and in 1817 he located; but was readmitted in 1819, and again appointed presiding elder on the Genesee District, to which Lake and Chautauqua Circuits were attached in 1820. We have no information worth recording relative to his labors on these two circuits this year, except the holding of a camp-meeting at North East, Pa., of great interest. His preaching was attended with much success. He located again in 1822.

Rev. PHILETUS PARKUS was admitted on trial in the Genesee Conference, held in Niagara, Upper Canada, July, 1820, and appointed to the Chautauqua Circuit, where he labored alone with great acceptance. He was received into full connection and ordained a deacon in 1822, and an elder in 1825, and died in holy triumph during the year 1827.

Rev. WILLIAM SWAYZE, Presiding Elder on the Ohio District, located his family on a small farm which he purchased on the south side of the Mahoning River, one mile and a quarter south of the center of Deerfield, Portage County, Ohio, in a retired and romantic place, where they continued to live until some years after the elder died. But it was but very little time he spent upon it. So interested was he in the work of the Lord going on upon his district that he must be in it night and day, leaving his family, with what help the kind neighbors could render, to take care of themselves. He was now in the prime of life, and almost constantly laboring in revivals of religion on his district. We regret much that his papers relating to this period of his life have been lost, so that we shall not be able to do anything like justice to the memory of this great and good man.

Rev. CHARLES ELLIOTT, second preacher on the Erie Circuit, was born in Ireland May 16, 1792. In early life he heard the Gospel preached by the ministers of the Methodist "societies," as they were then called, and while yet a mere lad was converted through their instrumentality. It was not long before he felt it his duty to preach the Gospel, and accordingly he entered upon a thorough course of preparatory study, thus laying the foundation of his subsequent extensive theological attainments. He pursued the regular collegiate course of studies until about his twenty-fourth year, having been refused admission to the Dublin University because he could not conscientiously subscribe to the "religious tests" required by its rules. In the year 1814 he emigrated to the United States of America, being at the time a local preacher, and proceeded immediately to Ohio, then almost a wilderness. He was admitted on trial in the Ohio Conference in 1818, and into full connection and ordained a deacon in 1820, and an elder in 1822. He is, I think, the first man from this field of labor who has merited and received the title of Doctor of Divinity.

Rev. ALFRED BRUNSON, in charge of the Cuyahoga Circuit, was born in Danbury, Conn., February 9, 1793, converted to God in Carlisle, Pa., February 3, 1809, licensed to preach in Hartford, Ohio, April 15, 1815, by Rev Jacob Young, ordained a deacon in Cincinnati, Ohio, July, 1819, was employed part of the following year by Elder Swayze on the Erie Circuit, where he succeeded in forming a class in Mercer, Pa., consisting of William Stephenson and wife, Joseph M'Dowell and wife, (now a preacher in Illinois Conference,) Robert Boice and wife, Sarah Stokely, Elizabeth Stokely, Polly Stokely, and Esther Stokely. Persecution ran high in Mercer at that time, and it was with much difficulty that a place was obtained in which to hold meetings. Churches, court-house, and school-houses were all refused. The society was organized in a small log-house a few rods from the place where the church now stands.

Mr. Brunson also formed a class on the Cassawago Creek, south-west of Meadville, Pa., consisting of Elisha Curtis and wife, David Bagly and wife, Nelson Smith and wife. Mr. Brunson was received on trial in the Ohio Conference in 1820, having been previously ordained a deacon, and into full connection, and ordained an elder in 1822. Although appointed to the Cuyahoga Circuit in 1820, he was subsequently removed by the presiding elder to the Mahoning Circuit.

Somewhere on the Erie Circuit there lived a landlord whose wife was a member of the Methodist Episcopal Church, but he was what we sometimes call a "clever sinner." He was very fond of the company of Methodist preachers, and they often found it quite convenient to stop with him, his house being much nearer the school-house where they preached than any of the brethren's houses. Mr. B., the circuit preacher, was a very pious man, but was pretty sharp occasionally in getting a good joke on whoever he was with. The landlord and he had several close encounters during the year, each occasionally getting the better of the other. The last appointment came, and Mr. B. preached a melting farewell sermon, and then went home with the landlord, who seemed unusually sober. As they pushed back from the breakfast table, having had prayers previously, the landlord said, "Well, Mr. B., this I suppose is your last time with us." "Yes," replied Mr. B., "I suppose it is." "Well, then," said the landlord, "we had better look over our accounts." Mr. B., with evident surprise, said slowly, "Yes, if we have any." "Step into the bar-room," said the landlord, "and we will see." As they approached the bar, the landlord stepped inside and took down his account book, and turning to the right page, began to read from it the date of each time Mr. B. had called with him, and the price of keeping his horse, supper, and breakfast. Mr. B. stood amazed at the amount of the bill that was coming against him. He had been but poorly paid on his circuit; had scarcely money enough to carry him to conference and back; and how should he manage to pay such a debt! The landlord finished the reckoning and announced the amount that was due him, looking seriously as though he expected prompt pay. "Well," said Mr. B., "I don't know what to do; I did not expect such a bill, and I have not money enough with me to pay it." "O stop," said the landlord; "you have some credits which will lessen the amount some." He then turned to another page, and began to read from it the date of each visit Mr. B. had made, with a description of each sermon he had preached, and each prayer he had offered, fixing the exact amount each were worth, during which Mr. B.'s countenance began to brighten. Finally, the landlord compared the two accounts, and pulling some change from his pocket, said, "here, Mr. B., I am in your debt just two dollars," handing him the money. Mr. B. received it thankfully, acknowledging himself outdone that time.

While Rev. A. Brunson was on the Mahoning Circuit, in 1820, the following incident occurred. Rev. Amos Smith, one of the first settlers in the town of Hubbard, Ohio, and one of the first members of the Methodist Episcopal Church in that town, had become so feeble in health as not to be able to attend public worship at the usual place of meeting, and Mr. Brunson made an appointment to preach in his house for his especial benefit. But while on his way thither Mr. Brunson became strongly impressed with the language of St. Paul to Timothy, "I am now ready to be offered, and the time of my departure is at hand." He concluded, however, that it would not be proper for him to preach from that text, as it would appear like preaching the good man's funeral sermon before he was dead. But he could think of no text but this on which he could receive any light. On arriving at the place, finding the congregation assembled, and being unable to find any other text that he could fix his mind upon, he proceeded to preach a very solemn and feeling sermon from the text we have named. At the close of the sermon Father Smith arose and spoke with great feeling, exhorting his brethren to live with the constant assurance of God's approbation, and assuring them that he was then "ready to be offered" if it was the will of his Master to take him home. He sat down in his chair, leaned his head back, and suddenly breathed his last, expiring without a struggle or a groan. And a member of the Church present, who was aroused from a backslidden state by his remarks, was suddenly killed at a raising a few days after this.

Rev. JAMES M'MAHAN closed his useful services within our bounds this year, but continued for many years a successful preacher and presiding elder in the Ohio and North Ohio Conferences.

Elder SWAYZE, in company with Mr. Green, visited Painesville, Ohio, in the fall of 1820, and preached several times, which produced an awakening among the people, and resulted in the formation of a class, consisting of Noah Nowland, leader, William Kerr, Anna Beckwith, Ellen Croft and daughter, Elizabeth Vanbenthusen, Charity Blodget, and Laura Armstrong.

Rev. JAMES HITCHCOCK, a local preacher, commenced preaching on Willoughby Ridge in the spring of 1821, and the following fall Mr. Green formed a class in that place, consisting of Lewis Miller, wife, and three daughters, Hezekiah Ferguson and wife, John L. Ferguson and wife, Samuel

Mapes and wife, Charles W Werrello and wife, Amasa Werrello and wife, William S. Werrello and wife, Reynolds Pratt, and Maria Bunt. The revival continued until over seventy were converted and added to the Church. There was also a revival in the town of Euclid, Ohio, which resulted in the formation of a class, consisting of Dennis Cooper and wife, Ruel House and wife, Betsey Bishop, Hannah Bishop, John E. Aikin, Father Woodworth and wife, Father Murray and wife, and Richard Curtis and wife.

Elder Swayze held a camp-meeting in Harpersfield, Ohio, in the summer of 1821, which is said by those who were present to have been a time of great power and of much good in that region. About one hundred souls were converted. Among them was Amos Parker, an infidel from Ashtabula, Ohio, who came to satisfy curiosity, but returned rejoicing in God. A. S. Gillet, of Mormon notoriety, was converted at this meeting. Elder Swayze also held a camp-meeting in Newburgh, near Cleveland, which resulted in the conversion of many souls. A small log meeting-house was erected this year in Mantua, Ohio, which became the birthplace of many souls.

Mr. Green formed a class in the town of Orange, Ohio, during the summer of 1821, consisting of Daniel Smith and wife, Caleb Leach and wife, Benjamin Jenks and wife, Jacob Gardner and wife, and Jesse Kimball and wife.

Rev. Samuel Brown, a local preacher, formed a class this year in Girard Hollow, Erie County, Pa., consisting of himself and wife, a Brother Shrives and wife, and a few others.

Mr. Booth, on the Mahoning Circuit, succeeded in forming a class in Canfield, Ohio, consisting of Dr. S. Bostwick, wife, and sister, C. Starr and wife, Ansel Beman and wife, and Ezra Hunt. Meetings were held in an old school-house. In the month of May, 1821, the eccentric Lorenzo Dow came to Canfield to visit Dr. Bostwick, they having been acquainted with each other in the East. He preached in the school-house, greatly amusing the people with his oddities. Mr. Elliott had a great revival in Mercer, Pa., this year.

The number of members reported this year was	3,344
Last year	3,144
Increase	200

The Missionary Society of the Methodist Episcopal Church was formed in 1819 in the City of New York, and from that time forward collections were taken on the different circuits in this territory; but the amount thus raised is not reported either in the minutes of Conference or the reports of the society, so that we cannot carry forward this part of our history.

1821.

The Genesee Conference met in Paris, N. Y., July 19, 1821, where the following appointments were made:

Erie District, Glezen Fillmore, Presiding Elder.
Lake Circuit, Nathaniel Reeder, Ira Brunson.
Chautauqua, Parker Buel.
French Creek, Zachariah Paddock.

The Ohio Conference met in Lebanon, Ohio, September 6, 1821, at which the following appointments were made:

Ohio District, William Swayze, Presiding Elder.
Erie Circuit, Ezra Booth, Charles Truscott.
Mahoning, Charles Elliott, Dennis Goddard.
Grand River, Alfred Brunson, Henry Knapp.
Cuyahoga, Ira Eddy.
New Castle, Samuel R. Brockunier.

A new circuit was formed this year, called French Creek, on the Erie District; and another, called New Castle, on the Ohio District.

Rev. GLEZEN FILLMORE, Presiding Elder on the Erie District, Genesee Conference, was "born in Bennington, Vermont, December 22, 1789. While yet an infant his parents moved to the State of New York," and settled about ten miles west of Rochester, then a wilderness, and their house for many years was "dignified with the name of *tavern*." Young Fillmore in his youth was so thin in flesh and feeble in structure as to cause those that knew him best to regard him as an almost certain victim of consumption; but in his maturity "his full and well-proportioned form showed most conclusively that whatever of consumption there was about him he was not the object consumed, settling down the scales when placed at the high figure of 228." And a more genial countenance, noble heart, generous spirit, and dignified person seldom greeted the eye of a delighted audience.

In 1807 the Philadelphia Conference, to whom the territory belonged, sent the Rev. PETER VAN NEST to form a circuit called the "Holland Purchase," embracing all that part of the State of New York lying west of the Genesee River. On his way to his field of labor he forded the river where Rochester now stands, and pursued his course west to Mr. Fillmore's. This house, though a tavern, became one of his frequent stopping places; and during the year young Mr. Fillmore became a subject of convicting and converting grace, and united himself with the Methodist Episcopal Church in the wilderness. In 1809 Mr. Fillmore was married, received a license to preach, and moved to the place where he now resides, in Clarence, Erie County, N. Y. He was undoubtedly the first person licensed to preach the Gospel by any Christian Church west of the Genesee River in the State of New York. The cabin in which he and "Aunt Vina" lived at this time was at some distance from that of any other human being, and yet they were by no means alone. Bears and wolves were companions, with which, whether agreeable or not, they were quite familiar. "On one occasion as a preacher was staying over night he was serenaded with a style of music to which he was not accustomed. On being informed it was a wolf concert, and seeing only a blanket at the door for safety, he inquired with evident alarm whether they could climb into the loft in which he was going to sleep. He regarded it as proof of a special providence that all were found safe next morning. Though Mr. Fillmore spent the first nine years of his ministerial life as a local preacher, his name and history are probably more intimately connected with the rise and spread of

Methodism in Western New York than those of any other man living or dead." * Mr. Fillmore was admitted on trial in the Genesee Conference in 1818, and having been ordained a deacon while a local preacher, he was received into full connection in 1820, and ordained an elder in 1821. He was stationed at Buffalo and Black Rock in 1818 and 1819, on Clarence Circuit in 1820, and on the Erie District in 1821. Mr. Fillmore was one of the most affable men, most captivating speakers, and most popular presiding elders we ever had the pleasure of listening to. He has for some years worthily carried the title of Doctor of Divinity.

Rev. NATHANIEL REEDER, in charge of Lake Circuit, was admitted on trial in the Genesee Conference in July, 1818, and into full connection and ordained a deacon in 1820, and an elder in 1822. He was an excellent man, a good sound preacher, health rather poor, and a little given to spleen.

Rev. IRA BRUNSON, second preacher on Lake Circuit, was admitted on trial in the Genesee Conference in July, 1820, and into full connection and ordained a deacon in 1822, and an elder in 1824. Though somewhat deformed in person he was an excellent preacher, and performed for many years much valuable service.

Rev PARKER BUEL, in charge of the Chautauqua Circuit, was admitted on trial in the Genesee Conference in July, 1818, and into full connection and ordained a deacon in 1820, and an elder in 1822. He was stout built, thorough going, and possessed

* Ladies' Repository, vol. xxi, p. 366.

a meek, amiable spirit; and performed the work upon the Chautauqua Circuit alone.

Rev. ZACHARIAH PADDOCK, in charge of French Creek Circuit, was born in Montgomery County, N. Y., December 20, 1798; was converted to God in the seventeenth year of his age in Paris, N. Y., occasioned by an ordination sermon preached before the Genesee Conference in session in that place by Bishop M'Kendree. He soon afterward united with the Methodist Episcopal Church, and commenced a course of preparation for the ministry. He was licensed to preach in Canandaigua, N. Y., in the spring of 1817. The year following he was employed by the presiding elder to labor on the Ontario Circuit. He was admitted on trial in the Genesee Conference in July, 1818, and ordained a deacon and received into full connection in 1820, and an elder in 1822. Mr. Paddock's history has been a brilliant one; but few men in the State of New York have excelled him. He is still in the active service of the Church, and worthily carries with his name the title of Doctor of Divinity. Through the instrumentality of Mr. Paddock a log meeting-house was built in the Pit-hole settlement, on the farm and near the house of old Mr. Dawson, two generations back from the present. Many seasons of great interest were enjoyed in this house by the good people who for ten miles around used to assemble and worship there.

A small class of six or eight members was formed about this time in the town of Napoli, Cattaraugus County, N. Y., but who the members were is not now known.

On the Ohio District, under the labors of Mr. Swayze, the work prospered gloriously. Several camp-meetings were held on the district that were seasons of great power. One was held in Mentor, Lake County, Ohio, at which a goodly number were converted, and soon after another was held in Concord, where a very large number were converted.

Rev. CHARLES TRUSCOTT was admitted on trial in the Ohio Conference in September, 1821, and appointed second preacher on the Erie Circuit, and for some reason unknown to us was discontinued at the end of his probation.

Rev. HENRY KNAPP, second preacher on the Grand River Circuit, was born at Saratoga, N Y. in August 9, 1796, and embraced religion when about nineteen years of age. In 1819 he was licensed to preach, and received on trial in the Ohio Conference in August, 1820, and into full connection and ordained a deacon in 1822, and an elder in 1824. Mr. Knapp was a young man of great promise, pious, zealous, talented, useful, and much esteemed by the people wherever he labored. His race was short but brilliant.

Rev. S. R. BROCKUNIER, in charge of the Newcastle Circuit, has already been introduced to the reader as a supply on the Chautauqua Circuit, appointed by Elder Finley in 1817 He was admitted on trial in the Ohio Conference in August, 1818, and into full connection and ordained a deacon in 1820, and an elder in 1822. This was the only year he spent within the bounds of the Erie Conference. He was a man of great physical strength, and an untiring laborer. The Cuyahoga Circuit at this time embraced all the country watered by the river of that name in Ohio, and was divided into two equal parts by the river. Mr. Eddy, who lived some distance from the river on the west side, found it necessary to have a colleague, to whom was committed the eastern side of the stream. Mr. Swayze, the elder, had a young man upon his district well fitted for the place, whom we will now introduce to the reader.

Rev. BILLINGS O. PLIMPTON was born in Sturbridge, Worcester County, Massachusetts, March 7, 1799. In 1815 the prayers and entreaties of his excellent mother on her dying bed was the means of his conversion to God, and soon after he was baptized and received into the Methodist Episcopal Church by Rev. Elias Marble, of the New England Conference. While in the twentieth year of his age, engaged in teaching a school in New Jersey, near New Brunswick, he received license to exhort, and immediately commenced calling sinners to repentance, and was favored with the conversion of several souls. He soon removed to Ohio, where he received license to preach at a district camp-meeting, in the summer of 1821, by Rev. William Swayze, who sent him on to the Cuyahoga Circuit the same fall. Among his converts this year was Dr. H. J. Clark, since president of Alleghany College. Early in the spring of 1822 Mr. Plimpton started to go through from Twinsburgh, Summit County, to Aurora, Portage County, Ohio, to preach to a small society then in that town. Having to follow a blind path, he missed his way, and night came on, which being exceedingly dark, he was compelled to stay in the woods. He selected a high piece of ground, tied his horse to a tree, and placing his portmanteau on the ground for a pillow, wrapped himself up in his cloak and lay down to sleep. But before getting to sleep a gang of six or eight wolves surrounded him and began to howl most piteously. His horse took fright and began to stamp and snort terribly. Mr. Plimpton jumped up and commenced hallooing with all his might, and he and his horse made the surrounding hills ring. The wolves took fright and fled, and Mr. Plimpton laid himself down and slept till morning, when he found he was but half a mile from the center of Aurora. From this place he was invited over to Bainbridge, where he established an appointment. Upon arriving at the house of Mr. Smith, where he had ordered the appointment to be made, he found a large crowd of people assembled, and among them Rev. Mr. Seward, a Presbyterian preacher from Aurora. Mr. Plimpton concluded that as the congregation was large and enjoyed preaching but seldom, they had better have two sermons, and accordingly invited Mr. Seward to preach first, to which he consented, and announced for his text, "Say ye to the righteous it shall be well with them." Isaiah iii, 10. His sermon was practical and earnest. Mr. Plimpton then took for his text, "Woe unto the wicked: it shall be ill with him," and in his rapid, earnest way, addressed himself to the wicked. From this meeting a general awakening spread through the community, which in a short time resulted in the formation of a class of thirty members. Harvey Baldwin was leader, Joseph Ely and wife, Philip Haskins and wife, Jonathan M'Farland and wife, Daniel M'Farland and wife, Wesley M'Farland, P D. M'Conney and wife, Asahel North and wife, Oren Henry, John Henry and wife, Gordon Kent and wife, Joseph Witter and wife, Oliver Wheeler and wife, were the principal members.

Rev. ELIJAH COLEMAN, a local preacher, formed a class this year in Punxutawney, Jefferson County, Pa., of ten members. It was connected with the Mahoning Circuit, Baltimore Conference.

That the reader may know what an amount of labor was performed by the itinerant Methodist ministers at this time, we will refer him to the Mahoning Circuit in 1821, when traveled by Messrs. Elliott and Goddard. It required six weeks to go round it, with forty-two regular appointments; and adding to these the various extra appointments, they were required to preach sixty-four times each round. And this was a year of wonderful success generally, but especially on the Mahoning Circuit, where there was an increase of near two hundred.

In the month of September, 1821, Mr. Swayze held a camp-meeting in the town of Mantua, Portage County, Ohio, which was a time of great religious awakening, and a multitude professed conversion.

A Methodist meeting-house was built this year in Ashtabula, Ohio, called the "Block Meeting-house," which served an excellent purpose in its day.

The membership on the Erie District this year amounted to..	1,309
Ohio District	3,455
Total	4,764
Last year	3,344
Increase	1,420

SECTION X.

FROM 1822 TO 1825.

"There is one joy the heart defines,
'Tis fellowship with kindred minds;
Sweet boon, by our Redeemer given,
To raise our hearts from earth to heaven;
For heaven's the source of living joy,
And heavenly friendships never cloy."

WHILE the founders of Methodism within the Erie Conference are deserving of much credit for the pious zeal with which they prosecuted their work generally, we are at the same time compelled to say that they made one sad mistake, in neglecting to erect our standard and to secure our full share of influence in the growing villages, and especially those that gave promise of becoming cities or centers of business to the surrounding country. When Methodism was first introduced upon this continent, New York, the commercial metropolis of the nation, was wisely selected as the base of their future operations. And when the intrepid Lee went to New England to plant our standard on Puritan soil, Boston, its largest commercial city, was the point from which it first waved, and the focus from which the light of truth was made to radiate. In this they acted wisely. A good commander will always look for the best place he can find as a base from whence to operate. And this is equally important in planting the Gospel in a new country. But in the Erie Conference it was otherwise. Shenango and Oil Creek, in Pennsylvania; Vernon and Deerfield, in Ohio; Sheridan and Villanovia, in New York State, were the starting points. Circuits and districts were formed, and the Gospel statedly preached through all the country, and societies formed in almost every settlement; while such places as Meadville, Erie, Jamestown, Akron, Ravenna, and Cleveland were unoccupied. In neither of these places had we any Church organization up to 1822.

1822.

The Genesee Conference met in Vienna, Ontario County, N. Y., July 24, 1822, where the following appointments were made:

Erie District, Glezen Fillmore, Presiding Elder.

French Creek, Josiah Keyes.

Lake, Richard Wright, Sylvester Cary.

Chautauqua, Parker Buel.

North East, Andrew Peck.

The Ohio Conference met at Marietta, Ohio, September 5, 1822, where the following appointments were made:

Ohio District, William Swayze, Presiding Elder.

Erie, William H. Collins.

Mercer, Samuel Adams.

Grand River, Edward H. Taylor, John Crawford.

Youngstown, William Tipton, Albert G. Richardson.

Deerfield, Ezra Booth, William Westlake.

Hudson, Ira Eddy.

New Castle, Thomas Carr.

The only alteration made in the work on the Erie District, Genesee Conference, was the division of Lake Circuit, calling the western part North East, our society in that place having become large and influential.

On the Ohio District several changes were made in the work. Erie Circuit was divided, the southern part called Mercer. Our society in that place, contending against the most violent Calvinistic prejudices, had grown rapidly.

The Mahoning Circuit was also divided, calling one part Youngstown and the other Deerfield. Cuyahoga was divided also; the eastern part was called Hudson, the western portion was not within our bounds. We now have eleven circuits on two districts, two presiding elders, and fifteen preachers.

Mr. Fillmore and Mr. Swayze continued to meet the demands of the work to the entire satisfaction of both preachers and people. Several camp-meetings were held, which resulted in a great amount of good.

One day when Elder Fillmore was on the south end of his district, he was traveling from Franklin, Pa., up to some point on the Alleghany River, which he had to cross in a ferry-boat. He encountered many difficulties amid the mountains during the day, and reached the river late in the afternoon; had some difficulty in making the ferryman hear, who was on the opposite side of the stream, which was very wide at that place. But getting safely over, and finding a kind family with whom to stay all night, he put up, and was treated to the best the house could afford. Some time during the night Mr. Fillmore commenced dreaming over the romantic scenes of the previous day, which it seems had made a very deep impression on his mind. In imagination he traveled over again the entire journey. On arriving at the river, in his dream, he concluded that it was so far to where the ferryman was on the opposite shore it would be very difficult to make him hear, and so prepared himself to make the loudest halloo in his power. He not only awoke himself by the effort, but he soon found the whole family astir. "What in the world is the matter?" inquired the affrighted man of the house. "O!" said Mr. Fillmore, as he settled back in his bed, "I was only dreaming." "Well," said the landlord, "that was the loudest dreaming I ever heard." The reader may judge of the truth of this remark when informed that Elder Fillmore has been heard two miles while preaching.

Rev. JOSIAH KEYES, in charge of the French Creek Circuit, was born in Canajoharie, N. Y., Dec. 30, 1799. He was converted to God and became a member of the Methodist Episcopal Church at twelve years of age. He was admitted on trial in the Genesee Conference in 1820, and into full connection in 1822, when he was also ordained a deacon, and an elder in 1824. In 1828, when the Oneida Conference was formed, he became a member of that body, in which he labored until he died. In 1831 he was appointed to the Black River District, and in 1833 to the Cayuga District, where he labored until called from toil to rest in heaven, which was on April 22, 1836. Mr. Keyes possessed an amount of intellectual strength and culture which are seldom excelled. By dint of industry, without instruction, he became a respectable Latin, Greek, and Hebrew scholar. He fell in his prime and in the midst of a glorious career. But he "conquered when he fell."

Rev. RICHARD WRIGHT, in charge of Lake Circuit, was admitted on trial in the Genesee Conference in 1820, into full connection and ordained a deacon in 1822, and an elder in 1824. He was a noble-looking man and a good preacher. He continued in the regular itinerant work until 1845, when he superannuated.

Rev. SYLVESTER CARY, second preacher on the Lake Circuit, was admitted on trial in the Genesee Conference in 1822, into full connection and ordained a deacon in 1824, and an elder in 1826. A fine appearing man, and well informed, but too moderate and tame in his address to suit the people of those times.

Rev. PARKER BUEL, in charge of the Chautauqua Circuit, closed his labor on that circuit this year. But he continued a faithful and successful laborer in the Genesee Conference until 1845, when, on account of ill health, he was superannuated.

Rev. ANDREW PECK was admitted on trial in the Genesee Conference in 1818, and into full connection and ordained a deacon in 1820, and appointed to North East Circuit, and was ordained an elder in 1825.

Rev. BENJAMIN P HILL was for several years a member of the New England Conference, but for some reason or other located, and in 1818 moved his family and settled them near Forestville, Chautauqua County, N. Y., where he commenced a career of great usefulness as a local preacher, defending the doctrine and discipline of the Methodist Episcopal Church wherever assailed, laboring in connection with the traveling preachers in revivals of religion all over the country, and attending the sick and preaching funeral sermons wherever called. In 1819 and 1820 he was employed by the presiding elder to labor on the Lake Circuit in connection with Mr. Hatton, where his labors were wonderfully successful. Societies were formed this year in Conewango, Westfield, Ripley, Gerry, and Portland, while those previously formed along the shore of Lake Erie, in Chautauqua County, were much strengthened. In 1822 he was again employed by Mr. Fillmore to labor on the Chautauqua Circuit in connection with Mr. Buel, where his valuable services were highly appreciated. He was a man of medium height, stout built, round featured, full favored, with his dark hair parted nicely on the top of his head, and hanging in graceful ringlets on his shoulders. He possessed a clear, graphic mind, well stored with Scripture knowledge. His preaching was argumentative, animating, and powerful. In private intercourse he was exceedingly pleasant and musical, possessing a rich fund of religious anecdotes, which he could tell with peculiar zest. He died in holy triumph in 1840, being sixty-five years of age.

> "Thy work shall live in souls redeemed
> While cycles roll along."

Mr. Fillmore held a camp-meeting this year on the banks of the Brokenstraw Creek, one mile west of Youngsville, Warren County, Pa., which resulted in much good. Our people in Fredonia, N. Y., commenced the erection of a church this year, which was finished and dedicated in 1824. It was situated on East Hill, half a mile east of the village, on the south side of the Buffalo Road, most of our people living in that direction.

Rev. WILLIAM H. COLLINS, in charge of the Erie Circuit, on the Ohio District, was admitted on trial in the Ohio Conference in 1821, into full connection and ordained a deacon in 1823, an elder in 1825, and located in 1827, cause not known.

Rev. EDWARD H. TAYLOR, in charge of the Grand River Circuit, was born in Washington County, Pa., August 25, 1796; embraced religion in 1813; was employed by Elder Finley on the Mahoning Circuit in 1817; was admitted on trial in the Ohio Conference in August, 1818, and into full connection and ordained a deacon in 1820, and an elder in 1822, when he was appointed to this charge.

Rev JOHN CRAWFORD, second preacher on the Grand River Circuit, was born in Fayette County, Pa., September 28, 1799. He was converted to God, through the instrumentality of the Methodist ministry, when about sixteen years old. He was licensed to preach, in company with B. O. Plimpton and A. G. Richardson, at a district local conference held by Mr. Swayze within the bounds of the Ohio District, in connection with a camp-meeting during the summer of 1821; was admitted on trial in the Ohio Conference in 1822, into full connection and ordained a deacon in 1824, and an elder in 1826. As a preacher his talents were of a very useful kind. Experimental and practical religion was his theme in the pulpit. He was remarkably agreeable in his manners, and much loved by the people.

Rev. William Tipton, in charge on the Youngstown Circuit, was admitted on trial in the Ohio Conference in September, 1821, and into full connection and ordained a deacon in 1823, and an elder in 1825. When the Pittsburgh Conference was formed he became a member of that body, where he continued a faithful laborer until he died.

Rev. William Westlake, second preacher on the Deerfield Circuit, was received on trial in the Ohio Conference in 1816, and into full connection and ordained a deacon in 1818, and an elder in 1820, and was expelled from the connection in 1824.

Rev. A. G. Richardson, second preacher on the Youngstown Circuit, was admitted on trial in the Ohio Conference in 1822, and into full connection and ordained a deacon in 1824, and located in 1825.

Rev. Thomas Carr, in charge of the New Castle Circuit, was born in Washington County, Pa., February 23, 1793, and was converted in early life at a camp-meeting held in Ohio by Rev. J. B. Finley. He was received on trial in the Ohio Conference in September, 1816, and into full connection and ordained a deacon in 1818, and an elder in 1820. Mr. Carr was small in stature, but a very pious, zealous preacher, and accomplished much good.

Rev. Elijah Ward was admitted on trial in the New England Conference, in company with Elijah Hedding and Martin Ruter, in 1801, and into full connection and ordained a deacon in 1803; but on account of the hardships he was compelled to endure his health failed him, and he was induced to locate in 1804. He continued, however, to preach as a local preacher very extensively up to 1822, when he removed his family to the West, and settled them on a farm one mile east of Willoughby, Lake County, Ohio, where he became extensively useful as an able and fearless defender of the doctrine and usages of the Methodist Episcopal Church. He was not favored with many literary advantages. His style was rough and severe, but he possessed a logical mind, and was entirely original, quick in thought and action, very sarcastic and odd, but at times eloquent and powerful. He was ordained an elder by Bishop Asbury in 1827. At a camp meeting in Concord in 1824 Father Ward preached from the "Holy City," and at the close of the sermon the whole ground seemed strewn with mourners. He died in peace in 1858, fully realizing that

> "The glorious, conquering King is nigh
> To take his exiles home."

Mr. Eddy, on the Hudson Circuit, established an appointment in the town of Edinburgh, at the house of Mr. Ely Booth, and soon after formed a class consisting of Ely Booth and wife, Mr. Pangman, wife, and daughter, which was soon increased by the addition of others. Preaching was continued at Mr. Booth's house for several years.

In the town of Brimfield, Portage County, Ohio, Father Shewel established an appointment as early as the summer of 1820 at the house of Mr. A. H. Lamphear, and in 1822 Mr. Lamphear became a happy subject of converting grace, and immediately invited the circuit preachers to his house. Mr. Eddy, on the Hudson Circuit, came in the spring of 1823, and organized a class consisting of Benjamin Mallory and wife, Amos Benedict and wife, John K. Chapman and wife, and A. H. Lamphear and wife. Others were soon added. Our people in Painesville, Lake County, Ohio, commenced building a church this year a little south and in the rear of their present church. Being unable to finish it they formed an alliance with the authorities of the town, permitting them to furnish a part of the funds, and to occupy the house a portion of the time as a town house. It was a frame building, inconveniently arranged, and jointly occupied for law and Gospel purposes for more than twenty years. On the Grand River Circuit there was an extensive revival this year. In the summer of 1823 Mr. Swayze held a quarterly meeting in the new meeting-house in Painesville, and a few weeks after he held a camp-meeting in Concord, at both of which a large number of souls were converted, increasing the society in Painesville to over one hundred members, and resulting in the formation of a class in the town of Kirtland. There was also a revival on the same circuit through the labor of Messrs. Taylor and Crawford, in the town of Orville, which resulted in the formation of a class consisting of John Babcock, leader, and wife and mother, Sarah Case, Julia A. Babcock, Buel Higbee, Lucinda Higbee, Samuel E. Babcock, and a few months after James Babcock and William R. Babcock were added. In the summer of 1823 Mr. Swayze held a camp-meeting in the town of Benton, which was attended with the most wonderful results, and still another on Willoughby Ridge.

A class was formed this year four miles north of Meadville, Pa., called the "State road" class. Its members were mostly taken from Father Brown's class, and a log meeting-house built, which was subsequently the scene of some glorious times.

From the Deerfield Circuit and the western half of the Cuyahoga there is no report of the number of members this year, or there would undoubtedly have been a handsome increase.

From the other circuits in the two districts there were....	4,131
Last year.	4,764
Decrease......................................	633

1823.

The Genesee Conference met at Westmoreland, Oneida County, N. Y., July 15, 1823, at which the following appointments were made:

Erie District, Glezen Fillmore, Presiding Elder.

Lake Circuit, Parker Buel, Richard Wright.

North East, to be supplied. Rev. Elijah Done, a local preacher, who resided on the Conewango Creek, one mile above Warren, Pa., was employed as a supply.

French Creek, Sylvester Cary.

Chautauqua, Asa Abel. Rev. John W Hill, son of Rev. Benjamin Hill, was employed as a supply with Mr. Abel.

The Ohio Conference met at Urbana, Ohio, September 24, 1823, at which the following appointments were made:

Ohio District, Charles Elliott, Presiding Elder.
Erie, John Summerville.
Mercer, Henry Knapp.
Grand River, Alfred Brunson, Robert Hopkins.
Youngstown, Samuel Adams, Sylvester Dunham.
Hartford, Charles Thorn.
Deerfield, Dennis Goddard, Elijah H. Field.
New Castle, Thomas Carr, Job Wilson.
Portland District, William Swayze, Presiding Elder.
Hudson, William H. Collins, Orin Gillmore.

The Youngstown Circuit was divided this year, and the north part called Hartford, to which was added a few appointments from the Grand River Circuit.

A new district was formed called Portland, and the Hudson Circuit connected with it; the remainder of the district principally lay west of the Ohio District.

Rev. ASA ABEL, in charge of the Chautauqua Circuit, was admitted on trial in the Genesee Conference at its session in Paris, N. Y., July, 1821, and into full connection and ordained a deacon in 1823, and an elder in 1825. He was noted for being a systematic preacher and a thorough disciplinarian, and has to this day maintained a very reputable position among the preachers of the Genesee Conference, having been several times presiding elder; but now gives evidence of age and hard wear, and of being a ripe Christian, but has withdrawn from the Church.

Rev Charles Elliott is now for the first time appointed presiding elder, a position for which his superior learning, ardent zeal, and robust Irish constitution eminently qualified him.

His speech was somewhat broken, giving unmistakable evidence of the country of his birth; his attitude and gestures were awkward and void of dignity; his appearance in and out of the pulpit indicated the most profound disregard for dress, being too much occupied with more important subjects than the wardrobe, the toilet, or looking-glass; and besides all this, his close application to study so affected the nerves of his face as to produce a most singular twitching, drawing his mouth and face into the most grotesque appearances imaginable. But he possessed a mind of gigantic strength, and his habits of study were systematic, rigid, and thorough, taking a wide range in both literature and theology. His sermons were generally argumentative, yet delivered in an attractive style and animating spirit, which made them very interesting to all except the unfortunate advocate of the doctrine he was opposing. But the various isms that happened to be floating in the public mind generally got a terrible scathing when he came round. "Calvinism," which was then believed and taught by the clergy of several leading denominations in its most extreme characteristics, furnished an abiding theme of discussion, against which Mr. Elliott's learning and talents qualified him to appear as an opposing champion. He was also a successful revivalist. He possessed a kind heart, a noble, generous spirit, and notwithstanding his foreign peculiarities, was immensely popular with the people generally.

Rev. ROBERT HOPKINS, second preacher on the Grand River Circuit, was received on trial in the Ohio Conference in July 1823, and appointed with Mr. Brunson to the above charge, where he labored one year with good success and general acceptability. Mr. Hopkins was a young man of more than ordinary promise; tall, stout built, and dignified in his appearance, social and gentlemanly in his deportment. He was received into full connection and ordained a deacon by the Pittsburgh Conference in 1825, and an elder in 1827. Mr. Hopkins has performed much valuable service in the last named Conference.

Rev. SYLVESTER DUNHAM, second preacher on the Youngstown Circuit, was admitted on trial in the Ohio Conference in September, 1823, and at the close of his second year of probation was, for some cause unknown to us, discontinued.

Rev. CHARLES THORN, in charge of the Hartford Circuit, was a man of perhaps medium size, but was not physically, mentally, morally, or socially, what his name indicates. In preaching he was not brilliant, but useful. He was admitted on trial in the Ohio Conference in August, 1820, and into full connection and ordained a deacon in 1822, and an elder in 1824. When the Pittsburgh Conference was formed in 1825 he became a member of that body, where he long labored with commendable zeal, and of which he is now a venerable superannuated member.

Rev. ELIJAH H. FIELD, second preacher on the Deerfield Circuit, was admitted on trial in the Ohio Conference in September, 1823, and into full connection and ordained a deacon in 1825, and an elder in 1826. In 1839 he was appointed presiding elder on the Kanawha District, where he remained two years. With this exception he labored in the regular work until his death.

Rev. JOB WILSON, second preacher on the New Castle Circuit, was an Irishman, born, converted, educated, and licensed to preach on the Emerald Isle. He was admitted on trial in the Ohio Conference in September 1823, and into full connection and ordained a deacon by the Pittsburgh Conference in 1825, and an elder in 1827. He was a rugged, stout-built man, face badly pockmarked. He possessed a mind of more than ordinary capacity, was remarkably fond of controversy, seemed never to be satisfied in the pulpit or in private circles unless opposing the views or criticising the opinions of others, and often with a severity and abruptness that gave offense. He was located in 1837, and lived and died near Meadville, Crawford County, Pa.

Rev. ORIN GILLMORE, second preacher on the Hudson Circuit, was admitted on trial in the Ohio Conference in 1820, and into full connection and ordained a deacon in 1822, an elder in 1825, and located in 1826. A good and useful man while in the work.

Rev. NICOLAS GEE, born in the State of New York in 1782, was converted and joined the Methodist Episcopal Church in 1804, and licensed to exhort in

1808, moved to Ohio, and settled in the town of Ellsworth, Mahoning County, in 1823; was licensed to preach by Rev. Charles Elliott, Presiding Elder, in 1824, and was ordained a deacon by Bishop Roberts in 1836. Rev. Samuel Adams being obliged to leave the Youngstown Circuit in the spring of 1824, Mr. Gee took his place until conference. Mr. Gee enjoyed but few literary advantages, and was a man of moderate preaching abilities; but his deep, uniform piety, earnest devotions, and burning zeal made him a very acceptable and useful local preacher. He assisted very much in carrying the Gospel to and establishing Methodism in Ellsworth, Berlin, Lordstown, Jackson, and other neighboring towns; and at the present time, though advanced in age, is much beloved by a large community.

During the spring and summer of 1824 the presid ing elder removed Mr. Peck from the Boston Circuit, and sent him to organize a new circuit out of territory that had been partly occupied in the Chautauqua and Lake Circuits, which will hereafter appear on the Minutes of Conference as "Conewango" Circuit. It embraced Conewango, Kennedy's Mills, Randolph, Ellery, Little Valley, Napoli, and Cold Springs, at all of which places classes had been formed. A class was also formed this year in Poland, Ohio, names of members not known.

A class was formed this year by Rev. Henry Knapp at Charleston, Mercer County, Pa., consisting of James Montgomery, leader, Father Jennings and wife, Mr. Brunson and wife, John Robbins and wife,

Mrs. Creary, Mrs. Saffer, Benjamin Canfield, and William Coon.

The number of members in society on the Erie District were.	1,346
Ohio District........................	3,332
Total	4,678
Last year....................	4,131
Increase	547

1824.

The Genesee Conference met in Lansing, N. Y., July 25, 1824. The appointments were as follows:

Erie District, Glezen Fillmore, Presiding Elder.
Lake Circuit, Josiah Keyes.
North East, Peter D. Horton.
French Creek, To be supplied.
Chautauqua, Nathaniel Reeder.
Conewango, William Fowler.

The Ohio Conference met in Zanesville, Ohio, September 2, 1824. The following are its appointments:

Ohio District, Charles Elliott, Presiding Elder.
New Castle, Henry Knapp, Joseph S. Barris.
Youngstown, John Summerville, Alfred Brunson.
Hartford, Thomas Carr.
Deerfield, Ira Eddy, Billings O. Plimpton.
Hudson, Philip Green, William C. Henderson.
Grand River, David Sharp, Sylvester Dunham.
Erie, John P Kent.
Mercer, Charles Thorn, Job Wilson.

Rev. WILLIAM SWAYZE was superannuated this year, his health having become much impaired; but he still resided on his little farm in Deerfield, Ohio,

Rev. GLEZEN FILLMORE concluded his valuable labors as presiding elder on the Erie District this year. He continued, however, to occupy districts most of the time for thirty years or more in the Genesee Conference; and when not on a district has been stationed in Buffalo, Rochester, and Lockport, where his labors have been blessed with very extensive revivals of religion. While in the vigor of health he was uniformly elected by his conference to represent them in the General Conference of the Methodist Episcopal Church, where he was regarded as among its most talented and influential members. His friends have often spoken of him as a suitable person to be elevated to the office of bishop; but unfortunately his superior qualifications for that office were not known through the connection sufficiently to secure his election. He was a member of the General Conference in 1836, 1840, 1844, and 1848. He has for a few years past occupied a superannuated relation in the Genesee Conference, possessing the love and esteem of his brethren to an extent that must be very gratifying to him in the evening of a well-spent life.

"He blew the Gospel's silver trump
From Zion's crystal wall;
Glad thousands heard the hallowed sound,
And swift obeyed the call.
His lips were touched with holy flame,
The altar fire of heaven;
And when he spoke the mighty bowed,
The heart of stone was riven."

Rev. PETER D. HORTON, in charge of North East Circuit, was born in Orange County, N. Y., December 11, 1796, was born of the Spirit April 19, 1819, and united with the Methodist Episcopal Church in Ontario County, N. Y., the following June. He was licensed to exhort in 1821, and to preach by Rev. Abner Chase, Presiding Elder, and recommended to the Genesee Conference, where he was admitted on trial June 4, 1824, and into full connection and ordained a deacon by the Pittsburgh Conference in 1826, and an elder in 1828. Mr. Horton was a very tall, slim man, of delicate health, and had a feeble voice; was exceedingly modest and timid, a close student, with a kind heart, systematic and concise in the delivery of his sermons, which were usually short and edifying. But very few men have lived a more pious and inoffensive life. He now (1864) holds a superannuated relation to the Erie Conference, residing in Nelson, Ohio.

Rev. WILLIAM FOWLER, in charge of Conewango Circuit, was admitted on trial in the Genesee Conference in 1822, and into full connection and ordained a deacon in 1824, and an elder in 1826. Mr. Fowler spent but one year in this section of the work, at the close of which, on account of the failure of his health, in consequence of the severity of his labors, he superannuated.

Rev CHARLES ELLIOTT, on the Ohio District, continued to prosecute his work with marked ability and general success.

> "Through the glens
> And on the mountains, by the lakes and rivers,
> And through the hush of the primeval woods,"

he continued to wend his way on horseback in search

of the "lost sheep of the house of Israel." A camp-meeting was held some time this year by Mr. Elliott on the bounds of the Erie Circuit, not far from the Ohio state line, which resulted in the conversion of a great number of souls, and after the meeting closed the work spread through the neighboring towns; other Christian denominations became aroused and entered the work, and gathered a rich harvest. It was supposed that between three and four hundred were gathered into the different churches in that region as the result of this camp-meeting.

Rev. JOSEPH S. BARRIS, second preacher on New Castle Circuit, was admitted on trial in the Ohio Conference in 1824, and appointed, with Mr. Knapp, to the above circuit. In 1826 he was received into full connection in the Pittsburgh Conference and ordained a deacon, and an elder in 1828. He was small in stature, but possessed a remarkably clear, pleasant, and interesting style of address, was very witty, musical, and social in his intercourse with the people, and soon became a universal favorite on each circuit he traveled. He rose rapidly in the conference until he became one of its most influential members.

Rev. WILLIAM C. HENDERSON, second preacher on the Hudson Circuit, was admitted on trial in the Ohio Conference in 1824, and appointed, with Mr. Green, to the above-named circuit. He was received into full connection by the Pittsburgh Conference in 1826, and ordained a deacon, and an elder in 1828. He was a stout-built man, a little above medium size, a good, plain, useful preacher, and has performed many years of faithful service on the Pittsburgh Conference.

Rev. DAVID SHARP, in charge of the Grand River Circuit, was admitted on trial in the Ohio Conference in 1813, and into full connection and ordained a deacon in 1815, and an elder in 1817. He was a short, heavy-built man, plain, earnest, and impressive in his manner, and was long an efficient laborer in the Pittsburgh Conference. After serving the Church effectually forty-seven years he was superannuated until April 21, 1865, when his useful and almost spotless life closed in death.

Rev. Messrs. Eddy and Plimpton, on the Deerfield Circuit, established an appointment in the town of Charlestown, Portage County, Ohio, where a Congregational Church, organized in Massachusetts and thence emigrated to this town, held almost unlimited sway, and were determined to keep the Methodists out anyhow. Soon a revival of religion commenced, which continued through the winter, and resulted in the formation of a class consisting of Claudius Coe and wife, Alpheus Baldwin, Adna C. Coe and wife, Luke Hall and wife, Sarah C. Coe, John Judson Steadman, Edward Steadman, and to this little band others were soon added, among them Dennis Steadman and wife, Watson Steadman, Diodama Steadman, and two young ladies by the name of Hall.

In the month of January Elder Elliott came to Charlestown to hold a quarterly meeting. At the close of service on Saturday Mr. Elliott was gravely informed that he could not occupy the little schoolhouse on the coming Sabbath, because the "Congregational minister, having the oldest right, claimed it." The old warrior understood things too well to dispute claims in such a case, and inquired if there was not some barn that could be obtained. A gentleman arose and offered his barn, the floor of which was seated and made comfortable for the women, and a few bundles of straw were spread upon the ground in front of the door for the men to stand on. Providence favored them with a fine mild day, and a large congregation assembled, leaving the little schoolhouse not half filled, and Mr. Elliott taking his stand near the barn door, so that all could both see and hear, showed up the peculiarities of Calvinism in such a manner as will never be forgotten by those that heard him. Soon after this the members of the little class met and appointed five trustees, who determined to build a church. After much difficulty they succeeded in getting a lot at the south-west corner of the square, on which they erected a neat little brick church, in which the society worshiped for many years, and enjoyed several good revivals of religion. The year closed with between thirty and forty members in the class. An extensive revival of religion took place this year in the town of Napoli, N. Y., at which from forty to fifty souls were converted and added to the Church in that place.

Rev. NELSON SMITH was born in Cairo, Greene County, N. Y., in 1791, moved into Pennsylvania, and settled in Crawford County, on the waters of Cassawago Creek, in 1815. In 1819 he heard a sermon from Rev. A. Brunson which arrested his attention, and soon afterward experienced religion, and united with the Methodist Episcopal Church then being formed in that place. He was licensed to preach in 1824 as a local preacher, and ordained a deacon in 1833. Though a moderate preacher, he has been very useful in helping to build up the cause of Christ in that region.

Mr. Lyman Crane, an exhorter in the Methodist Episcopal Church, settled his family in Jamestown, Chautauqua County, N. Y., in 1823, and commenced holding meetings, which were continued, and circuit preaching enjoyed occasionally up to the winter of 1824–5, when there was quite a revival, and a class was formed by Mr. Reeder consisting of Lyman Crane and wife, Edward Work and wife, Phineas Stephens and wife, Abram Jones, Day Knight, Rebecca Fenton, Elizabeth Knight, and several others.

The General Conference of the Methodist Episcopal Church, which met in Baltimore in May, 1824, formed the Pittsburgh Annual Conference out of portions of the Baltimore, Ohio, and Genesee Conferences, embracing the entire territory now occupied by the Erie Conference. We must therefore bid a reluctant adieu, as the good people on the Erie District then did, to Messrs. Fillmore and Keyes, who retained their connection with the Genesee Conference. At its session at Lansing, N. Y., September 14, 1825, the Genesee Conference made the following appointments, in connection with the Buffalo District, with the understanding that they were to be subject to the Pittsburgh Conference thereafter.

Lake Circuit, John Scott.

North East, Nathaniel Reeder.

Chautauqua, Peter D. Horton.

Conewango, John W Hill.

French Creek, Robert C. Hatton.

The Methodist Episcopal Church in Youngsville, Warren County, Pa., was commenced this year, but was not finished until several years later.

MEADVILLE, Pa., where various unsuccessful efforts had been made to establish Methodism, was this year, through the labors of Mr. Hatton, blessed with a revival of religion which resulted in the formation of a class consisting of John Lupher, leader, and wife, Wesley Bowman and wife, Griffeth Bennett and wife, Hannah Lowrey, "Blind Betty," Sarah Johnson, Margaret Johnson, and soon after, Nancy Mattocks, Richard Hope and wife, Isaac Myers and wife, Robert Adrain and wife, Jabez Goodrich and wife, and Thomas Benn. Their first meeting place was in the loft of a blacksmith's shop fitted up for that purpose; a humble beginning, but they have since been "exalted."

AKRON, Ohio, was frequently visited by Methodist preachers, who found a welcome home in the house of Mr. Paul Williams, yet no society was organized there until this year. Rev. James M'Intire, on the Huron Circuit, Ohio Conference, succeeded in forming a class consisting of Mr. Singler and wife, Mr. Barkdull and wife, and a few others.

In AURORA, Ohio, Rev. B. O. Plimpton formed a class this year. The members were Dudley Hollister and wife, Reuben Henry and wife, Mr. Steadman and wife, Maria Ferguson, and some others.

Mr. Thorn formed a class this year in South Shenango, Crawford County, Pa., subsequently known as the North Bank appointment. The members were, Charles Campbell, leader, and wife, James Fonner, Leah Fonner, Rebecca Fonner, Hannah Rcyal, Mark Royal, Margaret Fonner, Aaron Harriett, Sisson Harriett, Christian Fonner, Charlotte Royal, Elizabeth Royal, William Fonner, James Espy, Naney Espy, Francis Fowler, Edney Harriett, Rachel Harriett, Polly M'Guire, and George Espy.

The number of members this year were, Erie District.	1,466
Ohio	4,375
Total	5,841
Last year	4,678
Increase	**1,163**

SECTION XI.

FROM 1825 TO 1828.

"The morning light is breaking,
The darkness disappears;
Columbia's sons are waking
To penitential tears."

1825.

THE Pittsburgh Conference held its first session in Pittsburgh, Pa., September 15, 1825, more than a year after its organization by the General Conference. Bishop George presided, and Asa Shinn was elected secretary. Thirty-five members answered to their names. The appointments for this territory were as follows:

Erie District, William Swayze, Presiding Elder.
Erie, Nathaniel Reeder, Zachariah Ragan.
North East, John P Kent.
Chautauqua, Peter D. Horton, Joseph S. Barris.
Conewango, John W Hill.
Lake, Henry Knapp, John Scott.
French Creek, Robert C. Hatton.
Mercer, Alfred Brunson, Edward Stevenson.
Mahoning, Ignatius H. Tacket.
Ohio District, Charles Elliott, Presiding Elder.
Grand River, Philip Green, Joseph W Davis.
Deerfield, John Summerville, Ira Eddy, sup.
Hudson, Robert Hopkins.
Hartford, Thomas Carr, John Chandler.

Youngstown, Edward H. Taylor, William R. Babcock.

New Castle, Samuel Adams, James Babcock.

The Erie District had one additional circuit beyond our bounds, and the Ohio District had three. We now have an array of two districts and fourteen circuits, two presiding elders and twenty-three preachers.

The Mahoning Circuit was formed in 1812, and remained in connection with the Baltimore Conference until 1825. It was named after the Mahoning River, in Pennsylvania, which now forms part of the southern boundary of the Erie Conference from the Alleghany Mountains to the Alleghany River. All of its territory, however, lay south of the Alleghany River until 1817, when an appointment was established near the mouth of Red Bank, and in 1822 another at the house of Mr. Hoover, in Punxutawny, Jefferson County, Pa. In 1824 Mr. Dorsey, of the Baltimore Conference, also formed several classes, and established preaching at a number of places. In 1825, when Mr. Tacket was appointed there, the preaching appointments were as follows: Punxutawny, Mr. Lieser's, Mr. Lawson's, Mr. Stoner's, Mr. Young's; at Shippensville, at Mr. Armstrong's, Mr. Sulonger's, Mr. Smith's, Mr. Shouse's, Mr. Hoffman's, Mr. Smullen's, and at Mr. Critzer's, all within the bounds of our territory.

Rev. Zechariah Ragan, second preacher on the Erie Circuit, was admitted on trial in the Pittsburgh Conference in September, 1825, and appointed to the above charge. He was received into full connection and ordained a deacon in 1827, but on account of some unpleasant difficulty he was permitted to locate in 1828, and soon after joined the "Protestant Methodist Church," in whose service he has spent his subsequent life in the ministry. Mr. Ragan was a good-sized and good-looking man, with very respectable preaching talents.

Rev. JOHN W HILL was the son of Rev. Benjamin P Hill, and was born in the town of Preston, New London County, Mass., March 26, 1802. He was converted, in company with seven other persons, in a week-day prayer meeting in Brookfield, Madison County, N. Y., July 17, 1815. He removed with his parents into Chautauqua County, N. Y., in 1818, where he was licensed to exhort in 1820, and to preach in 1821. He was employed by the elder on the Chautauqua Circuit in 1823, was admitted on trial in the Genesee Conference in 1824, and into full connection and ordained a deacon in 1826 by the Pittsburgh Conference, and an elder in 1828. Mr. Hill was below medium size, was very pious and zealous, and a very useful practical and experimental preacher.

Rev. JOHN SCOTT, second preacher on Lake Circuit, was born in Ireland of pious parents, belonging to the Presbyterian Church; was converted in his seventeenth year, and united with the Methodist Church. In 1819 he emigrated to New Brunswick, where he was licensed to exhort, and soon after to preach. He then came to the United States, and proceeded westward, until he came within the bounds of the Erie District; and in 1824 Mr. Fillmore employed him to assist Mr. Reeder on the Chautauqua Circuit; and in September, 1825, he was admitted on trial in the Genesee Conference, appointed to the Lake Circuit, and then transferred to the Pittsburgh Conference, where he was received into full connection and ordained a deacon in 1827, and an elder in 1829. Mr. Scott was a short, stout-built Irishman; a fine specimen of an honest, simple, conscientious Christian; in his preaching, quaint, original, and practical. His speech and general appearance clearly indicated his country.

Rev. EDWARD STEVENSON, second preacher on the Mercer Circuit, was admitted on trial in the Pittsburgh Conference, at Pittsburgh, Pa., in September, 1825, and appointed to the above charge. He was received into full connection and ordained a deacon in 1827, and located in 1830.

Rev. IGNATIUS H. TACKET, in charge of the Mahon ing Circuit, was born in Monroe County, Virginia, the 19th of August, 1798, was converted in the seventeenth year of his age, and after graduating in the ministry in the usual way was admitted on trial in the Baltimore Conference in March, 1824, and into full connection and ordained a deacon in the Pittsburgh Conference in 1826, and an elder in 1828. Mr. Tacket was a young man of medium size, good address, and of much promise. If possessed of a sufficient amount of energy and application he might have risen to a position of eminence in his conference. He had a very successful year on the Mahoning Circuit.

Rev. JAMES BABCOCK, second preacher on the New Castle Circuit, in company with his father's family, emigrated from some of the eastern states, and settled in the town of Orwell, Trumbull County, Ohio, where, during a gracious revival of religion in 1822, through the labors of Rev. E. H. Taylor and Rev. J. Crawford, he was made a subject of converting power through faith in Jesus Christ, and immediately united with the Methodist Episcopal Church then being organized in that place, and after giving good evidence of Christian character, and of possessing talents and attainments that would be useful in the ministry, he was duly licensed to preach, and admitted on trial in the Ohio Conference at Zanesville, September, 1824, and into full connection and ordained a deacon by the Pittsburgh Conference in 1826, and an elder in 1828. Mr. Babcock was a tall, well-built, and dignified-appearing man, of deep piety, and earnest zeal, and was highly esteemed as a minister.

Rev. WILLIAM R. BABCOCK was a brother to James, was tall but more slender, quick in his movements, excitable in his feelings, and quite genteel in his manners. He was converted among the Freewill Baptists, but united with the Methodists in 1822. He was admitted on trial in the Ohio Conference in 1824, and into full connection and ordained a deacon in the Pittsburgh Conference in 1826, and an elder in 1828. He had a sharp voice, spoke rapidly, and often with powerful effect. He was a good preacher.

Rev. JOHN CHANDLER, second preacher on the Hartford Circuit, was a small, slim man, rather awkward in his movements, his under jaw a little turned to one side, but possessed a clear, strong mind, deep piety, full of zeal, apt in controversy, and at times was terribly severe and scathing; an ardent lover of Methodism, and regarded by other denominations as too sectarian. He was admitted on trial in the Ohio Conference in 1824, and into full connection and ordained a deacon by the Pittsburgh Conference in 1826, and an elder in 1828.

CAMPBELLISM.—About this time a new element of religious controversy developed itself in that part of our conference known as the "Western Reserve." A new sect sprang up under the leadership of Rev. Alexander Campbell, a Scotchman of a good deal of learning and respectable controversial talents, who left the Baptist Church and commenced a new organization, at first called "Campbellites," but finally calling themselves "*Disciples.*" On the "Western Reserve" Rev. Sidney Rigdon, residing in Mentor, Lake County, Ohio, who was once also a Baptist minister, but was now in union with Mr. Campbell in this enterprise, was their principal champion.

They claimed not to design the formation of a new sect, but to unite in one all denominations of Christians, without any articles of faith or rules of Church government except the New Testament; but unfortunately, they proclaimed doctrinal views on the subject of Christian baptism and of the Holy Spirit's influence and agency in convicting and converting sinners, and in remitting sins, which evangelic Christians could not receive or fellowship, and their zeal in controversy on these points knew no bounds. They seemed to possess a kind of religious frenzy on the subject of baptism, which they administered invariably, and at all times of day and night, by immersion.

The Methodist ministry on the "Western Reserve" harnessed themselves for the conflict, and engaged in the controversy with a zest and zeal which indicated both talents of a superior order and an unflinching regard for "the truth as it is in Jesus." Seeing the wrong use that was being made of water, they seemed the more in earnest for the baptism of the Holy Spirit sent down from heaven. At camp-meetings, quarterly meetings, and on all occasions, this seemed to be the constant theme of all the preachers. Under such preaching revivals of religion were frequent and powerful. Our people, too, were clearer in their views of Christian experience in consequence of hearing the subject discussed so much, and with such ability.

Rev. JOSEPH W DAVIS, second preacher on the Grand River Circuit, was born in Berkshire County, Mass., April 30, 1791, embraced religion in June, 1809, removed to Ohio in 1816, received license to preach in 1821, was admitted on trial in the Pittsburgh Conference at its session in Pittsburgh, September, 1825, and into full connection and ordained a deacon in 1827, and an elder in 1829. Mr. Davis was a tall, stout-built man, not brilliant in the pulpit, but a good practical preacher.

Rev. JOHN SUMMERVILLE at the close of this year was removed further south, and never again occupied a circuit within our limits. He continued a faithful laborer in the Pittsburgh Conference until he died, October 6, 1850.

Elder Swayze held a camp-meeting on the campground in Frank's Settlement, three miles south-west of Jamestown, N. Y., which commenced the 11th of June, 1826, and was a meeting never to be forgotten by multitudes of people, and especially by the writer of these pages. We attended the meeting, not from choice, nor by compulsion, but because our good father promised us a new hat, to be bought in Jamestown, N. Y The new hat was obtained, and so was a new heart. On Monday evening, June 13, 1826, Mr. Swayze preached one of his awful sermons. The congregation, which was very large, became terribly excited, most of them upon their feet, many, however, strewed the ground; some groaning in agony, others pleading for mercy, while many shouted for joy. The writer was seated on a slab some distance from the speaker's stand, where he could witness the whole scene. The last half hour of the sermon the preacher was engaged in delivering the most solemn appeals of warning and expostulation to the wicked, clothed with the most terrific language and figures, and with such pathetic tones of voice as no heart could withstand. In that vast crowd no one was unmoved. At the close of the sermon Swayze leaped from the stand to the ground in front, and up the center aisle he went toward the large altar, with his voice of invitation to sinners distinctly heard above the continuous roar of the multitude; at the same time six or eight ministers, who had been stationed at different places in that vast crowd, and wholly unobserved until Swayze sprang from the stand, were now moving slowly forward toward the altar exhorting sinners with all their might. The scene at this time was truly awful. We became so alarmed as we saw one of the ministers approaching the place where we stood that we wheeled round and ran with all our might into the woods and climbed on a stump, where we stood for some time listening to the terrific roar of voices, as the revelator says, "like the sound of many waters." At length the exhorting ceased, and a hymn was sung. It was the hymn commencing

> "Show pity, Lord, O Lord forgive,
> Let a repenting rebel live,"

sung to "Old Hundred;" and such majestic music as those hundreds of voices sent up to heaven we never heard before nor since. We there determined to seek our soul's salvation come what may, and coming down from the stump, we walked deliberately back to the ground and stood for a time looking in wonder at the scene. Not less than fifty persons, male and female, were on their knees in the altar pleading for mercy, while perhaps three hundred Christians were engaged in talking with and praying for these penitents. A lady of our acquaintance happening to see us looking very solemn came and took us by the hand, and kindly invited us to go with her to the altar. We went, and soon from a kneeling posture we lay flat upon the ground, with our head pillowed upon the roots of a large maple-tree, where we remained in great distress of mind until about midnight, when suddenly a stream of light, much the color of gold, came down from heaven and penetrated our dark, hard heart, and permeated our whole soul and body. We immediately sprang to our feet, giving "glory to God in the highest" for his goodness and mercy. After a few hours of sweet rest we awoke in the morning and walked forth in what appeared like a new world. That day we returned home with many others, with but little to say, but full of peace and good resolutions for the future, little imagining, however, what that future with us would be. Next Sabbath Rev. Peter D. Horton received us on trial in the Methodist Episcopal Church in, Youngsville, Warren County, Pa.

A small class was formed this year by Mr. Eddy in Huntsburgh, Ohio, consisting of Josephus Kile, Anna Kile, Villitina Kile, Frances L. Dixon, Mrs. Graves, Lee Kile, and Chloe Dixon. A class was also formed by Mr. Horton in Panama, Chautauqua County, N. Y., consisting of S. L. Paddock and wife, James Sweet and wife, Henry Crane and wife. S. L. Paddock was appointed leader. A camp-meeting of unusual interest was held this year in the town of Burton, Ohio, by Elder Swayze. While the elder was delivering one of his powerful exhortations one hundred persons came to the altar, seventy-five of whom were converted before the meeting closed. He held another camp-meeting after harvest near Titusville, on the banks of Oil Creek. Bishop Roberts was present, and preached on Sunday at eleven o'clock. He was then in the vigor of his manhood, a perfect giant. His sermon was solemn and eloquent, yet simple and impressive.

Our people in Hudson, Ohio, commenced the erection of a church this year. It was a small plain frame building, located near the south-west corner of the square. A small church was built this year at the center of Burton, Ohio. A much better church than either of those was commenced in the village of Jamestown, N. Y

As but few persons have any idea of the amount of labor performed by the preachers of former years, I will here give the plan of the Old Chautauqua Circuit, when Messrs. Horton and Barris traveled it in 1825 and 1826 :

Youngsville, Sunday, 10 o'clock A. M.; Warren, 3 o'clock P. M.
Chandler's Valley, Monday, 3 o'clock P. M.
Yankee Bush, Tuesday, 10 o'clock A. M.; Joseph Mead's, 4 o'clock P. M.
Kinzua, Wednesday, 3 o'clock P. M.
Dougherty's, Thursday, 3 o'clock P. M.; no class.
Braley's, Friday, 3 o'clock P. M.
Gilson's, Saturday, 3 o'clock P. M.; no class.
Hitchcock's, Sunday, 10 o'clock A. M.; Jamestown, 3 o'clock P. M.
Bentley's, Monday, 10 o'clock A. M.; Chautauqua Ridge, 3 o'clock P. M.
Vermont Settlement, Tuesday, 10 o'clock A. M.; St. Clairville, 3 o'clock P. M.
Judge Burnel's, Wednesday, 3 o'clock P. M.
Richard's, Thursday, 3 o'clock P. M.
Carpenter's, Friday, 8 o'clock P. M.
Frost's, Saturday, 3 o'clock P. M.
Miles's, Sunday, 10 o'clock A. M.; Mayville, 3 o'clock P. M.; no class.
Hitchcock's, Monday, 3 o'clock P. M.
Lewis's, Tuesday, 3 o'clock P. M.
Panama, Wednesday, 3 o'clock P. M.
Wilcox's, Sunday, 10 o'clock A. M.; Phillips's, 3 o'clock P. M.
Bullock's, Tuesday, 3 o'clock P. M.
Lott's, Wednesday, 3 o'clock P. M.
Columbus, Thursday, 3 o'clock P. M.; class formed this year.
Irwin, Friday, 3 o'clock P. M.

Thirty regular appointments each round, besides funeral and other extra sermons.

Mr. Carr formed a class this year near the center of North Shenango, Crawford County, Pa., consisting of John Thayer, leader, and wife, Harris Taylor and wife, Jacob Stitson and wife, James Angelo and wife, Hannah Burwell, Rachel Burwell, A. Wiser, C. Honsal, Maria Angelo, Edmund Williams, and Lucinda Williams.

The numbers reported this year were...........	5,834
Last year.	6,268
Decrease......	434

1826.

The Pittsburgh Conference met in Washington, Pa., August 22, 1826. The following were the appointments:

Erie District, William Swayze, Presiding Elder.

Erie, Nathaniel Reeder, Edward Stevenson.

North East, Henry Knapp.

Lake, Job Wilson, John P Kent.

Chautauqua, Joseph S. Barris, Zechariah Ragan.

Meadville, John W Hill, Ignatius H. Tacket.

Mercer, John Leach, Hiram Kinsley.

Ohio District, Charles Elliott, Presiding Elder.

Grand River, Thomas Carr, John Scott.

Deerfield, Philip Green, Peter D. Horton.

Hudson, John Crawford, William R. Babcock.

Hartford, William C. Henderson, Joseph W. Davis.

Youngstown, Robert C. Hatton, Robert Hopkins.

New Castle, Alfred Brunson.

The only changes made in the circuits this year were in the change of the name of "French Creek" to Meadville, a town too long deprived of this honor; "Conewango" was submerged in the Chautauqua and Lake Circuits; and "Mahoning" is called Shippensville, and connected with the Pittsburgh District, James Babcock, preacher, and Thornton Fleming, Presiding Elder.

Rev. HENRY KNAPP, in charge of North East Circuit, closed up his valuable services as a minister of the Gospel this year. He had spent seven years in the itinerant work. He was acceptable and useful, and possessed talents that would have placed him high in his conference if he had lived to develop and cultivate them. He died in Wesleyville, Erie County, Pa., May 20, 1827, after suffering severe afflictions, which he bore with Christian fortitude.

> "They bore him from the field of strife:
> His day of toil was past;
> His work of love was done for aye,
> A rest had come at last."

His final resting-place may be found in the rear of the Methodist Episcopal Church in Wesleyville, Erie County, Pa.

Rev. JOHN LEECH, in charge of Mercer Circuit, was admitted on trial in the Pittsburgh Conference in August, 1826, and appointed to the above charge, being at the time a local deacon. He was received into full connection and ordained an elder in 1828. In 1829 he was left without an appointment on account of affliction, and located in 1830, and still resides in Clarion County, Pa.

Rev. HIRAM KINSLEY, second preacher on the Mercer Circuit, was born in the town of Fairfield, Franklin County, Vermont, November 17, 1799. His religious education was somewhat Calvinistic. Possessing a vigorous mind, accustomed to investigate subjects for himself, he saw in that system doctrines which he could not reconcile with the attributes of the Deity, and at times was strongly inclined to infidelity. He came from the east into Chautauqua County, N. Y., and engaged in teaching school, and soon became acquainted with the Methodists and with their doctrine. One day, when all alone in the woods, after reflecting seriously on the subject, he deliberately made up his mind to seek religion, and immediately commenced praying for it in good earnest. One day, in the month of December, 1823, while listening to a class reading their spelling lesson, about 4 o'clock P M., the Lord answered his prayer, and sent peace to his soul. He immediately united with the Methodist Episcopal Church at Forestville, Chautauqua County, N. Y., and received license to exhort in 1824, and to preach at a local preachers' conference, held in connection with a camp-meeting at Wesleyville, Erie County, Pa., in 1825; was admitted on trial in the Pittsburgh Conference in 1826, into full connection and ordained a deacon in 1828, and an elder in 1830. Mr. Kinsley was rather below medium size, but well built for hard service; was a close student, which made him appear unsocial. He soon became one of the closest thinkers, best debaters, and most powerful doctrinal preachers in the Conference.

Rev. CHARLES ELLIOTT, Presiding Elder on the Ohio District, closed up his valuable labors on the district this year, and has never since occupied a field of labor within our bounds. From 1827 to 1831 he served the Church as a Professor of Languages in

Madison College, it being then under the patronage of the Pittsburgh Conference. He was then two years presiding elder on the Uniontown District. In 1833, when the "Pittsburgh Conference Journal" was commenced, he was appointed its editor, where he remained until 1836, when the General Conference appointed him editor of the "Western Christian Advocate," published at Cincinnati, Ohio. In this office he remained twelve years, or to 1848. He then returned to the regular work as pastor and presiding elder in the Cincinnati Conference until 1852, when the General Conference reappointed him editor of the Western Christian Advocate, where he remained until 1856. He was soon after elected president of the "Iowa Wesleyan University," in whose service he remained until 1860, when he was elected by the General Conference editor of the "Central Christian Advocate," published at St. Louis, which he has conducted with uncommon skill through this terrible rebellion and war. Forty-six years he has spent in effective service in the ministry, in colleges, and in the editorial chair; he has been a member of the General Conference in 1824, 1828, 1836, 1844, 1848, 1852, and in 1864. In the midst of all this labor Dr. Elliott has become an author of much notoriety. His chief works are, "Delineations of Roman Catholicism;" "Sinfulness of American Slavery;" and "The History of the Great Secession;" all giving evidence of vast research, and each containing an exhaustless store of the most valuable information. May his bright sun set in peace!

An extensive revival of religion was experienced during the fall of 1826 on the North East Circuit, through the instrumentality of Mr. Knapp. It commenced at Habor Creek, four miles below Erie, Pa., now called Wesleyville. A society was formed in this place by Mr. Knapp, consisting of Mr. Flower and wife, A. Shaddock and wife, David Chambers and wife, William Campbell and wife, Ezekiel Chambers, and others.

ERIE, Pa., was a flourishing village, in which, though Methodist preaching had frequently been enjoyed by the people, no permanent organization had been made until this year. Mr. James M'Conkey and wife, members of the Methodist Episcopal Church in Baltimore, moved to Erie to reside; and Mr. David Burton and wife attended the meeting at Harbor Creek, and were there converted, and invited Mr. Knapp to establish an appointment in Erie, and the same winter a class was formed composed of the above-named persons and a few others. Mr. M'Conkey was appointed leader, and soon after secured to the Church the lot on Seventh-street, on which their first church was subsequently built; the cost was $300.

CLEVELAND, Ohio, the most important place within the bounds of our conference, was among the last to be permanently occupied by us. Its inhabitants were mostly from New England, and not inclined to favor Methodism. A gentleman residing in one of the Eastern states, and owning real estate in Cleveland, being anxious to see the Methodist Episcopal Church established there at the time the Presbyterian and other Churches were being organized, sent to a person residing in the place a deed of the lot on the corner of Ontario and Rockwell streets, where Mr. Crittenden's dwelling-house now stands, which would have been the best location in the city for a Methodist Episcopal Church; but no one could be found that was willing to pay the postage on the package, or the recorder for recording the deed, and it had to be returned to its generous donor. In 1822 Captain William C. Johnston moved from Detroit, Michigan, to Cleveland, Ohio; his wife, Mrs. Grace Johnston, was at the time a member of the Methodist Episcopal Church, and remained the only one in the place for several years. The following year Cleveland was made a preaching appointment and attached to the Hudson Circuit. Preaching was continued regularly with but little apparent success until the spring of 1827, when, in consequence of several Methodist families moving into the place, Mr. Crawford succeeded in forming a class consisting of Andrew Tomlinson, leader, Grace Johnston, Eliza Worley, Elizabeth Southworth, Rev. Joel Sizer and wife, and Lucy Knowlton.

At Doan's Corners, now East Cleveland, a class was formed this year also, consisting of Aaron Hubbard, leader, and wife, James Sawtel and wife, Oliver Marshal, Israel Hubbard and wife, Anna Cozard, Elener Collier, Philinda Gould, William Mitchell and wife, Timothy Hurlbut and wife, Samuel Bond, Florilla Searls, Samuel Harris and wife, Harriet Slate, and Nathan Smith and wife. The meeting place for this society was finally removed to the Hubbard settlement on Kinsman-street, south-east from Cleveland. A class was also formed in Tallmadge, Summit County, Ohio, this year by Mr. Plimpton, on the Canton Circuit. The members were Philo Stone and wife, Joseph Blacksley, Ephraim Clarke, Allen Clarke, Sylvester Barnes, Mother Griswold, Lucy Bradly, Henry Stevens and wife, and Shubel Lowry and wife.

In closing up the year Elder Swayze says: "We have had five camp-meetings, three of which may be considered as beginning, continuing, and ending in the spirit of reformation. At these, three hundred and fifty were hopefully converted to God. One hundred and fifty came forward and put themselves under the watch-care of the Church, preferring in that consecrated spot to cast in their lots with the people who had taken such unwearied pains to bring them from darkness to light. Our other two meetings were equal as relates to appearance, good order, and evangelical preaching. We think we speak within bounds when we say four hundred were converted at our five camp-meetings."

There was a revival of religion this year on the Grand River Circuit. About sixty souls were converted, most of whom united with the Methodist Episcopal Church. At Youngsville, on the Chautauqua Circuit, on the 13th and 14th of January, 1827, Elder Swayze held a quarterly meeting of great interest. Mr. Barris, then preacher in charge, says: "It began in power, continued in power, and ended in power; and, glory to God! the work goes on there yet in power. It was the best quarterly meeting I was ever at, and so said more of my brethren in the ministry. In the love-feast we had eighteen to come forward as candidates for probation, and it was a love-feast indeed. I think near twenty were converted to God during the meeting, while all were quickened. Our beloved Elder Swayze, who preached, is on the wing for glory. May the Lord attend him, and make him continue what he has been, a flaming torch on the district." The "Bethel Chapel," a plain brick structure, was erected in Canfield, Ohio, this year, principally through the exertions of Dr. Bostwick, who gave the land.

Rev. ROBERT HOPKINS at the close of this year was removed further south, not returning again within our limits, but continued to labor and to rise in popular influence in the Pittsburgh Conference, discharging for many years the responsible duties of presiding elder on its best districts until failing health compelled him to desist. He has been five times a member of the General Conference. He now sustains a superannuated relation.

During the year 1818 Rev. William Horton, a local preacher, commenced preaching at a place called Brady's Bend, or Great Western, in Armstrong County, Pa., and in 1825 was instrumental in forming a class consisting of William Horton, wife, and two daughters, Samuel Lafevre, wife, and daughter, Samuel Phillips, Thomas M'Clure and wife, Robert Phillips and wife, John Phillips, Thomas Phillips.

Rev. Mr. Chandler, on the Butler Circuit, this year established circuit preaching there.

The members returned this year were, Erie District ..	3,563
Ohio..	2,853
Total	6,416
Last year	5,834
Increase	582

1827

The Pittsburgh Conference met in Steubenville, Ohio, August 22, 1827. The following are the appointments for this work:

Erie District, William Swayze, Presiding Elder.

Erie, Job Wilson, Joseph W Davis.

North East, Wilder B. Mack, John C. Ayres.

Lake, Joseph S. Barris, Zechariah Ragan.

Chautauqua, John Chandler, John Johnson.

Meadville, John Leech, Ignatius H. Tacket.

Mercer, John P Kent, Samuel Ayres.

Shippensville, James Babcock.

Ohio District, Daniel Limerick, Presiding Elder.

New Castle, Charles Thorn, J. Holt.

Youngstown, R. C. Hatton, S. Adams.

Hartford, Nathaniel Reeder, Hiram Kinsley.

Grand River, T. Carr, W R. Babcock.

Cleveland, John Crawford, Cornelius Jones.

Deerfield, Edward H. Taylor, George W Robinson.

Windsor, William C. Henderson.

There was no change in the work on the Erie District, except that the Shippensville Circuit is transferred back to it from the Pittsburgh District. On the Ohio District Cleveland takes the name of the circuit in place of Hudson, and Windsor is a new circuit formed out of part of Grand River.

Rev. Wilder B. Mack, in charge of the North East Circuit, was born, raised, educated, and converted to God amid the Green Mountains, in the State of Vermont. He was a small man, neat in appearance, and gentlemanly in his deportment. He possessed one of the sweetest, mellowest, sympathetic voices we ever heard in the pulpit; which, together with his fine descriptive imagination, enabled him to work upon the feelings of a congregation with wonderful effect. He was admitted on trial in the New England Conference, in company with Dr. Fisk, in June, 1818, and into full connection and ordained a deacon in 1823, and an elder in 1825 by the Maine Conference formed this year, and was transferred in 1827 to the Pittsburgh Conference, where he was appointed in charge of the North East Circuit.

Rev. John C. Ayres, second preacher on the North East Circuit, was born and raised in Pennsylvania, on the eastern side of the Alleghany Mountains. As he emerged to manhood, while engaged in the iron business in Bellefonte, Pa., he was powerfully awakened and converted to Almighty God in a revival of religion among the Methodists of that place. He immediately took up the "hammer of the word," and began to apply it with good effect to the hearts of the people. He was soon licensed to exhort, and sallied out in different directions in his master's work. Elder Swayze, in a tour on the east end of his district, found him and took him to several of his quarterly meetings, where he displayed great power in prayer and exhortation. He went a few times around the Chautauqua Circuit, was licensed to preach, and recommended to the Pittsburgh Conference, where he was admitted on trial August, 1827, and appointed to the above circuit. He was received into full connection and ordained a deacon in 1830, and an elder in 1832. Mr. Ayres was a small, compactly built man, of good health, capable of enduring a great amount of hard toil, and was very efficient in revivals of religion. He was a very social and agreeable person, and advanced steadily in the ministry and in his standing in the conference.

Rev. JOHN JOHNSON, second preacher on the Chautauqua Circuit, was admitted on trial in the Pittsburgh Conference in August, 1826, into full connection and ordained a deacon in 1828, and an elder in 1830, and located in 1834. Mr. Johnson was a very tall man, awkward in his movements, quite near-sighted, but a straightforward, deliberate, systematic preacher, and an amiable man; a close and thorough student, but had not animation enough for a Methodist preacher.

Rev. SAMUEL AYRES, second preacher on the Mercer Circuit, was admitted on trial in the Pittsburgh Conference in August, 1827, into full connection and ordained a deacon in 1829, and an elder in 1831. Mr. Ayres was a tall man, of rather poor health, wanting in self-confidence, easily discouraged, but a most amiable Christian gentleman, and a good, sound preacher. He was superannuated two years; gave his attention to the study of medicine, located in 1832, was readmitted in 1835, located again in 1836, when he engaged in the practice of medicine.

Rev. DANIEL LIMERICK, Presiding Elder on the

Ohio District, was admitted on trial in the Ohio Conference in August, 1820, into full connection and ordained a deacon in 1822, and an elder in 1824. Mr Limerick was a thick, solid built man, of medium height, and reputed a good, practical preacher. He spent but one year in this work, but was long a useful and influential preacher in the Pittsburgh Conference. Unfortunately I do not find any obituary of him in the regular minutes, and therefore can give no account of his death, which occurred in 1837.

"His soul to him who gave it rose;
God led it to its long repose,
Its glorious rest!"

Rev. JONATHAN HOLT, second preacher on the New Castle Circuit, was admitted on trial in the Baltimore Conference in August, 1824, and into full connection and ordained a deacon by the Pittsburgh Conference in 1826, and an elder in 1828. He was only one year connected with this work, and we have been able to learn but little of his subsequent history.

Rev. CORNELIUS JONES, second preacher on the Cleveland Circuit, was born May 20, 1800, in Hinsdale, Berkshire County, Mass. In 1820 he moved to Chardon, Geauga County, Ohio. On the 24th of February, 1821, he attended a meeting held by Rev. Alfred Brunson, to hear the discussion of some doctrinal points by that able theologian; and while the sacrament of the Lord's supper was being administered by Messrs. Brunson and Brown, his mind became seriously awakened to a sense of his lost condition, and after returning home, while engaged in earnest prayer, God gave him an evidence that his sins were all forgiven, and soon after he became convinced that God had called him to the work of the ministry. He was licensed to preach at Rootstown, Portage County, Ohio, June 17, 1825, and the year following was employed by the presiding elder to labor on the New Castle Circuit. He was admitted on trial in the Pittsburgh Conference in August, 1827, and into full connection and ordained a deacon in 1829, and an elder in 1831. Mr. Jones was remarkable for his deep, uniform piety. For several years his theme both in and out of the pulpit was *perfect love*, of which he was a living witness. Religious success attended his labors wherever he went.

Rev GEORGE W ROBINSON, second preacher on the Deerfield Circuit, was admitted on trial in the Pittsburgh Conference in August, 1825, and into full connection and ordained a deacon in 1827, and an elder in 1829. He spent but this one year within the bounds of this conference.

Rev. NATHANIEL REEDER was superannuated at the end of this year, in which relation he remained until 1834, when he located. We have not been able to get the time nor place of his death.

Rev. ELISHA WARNER. We do not know the exact time when this good brother was licensed to preach, but have concluded here to insert a short account of him as a local preacher, written by the Rev. William M. Osborn, of Wisconsin Conference: "Among the early Methodist local preachers in Trumbull County, Ohio, was the eccentric Elisha Warner, who still lives at a good old age to blow the Gospel 'ram's horn' on the banks of the Upper Mississippi. One of his early acquaintances in Ohio was Hon. Elisha Whittlesey, who had then an attorney's office in Canfield, Ohio. Hearing that his friend, Elisha Warner, had been authorized to preach, he resolved on the first opportunity to test Mr. Warner's ecclesiastical qualifications for the office and work to which he professed to be called. Such an opportunity was not long wanting, for on the first meeting in Judge Whittlesey's office something like the following examination took place:

"*Judge W* Well, Mr. Warner, I am informed that you have been authorized by the Methodist Episcopal Church to preach the Gospel. What do you think you can do?

"*Brother W* Why, yes, judge, in a big house there are not only vessels of honor, but also of dishonor. The china ware, you know, is employed to set before lawyers, doctors, and great ones of the earth; but you must recollect that pewter platters performed just as important offices in our mother's households as those of a more genteel and elegant character. Your 'established clergy' comprise in our religious households the china ware, while your obedient servant passes only for a pewter platter.

"*Judge W* But really, friend Warner, do you possess sufficient learning to handle such a polished instrument as the silver trumpet of the Gospel? Remember, 'No man taketh this honor to himself but he who is called of God, as was Aaron.'

"*Brother W* True, sir; but consider how it was under the law. Silver trumpets were ornamented and beautiful, but you are aware that the priests sometimes employed a less comely instrument in the worship of God, even the uncouth and crooked *ram's horn;* and I leave you to decide which of the two was most effective when the Lord overthrew Ai and demolished the walls of Jericho. If Elisha Warner were to sound the silver trumpet of the Gospel it would be as inharmonious as the notes of a raven; but with the God-given ram's horn he may make the walls of a second Jericho tremble before he dies.

"*Judge W* Friend Warner, will you be so good as to inform me in what college you received your education? None, you know, are thought fit to preach the Gospel unless they are liberally educated; pray tell me what are your attainments?

"*Brother W* At a rather late day, sir, I took my position as a student in *Brush College*, an institution of natural learning situated in the beech woods of Ohio, under the superintendency of one Professor *Hard Work*, an excellent tutor, but exacting to a fault; and these brawny hands and sun-burnt brow of mine will evidence to you, sir, that I performed well my task. For many years I toiled in darkness before I obtained sufficient knowledge of myself and God to know 'that the just shall live by faith.' Having suddenly advanced to the 'believer's degree,' I received a 'diploma,' which I always carry in my bosom, which reads: 'The Spirit itself beareth witness with our spirit that we are the children of God.' 'Be thou faithful unto death and I will give thee a crown of life.'

"*Judge W* Very well, Mr. Warner; be so kind as to give me some information concerning your knowledge of mathematics. As an English student I dare say you are well posted in this branch of science.

"*Brother W* You know, sir, this is an age of progress, and instead of bothering my head with a multiplicity of rules, I have merged them all in one, which for convenience' sake we denominate the 'Golden Rule,' found in Matthew's Gospel: 'Therefore all things whatsoever ye would that men should do to you, do ye even so to them; for this is the law and the prophets.'

"*Judge W* Well done, sir; your Gospel mathematics is better than Euclid's. Now be good enough to inform me what grammar you studied, and what are its principal parts of speech?

"*Brother W* I regret to say, sir, that the edition of my grammar is one with which lawyers and doctors are ill acquainted, as it is the grammar of the Holy Ghost, and its principal parts of speech are but three, 'Faith, hope, and charity, these three; but the greatest of these is charity.'"

Here ended the examination, which impressed the judge so favorably as to bring from him the declaration that "Mr. Warner would pass, for he had shown himself a scholar, and a workman that had no reason to be ashamed."

While the Methodist ministry from the beginning has been favored with some of the best scholars in the country, and while the Methodist Episcopal Church has been a constant and successful patron of education, she has at the same time reaped largely from a class of men in her local ministry, like Mr. Warner, with but little education, except what they have obtained through their own industry, especially by the reading of the Holy Scriptures. These local brethren have been the advance guard in new settlements.

In August, 1828, a camp-meeting was held on the New Castle Circuit by Elder Limerick, at which "it was thought that fifty souls were converted to God."

Rev. R. C. HATTON closed up his erratic career among us this year. After spending three years south of us in the Pittsburgh Conference, he finally withdrew again from the Methodist Episcopal Church in 1831, and united with the Cumberland Presbyterian Church.

A class of six members was formed in 1828 in Brookville, Pa., and David Butler was appointed leader. Their meetings were held for some time in an old mill a little north of the present village. A Sunday-school was formed soon after, Cyrus Butler superintendent.

The membership on Erie District this year was.	4,747
Ohio......	3,055
Total.................	7,802
Last year	6,416
Increase...................................... ..	1,386

SECTION XII.

FROM 1828 TO 1831.

"Then sink not in sorrow, despond not in fear;
A glorious to-morrow is brightening and near;
When a blessed reward for each faithful endeavor,
Christians with Christ shall be soon and forever."

1828.

THE year 1828 was rendered memorable in the annals of Methodism on account of the secession of what was called the "Radical Party" from the Methodist Episcopal Church, and the formation of the "Protestant Methodist Church," which took place soon after the close of the General Conference, which sat in Pittsburgh, Pa., May, 1828. They were called "Radicals" on account of radical changes they sought in the economy of the Church, by dispensing with the offices of bishops and presiding elders, and the introduction of an equal number of laymen with the ministry into the Annual and General Conferences.

This secession did not affect us as injuriously within the bounds of the Erie Conference as in some other portions of the Church; but yet in a few prominent places the work was seriously embarrassed for several years.

The Pittsburgh Conference met in Salem, formerly called Shenango, Mercer County, Pa., August 21, 1828, Bishop Roberts presiding. This was the first annual conference that was ever held within the present limits of the Erie Conference, and it was a remarkable coincidence that it was held in the old "Shenango settlement," where the first Methodist class was formed, now called Salem, and was presided over by the first "leader" of that class, now Bishop Roberts.

Dr. C. Cook, secretary of conference, writes: "The Pittsburgh Conference, which commenced its session at Salem, Mercer County, Pa., August 21, adjourned on Wednesday, 27th. Salem is only a house of worship, remote from any town or village, and our conference was held in connection with a camp-meeting. The brethren in the neighborhood and on the ground entertained the preachers with great urbanity and good feeling, which did honor to themselves. There were about one hundred tents, and the number of conversions it was supposed more than averaged one to a tent." The appointments were as follows:

Erie District, Wilder B. Mack, Presiding Elder.

Erie, Joseph W Davis, Joel Jones.

North East, David Preston, J. Maffit.

Lake, Joseph S. Barris, Samuel Ayres.

Meadville, Job Wilson, William R. Babcock.

Youngsville, Hiram Kinsley, John Johnson.

Jamestown, James Gilmore.

Franklin, Aurora Callender.

Shippensville, Nathaniel Callender.

Ohio District, Ira Eddy, Presiding Elder.

Youngstown, Billings O. Plimpton, Edmund W. Sehon.

Hartford, John Summerville, John Scott.

Mercer, Thomas Carr, R. Armstrong.

New Castle, Samuel Adams, William C. Henderson.

Canton District, William Swayze, Presiding Elder.

Deerfield, John W Hill, John C. Ayres.

Windsor, John Chandler.

Cleveland, Ignatius H. Tacket, Cornelius Jones.

Grand River, John Crawford, Lorenzo Dow Prosser.

We now have parts of three districts, with three presiding elders; sixteen circuits, with twenty-eight preachers. The Chautauqua Circuit is divided, and one part called Youngsville, and the other Jamestown.

Rev. WILDER B. MACK, the new presiding elder on the Erie District, had labored but one year in this conference, and was, therefore, comparatively a stranger. But that year was one of great success, and his fame as a preacher had spread with wonderful rapidity. He had attended several camp-meetings, where his preaching was universally admired; so much so that the people on the Erie District were greatly rejoiced when the appointment was made. Mr. Mack did not possess the moving power of Swayze, nor the dignified address of Fillmore; but he possessed an original charm in his voice, and his manner of speaking, and had a control of the feelings of his audience that neither of them had, and attracted as large crowds to hear as either of his illustrious predecessors. The year was one of great religious prosperity.

Rev. JOEL JONES, second preacher on the Erie Circuit, was admitted on trial in the Pittsburgh

Conference at its session in August, 1828; labored but one year, and was then discontinued. A very good but eccentric sort of a man.

Rev. DAVID PRESTON, in charge of the North East Circuit, was born in Washington County, N. Y., in 1785. He was converted in early life, and then backslid and became quite skeptical, reading with close attention all the prominent infidel writings of the day, which circumstance prepared him to become a most able and successful combatant of these errors when he became a minister. He was reclaimed and soon after licensed to preach, but when or where we do not know. He moved into the town of Harmony, Chautauqua County, N. Y., in 1824, and soon made himself known as a talented and useful local preacher. In 1827 he was employed by the elder to labor on the Youngsville Circuit, and in 1828 was received on trial in the Pittsburgh Conference, and into full connection in 1830. He was ordained a deacon while a local preacher, and was made an elder in 1832. Mr. Preston was about medium in size, disposed to stoop some, possessed a vigorous mind, and a terse, forcible style. His thoughts were brilliant, and were presented with a warmth of feeling that deeply impressed audience.

Rev. J. MAFFIT, second preacher on the North East Circuit, was an Irishman; was admitted on trial in the Pittsburgh Conference in 1827, and into full connection and ordained a deacon in 1829, and an elder in 1831.

Rev. JAMES GILMORE, in charge of the Jamestown Circuit, was born in the town of Chester, Hampshire

County, Mass., June 2, 1790; was converted to God, under the ministry of Rev. Billy Hibbard, in his eleventh year, when he united with the Methodist Episcopal Church. In about three years he backslid, and remained in that condition about five years. He had in the mean time, in connection with his father's family, removed and settled on the bank of the Alleghany River, near the line of the State of New York. From thence he went over to the Susquehanna River, where it pleased God to reclaim him. Soon after this he became acquainted with Henry B. Bascom, took him home with him to his father's house, and there they spent a year together in studying for the ministry, and laboring as exhorters wherever an opportunity presented. Mr. Gilmore was licensed to preach in 1812, admitted on trial in the Genesee Conference in 1813, and into full connection and ordained a deacon in 1815, and an elder in 1817. Mr. Gilmore labored in connection with the Genesee Conference until 1828, when he was transferred to the Pittsburgh Conference, and appointed to labor on the Jamestown Circuit. Mr. Gilmore was very tall, slim, and straight, and made a very dignified and commanding appearance. He possessed more than ordinary mental power, understood well the doctrines of the Bible, and could defend them against infidelity and the various isms of the day with tremendous effect. Calvinism was his hobby. When he came to Jamestown Circuit New-School Calvinism was exerting a tremendous influence. The way Mr. Gilmore exposed its peculiar characteristics will never be forgotten by those that heard him. During the year he held a camp-meeting a few miles from Jamestown, in a place called "Louk's Hollow." On Sabbath evening there was a vast crowd in attendance, and many of them very disorderly, who could not be induced to be seated or quiet. Mr. Gilmore went into the stand, and announced for his text, "Rejoice, O young man, in thy youth; and let thy heart cheer thee in the days of thy youth; and walk in the ways of thy heart and in the sight of thine eyes;" saying nothing about the remainder of the verse until he had talked perhaps half an hour to the young people, lauding and admiring the various sinful amusements and errors practiced and believed by them. While upon this theme the crowd rushed up as close as they could get to him and listened with astonishment and delight. Christians stood and wondered what the man could mean by such an apparent approval of all that was bad. All at once he paused, and recited the remainder of the verse, "but know thou that for all these things God will bring thee into judgment." The attention of all had become so perfectly secured by this time that the most profound silence prevailed all over the ground. He then went into such a description of the final judgment day—Gabriel blowing the trumpet—suiting his action and voice to the occasion, as to make the scene most awful and terrific. Tears flowed down many faces; sobs and groans could be heard in all directions. The countenances of the wicked were the pictures of sadness; as he proceeded cries for mercy were heard in all directions, and as he closed up a large number rushed to the altar of prayer, and the night passed away with singing, praying, and shouting, that made the adjoining mountains ring and listening angels rejoice. Mr. Gilmore attended a camp-meeting near Youngsville, Warren County, Pa., where he was a perfect stranger, and got up in the stand to preach. He informed the people that he had enjoyed but few literary opportunities when a boy, but that he had learned a few rules in arithmetic that were of great use to him in religious matters as well as in temporal business. He then read for his text the language of Peter: "Add to your faith, virtue; and to virtue, knowledge; and to knowledge, temperance," etc. He said, "We will now employ the rules of arithmetic in explaining this text:

"1. We will apply to it the rule of *addition*." He then proceeded to "add" these graces together, and to show what a man would be who possessed all of them. He then said, "We will apply,

"2. The rule of *subtraction*," and proceeded to subtract these graces from their opposite vices, and to show what a man would be without them, possessing all of their opposites. He then said, "We will apply,

"3. The rule of *multiplication*," and then endeavored to show how the good that a man does, who possesses these graces, will increase, multiplying both before and after he dies.

4. He applied the rule of *division*, by gathering all nations at the judgment-seat of Christ, and separating those that possessed these graces from those that did not possess them, showing their comparative position on the right and left of Christ.

5. He applied the rule of loss and gain, showing

what the one class would gain and what the other would lose. The whole was carried through in such a novel and ingenious way as to please all that heard it, while the winding up was thrilling and powerful.

Rev. AURORA CALLENDER, in charge of Franklin Circuit, was received on trial in the Pittsburgh Conference in 1828, and appointed to the above charge. He was received into full connection and ordained a deacon in 1830, and an elder in 1832. Mr. Callender was a large fleshy man, pleasant and social in his manners, and a good preacher.

Rev. NATHANIEL CALLENDER, in charge of the Shippensville Circuit, was received on trial in the Pittsburgh Conference in 1825, and into full connection and ordained a deacon in 1827, and an elder in 1829. He was a brother to Aurora Callender, but did not in any respect resemble him. Nathaniel was a small, sprightly man, with a clear, sound head, and was a fine speaker. He, however, spent but little of his time with us in this part of the work; nearly all of his labor has been performed within the Pittsburgh Conference. He is now (1864) connected with the Cincinnati Conference.

Rev. IRA EDDY, the new Presiding Elder on the Ohio District, has by this time become quite familiar to the reader, whether ever personally acquainted with him or not, as nearly all of his time since 1817 has been spent on this field, and in it he has almost constantly served as a pioneer, forming new circuits and new societies continually With all this labor he found time to read a vast amount, and to become a well-informed minister of Jesus Christ. Indeed, no man could apply himself more closely to reading and to his work than Mr. Eddy. And although he never was a profound theologian nor a systematic sermonizer, yet he did burn with zeal for his Master, and was a powerful and interesting preacher. He was very tall, straight, and dignified in appearance, early inclining to be gray, and full of religious anecdotes and stories about the past.

Rev. EDMUND W SEHON, second preacher on the Youngstown Circuit, was received on trial in the Pittsburgh Conference in 1828, and appointed to the above charge, where he labored but one year, the only year he ever served in this work. He graduated in the usual way in the conference, displayed unusual powers as a speaker, was appointed agent for the American Bible Society in the State of Ohio, in which capacity he labored for several years. In 1845, when the southern portion of the Church seceded from the Methodist Episcopal Church, he went with them, and served that Church as Missionary Secretary up to the time the late rebellion commenced. The government authorities had him for a time in prison on account of his rebel propensities, beyond which we have no desire to trace his history.

Rev. RICHARD ARMSTRONG, second preacher on the Mercer Circuit, was an Irishman, of moderate abilities. He was received on trial in the Baltimore Conference in 1819, in which conference he graduated, and labored until 1825. When the Pittsburgh Conference was formed he fell into that body, of which he is now (1864) a superannuated member.

Rev. LORENZO D. PROSSER, second preacher on

the Grand River Circuit, was born in Petersburgh, Rensselaer County, N. Y., in 1804. He was converted in the town of Edmonson, Otsego County, N. Y., in 1818; baptized and received into the Methodist Episcopal Church by Rev. Daniel Barnes, and one year after, in company with his father's family, moved into Chautauqua County, N. Y., and settled in the town of Villanovia. He received license to preach in 1825, and was received on trial in the Pittsburgh Conference in 1827, and into full connection and ordained a deacon in 1829, and an elder in 1831. Mr. Prosser was a very small man, and very eccentric. He sometimes would astonish and thrill his congregation with his eloquence, while at other times he could say nothing, and perhaps leave the congregation and flee to the house or the woods. As he grew older he became more reliable. Revivals were his delight, and when in them he would labor so hard as to disqualify himself for other parts of his work.

Rev. James Babcock, who superannuated at the last conference, closed his itinerant career in death at Butler, Pa., February 8, 1829. He spent two years alone on the Shippensville Circuit, on the east side of the Alleghany River, a large circuit in a new wilderness, mountainous country, with very little assistance from the presiding elder. He was also a close student, his thirst for knowledge interfering much with his hours of rest; and between hard labor, much exposure, and severe study, his manly frame gave way, and consumption and death ensued.

"He's gone! The spotless soul is gone
Triumphant to his place above."

Rev. JACOB BEAR was converted at a camp-meeting in Dauphin County, Pa., in 1818, where he immediately united with the Methodist Episcopal Church. He moved to Mount Jackson, Lawrence County, Pa., in 1825, and was the first Methodist and first class-leader in that town. The first Methodist preaching in that place was by Elder Eddy and B. O. Plimpton. A class was formed in 1828, consisting of Jacob Bear and wife, Stephen Bryan and wife, Louis Haulette, Isabella M'Gill and two daughters. This class was about one mile north of the village, and the meetings were held at Mr. Bear's log-house until 1838. About the time the class was formed Mr. Bear received license to preach, which he continued to do until he died, in 1858.

Mr. Davis formed a class, in the spring of 1829, in Conncautville, Crawford County, Pa., consisting of Jesse Danby, leader, and wife, Thomas Landon, wife, and daughter, and George Nelson and wife.

Very extensive revivals of religion were experienced on several of the circuits this year. A camp-meeting was held in Villanovia, at which "seventy or eighty" experienced religion, and on the Forestville Circuit there was an "increase of about one hundred and fifty." At a camp-meeting held on the Chautauqua Circuit "about one hundred were converted." On the Meadville Circuit it was thought that "at least one hundred souls were converted." A moderate sized brick church was erected at Wesleyville, Erie County, Pa., and at a quarterly meeting held in it late in the fall thirteen were hopefully converted. Two young men while at work in the brickyard making the brick for the above church were powerfully awakened and converted, one of whom is now an able preacher of the Gospel, and a member of the Erie Conference. A camp-meeting was held in Mentor, Lake County, Ohio, in June, 1829, at which forty or fifty were converted. There was also a revival in Hamden and in Ashtabula this year. A church was commenced this year in Westfield, Chautauqua County, N. Y., on the west side of the "great gulf," extending across the west end of that village, on account of the society living mostly on that side. This mistake kept Methodism out of that beautiful village for several years. At Forestville, Chautauqua County, N. Y., a church which had been reared a few years previously, but was unfinished, took fire and burned down in the midst of a protracted meeting that was going on in it in the winter of 1828–9, and a new one was built the following summer.

The number of members on the Erie District this year is.	3,945
Canton	1,848
Ohio	1,876
Total	7,669
Last year	7,802
Decrease	133

1829.

The Pittsburgh Conference met in Wheeling, Va., July 16, 1829. The appointments are as follows:

Erie District, Wilder B. Mack, Presiding Elder.
Springfield, Samuel Ayres, D. C. Richey.
North East, Joseph S. Barris.
Forestville, James Gilmore, Alured Plimpton.

Meadville, Nathaniel Callender, Aurora Callender.
Youngsville, John P Kent.
Jamestown, David Preston, William Butt.
Franklin, Hiram Kinsley, William R. Babcock.
Shippensville, John Johnson, John C. Ayres.
Ohio District, Ira Eddy, Presiding Elder.
Youngstown, B. O. Plimpton, Richard Armstrong.
Hartford, Job Wilson.
New Castle, Joseph W Davis, Jacob Jenks.
Mercer, Thomas Carr, Isaac Winans.
Canton District, William Swayze, Presiding Elder.
Deerfield, John W Hill, C. Jones.
Windsor, John Scott.
Cleveland, John Chandler, J. M'Lean, T. Vaughn.
Grand River, John Crawford, Caleb Brown.

The only change there is in the work this year is in the names of two circuits: "Erie" is called "Springfield," and "Lake" is called "Forestville." The presiding elders are the same as last year.

Rev. D. C. Richey, second preacher on the Springfield Circuit, was received on trial in the Pittsburgh Conference in 1829, and into full connection and ordained a deacon in 1831, and an elder in 1833. Mr. Richey was a small man, of moderate attainments and preaching abilities, but a very amiable and ex cellent man, and loved to do good whenever it was in his power.

Rev. Alured Plimpton was brother to Billings O. Plimpton. He was a regularly read physician, but abandoned the practice of medicine for the ministry of the word, and was admitted on trial in the Pittsburgh Conference in 1829, and into full connection and ordained a deacon in 1831, and an elder in 1833. Mr. Plimpton was below medium size, and had an impediment in his speech, which lessened his efficiency as a public speaker; but he was an accomplished gentleman, had an amiable disposition, was a close student, and was highly esteemed.

Rev. WILLIAM BUTT, second preacher on the Jamestown Circuit, was born, raised, converted, and graduated to the ministry in North East, Pa., and was received on trial in the Pittsburgh Conference in 1829, and into full connection and ordained a deacon in 1831, and an elder in 1833. Mr. Butt was a short man, of Dutch parentage, of limited attainments, and a passable preacher; rather abrupt in his manners, which often gave offense.

Rev JACOB JENKS, second preacher on the New Castle Circuit, was received on trial in the Pittsburgh Conference in 1829, and into full connection and ordained a deacon in 1831, and an elder in 1833, superannuated in 1836, and located in 1837. Mr. Jenks was a very tall and slim man, rather dull as a preacher, but esteemed a good man.

Rev. ISAAC WINANS, second preacher on the Mercer Circuit, was received on trial in the Pittsburgh Conference in 1829, and into full connection and ordained a deacon in 1831, and an elder in 1833. Mr. Winans was a tall, stout-built man, of more than ordinary promise.

Rev. JOHN M'LEAN, second preacher on the Cleveland Circuit, was born in the Shenango settlement, Mercer County, Pa., July 22, 1805. His parents were members of the first class formed within the bounds of the Erie Conference. He was converted to God in the same neighborhood in 1821. He was licensed to exhort in 1826 and to preach in 1827, and was employed by the elder to labor on the Forestville Circuit one year. He was received on trial in the Pittsburgh Conference in 1828, and into full connection and ordained a deacon in 1830, and an elder in 1832. Mr. M'Lean was a middling tall man, of good sound sense, maintained a uniform Christian character, and was a good preacher, excelling more in goodness than in eloquence.

Rev. T. VAUGHN, third preacher on the Cleveland Circuit, was admitted on trial in the Pittsburgh Conference in 1828, and was discontinued in 1830.

Rev. CALEB BROWN, second preacher on the Grand River Circuit, was born in Butler County, Pa., November 7, 1802, and was converted to God at a camp-meeting near King's Chapel, in Lawrence County, Pa., October 7, 1824. He was licensed to exhort in 1827, and soon afterward was employed by Elder Swayze to labor on the Meadville Circuit, where he was licensed to preach. He was received on trial in the Pittsburgh Conference in 1828, and into full connection and ordained a deacon in 1830, and an elder in 1832. Mr. Brown was more than medium in height, otherwise well-proportioned in size, gentlemanly in his deportment, pleasant in his address, truly pious, and was a good preacher. He accomplished much good on the circuits he traveled.

This, too, was a year of revivals. Mr. Johnson, on the Shippensville Circuit, writes September 30, 1829: "Our quarterly meeting for this circuit was a time of rejoicing. At the close of the love-feast more than twenty presented themselves at the altar. God has wonderfully favored us by raising a general revival around the circuit." Rev. S. Ayres, on the Springfield Circuit, writes: "For the first time we held a quarterly meeting in Monroe, Ohio, and the Lord was present in very deed. Seventeen or eighteen professed to find peace in believing." A revival of religion took place in Smethport, Pa., in October, 1829, which resulted in the formation of a class of seventeen members, Richard Chadwick, leader.

Our society in Euclid, Ohio, had succeeded in rearing and inclosing a church about one mile west of the present village, where a meeting was held in the fall of 1829 by Mr. Prosser, which resulted in a good revival of religion. Mr. Barris writes that a quarterly meeting was held in Quincy, N. Y., in December, 1829, which resulted in the conversion of twenty souls.

Rev. WILLIAM SWAYZE closes up his long term of service in the office of presiding elder this year. He broke down prematurely—in mind more than in body—and, as is common in such cases, he could not see it as others did, and consequently it was to him an awful affliction to be laid aside as a broken reed.

The conference, whose judgment had to determine the case, concluded that he could serve the Church to the best advantage as a "conference missionary," to travel where he pleased, and preach and hold protracted meetings wherever the preachers and people desired it. In this way he spent a few years, and accomplished some good, but was not as formerly in his element.

A class was formed about this time in Twinsburgh, Ohio, consisting of Solomon Upson and wife, Emory Alger and wife, Proctor Clark and wife, and a few others. Soon after this a camp-meeting was held by Elder Eddy in Twinsburgh, at which it was supposed about eighty were converted. On Sabbath evening the whole ground was strewn with mourners.

A class was formed either in 1828 or 1829, at Cuyahoga Falls, Ohio, consisting of Norton Hamline, leader, wife, and mother, John Rumrell and wife, Timothy Starr and wife, David Wadsworth and wife, Appolis Wadsworth and wife, Elenor Elmer, Waldo Elmer, Charles Hamline, Mary Hamline, John Mariner and wife, Catherine Yorkey, Mary Edie, Thomas Turner and wife, Allen Fouts and wife, Mary Wilcox, Sarah Jenkins, John and Sarah Ward, and William Teal. During this year our people commenced the erection of a church in Edinburgh, Ohio. It was a large frame structure, but they were several years in completing it. During this year Mr. Summerville, on the Butler Circuit, held the first quarterly meeting ever held at Brady's Bend, or Great Western as now called, which was followed by a revival of religion, at which forty souls were converted and added to the Church. Our people in Mercer, Pa., commenced the erection of a church this year, a frame structure thirty-four feet by forty; also, a church was built by our people in Ashtabula, Ohio.

During the summer of 1830 a class was formed in Troy, Jefferson County, Pa., in connection with the

Shippensville Circuit, consisting of Philip Clove and wife, Abram Miller and wife, John Welch and wife, Father Carrier and wife, E. Carrier and wife, Mrs. M'Elvain, James M'Elvain and wife, with some others.

The number of members this year was: Canton District	2,146
Ohio	1,881
Erie	4,214
Total	8,241
Last year	7,669
Increase	572

1830.

The Pittsburgh Conference met in Uniontown, Fayette County, Pa., August 20, 1830. The appointments were as follows:

Ohio District, Ira Eddy, Presiding Elder.
Cleveland Station, Billings O. Plimpton.
Cleveland Circuit, Caleb Brown, John Ferris.
Grand River, John W Hill, John M'Lean.
Deerfield, Cornelius Jones, John Maffit.
Youngstown, A. Brunson, T. Carr.
Windsor, P. Green, P D. Horton, sup.
Hartford, James Hitchcock, D. C. Richey.
Mercer, John Summerville, L. D. Prosser.
New Castle, Richard Armstrong, one to be supplied.
Erie District, Wilder B. Mack, Presiding Elder.
Erie, Joseph S. Barris, Alcinous Young.
North East, John Chandler, one to be supplied.
Springfield, S. Ayres, J. C. Ayres.
Meadville, Aurora Callender, Alured Plimpton.
Forestville, David Preston, Samuel E. Babcock.

Jamestown, Hiram Kinsley, J. Scott.

Napoli and Smethport, John P Kent, one to be supplied.

Youngsville, James Gilmore, John J. Swayze.

Franklin, William R. Babcock, John Robinson.

Clarion, Job Wilson.

William Swayze, Conference Missionary.

We now have but two districts and two presiding elders. Those circuits lying within our bounds, which were connected with the Canton District, were at the last conference connected with the Ohio District; and all, except one, that were connected with the Ohio District, which were not within our bounds, were at this conference removed from it, leaving our work more compact and less connected with other territory. Mr. Eddy and Mr. Mack continued to serve the Church efficiently on their respective districts, and each witnessed another prosperous year.

CLEVELAND, Ohio, is formed into a station this year, under the pastoral care of Mr. Plimpton, our society having increased rapidly since it was formed in 1827. But the radical secession from the Methodist Episcopal Church, which took place soon after the General Conference of 1828, had seriously affected our Church in Cleveland, and during this year a large portion of our members withdrew from our Church, and formed a "Methodist Protestant Church," procured preaching by ministers from this new connection, formed a joint stock company, purchased a lot, and commenced the erection of a large brick church on the north side of Prospect-street, a few rods west of Erie-street. But after getting the walls up and the roof completed the company disagreed, broke up, and the Church scattered, leaving the house without a door or window in it, to stand for years as an unsightly monument of their folly It was finally purchased and finished by the Universalist society, but is now (1864) occupied by the "Plymouth Church." Mr. Plimpton closed his year with thirty-five members, and Cleveland was put back into a circuit again.

In Youngstown, Ohio, another secession took place July 5, 1830, of about fifty members, out of which two classes were formed. They worshiped for a time in a small house fitted up for them by Mr. Wilson S. Thorn, until a larger church was built on shares of ten dollars each; the shareholders holding a deed of the property, so that it could not revert from them. And there it now stands (1864) a monument of their folly. No other secessions of any note took place within our bounds in favor of the "Methodist Protestant Church."

The Springfield Circuit, on the Erie District, was divided, and the east half called "Erie," and a new circuit was formed out of a part of "Forestville" called "Napoli and Smethport." The two extreme points of this last circuit were perhaps a hundred miles apart.

Rev JOHN FERRIS, second preacher on the Cleveland Circuit, was received on trial in the Pittsburgh Conference in 1830, and was discontinued at the close of the year.

Rev. JAMES HITCHCOCK, in charge of the Hartford

Circuit, was an experienced and talented local preacher of several years' standing; was a deacon when received on trial in the Pittsburgh Conference in 1830, and was received into full connection and ordained an elder in 1832.

Rev. ALCINOUS YOUNG was a pious member of the Presbyterian Church, residing near Wattsburgh, Erie County, Pa.; but under the preaching of Mr. Barris became so changed in his views in relation to the Calvinistic doctrines of his Church that he withdrew from it and united with the Methodist Episcopal Church; was soon afterward licensed to preach, and received on trial in the Pittsburgh Conference in 1830, and appointed with Mr. Barris on the Erie Circuit; was received into full connection and ordained a deacon in 1832, and an elder in 1834. When the Erie Conference was formed in 1836 Mr. Young remained in the Pittsburgh Conference for several years, and then took a transfer to the Iowa Conference, in which he spent several years of efficient service, and then superannuated.

Rev. SAMUEL E. BABCOCK, second preacher on the Forestville Circuit, was converted to God in the town of Orwell, in Ohio, during a revival of religion which took place there in 1822, and soon after, in company with his brothers James and William R. Babcock, helped to form the Methodist society in that place. Mr. Babcock was quite young at the time of his conversion, which gave him several years to prepare for the ministry. He was received on trial in the Pittsburgh Conference in 1830, into full connection and ordained a deacon in 1832, and an elder in 1834.

When the Erie Conference was formed in 1836 he remained in the Pittsburgh Conference, where he continued a faithful laborer, except a few years in which he was superannuated, until the spring of 1864, when he experienced a most honorable discharge from his toils by a most happy and triumphant death. Mr. Babcock was a very talented, powerful, and successful preacher, being instrumental in the conversion of a great many souls to God.

> "And shouting on angelic wings he flew,
> And gained the rest in Paradise."

Rev. JOHN J. SWAYZE was an only son of Elder William Swayze, born in Poughkeepsie, Dutchess County, N. Y., August 30, 1812. The time of his conversion is not positively known. He was licensed to preach in Euclid, Ohio, June 14, 1830; was received on trial in the Pittsburgh Conference in August, 1830, and into full connection and ordained a deacon in 1832, and an elder in 1834. He was a tall, straight, gentlemanly appearing young man, possessed a fine, descriptive, poetical imagination; an eloquent speaker, but did not possess the power and pathos of his father. He spent only one year within the bounds of the Erie Conference, but became a very popular and useful man in the Pittsburgh Conference. He died February 18, 1853, in the prime of life.

> "The prison walls are broken down;
> The angels speed his swift remove."

Rev. JOHN ROBINSON, second preacher on the Franklin Circuit, was born in Ohio County, Virginia,

June 29, 1806, and was converted to God at a camp-meeting held by Rev. George Brown, in Brook County, Virginia, August, 1824. Being anxious to qualify himself in the best way he could for the ministry, Mr. Robinson spent about three years at Madison College, at Uniontown, Pa., where he received license to exhort from Rev. Charles Elliott, and in 1829 was licensed to preach, and employed to labor on the Harrisonville Circuit. He was received on trial in the Pittsburgh Conference in 1830, and into full connection and ordained a deacon in 1832, and an elder in 1834. Mr. Robinson was a young man of good size, and well proportioned. He possessed a good mind, well cultivated, was an able preacher, and generally much beloved. His feelings were ardent, and he wept a great deal while preaching, and caused others to weep. He was very useful in revivals of religion.

Mr. Mack, in describing the work on the Erie District, says: "Our heavenly Father has been pleased to favor us with a very gracious revival of religion within the bounds of this district this year. Forestville, North East, and Erie Circuits have been favored with a fertilizing shower of divine grace. About five hundred have been received as probationers for membership in our Church as fruits of this revival. There has been a gradual increase to our membership on almost every circuit on this district since conference. I have recently attended a four days' meeting at Portland, Chautauqua County, N. Y., which was one of the most interesting seasons I ever witnessed. Our congregations were unusually large, solemn, and attentive. Seventy during the meeting found peace in believing. It would be impossible to describe the scene. The last day was truly the great day of the feast. Many were induced to say, 'What hath God wrought!'" Mr. Chandler writes, April 16, 1831: "We are cheered with a gracious revival on North East Circuit. About one hundred have united with the Church on probation." June 7, 1831, he again writes: "More than two hundred have united themselves with us, and new recruits are coming almost every day." Mr. Kinsley, on the Jamestown Circuit, writes August 6, 1831, that "God has favored us the past year with more than one hundred church members," and that a "revival is now progressing in Jamestown." Mr. Green writes from Painesville, Ohio, August 8, 1831, "The Lord is graciously reviving his work, and not less than one hundred have joined the Church." Mr. Young writes from Erie, Pa., April 20, 1831: "A two days' meeting has been held in this place, which was attended with very happy effects. Our Presbyterian brethren have entered heartily into the good cause. The large brick church, the court-house, the academy, and the private school-rooms are thronged with deeply attentive hearers and with weeping penitents."

NEW DIVINITY.—The Presbyterian and Congregational Churches were extensively engaged at this time in holding protracted meetings, which lasted sometimes three or four weeks, with a great amount of religious excitement, and resulting in many additions to their Churches. Evangelists were employed who possessed talents peculiarly fitted for such meetings; denouncing the old Calvinistic dogmas, and running to the opposite extreme of Pelagianism, giving to the sinner a "natural ability" to turn himself to God at pleasure. Their zeal at these meetings ran clear beyond what they had so long complained of among the Methodists. And applicants for membership in their Churches were not required to subscribe to their ordinary confession of faith; but each Church, with its pastor, manufactured articles that any person that was a Christian could subscribe to. While these Churches were in this way being greatly strengthened, our preachers and people were by no means idle. Our ministers, expert in argument, made a general telling attack upon this "new divinity," which saved the country, and the Presbyterian and Congregational Churches themselves, from rushing headlong into Pelagianism; and in the mean time revivals of religion were everywhere prevalent among us.

Rev. JOHN MAFFIT closed his labors with us this year. In 1832 he was compelled to take a supernumerary relation; but consumption had seized him as its victim, and he continued steadily to decline until the 3d of March, 1834, when he fell asleep in Jesus.

Our people in Meadville, Pa., commenced the erection of a large brick church this year, which they were several years in finishing. It stood on Arch-street, and in size was forty by sixty.

NORTHFIELD, Ohio. A class was formed in this town as early as 1816, but got into trouble and failed. In August, 1831, Mr. Brown, on the Cleveland Circuit, reorganized a class in this place, consisting of Abner Hunt, leader, and seventeen other members. When Mr. Gilmore came to the Youngsville Circuit he found a small class of about a dozen members two or three miles below Warren, Pa., the remnant of the one formed by Mr. Eddy in 1817, but none in the village of Warren. But during the year there was a great revival in the place, both among the Methodists and the Presbyterians. The small class referred to above was brought into the village and increased to seventy members before the close of the year. Mr. Carr writes from Deerfield, Ohio, saying that "at a four days' meeting held on that circuit in June, 1831, about fifty souls professed to find peace in believing." He also says that "an innkeeper of that place, who had frequently been seen among the mourners, in the evening of the last day came forward with nine others to be prayed for. The people of God struggled in prayer until nine were cleansed, but this man remained uncomforted. One of his children, a daughter, about fourteen years of age, just converted, kneeled down by his side and most fervently prayed for his salvation. In less than an hour his soul was enabled to rejoice in God. A professed infidel in beholding it was powerfully awakened, came forward to the mourners' bench, and in a short time was made happy in the love of God." Mr. Carr also speaks of attending three camp-meetings in that region, at each of which from sixty to one hundred were converted.

Our people in Clarkesville, Mercer County, Pa., commenced the erection of a church this year. It was a frame house of moderate size, a short distance east of the village.

The number of members this year were, on Ohio District.	4,949
Erie	5,188
Total	10,137
Last year	8,241
Increase	1,896

SECTION XIII.

1831 AND 1832.

"O, it is sweet to watch the world's night wearing,
  The Sabbath morn come on;
And sweet it were the vineyard labor sharing,
  Sweeter the labor done!
All finished! all; the conflict and the sorrow,
  Earth's dream of anguish o'er;
Deathless there dawns for thee a nightless morrow
  On Eden's blissful shore."

As early as 1820 Sunday-schools began to be organized in different parts of our work, not however by spontaneous growth, without effort on the part of friends, nor without stern and determined opposition from sources that should have been friendly. Some supposed that they were violating the sanctity of the Sabbath by collecting such groups of noisy children on that day: while others thought it well that the children of the poor should be collected together on the Sabbath and taught, but that persons able to pay for the instruction of their children should have it done on some other day. The writer entered the first Sunday-school he ever knew, and continued in it, either as a scholar or teacher, until he entered the ministry. But we are unable to give any minute account of the growth of the institution in connection with our work for the want of suitable statistics. They were not taken and published in our conference minutes, nor in our Sunday-school reports so as to be available here. But they constantly increased from year to year as their usefulness became more apparent to our people. Some of our ministers were active in getting them organized, while many of them treated the institution with cold indifference.

1831.

The Pittsburgh Conference met in Pittsburgh August 17, 1831, when the appointments were made as follows:

Ohio District, Ira Eddy, Presiding Elder.

Youngstown, Cornelius Jones, John Luccock.

New Castle, John Scott, Richard Armstrong.

Centerville, Thomas Thompson, John Summerville.

Mercer, James Hitchcock, William Butt.

Ashtabula, Caleb Brown, P D. Horton.

Windsor, Daniel C. Richey, John E. Aikin.

Chardon, Isaac Winans, J. M'Lean, Thomas Jamison.

Deerfield, Billings O. Plimpton, Thomas Carr.

Euclid and Cleveland, Alfred Brunson, Dennis Goddard, John J. Steadman.

Hudson, John W Hill.

Hartford, Philip Green, William Carroll.

Erie District, Wilder B. Mack, Presiding Elder.

North East, Hiram Kinsley, John H. Ebert, Andrew M'Cammon.

Erie, John P Kent, Alured Plimpton.

Springfield, Theodore Stow, William R. Babcock.

Meadville, Joseph S. Barris.

Meadville Circuit, Alcinous Young, Benjamin Preston.

Forestville, David Preston, John Robinson, Nelson Henry.

Jamestown, John Chandler, Almon C. Barnes.

Napoli, John K. Hallock.

Youngsville and Smethport, John C. Ayres, Samuel E. Babcock.

Franklin, Samuel Ayres.

Clarion, Job Wilson.

William Swayze, Conference Missionary.

We have now twenty-two circuits on two districts, with forty-two preachers and two presiding elders, where thirty years before one man stood alone. Mr. Eddy closed his presiding eldership with this year, but continued his valuable service in the regular work.

Rev. JOHN LUCCOCK, second preacher on the Youngstown Circuit, was born, reared, educated, converted, and licensed to preach in England. On coming to this country he made a brief stop at Franklin, Pa., where he was recommended to the Pittsburgh Conference and received on trial in 1831, and into full connection and ordained a deacon in 1833, and an elder in 1835. Mr. Luccock was a middling tall, stout-built man, rather rough in his features, abrupt in his manners and address; was shrewd and witty, excessively fond of controversy, and possessed a talent of superior ability for such preaching. The Lord pity the Universalist, Campbellite, or Calvinist that fell in his way. He soon became a strong man in the conference.

Rev. THOMAS THOMPSON, in charge of the Centerville Circuit, was born in Beaver County, Pa.;

experienced religion at one of Elder Swayze's camp-meetings, was received on trial in the Pittsburgh Conference in 1830, and into full connection and ordained a deacon in 1832, and an elder in 1834. He fell into the Pittsburgh Conference in 1836, and died in peace in Richmond, Jefferson County, Ohio, February 13, 1851.

Rev. JOHN E. AIKIN, second preacher on the Windsor Circuit, was converted to God during a revival of religion in Euclid, Cuyahoga County, in 1820, and immediately united with the class then being formed, and served the Church as a leader and exhorter, and was licensed to preach in Twinsburgh, Ohio, July 4, 1831, and the same year admitted on trial in the Pittsburgh Conference, and into full connection and ordained a deacon in 1833, and an elder in 1835. Mr. Aikin was quite tall, and otherwise middling sized; a very modest man, and did not pass in conference for all he was worth. He was a good man and a good preacher.

Rev. THOMAS JAMISON, third preacher on the Chardon Circuit, was received on trial in the Baltimore Conference in 1817, and into full connection and ordained a deacon in 1819, and an elder in 1821, and transferred to the Pittsburgh Conference in 1825. Mr. Jamison was but one year within our bounds, and a supernumerary at that.

Rev. JOHN J. STEADMAN, third preacher on the Euclid and Cleveland Circuit, was born in Cattaraugus County, N. Y. Both of his parents died while he was quite young, and the remainder of the family moved to Ohio and settled in Charlestown, Portage

County, where young Steadman was converted during a revival of religion which occurred in that town in 1824–5, principally under the labors of Rev. B. O. Plimpton. Mr. Steadman immediately united with the class which was then being formed, and gave himself up wholly to the service of God. Attending meetings of every kind, praying, exhorting, and laboring for the conversion of sinners, was his chief delight. He also devoted his time to reading useful books, but especially the Bible. He found an excellent home for a time at the house of A. C. Gardner, Esq., in Parkman, Ohio, where he could do some work and give the remainder of his time to study and to meetings. He improved rapidly, and the people everywhere were delighted with his exhortations and prayers. Mr. Gardner says that his thirst for knowledge was surprising. When in the barn, the field, or the woods at work, his book was with him, and every few minutes he would be reading it; and at night, late and early, he was engaged in reading and studying. We cannot give the time nor place in which he was licensed to exhort and to preach, but so great was his improvement that when he entered the conference he was a young man of superior talent and promise. He was received on trial in the Pittsburgh Conference in 1831, and into full connection and ordained a deacon in 1833, and an elder in 1835. Mr. Steadman was below medium size, except his head, which was very large, presenting a noble, well-developed forehead, in which was housed a gigantic intellect, which was always busy. Among the many men we have become acquainted with in our day we never knew a better logician. His love of controversy and his success in debate were truly surprising. The generation of Universalists and Disciples that were cotemporary with Mr. Steadman will never forget him. In conference his influence was unbounded. There the slavery question became his hobby. He had much to do in giving the Erie Conference the pro-slavery character which it once bore, and also in making it the strong antislavery body it now is. For Steadman changed on this subject, although he did not like to own it, and so has the conference changed. If an unfortunate brother got into trouble, and was complained of to conference, his first resort was to Steadman for help, and he was sure to get it; for Steadman's great, noble heart was full of kindness and sympathy for his brethren. He never was known to take up a case against a member of his conference. If he could not help him he would not oppose him.

Rev. WILLIAM CARROLL, second preacher on the Hartford Circuit, was for several years a useful local preacher residing in Mercer County, Pa., and in that capacity received ordination both as a deacon and an elder. He was admitted on trial in the Pittsburgh Conference in 1831, and into full connection in 1833. He was middling in height, but otherwise large and stout; and was a good practical preacher.

Rev. JOHN H. EBERT, second preacher on the North East Circuit, was received on trial in the Pittsburgh Conference in 1831, and into full connection and ordained a deacon in 1833, and an elder in 1835. He was a slim young man, of moderate height, light complexion, fair countenance, kind hearted, genial, affable, and gentlemanly, and a good warm, interesting preacher.

Rev. ANDREW M'CAMMON, third preacher on the North East Circuit, was born January 1, 1810. About the eighteenth year of his age he experienced the pardon of his sins through faith in Christ. He received license to preach in June, 1830, and was received on trial in the Pittsburgh Conference in 1831, and into full connection and ordained a deacon in 1833. Mr. M'Cammon was a very tall, firmly built, robust young man, noble and dignified in his appearance. He possessed a good mind, a strong voice, with untiring zeal in his work. The North East Circuit was wonderfully favored this year. It had three talented young preachers, had several good revivals, and good times generally.

Rev. THEODORE STOW, in charge of Springfield Circuit, was received on trial in the Pittsburgh Conference in 1830, and into full connection and ordained a deacon in 1832, and an elder in 1834. Mr. Stow was a very tall, slim, spare man, with light complexion. He was a man of considerable reading, a fair speaker, but wanting in energy, a quality so essential in a Methodist preacher.

Rev. BENJAMIN PRESTON, second preacher on the Meadville Circuit, was the son of Rev David Preston; was converted at one of Elder Swayze's quarterly meetings on the Chautauqua Circuit, I think, in 1828; licensed to preach in 1831, and recommended to the Pittsburgh Conference, where he was received on trial the same year, and into full connection and ordained a deacon in 1833, and an elder in 1835. Mr. Preston was not more than eighteen or nineteen when he entered the ministry. He was a stout-built young man, of medium height, full of good-humor; possessed excellent natural abilities, and with close application to study might have been brilliant; could preach a good strong sermon.

Rev. NELSON HENRY, third preacher on the Forestville Circuit, was converted and united with the Methodist Episcopal Church in Bainbridge, Ohio, where he graduated to the ministry; receiving license to preach in Twinsburgh, Ohio, July 4, 1831, and the same year was admitted on trial in the Pittsburgh Conference; was received into full connection and ordained a deacon in 1833, and an elder, by the Missouri Conference, in 1835. Mr. Henry was a stout-built man, of medium height, a plain, practical, earnest preacher, and a good and useful man.

Rev. ALMON C. BARNES, second preacher on the Jamestown Circuit, was received on trial in the Pittsburgh Conference in 1831, and into full connection and ordained a deacon in 1833, and expelled from the connection in 1835.

Rev. JOHN K. HALLOCK, in charge of the Napoli Circuit, was born in Peru, Clinton County, N. Y., February 2, 1798. His parents were Quakers, and his religious training was in accordance with that faith. He moved into Erie County, Pa., and settled in the township of M'Kean in 1820, and in 1826 attended a camp-meeting in Fairview, Pa., held by Elder Swayze, at which he became awakened to see and feel his need of salvation, and after his return home, while at family prayer, he received pardon, peace, and the witness of the spirit that he was a "child of God." He was licensed to preach in 1828, and was employed by the elder on the Meadville Circuit in 1829, and on the North East Circuit in 1830, received on trial in the Pittsburgh Conference in 1831, and into full connection and ordained a deacon in 1833, and an elder in 1835. Mr. Hallock, when a young man, was of medium height, but heavily built, inclined to be fleshy, and was in maturity quite corpulent. As a preacher he was self-confident, full of zeal, and quite inclined to be a theological combatant, attacking error, in whatever form it might assume, with intent to destroy. But he could preach a very good sermon if given time enough.

Rev. JOSEPH T. HOLLOWAY, a local preacher of several years' standing in Stark County, Ohio, moved his family to the village of Cuyahoga Falls some time in 1831, where he has since resided, serving the Church in that region faithfully, acceptably, and usefully. He was ordained a deacon by Bishop Soule in 1834, and an elder by Bishop Waugh in 1838. He is now advanced in years, but carries with him a youthful, buoyant, happy spirit. May his sun set in glorious brightness!

Rev. SAMUEL ADAMS, after spending a number of years of faithful and successful toil in this field, was obliged by the infirmities of age and declining health to take a superannuated relation in 1829, which was continued in 1830 and 1831. During the winter of 1831–2 he was afflicted with a cancer in his knee which caused the limb to be amputated, and was followed by death on the 6th of March, 1832, in the sixty-sixth year of his age.

> "Night dews fall not more gently to the ground,
> Nor weary, worn-out winds expire so soft."

Rev. JOHN CRAWFORD spent most of his time during the ten years of his ministry laboring within our bounds. At the conference of 1831 he was appointed to the New Lisbon Circuit, where, after an illness of thirteen days, caused by typhus fever, he finished his course in great peace February 29, 1832. He said to his brothers, "Tell my aged father that the doctrines of the Gospel, and the religion of Jesus Christ, which I have preached to others, are now my comfort in a dying hour."

> "My ransomed soul shall soar away
> To sing God's praise in endless day."

A camp-meeting was held in Aurora, Portage County, Ohio, where Mr. Cranmer and Mr. Drake, from the town of Freedom, invited Messrs. Plimpton and Carr to preach in that place, and an appointment was accordingly made, and before the year closed a class was formed, consisting of Charles Cranmer and wife, Ira Chamberlin and wife, O. L. Drake and wife, Lester Granger, and Esther Sherman.

The society formed in the western part of the town of Milton, Ohio, had been divided, and the east society commenced the erection of a brick church this year in the north-east part of the town, thirty by forty feet, but it was not finished until 1837.

RAVENNA, Portage County, Ohio, enjoyed the advantages of Methodist preaching occasionally for many years, and a class at one time existed in the north part of the town; but during this year Mr. Samuel Foljamb, an Englishman, for several years a member of the John-street Methodist Episcopal Church, in New York, and then a member of the Franklin Mills class, moved to Ravenna, and invited the circuit preachers to make a permanent appointment in the village, which they did, and soon a class was formed, consisting of Samuel Foljamb and wife, Susan Brown, Dennis Sutliff and wife, Darius Ely, Edwin Bostwick, Hannah and Sarah Sapp, and soon after Cyrus Prentis and wife.

A class was formed during this year in Springfield, Summit County, Ohio, by Rev. A. Callender, on the Canton Circuit, names not known.

A class was formed this year in Espyville, Mercer County, Pa., by transferring the following members from the North Bank class to that place: A. H. Harriett, leader, and wife, George Espy, John Espy, Sidney Harriett, Rachel Harriett, and Francis Fowler.

Rev. JOHN P KENT closed his long and valuable labors within our bounds this year. He continued to labor in other parts of the Pittsburgh Conference until 1840, when he was transferred to the Genesee Conference, of which he is now (1864) a superannuated member. Long and faithfully has he labored in the cause of Christ, and an accomplished gentleman and charming preacher he was in his prime.

Rev. RICHARD ARMSTRONG left this field at the conference of 1832 to labor the remainder of his itinerant life in other parts of the Pittsburgh Conference.

A class was formed in Newburgh, Cuyahoga County, Ohio, as early as 1818, which after experiencing various vicissitudes became extinct. In the fall of 1831 Mr. Lyman Ferris moved from the State of Vermont and settled his family in Newburgh, and on the 1st day of January, 1832, went to Cleveland, and invited Mr. Goddard, one of the circuit preachers, to resume the appointment, which he did, and a class was formed consisting of Lyman Ferris and wife, Stephen Ames and wife, Cyrus Chapman and wife, Mrs. Dr. Henderson, and Mrs. Wills.

The number of members in society on the Erie District were	6,230
Ohio District	5,410
Total	11,640
Last year	10,137
Increase	1,503

1832.

The Pittsburgh Conference met in Wellsburgh, Va., August 16, 1832, where the following appointments were made:

Warren District, W B. Mack, Presiding Elder.

Cleveland, John M'Lean, John E. Ebert.

Hudson Station, John Luccock.

Hudson Circuit, Thomas Carr, John E. Akin.

Chardon, Billings O. Plimpton, Thomas Stubbs.

Youngstown, Philip Green, Caleb Brown.

Hartford, Isaac Winans, L. D. Prosser.

Deerfield and Ravenna, Ira Eddy, John W Hill, Peter D. Horton.

Ashtabula, James Gilmore, A. M. Brown.

Windsor, Dennis Goddard, one to be supplied.

Brookfield, John J. Steadman.

Erie District, Joseph S. Barris, Presiding Elder.

Erie, John Chandler, E. P Steadman.

Springfield, Jacob Jenks, one to be supplied.

Youngsville, Alcinous Young, Thomas J. Jennings.

Smethport, William Butt, Samuel Gregg.

North East, William R. Babcock, B. Preston.

Westfield, Theodore Stow, A. M'Cammon.

Forestville, John K. Hallock, Daniel M. Stearns.

Jamestown, John C. Ayres, John L. Holmes.

Napoli, Nelson Henry, John Prosser.

Cambridge, Hiram Kinsley, Joseph E. Lee.

Meadville District, Zerah H. Coston, Presiding Elder.

Meadville, David Preston.

Franklin, Job Wilson, J. Hitchcock.

Clarion, Abner Jackson, A. C. Barnes.

Mercer, C. Jones, Thomas Thompson.

New Castle, D. C. Ritchie, Ahab Keller.

Centerville, John Scott, John Robinson.

We now have two full districts, and part of a third within our territory. Hudson and Meadville are stations. Meadville is the first station within our bounds that has remained so permanently. Ashtabula and Brookfield, on the Warren District, are new circuits formed this year, and so is Smethport, on the Erie District. Cambridge is a new name to the old Meadville Circuit. Centerville, on the Meadville District, is a new circuit formed out of portions of Mercer and New Castle Circuits. The number of preachers stationed this year is fifty-one, an increase of seven.

Rev. JOSEPH S. BARRIS, Presiding Elder on the Erie District, had in seven years made rapid advancement in improving his preaching talents, and in securing the confidence of his conference. He had traveled most of the circuits on the district, and was therefore well known to the people; and it is doubtful whether any man could have been sent by the conference that would have been as acceptable, or would have filled the place of Elder Mack as perfectly. The people were more than pleased—they were delighted. Mr. Barris continued but this one year in the eldership, his services being needed more in another department of the work.

Rev. ZERAH H. COSTON, Presiding Elder on the Meadville District, was received on trial in the Ohio Conference in 1820, and into full connection and ordained a deacon in 1822, and an elder in 1824. When the Pittsburgh Conference was formed he fell into that body, in which he has labored many years, and of which he is still a superannuated member. Mr. Coston was rather more than a middling sized man, well proportioned, and though not handsome had a good wholesome appearance, was very affable, and blessed with a great deal of good pleasantry, the life of any company he was in, and was sufficiently intelligent and communicative to make himself agreeable to everybody of respectability. He was also a very talented and useful Methodist preacher. He married a lady of wealth, which gave him the means of giving liberally, and of appearing to advantage.

He labored, however, but this one year on the Meadville District.

Rev. WILLIAM SWAYZE, at his own request, was transferred to the Ohio Conference this year, and in 1834 was transferred back again to the Pittsburgh Conference. Father Swayze was not contented nor happy in his work after leaving the district; the two years he was in the Ohio Conference he was on a circuit, but this work did not suit him; consequently, upon returning to the Pittsburgh Conference he resumed his position as "Conference Missionary." When the Erie Conference was formed in 1836 he fell into it.

Rev. THOMAS STUBBS, second preacher on the Chardon Circuit, was born, educated, converted to God, and licensed to preach in England. On coming to this country he moved west to Ohio, where he united with the Methodist Episcopal Church, and being recommended to the Pittsburgh Conference, was admitted on trial in 1832, and into full connection and ordained a deacon in 1834, and an elder by the Erie Conference in 1836. Mr. Stubbs was a middling sized man, well proportioned, very gentlemanly and agreeable, and possessed a fine imagination, with a warm, glowing heart, which enabled him to move the feelings of an audience sometimes to tears and at others to joy, and generally leaving them both interested and profited.

Rev. ARTHUR M. BROWN, second preacher on the Ashtabula Circuit, was received on trial in the Pittsburgh Conference in August, 1831, and appointed to Summerfield Circuit. He was received into full connection and ordained a deacon in 1833, and an elder in 1835. Mr. Brown was very tall, manly, and dignified, with a heavy voice, full of motion, talented and promising, and an excellent preacher.

Rev. ELKANAH P STEADMAN, second preacher on the Erie Circuit, was for several years a successful practitioner of medicine in Mayville, Chautauqua County, N. Y. He was quite inclined to infidelity; but by the conversion of his wife in a revival of religion, which took place in the winter of 1831–2, was induced to attend the meetings, and was soon awakened and powerfully converted to God. He immediately united with the Methodist Episcopal Church, gave up a lucrative business, received license to preach, was admitted on trial in the Pittsburgh Conference in 1832, and into full connection and ordained a deacon in 1834, and an elder by the Erie Conference in 1836. Mr. Steadman was a tall, slim man, full of energy and zeal, and was a good preacher, except that he was rather monotonous in his style of speaking. He was very active in Sabbath-schools, and the few years he was with us gave them a great start within our bounds; one too that was greatly needed, as the ministry generally thought they had enough else of more importance to attend to, but were stirred up to greater activity in their behalf through his instrumentality.

Rev. THOMAS J. JENNINGS, second preacher on the Youngsville Circuit, was admitted on trial in the Pittsburgh Conference in 1832, and into full connection and ordained a deacon in 1834, and an elder by the Erie Conference in 1836. Mr. Jennings was extremely tall and slim, a correct speaker and sermonizer, but slow and wanting in zeal. He was a very amiable, straightforward man, of good sense.

Rev. SAMUEL GREGG, second preacher on the Smethport Circuit, was born near Youngsville, Warren County, Pa., March 13, 1810, and embraced religion at one of Elder Swayze's camp-meetings held near Jamestown, Chautauqua County, N. Y., June 13, 1826, and received into the Methodist Episcopal Church the Sabbath following at Youngsville by Rev. P D. Horton, and was licensed to exhort by Rev. John P Kent in the spring of 1830, and to preach at a camp-meeting held by Elder Mack, in the town of Randolph, Crawford County, Pa., July 4, 1832, and at the same time recommended to the Pittsburgh Conference. He had been employed a few months to labor on the Franklin Circuit in the place of Rev. Samuel Ayres, whose health had failed. His first effort at preaching was at Franklin, Pa., in the old stone court-house, crowded full of people on Sabbath evening to hear the youthful stranger. On arriving at the place, and seeing the number and character of the congregation, he was so frightened that when he undertook to commence service he could not arise without assistance, which was readily furnished by Mr. Ayres, who fortunately sat by his side. After announcing his second hymn he sat down to find the text he had intended to preach from, but in his fright he had forgotten the place. Turning rapidly toward the back part of the Bible, his eye happened to light upon the words of our

Saviour recorded in Revelation iii, 20: "Behold, I stand at the door, and knock: if any man hear my voice, and open the door, I will come in to him, and will sup with him, and he with me." To this text his attention was suddenly fixed. He at once inquired, Who is it that is "knocking?" The answer came, It is Jesus; and several things were suggested that he could say about Jesus. The second inquiry was made, At what "door" does he knock? The answer came, The sinner's heart. Several things came to his mind that he could tell the sinner about how to open his heart. The third .inquiry, which immediately followed, was, What does he desire to "come in to him" for? The answer was, To establish a feast, "to sup with him." This is religion, about which he could say several things. That moment the congregation ceased singing, and sat down. He arose and read the text, and then proceeded to talk upon those several topics as well as he could for about twenty-five or thirty minutes.

He preached one day where Oil City now stands to one man and forty women, all the other men in the place being at work in an iron furnace. He was received on trial in the Pittsburgh Conference in 1832, and into full connection and ordained a deacon in 1834, and an elder in 1836, by the Erie Conference at its first session.

Rev. Daniel M. Stearns, second preacher on the Forestville Circuit, was raised, converted to God, and united with the Methodist Episcopal Church in the town of Gerry, Chautauqua County, N. Y., where he was also licensed to exhort and to preach. He was employed by the elder to labor on the Clarion Circuit in 1831, and was received on trial in the Pittsburgh Conference in 1832, into full connection and ordained a deacon in 1834, and an elder by the Erie Conference in 1836. Mr. Stearns was a tall, stout-built young man, rather coarse featured, but made a favorable appearance in the pulpit; possessed mental powers and preaching talents of a respectable order, and became a useful and acceptable Methodist preacher; had a heavy voice, and used it freely in preaching.

Rev. JOHN L. HOLMES, second preacher on the Jamestown Circuit, was converted to God and united with the Methodist Episcopal Church, and received license to preach somewhere in our work in Ohio; was received on trial in the Pittsburgh Conference in 1832, and into full connection and ordained a deacon in 1834, and an elder by the Erie Conference in 1836. Mr. Holmes was a middling sized, well appearing young man. Talents every way respectable.

Rev. JOHN PROSSER, second preacher on the Napoli Circuit, was brother to Rev. L. D. Prosser; was born in Otsego County, State of New York, in 1807; moved with his father's family into Chautauqua County, N. Y., and settled in the town of Villanovia, where he was converted in 1825, and licensed to preach in 1832; was admitted on trial in the Pittsburgh Conference in 1832, but on account of poor health was not received into full connection in the Erie Conference until 1837, where he was ordained a deacon, and an elder in 1839. Mr. Prosser was a small, feeble man, deeply pious, and of a heavenly spirit; a sweet singer, and a good exhorter; prayed and spoke with a good deal of feeling.

Rev. JOSEPH E. LEE, second preacher on the Cambridge Circuit, was for several years a local preacher, residing in North East, Erie County, Pa. He was received on trial in the Pittsburgh Conference in 1832, and appointed to the above circuit; but his health soon failed, and he returned home, and was discontinued by the conference in 1833. He continued to serve the Church for a number of years in a local capacity. He was a man of respectable talents. Died some years since.

Rev. AHAB KELLER, second preacher on the New Castle Circuit, was received on trial in the Pittsburgh Conference in 1832, and into full connection and ordained a deacon in 1834, and an elder by the Erie Conference in 1836. Mr. Keller was a middling sized man, compactly built, of good health, well qualified for hard service; was full of zeal, a true and earnest defender of Methodist doctrines; his style of preaching was rather rough, but evincing a good deal of talent, and he was a very laborious and useful man. We think he was among the first preachers raised up among us east of the Alleghany River, a region which has since been very productive of preachers.

Rev. ABNER JACKSON, in charge of the Clarion Circuit, was for several years a reputable local preacher in Springfield, Erie County, Pa.; he labored a part of 1831 on the Franklin Circuit as a supply; was received on trial in the Pittsburgh Conference in 1832, and into full connection in 1834, and ordained an elder in 1836. Mr. Jackson labored with us but two years, being sent south of our line in 1834, where he has remained ever since, now (1864) superannuated.

Rev JOHN H. EBERT was also sent south of our line in 1833, and has never performed service with us since. He is now (1864) superannuated.

We feel inclined here to relate a little of our personal experience. In connection with Mr. Butt, we were sent by the conference to form a new circuit on the headwaters of the Alleghany River, along the Tunungwant Creek, up and down the different branches of the Sinnemahoning Creek, embracing Potato Creek, and on the intervening ridges of mountains, with Smethport, Pa., for our head-quarters. As yet there was but one society formed in this region, and it was at Smethport, consisting of about twenty-six members. Our circuit, when formed, gave us a ride of three hundred miles, crossing large bridgeless streams thirty times, and preaching from thirty to forty sermons every four weeks, and in several places we were compelled to travel from fourteen to eighteen miles without an inhabitant. The second Friday after conference adjourned found us late in the evening at Smethport, having traveled during the day on horseback from Kenzua, on the Alleghany River, a distance of thirty miles, along a blind footpath, over rugged mountains, without finding a single inhabitant.

The first and second Sabbaths we spent upon our new charge we were at Coudersport, county seat of Potter County, Pa., situated on the Alleghany River, six or eight miles from its head spring. At this time there was not a court-house, church, schoolhouse, nor a religious society in the place. We preached twice each day in Mr. Carty's bar-room to a small congregation; but we left a society of forty members in that place at the close of the year.

The second time we were at the mouth of the first branch of the Sinnemahoning, after a hard day's travel, having put up for the night at a friend's house, we were sitting in rather a desponding mood, our thoughts running on this wise: Here we are, far from home and friends, clothes nearly worn out, no money to get new ones with, and no societies to look to for help; a cold winter is approaching; we must perish in these long wilderness rides as we are now clad; our cheeks had several times been wet during the day as they then were. Suddenly in came a young man and took hold of our hand and shook it heartily, saying that since we were there before he had been reclaimed from the backslidden state he was then in, and was now happy in the enjoyment of religion. After a few other remarks he invited us to walk down street with him, which we did. He took us into a tailor's shop and ordered down a roll of cloth he had left there, and told the tailor to measure this man, and make him a new suit of clothes throughout, coat, pants, and vest, and to have them ready next time he came round. It was done as ordered, and never was an act of the kind more unlooked for, more needed, more providentially sent, or more thankfully received.

One cold, blustering day about the middle of March we were under the necessity of riding on horseback from Smethport, about fourteen miles, to a settlement on the Tunungwant Creek, where we had an appointment to preach the next day, there being no human habitation between the two settlements. About four miles this side of the place of our destination we came to the Tunungwant Creek, which must be crossed. The creek was badly swollen, and the water was clear over its banks at the place of crossing, it having rained hard the day before. There was a poorly constructed bridge across the stream, consisting of loose plank laid across round logs, which served as sleepers; but the water was running around both ends of the bridge. We succeeded in getting our skittish horse on the bridge and part way over it, when he suddenly took fright at a limb of a tree which lay at our right, and sprang furiously in the opposite direction. We saw that he would go off the bridge, and so drew our feet from the stirrups, and as the horse went down into the water we caught hold of a sleeper and held fast, so as not to go entirely under the water, thoughtfully retaining hold of the horse's bridle in one hand. We soon drew ourself up on the log and started for the dry land, leading our horse, who soon reached the bank, and clambered up on it, and over logs and brush partly covered with water, until we reached a dry place, where we tied him to a small tree and returned to get our saddle and portmanteau. As the horse went off from the side of the bridge the girth gave way, and both the saddle and postbags had fallen on a plank which the horse had tipped into the water, and which had kept them from sinking or floating away.

We soon got hold of them and placed them on the horse, mounted, and rode him as fast as he could run the remaining four miles, halting at the first inhabited log-house we came to, so nearly perished that the good people had to help us dismount and into the house, where our frozen clothes had to be thawed before a good hot fire. After getting some refreshments we kneeled down with the family and thanked our kind heavenly Parent that it was no worse with us.

At the end of the year we left twelve societies, containing two hundred and five members, on our new circuit. This year was one of great prosperity throughout our work.

During this year Rev. Aurora Callender, on the Canton Circuit, established an appointment in Middlebury, Summit County, Ohio, where he soon after was enabled to form a class consisting of John Britton, wife, and two daughters, Bennet Vial, wife, and daughter, Thomas C. Southerland and wife, Richard Biggs, and Thomas Bull.

Some time during the summer of 1833 our people in Ravenna, Ohio, commenced the erection of a moderate sized frame church, which stood near the spot on which their present more sightly brick edifice stands, which was completed the following year.

We regret that throughout this volume we have been unable to enrich our pages with an account of the amount collected for the various benevolent institutions connected with our work. The Missionary Society acted independently, but the Bible, Sunday-School, and Tract causes were in these days conducted by one organization, located in the city of New York, to which all the preachers forwarded the moneys collected on their several fields of labor, or sent them through a committee at conference.

This year is the first in which the amount of missionary money raised by the conference is published in the General Minutes. The whole amount is $597 34, but how much of this was raised in our bounds we have no means of knowing. For the Bible, Sunday-school, and Tract causes there was raised in all $69 65 in the whole conference.

The numbers reported this year were,	
Warren District	4,674
Erie	5,605
Meadville	2,596
Total	12,875
Last year	11,640
Increase	1,235

SECTION XIV.

1833 AND 1834.

"Good words, if persuasive, are laden with power,
Like the heaven-given dew to the perishing flower;
And the heart of the loving can often present
The truth in such beauty that bad men repent."

1833.

THE Pittsburgh Conference met in Meadville, Pa., July 17, 1833, Bishop Roberts presiding; being the second time it met within the bounds of the present Erie Conference, Bishop Roberts presiding both times. The following are the appointments for this work:

Warren District, Wilder B. Mack, Presiding Elder.
Youngstown, David Preston, John L. Holmes.
Warren, Isaac Winans, James H. M'Mechen.
Deerfield, A. Young, John E. Akin.
Ravenna, John M'Lean.
Hudson, John Luccock.
Twinsburgh, Thomas Carr, L. D. Prosser.
Cleveland, John W Hill, Milton Colt.
Chardon, Billings O. Plimpton, Thomas Stubbs, A. Plimpton.
Ashtabula, John C. Ayres, A. M. Brown.
Gustavus, Caleb Brown, Alfred G. Sturgis.
Windsor, James Hitchcock, one to be supplied.
Erie District, Hiram Kinsley, Presiding Elder.
Springfield, William Todd, one to be supplied.
Erie, John Chandler, Samuel Gregg.

North East, P D. Horton, one to be supplied.

Westfield, Darius Williams, Francis A. Dighton.

Forestville, John K. Hallock, Ignatius H. Tacket.

Napoli, Andrew M'Cammon.

Olean, Nelson Henry.

Smethport Mission, T. J. Jennings, B. Preston, one to be supplied.

Youngsville, H. Luce, D. Pritchard.

Warren, Elkanna P Steadman.

Jamestown, John J. Steadman.

Gerry, William R. Babcock.

Meadville District, Alfred Brunson, Presiding Elder.

Meadville, Homer J. Clarke.

Franklin, Rouse B. Gardner, A. Keller.

Centerville, Daniel Richey, Samuel W Ingraham.

Mercer, Ralph Clapp.

New Castle, Thomas Thompson.

Alleghany District, Zerah H. Coston, Presiding Elder.

Brookville and Ridgeway Mission, A. Jackson.

Shippensville, John Scott.

Joseph S. Barris, Agent for Alleghany College.

We now have two whole districts, with parts of two others. Ravenna, on the Warren District, Warren and Jamestown, on the Erie District, and Mercer, on the Meadville District, are formed into stations this year. The other single charges have more work than the places named connected with them. There were fifty preachers appointed by the conference, and four to be supplied by the presiding elders. The Brookfield Circuit is enlarged and called Gustavus.

The Olean Circuit is a new one formed in the region of Olean, on the Alleghany River, in the State of New York. Brookville and Ridgeway Mission is a new charge formed out of part of Clarion Circuit in Pennsylvania.

Rev. HIRAM KINSLEY, after seven years of close application to study, and faithful labor in the ministry, is this year appointed presiding elder on the Erie District, a position in which he soon distinguished himself. His thorough knowledge of the laws of the Church, and his tenacious adherence to them, made him an excellent presiding officer in the quarterly conference. And the superior ability with which he handled the various systems of error prevalent, made him a much esteemed champion in the defense of our doctrines. His close application to study rendered him too unsocial to be a popular circuit or station preacher, but it only qualified him the better for the presiding eldership. His brethren soon saw that he was in the right place, and have on that account continued him in that office an unusual length of time.

Rev. ALFRED BRUNSON, after serving the Church several years as a local preacher, and then laboring thirteen years with distinguished ability on circuits and stations, was this year appointed presiding elder on the Meadville District. Mr. Brunson was a very large, compactly built man, possessing a bold, fearless spirit, ambitious and resolute, and was sure to keep something astir wherever he was. He took a lively interest in the "temperance cause," treating rum-drinkers and rumsellers with such severity as to give great offense, for unfortunately there was a large number of both in the Church, as well as in the community. At Meadville, Pa., the Cumberland Presbyterians held a meeting of some interest, to which the people were very generally drawn by the religious excitement. Mr. Brunson's "quarterly meeting" came on in the midst of their meeting, which they refused to adjourn, as they had engaged to do. On Saturday there was but a small congregation out to hear Mr. Brunson, and the appearance of things indicated a slim attendance on the Sabbath. The elder was made of a kind of material that could not calmly submit to a defeat of that kind; so on Saturday afternoon, and again in the evening, he announced that on the coming Sabbath, at 11 o'clock, he would "preach the devil's funeral sermon in that house," and strongly urged "the children and particular friends of the old evil majesty to be present and show him due respect." At the appointed hour a vast crowd assembled, the appointment having spread rapidly through the town; and some rude fellows, anxious to make the thing as ridiculous as possible, went and procured a coffin and placed it in the churchyard. Mr. Brunson went into the pulpit, not in the least daunted at what he saw, and commenced service, reading for his text Revelation xx, 1–3: "And I saw an angel come down from heaven, having the key of the bottomless pit, and a great chain in his hand. And he laid hold on the dragon, that old serpent, which is the devil, and Satan, and bound him a thousand years, and cast him into the bottomless pit, and shut him up, and set a seal upon him, that he should deceive the nations no more, till the thousand years should be fulfilled." In his introduction Mr. Brunson expressed his gratification that the "children of the devil" were there, and had made such ample preparations for his funeral and burial, but said that "he must inform them that the devil was not dead yet, and consequently they could not bury him now; but that he was under sentence of death, and as criminals had their funeral service performed before they were executed, he should proceed to preach his funeral sermon." Mr. Brunson then proceeded to deal out such an awful discourse to the wicked present on their relation to, and sympathy with, the devil, as no one but Alfred Brunson could give.

Rev. ZERAH H. COSTON is again brought within our bounds by the connection of two circuits within our territory with the Alleghany District on which he presided. Once as Mr. Coston was on his way to a quarterly meeting at Curllsville he missed his way, and night coming on, he was obliged to sleep at a house where the family were Roman Catholics. They positively refused to put him on the right road, or to allow him to stay all night. But he assured them that he must stay, as he could not find the road in the dark. They then refused him any supper; but one of the girls managed to get him some privately. Mr. Coston was under the necessity of employing a pious, promising young man on the Ridgaway Mission, whom he had never seen, on the recommendation of other persons; and on his way to his first quarterly meeting, five or six miles from the place of meeting, the elder and the young minister unexpectedly came together, and without either one knowing or even suspecting who the other was, performed the remainder of the journey together. The young man was tall, poorly clad, and looking too green to cause the elder to think of him being a preacher, and the elder was too elegantly mounted to give the young itinerant the slightest impression that he was the looked-for presiding elder. Soon the young man inquired of the stranger where he was from, and where he was going. Mr. Coston, regarding his inquiries as being rather impertinent, gave them an evasive answer. Soon, however, the young minister, warm with love to his Master, inquired of the stranger if he was a professor of religion. Mr. Coston gave another evasive answer, leaving, however, the impression on the mind of the young man that he was not a Christian. Full of zeal in the cause in which he had so recently embarked for life, the young embassador for Christ began to exhort him to "repent, and give his heart to the Lord without delay." All of which Mr. Coston listened to with great respect, which led the young minister to suppose that his exhortation was producing the desired effect, and so continued his kind expostulations until they suddenly arrived at the place of meeting; when, to the surprise of the young man, the stranger dismounted, and with him entered the meeting-house, and in a moment went into the pulpit and commenced the service. When the quarterly conference was opened, the elder was about as much surprised to find that the young man that had belabored him so earnestly by the way was the preacher which was employed on the circuit by himself, as the preacher was to find that the stranger in whose spiritual welfare he had taken so much interest was his presiding elder.

Rev. James H. M'Mechen was received on trial in the Pittsburgh Conference in 1832, and into full connection and ordained a deacon in 1834, and an elder in 1836. He labored but one year within the bounds of the Erie Conference, and continued to labor in the Pittsburgh Conference but a few years. He withdrew from the conference in 1837 and united with the Protestant Episcopal Church, to whose ministry he was perhaps better adapted.

Rev. Milton Colt, second preacher on the Cleveland Circuit, was born in Oswego County, N. Y., in 1810. He was greatly favored with early religious instruction, especially by his pious mother, to whose prayers he always attributed his salvation. While young his parents moved into Chautauqua County, N. Y., where, when about twenty years of age, he sought and obtained God's pardoning mercy, and immediately united with the Methodist Episcopal Church. He received license to preach in 1830 from the North East quarterly conference, and in July of that year was employed by the elder to labor on the Leesburgh Circuit. During this year he professed to obtain the blessing of perfect love, which he continued to enjoy through life. He was received on trial in the Pittsburgh Conference in 1833, and into full connection and ordained a deacon in 1835. Mr. Colt was a small, well-appearing young man, deeply pious, and wholly devoted to his work. He was eloquent and powerful in the pulpit, and greatly beloved by the people. He formed the first Methodist Sabbath-school in Cleveland, Ohio, in 1833. The school was held for a time after it was formed in the "Infant school-house" on "Academy Lane," Mr. John Smith, superintendent.

Rev. ALFRED G. STURGIS, second preacher on Gustavus Circuit, was born in Uniontown, Pa., March 11, 1813, and experienced religion while at college at Uniontown, Pa., in the winter of 1829. He was licensed to exhort, and subsequently to preach, in 1832, and was soon afterward employed by Dr. Elliott, presiding elder, to form a new circuit in the region of Morgantown, Va. He was received on trial in the Pittsburgh Conference in 1833, and into full connection and ordained a deacon in 1835, and an elder in 1837. Mr. Sturgis was a young man of medium size, a finished gentleman in manners, quite good-looking, and a zealous, talented preacher.

Rev. WILLIAM TODD, in charge of the Springfield Circuit, was an Irishman, born, educated, converted, and licensed to preach in the Emerald Isle. He emigrated to this country, and united with the New York Conference on trial in 1823, was received into full connection and ordained a deacon in 1825, and an elder in 1827. He was transferred to the New England Conference in 1829, and located in 1832, and removed westward, and was readmitted into the Pittsburgh Conference in 1833. Mr. Todd was a middling sized man, of much religious experience, a good preacher, and had a remarkable gift in prayer. We have seen large congregations melted, moved, and excited while he was praying, to an extent we scarcely ever witnessed under the prayer of any other man; and at times he was powerful in exhortation.

Rev. Darius Williams, in charge of the Westfield Circuit, was received on trial in the Pittsburgh Conference in 1833, and continued in this part of the work two years, and was then discontinued at his own request, preferring the Genesee Conference, into which he subsequently entered.

Rev. Francis A. Dighton, second preacher on the Westfield Circuit, was born in North East, Erie County, Pa., October 7, 1812. His father dying when he was quite young, his education and religious training devolved principally upon his excellent mother. He embraced religion at a camp-meeting held in Villanovia, Chautauqua County, N. Y., June 4, 1827, and was licensed to preach in 1833, and the same year received on trial in the Pittsburgh Conference. He was received into full connection and ordained a deacon in 1835, and an elder in 1837. Mr. Dighton was quite tall, very gentlemanly and affable in his manners, possessed unusual gifts for public speaking, and was generally much admired and greatly beloved by the people.

Rev. Hiram Luce, in charge of the Youngsville Circuit, was born in Palmyra, Ontario County, N. Y., March 18, 1799. He embraced religion in his eighteenth year, in Vienna, Phelps County, N. Y., and was licensed to preach in 1828; labored in the local ranks until he was received on trial in the Pittsburgh Conference in 1833, and into full connection and ordained a deacon in 1835, and an elder in 1837. Mr. Luce was large and heavy in person, of moderate preaching abilities, but an excellent man, and has done what he could.

Rev. DANIEL PRITCHARD, second preacher on the Youngsville Circuit, was converted to God and graduated to the ministry in the town of Nelson, Portage County, Ohio, and was received on trial in the Pittsburgh Conference in 1833, and into full connection and ordained a deacon in 1835, and an elder in 1837. Mr. Pritchard was about medium in height, but stout and heavy, and possessed talents which with a suitable amount of energy and industry might have rendered him extensively useful and popular as a preacher.

Rev. ROUSE B. GARDNER, in charge of the Franklin Circuit, was received on trial in the Pittsburgh Conference in 1833, and into full connection and ordained a deacon in 1835, and an elder in 1837. Mr. Gardner was a tall, spare man, possessed some talents for preaching, especially for controversy, but was rather unhappy in his disposition, and did not pass smoothly among the people.

Rev. SAMUEL W INGRAHAM, second preacher on the Centerville Circuit, was for several years a local preacher on the North East Circuit, was received on trial in the Pittsburgh Conference in 1833, and into full connection and ordained a deacon in 1835, and an elder in 1837. Mr. Ingraham was tall and well-proportioned in size, his preaching talents were respectable, but he was embarrassed with some constitutional infirmities which lessened his acceptability.

Rev. RALPH CLAPP, stationed in Mercer, was a local elder when received into the Pittsburgh Conference on trial in 1833. He was received into full connection in 1835. Mr. Clapp was a man of more than medium size, and of superior preaching talents, and the short time he remained in the work was very useful; but in 1836 he located, and has most of the time since been engaged in making iron.

The place of the second preacher on the Springfield Circuit was supplied by the Rev. LEWIS TODD, who for several years had been a noted Universalist preacher in Jamestown, Chautauqua County, N. Y., but who professed a change of heart and of doctrinal views in 1832, and united with the Methodist Episcopal Church. He was soon after licensed to preach, and employed by the presiding elder on the above charge. During the year he published a book, evidencing a good deal of talent and research against Universalism, and much good would have resulted but for his subsequent vacillating course. At the close of the year he ceased to labor among us, and relapsed into Universalism again.

Rev. ANDREW M'CAMMON, in charge of the Napoli Circuit, was compelled to leave his charge early in the winter of this year on account of the failure of his health. His almost unbounded zeal in preaching had brought on consumption, and he came in a very feeble state to the house of a friend in North East, Pa., where he lingered until the 27th of May, 1834, when he calmly fell asleep in Jesus. His last words were, "My sufferings will soon be over; Lord Jesus, receive my spirit."

> "There is a world above,
> Where sorrow is unknown;
> A long eternity of love,
> Formed for the good alone."

Rev. CORNELIUS JONES, one of the good and faithful men who labored in this field from 1826 to 1833, was this year removed further south within the bounds of the Pittsburgh Conference, where he continued in the same heavenly spirit to labor until prostrated by bilious fever, of which he died August 27, 1835. Mr. Jones was a model man and minister. For several years he enjoyed the blessing of perfect love, and made it his principal pulpit theme.

> "And faith beholds him dying here,
> Translated to that glorious sphere."

Rev. WILLIAM R. BABCOCK, at the close of this year, obtained a transfer to the Genesee Conference, where he spent several years, and then moved south and connected himself with the Kentucky Conference of the Methodist Episcopal Church South, beyond which we cannot trace him.

Rev. NELSON HENRY at the end of this conference year was transferred to the Missouri Conference, in which he has spent many years of faithful service.

A camp-meeting was held this year in Hudson, Ohio, by Elder Mack, of unusual interest. Rev. John J. Steadman preached a sermon on the "final day of judgment" that will never be forgotten by many of those present. Just as he had got fairly engaged in his subject clouds began to arise and darken the sky; and as the preacher became animated in depicting the awful scenes of that day, peal after peal of thunder broke from the angry sky, which were instantly used by the speaker in describing God's fierce anger toward the wicked, and the crushing judgments that would fall from heaven upon them. The effect was grand, and a multitude was gathered to the altar of prayer. Another camp-meeting was held by Mr. Mack in Aurora, which was a season of great power.

ALLEGHANY COLLEGE, located at Meadville, Pa., was founded in 1815, and chartered by the legislature of Pennsylvania in 1817. Although the funds for building were in part supplied by the legislature of the state, the institution was exclusively under the control of the Presbyterian Church in Western Pennsylvania. The first president, elected in 1817, was the Rev. Timothy Alden, D. D.

The college building was located on the brow of the hill, about one mile west of north from Meadville, on the west side of the Pittsburgh and Erie Turnpike road, and presents a beautiful front end with two wings to the village. A very valuable library was soon collected, containing about eight thousand volumes. But the institution had no endowment, and was entirely dependent on the tuition fees and donations made by its friends and the state for its support; and the result was, a sickly existence of a few years, and an ultimate failure. The board of trustees made a generous offer to the Pittsburgh Conference in 1832 to place the college entirely under their control on condition that the conference would pay off its debts, and put the institution in a healthy, prosperous condition; the conference appointed a committee to examine into the condition of the college, with power to accept the proposal made by the trustees, and to adopt measures to open the college as soon as possible. Rev. H. J. Clark, a member of the committee, and a regular college graduate, was stationed at Meadville to take immediate charge of the college whenever it might be opened. All of which was duly accomplished, and the conference, at its session in Meadville, Pa., in 1833, ratified the contract entered into by the committee, and Rev. J. S. Barris was appointed agent of Allegliany College, which post he occupied two years, securing a large amount on subscription, and collecting enough to meet contingent expenses. The college being located near the center of the territory of the Erie Conference, became an object of great interest throughout our work, and has been of incalculable advantage to us. The preparatory department was opened the first Monday in September, 1833, and the college department on the first Monday in November following. The term opened with twenty-two students, and closed with sixty-two. The faculty was arranged as follows:

Rev. Martin Ruter, D. D., President, and Professor of Moral Science; Rev Homer J Clark, A. M., Vice-President, and Professor of Mathematics and Natural Science; Augustus M. Ruter, A. B., Professor of Languages and of Grecian and Roman Antiquities.

At this same conference measures were adopted to commence the publication of the "Pittsburgh Conference Journal," at Pittsburgh, Pa. Dr. Charles Elliott was appointed editor. The first number was issued November 15, 1833. The year was one of great prosperity. Powerful revivals spread through our entire work. Rev. B. O. Plimpton says that "rising of one hundred have come into our Zion on the Chardon Circuit within eight weeks." Elder Mack says that "a four days' meeting was held in Cleveland, at which more than forty were converted, many of whom united with the Church." Also "a refreshing shower was realized at Hartford, which extended to Vernon and to Fowler." At a quarterly meeting held at Geneva "more than one hundred experienced religion, forty-six were baptized in the house of God, and fifty were received on probation." "At Mesopotamia about fifty experienced religion," and at "Ravenna between thirty and forty were converted." Rev. J. C. Ayres writes February, 1834, that in the town of Madison "between fifty and sixty have been converted to God." Rev. R. Clapp writes that "the church in Mercer had been finished and dedicated, and as the fruits of a revival in that place he had received about one hundred and twenty souls into our Zion." Rev. Isaac Winans says that in Warren, Ohio, a meeting had been held for seven days, in which about eighty were converted, and on the entire circuit as many as one hundred and twenty. At Deerfield, Ohio, there were seventeen conversions, and at another place on that circuit, forty. Rev. T. Carr says that "a meeting was held at Twinsburgh, February 18, 1834, which lasted twelve days, and resulted in the conversion of forty souls." Rev. H. Luce reports that revivals have occurred at several places "on the Youngsville Circuit, resulting in the conversion of two hundred souls." Rev. J. J. Steadman says that on the "Jamestown Circuit a very interesting work of God had occurred, in which about one hundred souls were converted, and that sixty had united with the Church." Rev. John Scott baptized thirty-three on the Shippensville Circuit April 13, 1834. Rev. C. Jones says that "a revival had spread over Salem Circuit, and that two hundred had been received since conference." Rev. T. Thompson says that a revival had been enjoyed on the New Castle Circuit, and that over one hundred had been received on probation." Rev. D. Preston writes June 7, 1834, that revivals had occurred in Boardman and Youngstown, with forty conversions. Elder Brunson thinks that on the Meadville District one thousand souls had been converted during the year.

The members returned this year were, Erie District	6,064
Warren District	5,814
Meadville District	2,923
Alleghany District	523
Total	15,324
Last year	12,874
Increase	2,450

1834.

The Pittsburgh Conference met in Washington, Pa., July 16, 1834, Bishop Soule presiding, Charles Cook, secretary. The following is the list of the appointments for our part of the conference:

Ravenna District, William Stevens, Presiding Elder.

Cleveland Station, George M'Caskey.

Cleveland Circuit, William S. Worrallo.

Twinsburgh, Ira Eddy, one to be supplied.

Hudson, Milton Colt, George W Clarke.

Tallmadge and Middlebury, Billings O. Plimpton.
Deerfield, J. Hitchcock, D. Goddard.
Ravenna, Aurora Callender.
Chardon, John K. Hallock, John Luccock.
Warren District, Wilder B. Mack, Presiding Elder.
New Castle, R. B. Gardner, one to be supplied.
Youngstown, J. W Hill, B. Preston.
Warren, T. Stubbs, W Weigley.
Jefferson, John L. Holmes.
Windsor, A. M. Brown, L. D. Prosser.
Ashtabula, J. C. Ayres, Dillon Prosser.
Gustavus, John E. Akin, D. Pritchard.
Meadville District, A. Brunson, Presiding Elder.
Meadville, John Robinson.
Alleghany College, Martin Ruter, H. J. Clark.
Mercer, Ralph Clapp.
Salem, T. Stow, A. G. Sturgis.
Centerville, William Carroll, one to be supplied.
Franklin, S. W Ingraham.
Oil Creek, D. Reichey, R. Peck.
Harmonsburgh, G. Hills, Philander S. Ruter
Cambridge, Jacob Jenks, one to be supplied.
Springfield, John Chandler, one to be supplied.
Erie, E. P Steadman.
Wesleyville, Peter D. Horton, one to be supplied.
Jamestown District, Hiram Kinsley, Presiding Elder.
Jamestown, John J. Steadman, Lorenzo D. Mix.
Warren, A. Plimpton.
Youngsville, David Preston, one to be supplied.
Columbus, Darius Smith.

North East, T. J. Jennings, James E. Chapin.
Westfield, Caleb Brown, Simeon W Parks.
Fredonia, William Todd, Lorenzo Rogers.
Forestville, Hiram Luce, S. Gregg.
Napoli, D. Williams, Joseph A. Hallock.
Smethport, Ignatius H. Tacket, Brian S. Hill.
Alleghany District, Z. H. Coston, Presiding Elder.
Brookville, A. Keller.
Ridgeway Mission, G. D. Kinnear.
Shippensville, J. Scott, C. Morrison.

J. S. Barris and Isaac Winans, Agents for Alleghany College.

Ravenna District is formed this year out of the western part of Warren District in Ohio, and Jamestown District out of the eastern part of Erie District; the remainder of Erie was put into Meadville District.

CLEVELAND, Ohio, had so far overcome her injury received by the radical secession that she is again formed into a station. During the year the society succeeded in purchasing a lot for a church, situated at the north-west corner of the park on which the new county court-house now stands. The cost was $600. But they were not able to proceed with the erection of a church.

ERIE, Pa., is also made a station, but unfortunately the preacher stationed there did not go, his services being greatly needed at Warren, Pa., where, through his active exertions the previous year, a fine brick church was commenced, and the two presiding elders agreed to an exchange, placing Mr. Steadman at Warren again, and Mr. Plimpton at Erie; but Mr.

Plimpton not liking the change, and not regarding it lawful, did not go to Erie, and the place had to be supplied. Jamestown, N. Y., is again turned into a circuit. Tallmadge and Middlebury is a small circuit formed out of part of Canton Circuit. Warren Circuit was formed by dividing the Youngstown Circuit. Oil Creek Circuit is formed by dividing Franklin Circuit. Harmonsburgh received territory from several circuits. Wesleyville Circuit is the old Erie Circuit, Erie excepted. The Jamestown and Meadville Districts are complete; the Ravenna and Warren Districts have each two circuits more than are here given, lying beyond the bounds of the Erie Conference. The Alleghany District is all, except three circuits, beyond our present bounds. There are sixty-eight preachers stationed this year, and eight places to be supplied by the elders; making an increase of twenty-two men.

Rev. William Stevens, Presiding Elder on the Ravenna District, was born in Plymouth County, Mass., March 24, 1778. In the twenty-second year of his age he was led to seek the Lord, and obtained the pearl of great price; two years after he experienced the blessing of perfect love, and about the same time was licensed to preach. He was received on trial in the New England Conference in 1804, and into full connection and ordained a deacon in 1806, and an elder in 1808. In 1811 he located and moved to the West, where in 1821 he was readmitted into the Ohio Conference, and in 1825 fell into the Pittsburgh Conference, and was appointed to the Ravenna District in 1834. A man of superior talents.

Rev. GEORGE M'CASKEY, stationed in Cleveland, Ohio, was received on trial in the Pittsburgh Conference in 1827, and into full connection and ordained a deacon in 1829, and an elder in 1831. He was a good-sized man, with respectable preaching talents. He remained but one year within our bounds, but spent many years within the bounds of the Pittsburgh Conference.

Rev. WILLIAM S. WORRALLO, in charge of the Cleveland Circuit, was born in Gorham, Ontario County, N. Y., October 19, 1801. At the age of thirteen he moved with his parents to Willoughby Ridge, Lake County, Ohio, where at the age of eighteen he was converted under the preaching of Rev. James Hitchcock, and united with the Methodist Episcopal Church. After serving the Church as class-leader for seven years he was licensed to preach in 1832, was received into the Pittsburgh Conference in 1834, and into full connection and ordained a deacon by the Erie Conference in 1836, and an elder in 1838. He was a very good man, and a good preacher.

Rev. GEORGE W CLARKE, second preacher on the Hudson Circuit, was born in Starke County, Ohio, July 11, 1810, and embraced religion when about ten years of age; but his parents and many of his relatives belonging to the Presbyterian Church, he did not unite with the Methodist Episcopal Church until fifteen years old. Feeling it to be his duty to devote himself to the ministry, and being anxious to qualify himself for its responsible duties, he entered the "Western Reserve College" at Hudson, Ohio, where he remained until he reached the senior class. His friends in the ministry advised him to receive license to preach and unite with the conference on probation, and take an appointment requiring him only to preach occasionally on the Sabbath, which he could do without materially interrupting his studies. He accordingly was received on trial in the Pittsburgh Conference in 1834, and appointed to the Hudson Circuit, and in 1835 was appointed to Franklin, Pa., but spent a short time the first of the year at "Alleghany College," at Meadville, Pa., where he graduated. He was received into full connection and ordained a deacon by the Erie Conference in 1836, and an elder in 1838. Mr. Clarke was very tall and slim, dignified and gentlemanly in his manners; rather moderate in his address for a Methodist minister, but his discourses were so sound in theology and so replete with good sense as to make him a very acceptable preacher.

Rev. W WEIGLEY, second preacher on the Warren Circuit, was received on trial in the Pittsburgh Conference in 1834, and appointed as above, and into full connection and ordained a deacon in 1836, when he was transferred to the Illinois Conference, beyond which we cannot give his history.

Rev. DILLON PROSSER, second preacher on the Ashtabula Circuit, was born in Otsego County, N. Y., July 2, 1815, and moved with his parents into Chautauqua County, N. Y., in 1819, where he was converted to God under the ministry of Rev. John C. Ayres in 1828, and licensed to exhort by Rev. James Gilmore in 1830. After spending two years in close application to study at the Western Reserve Seminary in Ohio, he was there licensed to preach in 1833, and employed by the elder to labor on the Cambridge Circuit; was received on trial in the Pittsburgh Conference in 1834, and into full connection and ordained a deacon by the Erie Conference in 1836, and an elder in 1838. Mr. Prosser was a medium-sized man, firmly built, stout and spry, happy in his disposition; could sing sweetly, pray earnestly, had a pleasant voice and ready utterance; had a happy faculty to please and instruct children; took a great interest in Sabbath-schools; was in this particular never excelled in the conference; succeeded well in revivals of religion; a good preacher.

Rev. MARTIN RUTER, D. D., President of Alleghany College, was born in Charlestown, Massachusetts, April 3, 1785. His parents were pious, and he was early impressed with the importance of seeking his soul's salvation. In the autumn of 1799, when but fourteen years of age, he was made the happy subject of converting grace, and the following winter united with the Methodist Episcopal Church. He soon became impressed with the duty of devoting himself to the Christian ministry, and immediately commenced a course of study, which he rigorously pursued through life, to qualify himself for that work. He received license to exhort in the summer of 1800, and the same autumn was licensed to preach by the Rev. John Broadhead, Presiding Elder of the New London District, and was employed to labor on the Weathersfield Circuit, in Vermont. In June, 1801, he was received on trial in the New York Conference, being a little over sixteen years of age;

he was admitted to full connection and ordained a deacon in 1803, and an elder in 1805. In 1808 he was stationed in Boston, and in 1809 appointed presiding elder on the New Hampshire District. He was elected a member of the first delegated General Conference, in 1812, and also of 1816, and received the degree of Master of Arts from the Asbury College in Baltimore in 1818. He was again elected a delegate to the General Conference in 1820, and was there appointed book agent at Cincinnati. In 1822 the Transylvania University of Kentucky conferred on him the degree of Doctor of Divinity. In 1824 the General Conference, of which he was a member, re-elected him to the Western book agency; but before this term expired he was appointed President of Augusta College, Kentucky, where he remained over four years, and was then transferred to the Pittsburgh Conference, and spent two years in the regular work in the city of Pittsburgh, and was then, in 1834, elected President of Alleghany College, where he remained until the summer of 1837, when he resigned this position to take the superintendence of our missionary work in Texas, on which field he entered the following October. Here his labor was incessant and hard, and his exposures great, and the following spring he contracted a disease which terminated his useful life May 16, 1838. He professed strong faith in God, and a bright hope of future joy upon the bed of death. Dr. Ruter was more than a middling-sized man, though not large; was dignified, but affable and courteous. He stood for many years among the first men in the Methodist Episcopal Church, and furnished one of her best specimens of self-culture.

> "Calm on the bosom of thy God,
> Fair spirit, rest thee now."

Rev. R. PECK, second preacher on the Oil Creek Circuit, was admitted on trial in the Pittsburgh Conference in 1834, and continued to labor but two years, when, being somewhat advanced in years, he was discontinued. He continues to labor as a local preacher in Crawford County, Pa.

Rev. GUSTAVUS HILLS, in charge of the Harmonsburgh Circuit, was received on trial in the Pittsburgh Conference in 1834, and into full connection and ordained a deacon in 1836 by the Erie Conference, and then located.

Rev. PHILANDER S. RUTER was a son of Dr. Ruter, was a regular graduate, and a fine Christian gentleman. He was received on trial in the Pittsburgh Conference in 1834, but did not succeed well in preaching, and was discontinued at the end of the year.

Rev. LORENZO D. MIX, second preacher on the Jamestown Circuit, was converted, and licensed both to exhort and to preach in Sheridan, Chautauqua County, N. Y.; was received on trial in the Pittsburgh Conference in 1834, and into full connection and ordained a deacon by the Erie Conference in 1836, and an elder in 1838. Mr. Mix was a small man, of a bright intellect, rapid utterance, and a good preacher.

Rev. DARIUS SMITH, on the Columbus Circuit, was born in Pittsford, Monroe County, N. Y., July, 1805, and converted in a revival of religion which took place in the town of Chautauqua, Chautauqua County, N. Y., in the spring of 1827. He was licensed to preach in 1833, and the same year labored as a supply on the Napoli Circuit; was received on trial in the Pittsburgh Conference in 1834, and into full connection and ordained a deacon by the Erie Conference in 1836, and an elder in 1838. Mr. Smith was a tall, slim, spare man; sober, grave, and deeply pious. Preached with a great deal of zeal and pathos, was rather lengthy in his sermons, but always highly esteemed by the people as a prudent, conscientious, holy man.

Rev. JAMES E. CHAPIN, second preacher on the North East Circuit, was born in Wadesborough, Windham County, Vermont, February 15, 1810; was reared and educated under Calvinistic influences. He moved to Jamestown, Chautauqua County, N. Y., where he was converted in 1830. He united with the Presbyterian Church, and commenced a course of study preparatory for the ministry in that Church; but as he became acquainted with its doctrines they did not accord in his judgment with the Holy Scriptures, and consequently he sought admission into the Methodist Episcopal Church in 1833, and was soon afterward licensed to preach, and received on trial in the Pittsburgh Conference in 1834, and into full connection and ordained a deacon by the Erie Conference in 1836, and an elder in 1838. Mr. Chapin was of moderate height, slim and spare when young, but grew fat and lusty as he grew older; was exceedingly active and laborious, never easy unless he was building a parsonage, meeting-house, or in the midst of a revival; was very active in the Sunday-school work; as a good brother once said of him, "He knew how to get the fodder down low enough in the rack so that the small cattle could reach it."

Rev. SIMEON W PARKS, second preacher on the Westfield Circuit, was received on trial in the Pittsburgh Conference in 1834, and into full connection and ordained a deacon by the Erie Conference in 1836, and an elder in 1838, and located the same year. Mr. Parks was a tall spare man, of poor health; not able to endure the hardships and labor of a Methodist itinerant of that day. He was engaged in merchandising in Jamestown, N. Y., before entering the ministry, and after locating returned to it again.

Rev. LORENZO RODGERS, second preacher on the Fredonia Circuit, was born in Orange County, Vermont, March 12, 1804. His father died while he was quite young, and in his fifteenth year, in company with the remainder of the family, he moved to North East, Pa., where in his twenty-fourth year he went one Sabbath day to a neighbor's for a pail of water, and as he entered the house, behold there was a Methodist class-meeting in progress. He sat down and listened to the speaking and singing, and when they came to him he was so affected he could not speak; they kneeled down and prayed until he was converted, and like the woman in the Gospel "left his waterpot," and ran home to tell what the Lord had done for him. He was licensed to preach

August 1, 1832, and the year following was employed by the elder on the Springfield Circuit, and in 1833 on the North East Circuit. He was received on trial in the Pittsburgh Conference in 1834, and into full connection and ordained a deacon in 1836 by the Erie Conference, and an elder in 1838. Mr. Rodgers was of good size, stout-built, full of zeal, a very good preacher, and could pray with great power.

Rev. JOSEPH A. HALLOCK, second preacher on the Napoli Circuit, was brother to Rev. J. K. Hallock; was received on trial in the Pittsburgh Conference in 1834, and into full connection and ordained a deacon in 1836 by the Erie Conference, and an elder in 1838. Mr. Hallock was a tall, stout-built young man, of moderate abilities as a preacher.

Rev. BRYAN S. HILL, second preacher on the Smethport Circuit, was born in Windham County, Vermont, May 27, 1812. While quite young he moved with his parents to the town of Chautauqua, Chautauqua County, N. Y., where he was converted July 26, 1836, in the midst of a glorious revival of religion, which resulted from the labors of Rev. L. D. Prosser, in which there were perhaps sixty converted. He immediately united with the Methodist Episcopal Church, and was licensed to preach in Jamestown, N. Y., in 1833, and was employed by the elder to labor on the Forestville Circuit. He was received on trial in the Pittsburgh Conference in 1834, and into full connection and ordained a deacon in 1836 by the Erie Conference, and an elder in 1838. Mr. Hill was rather tall, otherwise of medium size, possessed an amiable disposition and a kind heart; became a good practical preacher, loved more for his many excellent traits of character than for eloquence or power in the pulpit. By diligence and perseverance he obtained a respectable standing in his conference, and long maintained it.

Rev. GIDEON D. KINNEAR, on the Ridgeway Mission, was born, educated, converted, and raised to manhood in Franklin, Pa., where he united with the Methodist Episcopal Church, and received license to exhort. He was employed by the elder in 1831 to labor on the Youngsville Circuit, where he received license to preach. He was received on trial in the Pittsburgh Conference in 1832, and into full connection and ordained a deacon in 1834, and an elder in 1836, and continues (1864) to labor in that conference.

Rev. CHESTER MORRISON, second preacher on the Shippensville Circuit, was received on trial in the Pittsburgh Conference in 1834, graduated in the usual way, and labored but one year in this part of the work.

Revivals of religion continued to cheer the hearts and crown the labor of God's ministers throughout our work. Rev. D. Smith writes December 12, 1834, that on the Columbus Circuit "about forty souls had been converted," and on the Salem Circuit Mr. Stow reports forty conversions. Rev. S. W. Ingraham writes December 30, 1834, that at a protracted meeting held in Franklin, Pa., there had been forty conversions. Rev. G. D. Kinnear writes January 9, 1835, a protracted meeting had been held at Punxutawney, which resulted in the addition of fifty-eight persons to the Church. Rev. G. W. Clarke writes that in January, 1835, at a protracted meeting in Hudson, Ohio, about forty were converted and added to the Church. Rev. A. Keller reports the conversion of between sixty and seventy on the Brookville Circuit. Rev. John E. Aikin says that a meeting had been held on the Williamsfield Circuit, in which one hundred had been converted, and another at which there were thirty conversions. Rev. Ira Eddy reports a revival on the Twinsburgh Circuit, resulting in the conversion of seventy or eighty. Rev. John Chandler reports the conversion of thirty at West Springfield, Pa., and Mr. Worrallo reports thirty converted at Newburgh, Ohio. Rev. A. Brunson writes that a meeting was commenced at Girard, Pa., April 24, 1835, which resulted in the conversion of forty-eight persons, who united with the Methodist Episcopal Church in that place. Two cases of religious swooning are given, which may interest the reader, as such cases are now rare.

The first was a young lady. She became so stiff in her joints that it was impossible to bend them, the sight of her eyes rolled back out of view, and no pulse was observable in her wrist. "I invited," says Mr. Brunson, "those that were skeptical to look at her and make any examination they pleased so that no abuse or insult was given. I remarked to them that if this was the work of the devil, when she came to she would use the language of profanity; but if it was the work of God she would speak to his praise. And some, whose doubts were hard to remove, continued by her side till she came to with the well-known language of 'Glory to God!'" The writer once saw a young lady in a similar state lie over three days and nights before she obtained self-control. Mr. Brunson says, "The other case was a young man; his father examined him, found his pulse regular, every joint as limber as a rag, and his breathing regular; indeed, his case was exactly opposite to the young woman's. He came to about 2 o'clock A. M. He said he was happy, heard and understood most of what passed about him, but he could not see or move in any way hand or foot." From this time our society in Girard forsook the old rusty-looking church standing near the west bank of the creek, and established their meetings in the East Village.

Rev. J K. Hallock reports the conversion of thirty at Middlebury, Ohio.

The number of members this year were, Ravenna District.	2,787
Warren District.	3,456
Jamestown District	3,819
Meadville District.	4,312
Alleghany District.	730
Total.	15,104
Last year.	15,324
Decrease.	220

SECTION XV.

1835.

"There are mansions of life in that realm of delight
Unsought by the angel of death in his flight;
O seek for those mansions celestial above,
Whose years are eternal, whose banner is love."

THE Pittsburgh Conference met in Pittsburgh, Pa., July 22, 1835, Bishop James O. Andrew presiding, Charles Cook, secretary. The appointments for this part of the conference were as follows:

Ravenna District, William Stevens, Presiding Elder.

Cleveland, Francis A. Dighton.

Cleveland Circuit, H. B. Stanard, one to be supplied.

Twinsburgh, Edward H. Taylor, John L. Holmes.

Hudson, Daniel M. Stearns.

Talmadge and Middlebury, John K. Hallock.

Deerfield, Rouse B. Gardner, Asahel Reeves.

Ravenna, Hiram Gilmore.

Chardon, Aurora Callender, James R. Lock.

Painesville, Arthur M. Brown, Joseph A. Hallock.

Warren District, Ira Eddy, Presiding Elder.

New Castle, William Carroll, Thomas Thompson.

Youngstown, John W. Hill, Thomas Stubbs, H. Elliott.

Warren and Hartford, John J. Steadman, E. Burkett.

Jefferson, Ira Norris.

Mesopotamia, John C. Ayres.

Newburgh, John E. Aikin, Thomas Carr, sup.

Ashtabula, Billings O. Plimpton.

Geneva, John Luccock, S. Card.

Gustavus, Stephen Hubbard, Edwin J. L. Baker.

Williamsfield, Benjamin Preston, Dillon Prosser.

Meadville District, Isaac Winans, Presiding Elder.

Meadville, Ralph Clapp.

Alleghany College, Martin Ruter, Homer J. Clark.

Mercer, Joseph S. Barris.

Salem, Ensign B. Hill, R. Peck.

Centerville, Joseph W Davis, Ahab Keller.

Franklin, Alfred Brunson, G. W Clarke, to change after six months with D. M. Stearns.

Oil Creek, Daniel Pritchard, A. Webber.

Randolph, Watts B. Lloyd.

Harmonsburgh, Gustavus Hills, Calvin D. Rockwell.

Cambridge, John Robinson, Daniel Richey.

Springfield, John Chandler, John Prosser.

Conneaut, John Bain, Wellington Weigley.

Erie, Alfred G. Sturgis.

Wesleyville, Peter D. Horton, Thomas Graham.

Jamestown District, Hiram Kinsley, Presiding Elder.

Jamestown, Samuel Gregg.

Gerry, Thomas J. Jennings, Bryan S. Hill.

Warren, Samuel Ayres.

Youngsville, William Todd, James E. Chapen.

Wattsburgh, Lorenzo D. Mix, Moses Crow.

North East, Caleb Brown, Theodore Stow.

Westfield, David Preston, Justus O. Rich.

Fredonia, Hiram Luce, one to be supplied.

Forestville, Lorenzo Rogers, I. H. Tacket, Darius Smith.

Fayette, Simeon W Parks.

Napoli, Josiah Flower, Horatio N. Stearns.

Smethport and Sinnemahoning Mission, M. Hannah, two to be supplied.

Kenzua, one to be supplied.

Alleghany District, Joshua Monroe, Presiding Elder.

Brookville, John Scott, Charles C. Best.

Ridgeway Mission, Alured Plimpton.

Shippensville and Tionesta Mission, S. W Ingraham, Lewis Janney.

E. P Steadman, Agent for Alleghany College.

William Swayze, Conference Missionary.

W B. Mack, J. Hitchcock, and W Whitney, transferred to the Illinois Conference.

We have now four districts, with part of the fifth, with eighty-seven preachers stationed by the conference, and five to be employed by the presiding elders. What a change in thirty-five years!

Painesville is a new circuit formed out of part of Chardon. Mesopotamia is part of the old Windsor Circuit; Williamsfield contains the remainder. Conneaut is a new circuit made out of part of Ashtabula. Jamestown is again formed into a station. Fayette as taken from Forestville Circuit.

Rev. ISAAC WINANS, after serving in the regular about seven years, is this year appointed presiding elder on the Meadville District, a position for which he had many of the necessary qualifications, having improved rapidly in preaching, and risen equally fast in the confidence and esteem of his brethren. He was at this time a very dignified, gentlemanly-appearing person, and a good preacher.

Rev. IRA EDDY is again promoted to the presiding eldership on the very ground where he had previously served four years. The name of the district is changed, and its territory not quite so large.

During this conference year was commenced the agitation of the slavery question. Messrs. Barris, Winans, and Clapp, espousing ardently the anti-slavery side of the question, felt it to be their duty, especially after the close of the General Conference, which sat in Cincinnati in May, 1836, whose action on the slavery question greatly offended them, to preach, lecture, pray, and talk much upon the evils of slavery, advocating immediate, universal, and unconditional emancipation of the slaves, on account of which they were called Abolitionists.

The action of the General Conference referred to is contained in the following resolutions:

"*Resolved*, 1. By the delegates of the Annual Conferences in General Conference assembled, that they disapprove in the most unqualified sense of the conduct of two members of General Conference, who are reported to have lectured in this city recently upon and in favor of modern abolitionism.

"*Resolved*, 2. By the delegates of the Annual Conferences in General Conference assembled, that they are decidedly opposed to modern abolitionism, and wholly disclaim any right, wish, or intention to interfere in the civil or political relation between master and slave as it exists in the slaveholding states of this Union."

The offending brethren referred to in these resolutions were the Rev. Orange Scott and the Rev. Leroy Sunderland, both members of the New England Conference, and delegates to the General Conference, who had each delivered a brief lecture one evening at a public antislavery meeting held in the city during the session of the General Conference.

The passage of these resolutions was one of the most unwise and mischievous things ever accomplished by the General Conference of the Methodist Episcopal Church. If no notice had been taken of those brethren or of their lectures they would never have been heard of beyond the city of Cincinnati; but being thus arraigned they must defend themselves to any extent they pleased, and their speeches were published and scattered broadcast over the country, and read by thousands of our people, who saw in them the very doctrine advocated by Mr. Wesley, Dr. Clarke, Bishop Coke, and former General Conferences, and ardently sympathized with these bold champions of freedom for the oppressed. But a majority of our preachers and people being connected with the two great political parties of the country, which were ruled by the South, and being anxious to keep at peace with slaveholders in Church and State, upheld the action of the General Conference, and condemned the abolitionists. The leaders on this side of the subject were Messrs. Stevens, Eddy, Plimpton, Kinsley, Ayres, Chandler, and J. J.

Steadman. It is due these brethren, however, to say that they were not in favor of slavery, but did not admit its necessary and universal sinfulness, nor did they believe universal and unconditional emancipation practicable or expedient, and were opposed to the spirit, language, and irregularities practiced by the abolitionists. But most if not all of them have greatly modified their views since that day.

Rev. H. B. STANARD, in charge of the Cleveland Circuit, was received on trial in the Pittsburgh Conference in 1835, and after one year returned to the local ranks, and not long after left the Church.

Rev. EDWARD H. TAYLOR, in charge of the Twinsburgh Circuit, closed his labors this year, falling into the Pittsburgh Conference when the Erie Conference was formed. He remained a faithful member of that body until his death, which occurred June 13, 1853.

Rev. ASAHEL REEVES, second preacher on the Deerfield Circuit, was born in Turin, Lewis County, N. Y., July 6, 1810, and embraced religion March 13, 1823, and during the year united with the Methodist Episcopal Church. He was licensed to exhort in September, 1832, and then, removing to Ohio, received license to preach in Newbury, Ohio, June 15, 1833, W B. Mack being Presiding Elder, and was employed on the Twinsburgh Circuit in 1834, and admitted on trial in the Pittsburgh Conference in 1835, and into full connection and ordained a deacon by the Erie Conference in 1837, and an elder in 1839. Mr. Reeves was a small-sized man, with sharp features, clear in thought, a ready speaker, fervent in prayer, and deeply pious.

Rev. JAMES R. LOCK, second preacher on the Chardon Circuit, was received on trial in the Pittsburgh Conference in 1835, and into full connection and ordained a deacon by the Erie Conference in 1837, and an elder in 1839. Mr. Lock was a small, sprightly young man, but grew large and fleshy in riper years; was a good practical preacher, and did much good.

Rev. HIRAM GILMORE, stationed in Ravenna, was brother to Rev. James Gilmore, and was received on trial in the Pittsburgh Conference in 1831, and into full connection and ordained a deacon in 1833, and an elder in 1835. Mr. Gilmore was very tall and straight, with sandy hair and complexion. He possessed more than ordinary abilities as a preacher.

Rev. THOMAS THOMPSON, on the New Castle Circuit, at the close of this year fell into the Pittsburgh Conference, where he continued to labor until he died, which occurred in Richmond, Ashtabula County, Ohio, February 13, 1851.

> 'O sweet abode of peace and love,
> Where pilgrims freed from toil are blest!"

Rev. HENRY ELLIOTT, third preacher on the Youngstown Circuit, was received on trial in the Pittsburgh Conference in 1835, and into full connection and ordained a deacon in 1837 by the Erie Conference, and an elder in 1839. Mr. Elliott was rather below medium size, not brilliant in the pulpit, but was a plain, practical, useful preacher of moderate attainments.

Rev. EDWARD BURKETT, second preacher on the Warren Circuit, was an Englishman, converted, educated, and licensed to preach in England. He was received on trial in the Pittsburgh Conference in 1835, and into full connection and ordained a deacon by the Erie Conference in 1837, and an elder in 1839. Mr. Burkett was rather tall and slim, a beautiful speaker, and powerful preacher.

Rev. IRA NORRIS, in charge of the Jefferson Circuit, was received on trial in the Pittsburgh Conference in 1835, and into full connection and ordained a deacon in 1837 by the Erie Conference, and an elder in 1839. Mr. Norris was tall and well-proportioned, and possessed a good mind, a pleasant, forcible delivery; was very pious and useful as a minister.

Rev. S. CARD, second preacher on the Geneva Circuit, was received on trial in the Pittsburgh Conference in 1835, and at the end of two years was discontinued.

Rev. EDWIN J. L. BAKER, second preacher on the Gustavus Circuit, was born in the Wyoming Valley, Luzerne County, Pa., February 11, 1810. His parents were Moravians, and his father dying when he was quite young, left the education and religious training of the son upon the mother, who performed her duty with commendable fidelity. As Mr. Baker emerged to manhood he became acquainted with and interested in Methodism, and was induced to offer himself on probation in the Methodist Episcopal Church as a seeker of salvation in Center County, Pa., in 1831, and about the time his probation expired he was made happy in God's pardoning mercy, when he united in full connection with the Church in that place. In the spring of 1832 Mr. Baker came across the mountains to Franklin, Pa., where he united with the Church, and served as a class-leader, and received license to exhort. When Alleghany College was opened in 1833 he entered that institution as a student, and continued to apply himself closely to his studies until near the time of the session of the Pittsburgh Conference in 1835, when he was licensed to preach in Jamestown, N. Y., and recommended to the conference and was received on trial, and into full connection and ordained a deacon by the Erie Conference in 1838, having spent one of the three intervening years in college, and was ordained an elder in 1840. Mr. Baker was very tall and slim, but grew more fleshy as he became older. He possessed a mind of more than ordinary power and culture, an easy, forcible delivery, and was an excellent preacher.

Rev. ENSIGN B. HILL, in charge of Salem Circuit, was received on trial in the Pittsburgh Conference in 1835, and ordained a deacon, having held license four years as a local preacher. He was received into full connection and ordained an elder in 1837. Mr. Hill was a large, stout man, with zeal enough, and was a very passable preacher.

Rev. A. WEBBER, second preacher on the Oil Creek Circuit, was received on trial in the Pittsburgh Conference in 1835, and at the end of his second year on trial was discontinued by the Erie Conference.

Rev. WATTS B. LLOYD, in charge of the Randolph Circuit, was a local preacher within the bounds of the Wesleyville Circuit; was received on trial in the Pittsburgh Conference in 1835, and into full connection and ordained a deacon in 1837 by the Erie Conference, and an elder in 1839. Mr. Lloyd was a tall, stout-built man, with a good mind; of limited acquirements, but with proper culture and care might have made a very useful Methodist preacher; but his unbounded zeal in praying and speaking injured his usefulness and destroyed his health. He was a good man.

Rev. CALVIN D. ROCKWELL, second preacher on the Harmonsburgh Circuit, was converted to God in a revival of religion in Cambridge, Crawford County, Pa., which occurred in the spring of 1832 under the labors of Rev. Messrs. A. Young and B. Preston, at which place he resided, and received license to preach. He was admitted on trial in the Pittsburgh Conference in 1835, and into full connection and ordained a deacon in 1837 by the Erie Conference, and an elder in 1839. Mr. Rockwell was tall and slim, of moderate attainments and abilities as a preacher.

Rev. JOHN BAIN was born January 3, 1804, and raised and received his education in the highlands of Scotland. He emigrated to America in 1823, and settled in Saybrook, Ashtabula County, Ohio, in 1824, and the same year was converted to God and united with the Methodist Episcopal Church in that place. He was licensed to preach by Elder William Swayze in 1828, and labored extensively as a local preacher until 1834, when he was employed by the elder one year, and in 1835 was received on trial in the

Pittsburgh Conference, and into full connection and ordained an elder in 1837 by the Erie Conference, having been ordained a deacon while a local preacher. Mr. Bain was a thick, heavy-built man; his head and features as well as his language clearly indicated his native country. He possessed a more than usually strong, active, and shrewd intellect, a ready tact in debate, could preach strong doctrinal sermons, and could scathe terribly any false ism which came in his way. He soon became an influential member of the conference, always taking a lively interest, and exerting a controlling influence, in its business.

Rev. THOMAS GRAHAM, second preacher on the Wesleyville Circuit, was born in Butler County, Pa., October 8, 1810, and embraced religion in the twentieth year of his age in a Methodist prayer and class meeting. He was licensed to preach in 1834, and employed by Elder Brunson to labor on the Springfield Circuit, and was received on trial in the Pittsburgh Conference in 1835, and into full connection and ordained a deacon by the Erie Conference in 1837, and an elder in 1839. Mr. Graham was rather tall and slim, with light hair and complexion, a rapid, forcible speaker, with a good deal of shrewd mental power which made him a successful disputant. He was social and musical in his disposition, a close student, and an excellent preacher.

Rev. SAMUEL AYRES, stationed in Warren, Pa., located at the end of this year and returned to the practice of medicine.

Rev. MOSES CROW, second preacher on the Wattsburgh Circuit, was converted to God at a meeting held in Smethport, Pa., where he resided, in 1832, by Rev. Messrs. Butt and Gregg, and immediately united with the Methodist Episcopal Church, his parents being Presbyterians. He was licensed to preach and employed by the elder in 1834, and was received on trial in the Pittsburgh Conference in 1835, and into full connection and ordained a deacon by the Erie Conference in 1837, when he located for the purpose of attending Alleghany College, where he graduated in 1840, and soon after was readmitted into the Genesee Conference, where he soon became one of its most popular ministers. He was for several years Principal of the Genesee Wesleyan Seminary at Lima, N. Y., where he received the degree of Doctor of Divinity from Alleghany College; was then stationed in Geneva, N. Y., and was finally presiding elder on the Geneva District, where his health began to decline; he then went to the West, hoping to regain it, but returned and died with pulmonary consumption a few years since at Geneva, N. Y

Rev. JUSTUS O. RICH, second preacher on the Westfield Circuit, was educated, converted, and licensed to preach while residing at his father's in Napoli, Cattaraugus County, N. Y., and was received on trial in the Pittsburgh Conference in 1835, and into full connection and ordained a deacon by the Erie Conference in 1837, and an elder in 1839. Mr. Rich was a short, thick, well-favored young man, and studied to be an accomplished gentleman as well as an exemplary Christian. He was rather deficient in energy for a successful Methodist minister.

Rev. JOSIAH FLOWER, in charge of Napoli Circuit,

was born in West Springfield, Massachusetts, June 19, 1803, emigrated to Erie County, Pa., in company with his parents, in 1816; was powerfully awakened in Harbor Creek, to which place he had gone to assist in making brick for a Methodist meeting-house, while listening to a sermon preached by Rev. Joseph E. Lee, and was happily converted in the town of M'Kean, at a two days' meeting, on the 24th of May, 1828. He was licensed to exhort in May, 1829, and to preach at a quarterly meeting held by Elder Mack in Wesleyville, Erie County, Pa., June 25, 1831. In 1834 he was employed by Elder Kinsley to labor on the Forestville Circuit, and was admitted on trial in the Pittsburgh Conference in 1835, and into full connection and ordained a deacon by the Erie Conference in 1837, and an elder in 1839. Mr. Flower was an unusually compact, stout-built young man, and growing more fleshy became quite corpulent as he advanced in years. His voice was rough, at times grating, especially to the ear of an advocate of Universalism, or any other ism that might happen to be under review. He possessed a mind of uncommon strength, and could drive an argument with as much force and clinch it as tight as any other man. The good people were never known on any circuit he ever traveled to complain of any failure to fulfill that part of his ordination vows by which he promised to be "diligent to banish and drive away all erroneous and strange doctrines." Such men are rarely popular, but are nevertheless of great value to the cause of truth.

Rev. Horatio N. Stearns, second preacher on the

Napoli Circuit, was born in Wilmington, Windham County, Vermont, May 24, 1810, and moved with his parents, Daniel and Elizabeth Stearns, to Gerry, Chautauqua County, N. Y., in the fall of 1818, where he was converted in December, 1829, and received into the Methodist Episcopal Church in that place the following March. He was licensed to exhort July 4, 1832, and to preach June 7, 1834, and was employed by Elder Kinsley to labor one year on the Youngsville Circuit, Jamestown District, and received on trial in the Pittsburgh Conference in 1835, and into full connection and ordained a deacon by the Erie Conference in 1837, and an elder in 1839. Mr. Stearns was a brother of Rev. D. M. Stearns, was a small man, of a bright intellect, ready and eloquent in speech, full of zeal, and an excellent and powerful preacher.

Rev. M. HANNAH, on the Smethport Mission, was received on trial in the Pittsburgh Conference in 1835, and at the end of his second year's probation was discontinued by the Erie Conference, beyond which we have not been able to trace his history.

Rev. JOSHUA MONROE, who spent two years on this ground (1810, 1811) as a circuit preacher, is now again brought within our bounds as presiding elder, three circuits in the Clarion region being attached to the Alleghany District, on which he presided, and was as acceptable in that capacity as in the other.

Rev. CHARLES C. BEST, second preacher on the Brookville Circuit, was received on trial in the Pittsburgh Conference in 1834, and into full connection and ordained a deacon by the Erie Conference in

1836, and an elder in 1838. He was transferred to the Pittsburgh Conference in 1839, and a few years after to the Illinois Conference, and thence to the Rock River Conference, of which he is still (1864) a member.

Rev. LEWIS JANNEY, second preacher on the Shippensville Circuit, was received on trial in the Pittsburgh Conference in 1834, and into full connection and ordained a deacon in 1836, and an elder in 1838.

Rev. EDWIN J. KINNEY, second preacher on the Butler Circuit, only part of which came within this conference when formed, was born in Starkey, Yates County, N. Y., August 9, 1810. He embraced religion in the twenty-first year of his age and received license to exhort, and soon after entered the Cazenovia Seminary as a student, but soon was compelled to desist on account of ill health, and moved with his parents to Ohio, where he was licensed to preach in 1833, and employed by the elder on the Gustavus Circuit for a few months in 1834, admitted on trial in the Pittsburgh Conference in 1835, and into full connection and ordained a deacon by the Erie Conference in 1837, and an elder in 1839. Mr. Kinney was but a middling-sized man when young, but grew fleshy and corpulent. He possessed a strong, vigorous mind, was much inclined to religious controversy, espoused earnestly the antislavery cause, dealing withering blows at times upon the institution of slavery and its friends, which often gave offense. As a preacher he was neither systematic nor uniform, but at times when aroused would speak with great power, and became an influential member of conference.

Rev. Alfred Brunson at the close of this year obtained a transfer to the Illinois Conference, settled his family near Prairie du Chien, Wisconsin, and spent several years as a missionary among the Indians on the Upper Mississippi, then was presiding elder a while, then lawyer and state legislator, then returned to the regular work of the ministry, and now is superannuated, but vigorous in mind.

Speculation Mania.—The year 1836 and first part of 1837 will long be remembered by the people then residing along the shore of Lake Erie as the time of the great land speculation mania, when, abandoning almost every other business pursuit, they betook themselves to buying and selling real estate on credit at almost fabulous advances.

While religion suffered much generally from this cause, our Church was extremely unfortunate in a few places. In Cleveland, Ohio, the trustees, with the approval of their young and energetic pastor, determined to purchase a church lot on the corner of St. Clair and Wood streets, then quite in the suburbs of the city, surrounded with groves of small oak trees and bushes, and then to sell the lot they already possessed at the north-west corner of the park, hoping to realize a sufficient amount from its sale to enable them to pay for the new lot and assist in the erection of a large and sightly church upon it, which they began greatly to need, and were not able to build without some such assistance. And then everybody was getting rich by such bargains, and why not do something in that way for the Lord? The lot was purchased from Messrs. Canfield and Dennison for the enormous sum of thirty-six hundred dollars. Six hundred dollars was paid down, and two of the trustees, Messrs. Peet and Jones, gave their notes for the remainder.

A subscription paper was circulated obligating the trustees to build a house of specified dimensions and style, the contract for the building made, and the basement walls completed, when lo, it was ascertained that a mortgage of twenty-five hundred dollars covered the entire premises, given by Mr. Dennison to the "Ohio Life and Trust Company" before it was bought by the trustees. The builders were compelled to stop work until this difficulty was adjusted. The trustees finally assumed the payment of the mortgage debt of twenty-five hundred dollars, and Messrs. Canfield and Dennison released them from their obligations to that amount, leaving five hundred dollars for them still to pay, and which was finally paid by Mr. Jones, causing him to abandon the church before the trustees could refund the money. The trustees were so engrossed with these perplexing circumstances that they neglected to sell their lot on the corner of the park until the speculation turned, and land suddenly fell so low that it could scarcely be disposed of for cash at any price. In an extremity for money they mortgaged it for six hundred dollars, and finally were compelled to let it go to cancel the mortgage. This should be a warning at least to church speculators, for which purpose it is here inserted.

In Erie, Pa., where the speculating mania ran equally high, two of our trustees purchased a lot under very similar circumstances; but the remainder of the board refusing to sanction the purchase, left the two brethren to pay for the lot they purchased and endure the loss occurring in the fall of prices which followed, and thus saved the Church from disaster, but greatly afflicted the two brethren.

A camp-meeting was held this year in Hudson, Ohio, at which Dr. Ruter preached with wonderful power and success; many conversions occurred.

A class was formed by Mr. Thompson this year in Petersburgh, on the New Castle Circuit, consisting of James Wallace and wife, J. K. Swisher and wife, Hosea Hoover and mother, and Rachel Piatt.

Rev. Messrs. Callender and Lock, on the Chardon Circuit, report that a church was completed and dedicated in Chardon, Geauga County, Ohio, followed by a protracted meeting, in which between sixty and seventy souls were converted, and another church dedicated at Chagrin Falls, and the meeting protracted until between eighty and one hundred were converted. Revivals also took place at Thompson, Montville, Hamden, and Chester. In all of these places it was supposed that not less than three hundred and fifty souls were converted.

Rev. Messrs. Aikin and Carr, on the Newburgh Circuit, established an appointment at Parkman, Ohio, where they had a revival, resulting in the conversion of forty persons, who were formed into a class. Also a revival occurred in Troy, on the same circuit, which resulted in the erection of a church in that town. Rev. Messrs. Ayres and Crum held a meeting in East Farmington, at which between sixty and seventy conversions took place. At Southington a revival took place under the labors of Rev. D. Prosser, which resulted in thirty being added to the Church. Rev. S. Gregg reports a revival in Jamestown, N.Y., in which between thirty and forty were converted. A protracted meeting was held in Ashville, N. Y., by Rev. Messrs. Chapin and Gregg, in which sixty souls were converted. Youngsville, Pa., enjoyed a glorious revival through the labor of Rev. J. E. Chapin, in which one hundred were converted. In Palmyra, Ohio, a church was finished and dedicated, and followed by a revival, resulting in fifty conversions. A protracted meeting was held in Lennox, on the Jefferson Circuit, by Rev. J. Norris, at which eighty souls were converted. Revivals also occurred in Morgan and Rome, on the Jefferson Circuit. Elder Winans held a quarterly meeting at Pierpont, Ohio, at which forty were converted. Rev. J. Luccock held a meeting in a school-house on the Geneva Circuit, at which sixty were converted. Rev. W. B. Lloyd held a meeting at one of his appointments on the Randolph Circuit, resulting in thirty conversions. At a quarterly meeting held in Kinsman, Ohio, between twenty and thirty were converted. There were revivals also in Johnson and Mecca, on the Geneva Circuit. Rev. G. Hills reports sixty conversions at Bagley's settlement, and thirty at Hickernell's, on the Harmonsburgh Circuit. Rev. Messrs. Gardner and Reeves held a meeting at Charlestown, Ohio, at which there were eighty conversions.

The numbers reported this year were, Warren District	4,232
Ravenna District	3,408
Jamestown District	4,213
Meadville District	5,023
Total	16,876
Last year	15,104
Increase	1,772

Bishop R. R. Roberts, with whose early history Methodism commenced in our conference, deserves some further attention before we close this volume.

He was elected and consecrated to the office of a bishop by the General Conference in 1816, when he entered at once upon his large circuit, extending from Maine to Georgia, and from the Atlantic to the western frontier settlements, embracing eleven annual conferences, with two colleagues, Bishops George and M'Kendree, between whom the entire work was divided, and the traveling mostly accomplished on horseback. Bishop Asbury had died only in March previous to the election of Bishop Roberts; hence he may be said to be Asbury's successor. From 1820 to 1824 Bishop M'Kendree's health was quite poor, and consequently the brunt of labor and care fell upon Bishops George and Roberts, who had twelve conferences to superintend. And the most remarkable circumstance of all, is the fact that Bishop Roberts's salary up to 1824 amounted only to two hundred dollars and his traveling expenses. How he succeeded in furnishing himself with the horses and outfit necessary, and support himself and wife, is hard now to tell. In 1824 Elijah Hedding and Joshua Soule were added to the Episcopal board, while the number of conferences to be presided over were seventeen, in 1828 eighteen, and in 1832 they were twenty-two in number.

> "Let the mimic canvas show
> His calm, benevolent features; let the light
> Stream o'er his deeds of love that shunned the sight
> Of all but heaven; and in the book of fame
> The glorious record of his virtues write,
> And hold it up to men, and bid them claim
> A palm like his, and catch from him the hallowed flame."

THE END.

CPSIA information can be obtained
at www.ICGtesting.com
Printed in the USA
LVHW022012120422
716028LV00006B/222

9 783752 590180